Praise for Jonny Garza Villa

"Emotional, heartfelt, and at times heartbreaking, this vulnerable and ultimately hopeful story is healing. Jonny writes with clear care and intention for their younger readers. Beautifully done."

—Kacen Callender, author of *Felix Ever After* and *This Is Kind of an Epic Love Story*

"*Fifteen Hundred Miles from the Sun* is the gay happily-ever-after romance I longed for as a teen! With its fun and refreshing voice, the book depicts a long-distance relationship that is sweet and incredibly authentic for teens nowadays. This book tackles the intense, nuanced struggles queer Latinx kids face with care and compassion. It's a story of love, hope, and healing that we all need right now."

—Aiden Thomas, *New York Times* bestselling author of *Cemetery Boys*

"This book is a revelation. It's like Jonny Garza Villa wrote a book for seventeen-year-old me just as much as they wrote it for the person I am today. Told in a wildly entertaining, conversational style, it's equal parts heartbreak and joy, and it centers queer people of color in all their brilliant glory. It's the Whataburger to my In-N-Out, and I can't wait for the world to lose their shit over it."

—Mark Oshiro, author of *Anger Is a Gift* and *Each of Us a Desert*

"*Fifteen Hundred Miles from the Sun* perfectly captures everything bittersweet about digital dating and long-term long-distance relationships without sacrificing an ounce of romance. Jonny Garza Villa lights up the sky in a debut that's equal parts heartbreaking and healing, sincere and snarky, with a cast of teens you will want to fight for."

—Anna Meriano, author of *This Is How We Fly*

"*Fifteen Hundred Miles from the Sun* shines like a supernova. A heartfelt debut that sings with its authentic moments of discovery, pain, triumph, humor, and tender romance. Julián Luna's journey is universally relatable and deeply needed."

—Julian Winters, award-winning author of *Running with Lions*

"An emotionally honest book that captures both sides of coming out as a gay teen: the light, laughter, and joy, and the difficulties and devastation."

—Adiba Jaigirdar, author of *The Henna Wars*

"A refreshing addition to LGBTQ literature, Garza Villa's *Fifteen Hundred Miles from the Sun* authentically reminds us of the power of love, the strength of friendships (near and far), and most importantly, the complexities of living as our true selves. A book I wish I had when I was a teen, and a must read by all those, no matter their ages, working to define themselves in this messed-up, complicated, beautiful world."

—Kosoko Jackson, author of *Yesterday Is History*

FIFTEEN HUNDRED MILES FROM THE SUN

FIFTEEN HUNDRED MILES FROM THE SUN

a novel

JONNY GARZA VILLA

SKYSCAPE

SKYSCAPE

Published by Skyscape, New York

www.apub.com

ISBN-13: 9781542027052 (hardcover)
ISBN-10: 1542027055 (hardcover)

ISBN-13: 9781542027045 (paperback)
ISBN-10: 1542027047 (paperback)

Cover illustration by Jay Bendt

Cover design by Anna Laytham

Printed in the United States of America

First edition

To all the queer brown boys still waiting for their chance to bloom.

Quisieron enterrarnos, pero no sabían que éramos semillas.

AUTHOR'S NOTE

I want you to know that in the hundreds of pages that comprise this book, there is a lot of joy. *So much.* It is a journey of figuring out how to embrace who you are and of unexpected love, a celebration of those who adore and accept every part of us, and, if I can be so bold for a second, pretty fucking funny.

But it would be irresponsible of me to let you begin without also mentioning the sadness that is very much a part of this novel. Jules's story is mine in so many ways. The fears, the hiding, the hoping that one day we might reach greener grass. And, with that in mind, topics are going to arise that I want you to be prepared for, such as physical abuse and how that affects mental health, language used in a homophobic manner, and forced outing.

I'm not going to tell you *oh, it happens only once* or *it's not that big of a thing* because one, that would not necessarily be true, and two, for those of us who have experienced abuse and trauma, there is no system of measurement. There is no *I can handle x amount of this*. There is only *this is triggering*.

Many scenes in this book triggered deep, emotional reactions, both while writing and still when I go back and read. This story is more personal than I ever could have envisioned when I first started drafting, and much of it I'd never taken the time to process before. I say all this not to diminish the beauty of the aforementioned joy you will find here but to acknowledge the reality that for queer people of color, for queer Latinxs, Chicanxs, Mexican Americans, joy is very much tied to trauma. Two sides of the coin that is our lives.

So, as the writer of the words that form this journey, I ask you to do me a favor and check in with yourself before starting. And I want you to know that it's okay if you're not ready for this book yet. It's okay if you never are. No hard feelings. Te lo prometo y te quiero.

x Jonny

1

One question runs through my mind as I stare blankly at page eighty-seven of my *Fundamentals of Physics* textbook: *Why the fuck did I let my friends force me into taking this class?* I suck at math—am even worse at science—so process of elimination should have told me to stay far away from a subject that's literally the worst combination of both.

"It'll look good on your UCLA application," I mutter, mocking Itzel's know-it-all voice. I really let her convince me that taking AP physics would be a good idea.

Peer pressure is a perra.

After spending the least productive hour of my life wondering how large of a fire I could create with the book, I open Snapchat to take a picture of the homework gathered on my bed, adding the words SAVE ME and maximizing the font size for emphasis. It's sent to Itzel. Seeing as it was her idea, the least she could do is send some answers.

Pushing the textbook and papers to the side, I mentally take stock of all the homework I need to get done tonight and what's still left to do while I wait for her to reply.

I grab my copy of *Cien Años de Soledad* and flip to the dog-eared page marking where I last left off, humming along mindlessly to a playlist of those sort of soft, folksy pop, easy listening Spanish songs while

I read. Kind of wishing I had some mango slices con chile y limón to really complete this Latinx aesthetic.

The novel is fine. Likable in a Charles Dickens's *A Tale of Two Cities, all these old writers love to hear themselves talk* sort of way. Something about spending hundreds of pages rambling about José Arcadio Buendía's children, grandchildren, and great-grandchildren until I've forgotten who's dead or alive and who's sleeping with whom really gets Gabriel García Márquez going. In a way that seems almost irrelevant when we live in a society of Twitter character limits and curated Instagram captions.

I finish one final annotation when my phone vibrates underneath me, and I go to Itzel's reply: a picture of her completed homework—which I immediately screenshot—and a video message.

"We're not even a month into the year yet and you're already lost? You get this *one* free pass, Julián Luna. Next time, don't be a tonto and wait until Sunday night to start your shit because you had to, I don't know, probably binge-watch *Selena* for the twentieth time. 'Kay? 'Kay. Love you, mi pendejito. See you tomorrow!"

Ignoring her nags, I switch over to my photos, select the screen capture, and scribble her work onto my own paper as fast as I can. Not even worrying about trying to understand how she got these answers. That I can do tomorrow. Right now, the last thing I need is for Dad to barge in and see me copying my friend's homework.

Weekend assignments now complete, I come back to the app to record my response. "Yeah, Itzel, *I'm* the tonto." I pause to situate the curly bangs hanging down onto my forehead. "If I'm a tonto, it's only because I let you and Rolie and Jordan convince me to take physics instead of advanced biology. I could be coloring a plant cell right now!

"We made a deal," I say, brushing off her threats. "You said if I took this class with y'all, you'd help me when I don't understand the pinche assignments. Stop acting brand-new, pretending you didn't know that'd be an eternal mood. Anyways, thanks for the help, as always. I'm tired, so going mimis now. Te quiero mucho. See you in the morning."

After only half listening to her next response of "*listen here, coñito*" and "we're going over all of this at lunch tomorrow so you won't have to cheat next time," I get out of Snapchat and set all five of my morning alarms, labeled with varying degrees of urgency, starting with DESPIERTA BABOSO, then I KNOW YOU'RE AWAKE AND LYING IN BED ALL LAZY RN, and finally, GET YOUR ASS UP at the end. Then I get up to put my books and laptop in my bag, turn off the bedroom lights, carelessly toss the UCLA hoodie I'd been wearing somewhere in the direction of my closet, and throw myself back onto my bed.

As usual, I give it ninety seconds of making a half-assed attempt at falling asleep before I'm back on my phone, flipping through Instagram. I scroll past selfies of Itzel, random person, random person, random person, and—*oh*. A nearly naked Maluma. Screenshot that.

Another minute of scrolling and then I stop at a #ThrowbackThursday picture Jordan posted last week. It's from the final junior varsity soccer match of our freshman year. Both of us locked arms over shoulders with Itzel and Rolie, who've been going to every home game the past three years to cheer us on.

Itzel Santos is one of the prettiest girls in the entire school. In a Selena Quintanilla, Kali Uchis type of way (which is the *best* kind of pretty in my purely observational opinion). She's the smartest student in our grade too. Dad thought we were dating for a while, and I can't remember ever seeing him *that* genuinely impressed with me. I put off correcting him for months.

Rolie de Leon, or sometimes just Roe—whose actual name is Rolando, but he's always hated it—is a good eight inches taller than I am and is a little pudgy. But I like it. I once used his pancita as a pillow during a beach trip. Best. Nap. Ever. And puro güero. He spends half the year looking more red than brown. He's also the introvert of the group, but with this magnetic approachability. Plus, I dare you to try *not* to fall in love with him when he starts singing "Volver, Volver."

Staring at the photo, I'm reminded of how we spent an entire semester in the same Advanced Placement courses before soccer brought Jordan Thomas and me together. When I let my eyes glance a little too long at Trey Guerrero changing and the entire team started talking mess, Jordan came to my defense. Not prodding me to admit if I'm gay. Accepting me from the beginning.

Since then, he's been a constant presence in my life. Always there when I need someone to tell me to brush off my teammates' assholery or just to hang out. Few weekends pass where we aren't practicing or playing video games or helping each other with homework.

I double-tap our post-soccer-game throwback, since I failed to like the picture when he first posted it a few days ago, and close out of the app. Intent on that being the end of me destroying my retinas tonight. I *need* to go to bed.

I toss and turn, unable to find an ideal sleep position. More, unable to get shirtless Maluma off my mind. And other parts of my body.

I glance at my phone to check the time: 1:28 a.m. I'm going to regret not being asleep by now. But also, Maluma and me on our private yacht somewhere in the Caribbean. Clothing optional and *strongly* unrecommended.

Sleep can wait a few minutes.

~

"What should I wear today?" I ask myself out loud, looking through my closet full of forest-green, navy, and white shirts. Pretending that my Catholic school dress code doesn't suffocate my fashion sense.

I guess this. I pull out a dark-green button-up shirt, basing my decision completely on the fact that it's my least wrinkled option and I'm feeling too lazy to iron this morning.

A little smoothing out the front of the shirt with my hands and it's good to go. Then a pair of navy chino shorts that rise a couple of inches above my knees and show off my made-by-soccer butt. Being a towering five foot seven, that was basically the one sport Dad had any hopes of me ever being any good at.

My fingers brush through wavy curls of hair that go between black and a tinted dark, dark brown from sun and saltwater, attempting to create the perfect amount of disheveled that says *cool* instead of *just had sex* hair. Then I grab my backpack and slip on a pair of moccasins.

"Buenos días, mi'jo," Dad yells when he hears my bedroom door open.

"Morning, Dad," I reply, finding him in the kitchen. He hands me a tortilla with refried beans, avocado, and jalapeño slices and a Yeti cup filled with orange juice.

Dad pats me on the back a couple of times, and if he notices the way my eyes close and the muscles tighten where his hand hits, and how I don't even breathe until he stops, he doesn't say anything about it. Too in a hurry to get to the front door, already in a rush to hit the road.

We rarely see each other during the week, since he works at a chemical plant an hour and a half outside Corpus Christi and spends his days off driving for Lyft and Uber or taking on menial physical jobs around the neighborhood. His absence isn't exactly unwanted, though.

Our relationship has always been rocky. We have our good times, and it's not as if we don't get along at all. I could never *not* love him. But he's forever full of criticisms, and most days there's a tangible tension between the two of us.

Don't talk like a pinche sissy, he would say when he'd overhear Itzel and me FaceTiming.

And before going to Abuelita's funeral when he told me, *I better not see you acting all chillona.* One of the many times he's warned me against showing any emotions that could embarrass him.

Or in those rarer moments he gets physical. Like at Itzel's quinceañera, when he found me in the corner of the dance hall talking to one of her cousins, at exactly the moment his hand reached over to mine. I had to get pretty creative explaining the bruises at soccer practice the next day.

It's because he knows. He's known I'm gay even before I knew it myself. Before I knew what the word was. And he's intent on keeping me from acknowledging it. Intent on ensuring I hate that part of myself.

Seventeen years of pressure to be this rigid presentation of a heterosexual, machismo Mexican American young man. All in the name of paternal love and care.

Only one more year. And then graduation, and I can take a one-way flight to Los Angeles for college. Some distance would definitely do us both good.

2

Jordan and Rolie are busy chismeando with Itzel when I get to campus. She's going on about whatever weekend drama that is her life, leaning against Rolie's car, talking as much as she can before being forced to break for air. I turn in to my regular spot next to Jordan's Jeep, parking my dark-red Ford pickup that's older than I am. It was a sixteenth birthday gift from Dad and Güelo, who fixed it up, complete with working AC and Bluetooth stereo.

Dad swears that *real* men drive trucks. It only serves as a symbol of his efforts to keep me heteronormative. But I have to admit, I love it more than most things in my life.

Itzel shoves her phone into my face as soon as I step out, showing me an Instagram post her ex-boyfriend put up late last night. At the same time, Rolie is using my shoulder as an armrest and asking if he can compare answers for our government homework while Jordan is calling dibs on what's left of my orange juice. I take the phone from Itzel, hand Jordan my cup, and pivot to give Rolie access to my backpack.

The three of them have been great with helping better my ability to multitask.

"You know, drinking from the same cup as someone else is basically making out with them," Itzel tells Jordan as he drinks from my Yeti. Rolie tries to hold in his cackle at her comment.

"Don't be jealous I've made out with Luna before you have," he teases.

"That's exactly what it is. I'm *so* jealous," she replies. Itzel takes my hand, pulling me forward with her. "Jules is mine. Back off."

"We've all shared cups before," I tell them, trying to brush off the conversation. "It's not that big of a deal." I'm happy to not be facing any of them. Otherwise they'd see how embarrassed and off guard Itzel caught me with that comment, and even more with Jordan's response.

I'd be lying if I said I wasn't attracted to Jordan. Crushing on the hot, heroic, melanated, straight boy borders on being too cliché. The little bit of an accent he has that's a mixture of being raised in Houston until he was in eighth grade and what happens with regular trips to see the rest of his family in South Carolina and Georgia. The way he looks with those short sponge twists added to that constant smile, the silver studs he takes out every morning before class, and the athletic legs I'd spend my entire day staring at if he didn't sit behind me in every class.

I know nothing would ever happen, though. One: because I exist so deeply in the closet, I could be in Narnia by now. And two: Jordan is unquestionably straight.

But it doesn't hurt anyone to imagine making out. He's the one who brought it up.

"Thanks, Roe," Itzel and I say in unison as he holds the door open for us. Martin Catholic used to be a convent or monastery or something decades ago. Now dead racist nuns haunt and terrorize their home turned high school for underprivileged (read: brown and Black) teenagers whose families can't afford the cost of a private education at Saint Augustine's. For a Catholic school, it's pretty laid-back. Most theology classes revolve around helping the less fortunate and social justice rather than listing all the reasons the book of Leviticus says we're going to Hell. Not to say that we're without our more *aggressive faithful*, but after a few tense in-class debates over why condoms are definitely not destroying Christian society, those with differing philosophies agreed to keep some distance.

I've always believed morning classes on a Monday shouldn't be a thing. Staunchly against it. At least I have the easy ones first: Spanish, English, civic engagement. But then I get to calculus, and the mixture of never knowing what's going on and my growing impatience for lunch is a recipe for the least possible amount of productivity.

"Finally," I sigh when the bell rings, hopping out of my desk.

I stay a couple of steps ahead of my friends as we rush to the cafeteria. When we get inside, I separate from everyone, heading for the vegetarian line. I can always rely on it to be shorter than the regular lunch queues the other three fight their way through.

"Luna," I hear Jordan call out as he approaches, setting a cup under the Powerade nozzle. "Itzel and Rolie were behind me somewhere with Lou. Said they'd meet us at the table."

I nod and follow him outside to our regular bench.

Itzel sits between Jordan and me, and Roe and Lou plop onto the other side. Soccer teammates, a few student council kids, and some friends of friends take up the remaining spaces.

"Julito, you have to be the only one who goes through that vegan line," Lou mocks. She's that token chingona, extra, big personality, *way too much ninety-nine percent of the time* sort of person, and not exactly a friend in the way the others are, but as the school's life of the party, she always keeps things interesting when she's around. "I swear, you think you're saving all the chickens and piglets."

"It's vegetarian, Lou," I correct. "I don't have the willpower to give up cheese yet." A few years ago, seeing a cow head sitting on my abuela's kitchen counter scarred me for life. Since then, the idea of eating animals has lost all its appeal. "Plus, I don't have to spend half my lunch period standing in line for mediocre mystery meat."

Rolie stares at his forkful of chicken-fried steak before shrugging. "I don't know how he does it. I couldn't go a day without carnitas or asada."

"He did make those jackfruit tacos that I swear tasted exactly like—if not better than—any chicken I've ever had," Itzel rebuts. "Oh, and those . . . what were they, Jules? Black bean and soyrizo chiles rellenos you made us a few months back. Life changing."

"Damn, y'all. Thanks for the invite to all these meals with Chef Julito at Cocina Cochina," Lou says. Insulted that any plans involving a free meal wouldn't include her. "Was I supposed to put in a reservation?"

"Lou, we've invited you over lots of times. The door is always open," I reply.

"Mil gracias, chiquis," she says. Her smile is half-authentic at best. "Anyways, moving on to more important matters. My dad'll be in the Valley this weekend to visit a tía or prima or abuela or who knows who. I'm thinking kickback? I can have my brother buy us some beer and booze. Roe, you ask the same from yours. Julián Ramsey, quieres cocinar para nosotros, porfa?"

"There's no way I'm making dinner for an entire party, Lou."

"Ew, whatever. But still, party this weekend at my house. Jules, if you want cheese pizza or cómo que, tofu, that's on you." She doesn't notice my eye roll, tuning me out to talk about the details of her upcoming party and triple-check her makeup until it's time for us to get back to class.

Theology goes by at a glacial pace, and physics is unsurprisingly The Worst. Economics is just *slightly* more bearable, if only because of the relief at knowing the day's almost over and it's easier to daydream without getting caught. It takes only about two minutes before my mind is gone and I'm looking out the window for the rest of class.

That is, until the feeling of something wiggling in my ear makes me jump and I'm trying my hardest to hold in the cusses that stop at the tip of my tongue.

"Everything all right back there?" Mr. Ruiz asks, not bothering to look away from the projection screen and his PowerPoint.

"Yeah," I quickly reply. "I, uh—I thought I saw a bug."

Pay attention, Luna, Jordan mouths when I turn around to glare at him.

Pinche mamón.

~

"Beach?" Jordan asks Itzel and me as the three of us walk to our lockers. Ever since Rolie was the first to get his driver's license and car our sophomore year, taking that fifteen-minute drive from Oso Bay, where Martin Catholic's at, to McGee Beach has become our tradition. Especially on days as nice and sunny as these. So much so that Jordan, Roe, and I started keeping a couple of swim shorts in our lockers last year and Itzel, a few bikinis.

We both give enthusiastic yeses and hurry to pack our stuff. I grab all the books and binders I'll need for tonight and a pair of these four-inch-inseam burgundy shorts I bought from ASOS and rush to catch up to them, walking out together to our cars.

"McGee, Rolie!" Itzel yells when she sees him walking out of the band hall from mariachi.

He sticks both thumbs up. "I'll meet y'all at Sonic!"

That's step one to any great afternoon at the beach: Sonic Drive-In. We all order drinks in the largest size they have and take turns using their sketchy-*ish* bathroom at the back of the building to change. Step two, stay on Ocean Drive all the way up, heading toward downtown, the One Shoreline Plaza buildings, and the Harbor Bridge, but not quite that far. Only until it becomes Shoreline and the entrance to the beach is right there.

We spend the next few hours hanging out on the beach. The various shades of brown to black of our skin will become even more so by the time we leave. Except for Rolie, who will probably look like a tomate if he doesn't get some sunscreen on him ASAP. Jordan brings a Bluetooth speaker and a volleyball with him, going straight to Megan Thee Stallion (or, as he usually refers to her, his *future wife*) while we take selfies with Itzel and laugh at Rolie for getting a brain freeze because he started chugging his Ocean Water and Jordan and I practice throwing tater tots into each other's mouths until a volleyball court opens up and we play two on two for the rest of the afternoon, taking in the bright sun and salty air.

These are the moments I keep close. The times I can let my guard down around Itzel and Jordan and Roe, even Lou. When I'm not concerned with hand gestures or the tone of my voice. Or if my eyes happen to glance at an attractive boy passing by. When all that matters is that they're my friends and we're having the time of our lives right now.

I don't know if they realize how much I've relied on their friendship over the years. On something as simple as ignoring rumors or standing by me through insults or when someone tries to be an ass. I don't doubt they have their own suspicions about my sexuality, but I'm thankful they're allowing me to figure out when, where, and how I come to terms with and vocalize it.

3

Deep breath in. Deep breath out. Eyes locked onto the rearview mirror.

Time to compose myself.

Center myself.

Straighten myself.

This ritual has existed in some form since people started calling out any of my mannerisms that weren't *strictly masculine*. A way of keeping myself in check. And making sure that gay-Jules was securely locked back in his closet. Especially after a couple of hours with my three closest friends, when I'm not as likely to pay attention to how I act.

It's become a daily habit on the drive to school, where chances of getting called a fag or joto increase substantially. And something that precedes every interaction with Dad. Or like now, when I come back home to Güelo's truck parked in the driveway.

I don't think my grandfather would ever hate me. But he, like his son-in-law, is such a *man's man, hard day's work, can dismember a goat and will use every part of it in dinner tonight, asks for tools for Christmas* sort of guy. And the last thing I'd want to do is disappoint him or shatter our relationship because I'm a very different sort of *man's man*.

The aromas of burning wood and meat fill the air, and I can feel the vibrations of my stomach growling. As devoted as I am to the herbivore lifestyle, it'd be a lie to say I don't get very real barbecue withdrawals at times. I mean, I might be vegetarian, but I'm still human.

I call out for Güelo as I walk inside, getting only silence in response. Must be outside still.

A quick shower to get rid of the beach smell, and then I head to the dining table. I put in my AirPods, spread out what remains of my homework, and dive in. With my eyes stuck to books and papers, I don't see Güelo coming in from the back door, but the strong smell of fajitas calls me to attention.

He smiles and begins mouthing words I can't comprehend.

"Lo siento, Güelo," I say, taking out the earbuds. "No pude oírte. Music."

"Ay, bueno, mi'jito. Se me olvida que son wireless." He pats me on the back and tousles my hair, leaving the scent of charcoal and fire to linger on me. "Supper's almost ready. Asando setas y chiles para ti. H-E-B had the mushrooms you like, the long, white, más feo, but they grill good. And your sister's outside. I'll tell her you're home."

I close my laptop and books. Xochi being here means that it's not likely I'll be getting any more homework done soon. She walks in with an almost empty bottle of wine in one hand and a half-full glass in the other.

Yep. Putting the homework on hold.

I rush over to hug my older sister, about an inch taller than me; long, dark brunette hair; and brown freckles that come out in the sun.

"Was that bottle full when you got here?" I don't bother to hide my judgment.

"Te lo sico," she hisses. "You try making sure twenty-eight kindergarteners stay alive for eight hours, 'manito. This is self-care." She takes a seat on the couch, patting the spot next to her.

Xo moved back to Corpus this summer, after four years at the University of Texas in San Antonio and then three in Miami working for Teach for America. Not that I'd ever tell her, but she's an idiot for coming back home. I get that Florida will be underwater in a few years, but still. I'm for sure not making that same mistake.

"Forget them, though," Xo says. "Catch me up on you, 'Lito. I haven't seen you in weeks. School okay?"

"School's great," I tell her as she refills her glass, asking me if I want to join her. I decline, still on a sugar high from the large grape slush I had earlier.

"And you're on top of your scholarship apps, *right*?"

"Unless another good one comes up, I've only got two or three more." Thank God too. Three months searching for ways to get money for college with Itzel, Jordan, and Roe was *not* how I planned on spending the summer before my senior year.

"Good." She takes a sip from her glass. "And Papi? How're you two doing?"

Xo's always had a surface-level understanding of my and Dad's relationship. Although she hasn't been a huge part of my life for the past seven years, she was a buffer for me growing up. When Dad would yell at me before going to work, my sister would be right there with the Britney Spears Pandora station ready.

Baila conmigo, 'manito, Xo would demand. And she wouldn't let me stop until I started smiling again. Until she had physical proof that my happiness was returning.

Even after she left, I'm sure there were times at Christmases and during summer breaks when she felt the tension. Enough to still concern herself with our relationship.

"It's whatever," I answer. "Don't worry."

She gives me those eyes. That *don't tell your big sister what to do* look.

"I do what I want. Now, come on. Let's get your stuff off the table. Dinner's almost ready, y tengo mucha hambre," she whines. "You would not believe. Even after Güelo went into a very detailed story about the journey one of his pigs took from alive in his backyard to the grill outside."

~

"You ever think about her?" Xo asks. She and Güelo were on the way out when we got caught up looking at two pictures hanging on the wall in the entryway. Photos of Mom in a hospital bed holding a baby and Dad leaning in next to them. The only differences between the photos are the small variances in how the rooms look and that in the picture of me as a newborn, there's also a seven-year-old Xo sitting on the bed, smiling at the camera.

"Not in the same way you do," I tell her. Mom died when I was only a few months old. Way too young to have any memories of her.

But I do. I wonder how it would've been to grow up with her around, and to have been able to know her.

I like to think she would've been one of those loud sports moms: hollering and shaking cowbells, wearing one of those awful, homemade "#16's MOM" tees at my soccer games. We would've cooked together and listened to Selena at every opportunity. And she could've been my support and reassurance when I'm on the receiving end of Dad's regular irritability.

"Well, keep on. I'm sure she's exactly as you imagine her," she says. Xo's arm reaches around me, squeezing me into her as she kisses the side of my head. "Anyways, better go before Güelo falls asleep in the truck. Call me if you need anything, all right? Come stay over for a weekend."

"I will." Now that she's back—and tan tonta as I will always believe that is—I'm grateful to have her around making sure I'm not wallowing in loneliness. And that I know I can get some space from Dad.

Xo squeezes my cheek and hugs me one last time before catching up with Güelo. They both wave to me from his truck, and Güelo gives a couple of quick honks as he drives off. His ranchera music audible even after I can't see them anymore.

When I'm back inside, standing against the closed front door, the emptiness of the house feels huge without my sister's and Güelo's energies. Once in my room, I take off my T-shirt and hop into bed, lying down in front of my laptop, open to its regular lineup of websites, like my discreet Twitter account, @andwhataboutittt, which I use for gawking at hot boys, tweeting about Ariana Grande, and keeping up with a few drag queens and the popular Twitter gays. No pictures of me, though. Ever. In case someone who knows me accidentally ends up on it.

My regular Twitter profile, @laMalaLuna, is carefully curated with the opposite: only following friends, classmates, some musicians, and a handful of celebrities and soccer teams. Clean, low profile, and basic. Aside from Lil Nas X and a Frank Ocean fan account, there's not much that would give off even the smallest hint of homosexuality.

A one-eighty from the regular lineup of Lady Gaga and Mariah Carey memes and tweets about how much Pisces cry and how little Capricorns care about *anything* that fill my @andwhataboutittt timeline. Plus the occasional OnlyFans.com nude. A couple of funny Grindr message screenshots. Someone being real salty because *oomf trying to drag Nicki Minaj*. The usual.

Until I reach a set of pictures posted by this boy, @sunnysideup213. They're captioned T-minus 277 days to go until graduation. T-minus no more days until 18, adding a birthday cake and a balloon emoji to the end. I can't remember following him, but I have a habit of thirst-following a ton of guys at random without paying too much attention. If I had to guess, these are his senior pictures. And either he had an amazing photographer or he's incredibly photogenic.

Both. Definitely both.

The pictures are tagged at Venice Beach, which I know is in Los Angeles because of Lana Del Rey and my long-existing obsession with the city. It's been a goal for years now to move there after high school. I could have a chance to cultivate some sort of personal glow up without the constraints that exist at home. And I'm kind of envious of this boy who's already there.

@sunnysideup213 is wearing a light-blue linen button-up and slim khaki chinos rolled up a few inches past his ankle. He's Asian. His skin is close to my own year-long brown. His hair is faded on the sides like mine but pomaded on top and brushed up and all to one side. And his eyes are a pretty dark hazel. A little lighter than my own bordering on pitch-black eyes.

In the first picture, he's sitting in the sand, and a wave has come up to his feet. In the next, he's squatting in the middle of a sidewalk. Both pointer fingers gesture forward to the camera, shops lined along the background. He's in the sand again for the final picture, standing with arms outstretched, each hand holding a flag. One's solid red with a yellow star in the center. Maybe China? Or Taiwan? The other is a Pride flag, altered to include two extra stripes above the red: a black on top and a brown below that.

Shit. How long have I been staring at these pictures? Smiling back at his smile. Sensing myself beginning to create scenarios in my head involving the two of us. I bang my fingers against the mouse pad until I'm out of the maximized view. I don't need the NSA agent assigned to my laptop knowing I've been ogling this boy for an uncomfortably long time.

HAPPY BIRTHDAY! also YAS, SENIORS! I type and then add a little graduate emoji. At the same time imagining having the courage to comment on how good he looks. Then I like his post before continuing my nightly journey down the Twitter feed.

4

I wake up to a notification that @sunnysideup213 is now following @andwhataboutittt. Plus, another thanking me for the birthday wishes. And a third about him liking a few of my tweets. Primarily the ones about Ariana Grande deserving all the good things in this world and how Diego Tinoco could *get it*.

I try to refrain from becoming excessively ecstatic, but there's no calming me down. I'm going to be overhyping this interaction for a while.

I need to get myself together. He doesn't know who I am. I don't even know his name. But also, why is there no gay guy this attractive in Corpus Christi?

At any opportunity I find throughout the day, I'm scrolling through the pictures on @sunnysideup213's Twitter. He has his Instagram linked too, which is perfect for additional stalking.

But I have to be cautious about it. One wrong thumb glide and I'm liking a picture from 2016. Like a closeted, gay basura racoon dumpster diving.

Itzel forcefully slaps the lunch table to get my attention.

"AY LA VERGA," I scream at the same time Jordan yells, "JESUS F—" when I elbow him in the side as a frightened, unintentional reaction.

"I'm trying to ask you what you got on your theology paper!" she says, snapping her fingers near my ear.

"Well, you didn't have to slam the table. Chíngale," I gripe as I get the report out of my bag for her. "And I got a ninety-six."

"OMG, what? How? I got an eighty-nine! Ugh, he hates me, you know?" She grabs the papers and begins to skim through them, continuing her tirade as she reads.

At the student council meeting after school, I'm back to paying attention to nothing and no one besides my phone. Until I hear Mr. Harden, the StuCo faculty sponsor, clearing his throat. I can feel his eyes lasered on me.

When I look up, I see Mirella Garcia, our president, glaring at me.

"We're presenting a motion, Jules," she says. Her manicured fingernails tap the wood of the desk, and I can see in her eyes that whatever patience she came into this meeting with is about gone. "Since you're secretary, could we very quickly bother you to type this into the minutes?"

"Oh. For sure," I reply. I frantically shove my phone into my pocket and begin typing, eyes glued to my laptop. Trying not to think about how much I hate being the center of attention.

And back at home, I spend a few hours forgetting about an essay on voting rights that I should've started last week. My Microsoft Word window long ago minimized and Twitter covering my laptop screen. Liking, retweeting, and commenting on anything @sunnysideup213 posts is priority.

The *ding* of my phone breaks me from my obsessiveness.

Soccer fields tomorrow, Luna? Piña wants to put in some goalie prac, Jordan messages to our group text, "Itzel y Los Dinos" (leaving no confusion as to which one of us Selena stans last renamed the chat), followed by a separate text: Sry, didn't mean to send to group.

God, Jordan, Itzel replies with a bunch of bothered-face emojis. being such an unnecessary disruption to my evening.

Jordan responds with lines of middle-finger and broken-heart emojis in retaliation.

Sounds good, I type, ignoring their text war, followed by a thumbs-up emoji.

Cool. C U mañana bae. Every single time he does this playful bromo thing, I have to use all my strength to fight back a full-on gay implosion.

OMFG keep the sexting between y'all, Itzel sends to the group.

I'll do as I please woman. PS if U and Rolie wanna bring us sonic powerades I'll love U 4ever.

We'll consider it.

Y'all are too much, I type, I'm going to bed. See you tmrw.

MANDE? Rolie inputs, finally noticing the conversation. Wuts goin on tomorrow? Powerades? And TFTI to bed Jules.

Bro sleepover in Luna's bed! I call middle spoon, says Jordan.

Itzel's response of I need new friends is the last line I notice before clicking off my phone and tossing it to the side.

I fall back onto my bed, staring at the ceiling and then the wall on the left side of my bed, where soccer trophies and medals and academic awards fill a shelf a head taller than I am. Beside that, a Mexican flag hangs vertically down. Dad gave it to me when I went with Jordan and his family to see their national team and Argentina play.

And across from the bed, my desk with a small pile of textbooks next to a bookshelf filled with vegan cookbooks Xo got me a couple of Christmases ago when she found out I quit meat. Above those are some classics: *The House on Mango Street* and *Bless Me, Ultima* and a couple of others that've been handed down from Xo and older cousins.

I keep the ones I wouldn't want Dad questioning me about in a box under my bed. The stories that are more obviously gay. Where *Simon vs. the Homo Sapiens Agenda* and *Aristotle and Dante Discover the Secrets of the Universe* hide.

But up here is the life that I've created for mass consumption. A life where I get to witness Jordan—even Rolie sometimes—goof off and be secure in his straightness while I pretend to be someone I'm not. See them joke around and not think anything of it. It makes me wonder how everything could change if I were out. If *I* got to be secure in my sexuality. What lines they'd be afraid of crossing. And the possibility of them cutting ties altogether.

~

Reminder to never say yes to after-school practice with Jordan and Piña ever again.

Soccer in the South Texas September heat, mixed with Gulf Coast humidity, is a special form of torture. I didn't even know my body could sweat this much. I can feel a sun that has to be *extra close* to Texas coloring my skin a few shades darker.

Piña covers the goal, and with his six-foot stature, it's something that he excels at pretty well. His first name's Gabriel, but probably because of sports, almost no one refers to him by anything other than his last name. Besides Jordan, he's my favorite teammate. And those two together? The most questionable straight boys I've ever met.

Jordan and I go head-to-head, switching between offense and defense. I'm not one to brag, but—again, being completely modest—I can keep up with and best anyone on the team. *Except* for Jordan, who is without a doubt the most competitive person in existence and will go best one hundred and one out of two hundred if that's what he's got to do to win.

"Thank God," I huff when I see Rolie and Itzel approaching the practice fields, large Styrofoam cups in hand.

"Let's take ten," Jordan yells to Piña and me, running toward our friends to help carry the drinks.

He hands me one, and I don't bother with the straw and lid. They're only working against me. Plus, this is the best method for getting pieces of crushed ice too. Heaven.

"SLOW. DOWN. Pinche camellito!" Itzel yells, slapping the back of my head, realizing I've swallowed half my drink in seconds.

The quick breather turns into half an hour of Jordan and Piña debating most effective goalie maneuvers. Then Itzel tells us that Lionel Messi is inarguably the hottest man on the planet, and no one can tell her otherwise. A conversation on Shakira's hotness follows because Rolie doesn't know the difference between Messi and Gerard Piqué, which somehow becomes a belly dancing competition to Shakira's "Hips Don't Lie." Trying my best not to gawk at Piña and Jordan gyrating or think the thoughts filling my brain with their very visible dick prints. Roe's *attempt turned hilarious uncoordinated hula* leaves everyone rolling on the ground and grabbing our sides, unable to contain our laughter.

Itzel and I sit against the fence, ignoring the boys, who've now moved on to something about the Dallas Cowboys. She's telling me how her mom did something recently that *annoyed me so much, oh my God*, when Piña walks over, first using the bottom half of his shirt to wipe his face, showing the small but noticeable difference in the browns of his arms and stomach from being out here, and then holding out a hand to her.

"Can we talk?" he asks.

She gives an "mm-hmm," grabbing his hand to stand up. He points to the opposite end of the field, and they both start in that direction.

"What's up with them?" I ask.

"Piña's asking Itzel to homecoming," Jordan answers, not without the slightest bit of grief in his voice.

"But wait, weren't you and Itzel talk—"

Jordan cuts Roe off. "Don't—it's not a thing. She should do whatever she wants."

It's no secret that Jordan and Itzel have had a growing attraction to each other since freshman year. But almost no one knows about them going on a few dates the summer before junior year and a not-exactly-platonic sleepover the week his parents were on a cruise. And how Itzel's parents forbade her from dating him because *certain boys* weren't in her best interest. Especially *the negrito without a Spanish last name.*

They've both seen and dated other people since then. But it isn't too difficult to see that something still exists between them. The spark that shows up once in a while, when Itzel is at her happiest. And it seems as if nothing in the world could keep Jordan down.

I know he's not in the mood to discuss how prejudiced Latinx people can be, so I attempt to divert from Rolie's curiosity. "I guess this means we'll have to get homecoming dates too, then, huh?"

"I was thinking of asking Carolina from mariachi," Roe responds.

"And I asked Avery Aquino last week," Jordan says, letting me know that I'm way behind all my friends.

"Wow, guys, thanks for giving me a heads-up." The four of us, sometimes with the addition of Lou, have gone as a group to every school dance the past three years. Now I have to go put in actual effort.

I could see if Lou's still looking for a date. Pray that she hasn't said yes to anyone yet.

When Itzel makes it back with Piña, she's doing her best to avoid eye contact with Jordan.

"So, want to call it a day?" Piña asks as he grabs the soccer ball.

"Yes, please," I reply, already rushing toward the bleachers to grab my backpack, wanting nothing more than air-conditioning and a shower.

Piña offers to give Itzel a ride home, separating them from the rest of us as they walk to the opposite end of the parking lot. I follow Roe and Jordan to our cars lined up in a row close by.

I grab Jordan's arm as he's opening the door to his Jeep. "You good?"

"Yeah, bro. Everything's one hundred," he replies while waving at Rolie speeding out of the parking lot.

I know you're lying, I almost say.

"I guess I'll have to give you the benefit of the doubt this time?"

"Luna, Itzel's parents are assholes. We know this. But that doesn't mean that we can't still be friends. I'm not gonna lose her because I choose to stay stuck in my feelings."

I sigh. "As long as you're fine. But if you need to talk or vent, I'm here."

It might have been a year since they were close to anything official-adjacent, but it's still difficult to keep my opinions to myself. To not scream at them that they should do what makes them happy. Especially Jordan, who often makes it a habit to hide his emotions and pretend things don't bother him. He has his manhood and pride to keep intact, I guess.

"I'm—they shouldn't treat you like that, though. I'm sorry brown people are still out here acting like Donald Trump."

"That's why our generation's gonna come up and change the world, Luna," he replies as he settles into his vehicle and turns on the Jeep. The Jaden album he's obsessed with starts booming from his speakers, making any further conversation impossible.

5

I heave a couple of reusable Selena-edition H-E-B grocery bags onto the kitchen counter. Whatever I don't need right now goes into the fridge and pantry and the rest is spread out. Set my phone down, open Spotify, select my Cocina Party playlist, and start moving to the beat of "En el Dancefloor" while I begin mentally following a recipe I've had memorized for years now.

I turn one of the knobs on the stove, hearing the clicks of the gas and then seeing the small flame erupt under the range. Then I start cutting homemade corn tortillas into quarters and carefully place them in hot oil to fry, enjoying that angry bubbling sound that comes as soon as the two meet. At the same time, I fill another pan with jackfruit, onion, garlic, jalapeños, and bell pepper, sprinkled with salt, comino, chopped cilantro, and chili powder. Soon the kitchen is filled with mixtures of spicy, sweet, and sharp aromas that are so familiarly Mexican.

When the tortilla pieces are cooked enough, a spicy red salsa made with cayenne, tabasco, jalapeño, and habanero chilis is poured over them and brought to a simmer. Not too long, enough for them to soften.

Add some refried beans, queso fresco, and a fried egg, and I have my favorite breakfast-for-dinner meal: chilaquiles rojos.

Just as I'm taking a seat on the couch, warm bowl of chilaquiles in one hand and phone in the other, I get a Twitter notification that @sunnysideup213 has reposted one of my tweets. I set the bowl down, forgetting about the food for a second. Needing to know which tweet got his attention.

Thx @_michaelcimino_ for never getting back to me about being my HoCo date. Guess I gotta go with a girl.

He added a comment of his own: He never responded to my invite either and a video of Cardi B screaming, "What is the reason?"

@sunnysideup213 *and* Michael Cimino. That's something to keep for later tonight.

Dad's car pulls up into the driveway, earlier than usual. I stop "I Didn't Just Come Here to Dance" as he walks in carrying a gallon of rocky road ice cream.

"What smells good?"

"I made chilaquiles. There's some on the stove if you're hungry."

"Rojo o verde?"

"Rojos, of course," I answer. I know better than to make chilaquiles verdes in the home of a Tamaulipeco.

"Miles Morales tonight?" he asks, setting down his own plate of food. *Into the Spider-Verse* has been our go-to movie since it came out. We've seen it together at least a million times.

Watching movies is one of the few things that we both enjoy. Dad's too busy concentrating on the screen to fixate on whatever it is about me that's currently annoying or angering him. And I can actually enjoy his company for a change.

When we're both sitting on the edge of the couch during the fights at Aunt May's house and in the Super Collider. Or laughing at the diner scene with Peter B. Parker. And how he always whispers all the Spanish curses he knows during *that moment* with Miles and Prowler.

I try to convince myself that this is the real Dad. The one who knocks my arm with his elbow at his favorite parts. The one with the ecstatic smile who shakes my shoulder and can't stop telling me how proud he is after a good soccer game. The one whose eyes light up every time he sees my name in the top ten of the class list.

He switches the TV from Spider-Man to Pandora when the credits roll, going right to his 1980s station. We might've gotten our Selena obsession from Abuelita and introduced to norteños and mariachi from Güelo, but this was the music Dad grew up listening to and raised Xochi and me on. And sure, the songs are catchy, but if I have to hear "Take On Me" one more time—

"How's everything going?" Dad asks. That real vague question parents always ask and expect to get a full play-by-play on all that is their kid's life. *Can you be more specific, please?*

I give him a brief summary of my classes, practice with Jordan and Piña, and asking Lou to homecoming.

"Lucette? ¿La pendejita? Don't y'all go together every year, the five of you?"

"Jordan and Rolie both got dates this year and Piña asked Itzel."

Luckily, Lou was still juggling offers and wasn't a complete hassle to persuade. I owe her a personal three-course dinner, have to do her Spanish homework for a month, and convince Xochi to get us a couple of bottles for tomorrow's party, but whatever. At least I know I'll for sure have fun.

"You couldn't go with anyone else? Isn't there a girl you like who you could've asked? Or got to Itzel before she said yes to some other cabrón? You can't have been friends with her for this long and not have thought the two of you could be good together."

"We're just friends, Dad," I say. A hint of frustration comes out with the words. This isn't the first time he's tried to convince me to have some sort of romantic or even sexual attraction toward Itzel.

No heterosexual boy would be *just friends* with Itzel for three years and be content with it. My unchanging response has become a sensitive issue.

"You hang around her and that necia Lou all the time, never having a girlfriend, people will assume things, mi'jo. You—I wish you'd put yourself out there more. Be more of a man about things."

"I know, Dad." I know that he's not worried what people might assume. He's worried that they'll find out they're right. And that he won't have any choice but to confront it.

I sigh, considering all the reactions that might happen if I came out to Dad right now. Comparable to ripping off a Band-Aid: fast, flinching, and not without a sting. At least I'd spare us these talks about girls and relationships that'll never happen. But I don't see him loving the idea of me bringing a boy home. So for now, suffering through the constant interrogations is the best, safest choice.

Breaking my train of thought, Dad asks, "You've decided on the colleges you're applying to?"

"I have four or five in mind right now. I'm meeting with Mr. Calderón tomorrow to go over some options. I already mentioned UCLA, plus University of Southern California. And he brought up a Catholic college in LA that he wants me to do some research on. I'll apply to UT too. And Saint Edward's."

"You aren't considering the school here too, Julián?" He huffs and shakes his head. "Can't wait to be anywhere else once you graduate. Xo was the exact same. But it wouldn't be the end of the world, mi'jo. I get you're young and have this idea of some great life across the country, but a life here wouldn't be so bad, right?"

I know Dad only wants what's best for me. Or whatever concept of that that plays out in his head. But while my world might not end if I stay here, it's never going to begin either.

I want to tell Dad that no matter where I go to college, and for whatever amount of time I'm away from home, a part of my heart will always be in Corpus with him, even as often as I've felt devalued or not enough in his eyes. That things will change, and I doubt he'll like it. That I need to have a chance to figure myself out. To live and make decisions without worry of judgment.

That I want to finally be comfortable with who I am. And to date boys. To realize that some are complete trash while others are fairy-tale perfect. I can't do that here. I can't do that with him around.

I tell him that I will *think about* adding A&M Corpus Christi to my list of potential colleges, and Dad settles for that for now, sensing the building tension and choosing to quit the prodding for tonight. He mentions how he still doesn't understand why there's a pig Spider-Man and jokes about how he's beginning to get a stomach like Peter B. Parker. I notice his yawns and eyes getting heavy from a long day at work.

I stay in the living room when Dad goes to bed, not yet tired enough to go to sleep and too lazy to drag myself to my room. I look up the school my guidance counselor mentioned, Loyola something. It's pretty in a way that reminds me of home, except up on a hill instead of everything being at sea level, and you can see the mountains. There's a chapel right in the middle of campus. And the ocean in the other direction.

Not a first choice, but I'll add it to the list.

I switch to Instagram, where a photo of Angel Curiel being his usual flawlessly cute self pops up at the top of my feed. And then I *somehow* end up on his profile, looking through all his shirtless pics and videos of him speaking in that hot accent of his, when I get a notification that @sunnysideup213 has replied to another one of my tweets.

This one from earlier tonight: Who's gonna tell my dad I'm NOT staying in state for college?

His response: Cali's great if you tryna find yourself, with a Golden Gate emoji at the end. And then, PS the emoji might be misleading, I'd like to specify SoCal!

God is testing me. Seeing if I can hold a basic *not even in person* conversation with another gay person without looking all baboso.

LA is the dream! I type. Applying to a few schools there and crossing my fingers that at least one of them accepts me.

I almost add *maybe we can hang out when I go visit universities* but realize that might be a pretty big flex for a not-even-openly-gay kid hiding behind a secret Twitter account.

The tweet becomes an invite for anyone else with an opinion to share. @trashyHOEmo replies with a strong argument for why New York City is very much better than Los Angeles. @godstansLOONA and @GokusBabyMama are trying to convince me that the Bay Area is, by every measurable standard, the best part of California. And @LaReynaChicharron sides with @sunnysideup213, both firmly in the Los Angeles camp.

"Way too many thoughts," I mutter as I mute the conversation. I've lost all control of my social media to gay Twitter. They can keep debating. I'm going to bed.

6

Rolie and I run through the aisles at H-E-B, eager to get out and over to Lou's. We toss bags of regular wavy, limón, and jalapeño potato chips; Takis; Hot Cheetos; tortilla chips; and containers of salsa and ranch into our basket. And when we start walking to the self-checkout, he throws in a large bag of peanut M&M's and a Mexican Coke.

Our final stop is Papito's Pizza. Rolie holds the boxes toward me so I can place them on the back seat, overwhelming me with the smell of pepperoni and garlic inches from my face. And just before we get going, he turns around to open the topmost box, grabbing a slice of pizza. Led himself right into temptation.

"No me critiques, compa," Roe says, noticing my eyes saying all the judgmental things I won't say aloud. "I'm DD. I can do whatever I want tonight."

"Not arguing with that," I concede as we make our way to Lou's, no more delays keeping us from the chaos that I'm sure is waiting for us.

~

Some of my favorite things about the weekend are the reasons to wear clothes that aren't the same school-colors shirts, shorts, and chinos. All of us pulling out the Forever 21, H&M, and Urban Outfitters outfits we've been waiting for the chance to show off. Nothing like being told what to wear for five days to have Itzel giving her best Maddy-from-*Euphoria*-inspired look.

My least favorite thing? The hangover I already know I'll have in the morning when Lou greets Roe and me at the door, bottle of Patrón in hand.

"House rule: everyone takes a shot to enter!" she demands, yelling slurred Spanish curses when she almost trips over a step. Since Roe's driving, Lou amends the rule. I have to take my own shot plus one for the designated driver *and* an extra one for being her *HoCo Co-Ho*.

I glare at them while holding a cup half-filled with tequila. Hoping they might be joking or change their minds. Nope.

Lou and Roe both cheer me on as I shoot back liquor in her front yard. How *on brand* for one of her parties.

Rolie leads me to the kitchen with the groceries, pizza, and bottles Xochi and Roe's older brothers provided. I grab a slice of cheese and jalapeño pizza, empty the contents of a bag of red pepper flakes over it, and demolish the slice. The Patrón is already hard at work.

"There's no way I'm gonna be the first one drunk," I say, still chewing my food. Rolie watches me, looking awestruck at my eating ability.

I hear an already tipsy Jordan scream my name from behind me and feel his body crash into my own. His arms wrap around my stomach.

"Luna . . . Luna . . . *Bro*. Lou's brother hooked it up with some Jack and Absolut. You're taking a shot with me. Which one do you want?"

"He has to take one for me too, Jordan!" Rolie replies. "As designated driver, I'm naming Jules as my drinking proxy."

If looks could kill, I'd have murdered Roe plenty of times over right now.

"Yes!" Jordan shouts. He opens the whiskey and pours it straight into a Solo cup.

"JORDAN. STOP!" I shout when I realize he was planning on filling my entire cup with Jack Daniel's and not thinking twice about it. I take a deep inhale and say a quick prayer as we lift our cups.

"Arriba, abajo, al centro, y pa'dentro!" Jordan and I toast before swallowing the liquid. Fighting it for a second as it tries to come back up, covering my mouth with my arm so he and Rolie don't see me gagging.

As I reach for another slice of pizza, I'm finding it harder to believe that I'll remember any of this tomorrow. When Itzel and Piña arrive, Jordan doesn't let us go anywhere before doing a soccer team shotgun. He hands Piña and me each a can of Bud Light, not allowing either of us to decline. Then Lou forces everyone into a Waterfall-style group chug of trash-can punch, and I don't know why God is punishing me tonight, but I somehow pick the end spot.

Itzel, standing next to me, catches me taking only small sips of punch at a time. She starts tipping my cup up with her free hand, not letting me get away with babysitting my drink. By the time I'm finally able to stop, I've gone through nearly six refills.

It's been maybe more than an hour since arriving to the party, and I am more trashed than I've ever been in my life. Dancing along to a mixture of Cardi B, Years & Years, Jenni Rivera, and Khalid without any real care in the world. Itzel and Lou sandwich me in between them, and we sing incoherently along to the music. The strobe lights Lou's dad keeps for big parties flash around the room, adding to my dizziness.

I stumble into the bathroom, feeling the consequences of ingesting way too much alcohol on my bladder and kidneys. I've lost too many games of beer pong to count and, with my sobriety long gone, have been saying yes to anyone offering me a drink. I wash my hands and assess how intoxicated I look. Or, at least, *attempt* to assess how drunk I look. Staring into the mirror turns into checking myself out. The sleeves of my white-and-blue-striped shirt have been pushed above my elbows, and most of the buttons are undone. I'm almost certain this was Lou and Itzel's doing during our dancing.

And I'm feeling the look. Heavily.

"Hold on," I tell my reflection, one hand out like I'm telling myself *stop* and the other digging through my pocket for my phone. "Hold on. Hold on. *Hold on.*

"Why is it so fucking hard to get to the camera?" I continue, groaning as I keep tapping on the screen, missing the camera, and ending up at the calculator, then screen recording and the brightness bar before finally getting where I want. My mind is barely keeping up with me as I go through pose after pose in the mirror, taking I don't even know how many pictures.

Twitter! These deserve to go on Twitter. If I can just—*where is that stupid bird icon?*

Exiting the restroom, I spot Itzel and hand her my phone. "Itzel! Itzel! Itzel-y belly peanut butter and jelly! Hey, I noticed that I look cute AF, and we need to document this for the world. So take—get some pictures of me. And of us together! But mainly me."

She finishes what's left of her drink and grabs my phone. We make the entire house our backdrop. Jumping on Lou's brother's bed. In the backyard, where Lou helps me do a handstand and twerk against a tree. Lying across Piña, Jordan, and Roe on the couch and in the bathtub.

Itzel and I look through the pictures and pass a bottle of Smirnoff between us, still sitting in the tub. I'm telling her in slurred words how sincere I am that she should go work at *Vogue* with her professional-level photography skills and how happy I am that she's one of my best friends, along with more of the usual lovey drunk-Jules banter.

"Can I—can, can . . . will you be mad if I tell you something?" I struggle to ask. My voice has taken a cliff dive from airy to somber.

I know where my mind and mouth are steering me, as much as whatever sobriety left in me struggles to rein it in. Am I having this conversation right now? Drunk and in a bathtub?

"Jules, you know that I love you too much to be mad at you. *So much.* Like, this much." She extends her arms as far as possible, hitting me in the face in the process, causing both of us to laugh hysterically.

"Yo sé, but—I don't want anything to change. I don't want to screw everything up, you know?"

She scoots as close to me as she can. "You're my best friend. And there's nothing that could ever get in the way of that."

"Do you think Jordan and Rolie feel the same way?"

"Of course they feel the same way. Where—what's going on with you?"

The words want to come out. All the alcohol in my system is creating a waterslide for my truth to stream down from my brain, unable to process decision-making, to my tongue. "I—it's hard to say it, but—"

"What are you two doing? I gotta take a piss." Jordan looks at Itzel and me hanging out in the tub with intense interest on a face that's telling us he's gonna drop his pants whether he has company or not. He helps both of us out of the tub, the conversation now forgotten, and I'm back to happily animated. Itzel and I scream, trying to get Jordan to take a selfie with us while he shoves us out of the bathroom.

~

Props to sober-Jules's preparedness in asking Xochi earlier today if I could spend the night. Getting back home, drunk, and waking up Dad wouldn't have been a great start to my weekend. Her only stipulation was that we bring her Whataburger.

Itzel and Jordan leave Lou's with Rolie and me, and it takes all his effort to keep us from tearing into our food in his car.

"¡Dámelos!" he yells, taking all our bags and placing them at his feet so his vehicle won't end up covered in fries.

By the time we reach Xo's home, my eyes and head are becoming heavy. My vision and mind have been fuzzy since before we left Lou's, and I'm barely aware of Rolie carrying me over his shoulder and handing me a jalapeño cheddar biscuit as I belt Lorde's "Supercut" into my sober friend's ear. I'm even less aware of him tossing me onto the bed in Xochi's guest room. Itzel and Jordan hop onto the bed too with their food, whispering with Roe.

"Wha're—huh?" comes out of my mouth in a tired, mostly unconscious moan as what's left of me tries and fails to focus on the indiscernible words. Passing out thinking about how my phone won't stop vibrating in my hand.

7

I wake up feeling severely dehydrated, head pounding, and unsure of when I changed into one of Xo's UTSA shirts. And—*why is there half a biscuit in my hand?* Groaning, I turn over and am stunned by the light coming in through the window. I yell and reach for the closest pillow to hide myself in darkness.

The bedroom door opens, and a hand shakes my foot. I reply with muffled gripes into the cushion. *Leave me alone here to die.*

"Jules." It's Jordan. "Get up, dude. I have some water for you."

Jules? He never refers to me by anything other than *Luna* unless it's some important life discussion. I haven't heard him say *Jules* since the first time he told me not to let what our asshole teammates say bother me. Or when we talked about Itzel's parents.

I reluctantly toss the pillow aside and grab the cup from Jordan, downing it in seconds. He motions for me to scoot over, asking to join me on the bed. I feel so sick. But I'm not sure if it's because of the heavy drinking from last night or from the dread of whatever conversation he's wanting to have right now.

Is he about to tell me I threw up on Itzel?

"I, uh—I don't know if you remember anything from last night. You were pretty gone, bro. And I'm not sure you knew exactly what you were doing."

My memories are hazy, and even that might be understating it. But—oh my God, I hit on Jordan. When he had to go to the bathroom and Itzel and I were in the tub. And as he was shoving us out, I told him that he could—no, I thought I only dreamed that. But what if I did and—I won't be able to look him in the eyes ever again—

"Jules. Bro." Jordan calls me back to attention, shaking my arm. "Look, regardless, we don't think any different of you. Seriously. But do you remember posting on Twitter last night?"

I don't. I reach over Jordan to grab my phone, feeling an anxiety attack near. There are an endless number of notifications displayed on my lock screen and more still coming through. My finger jabs and swipes, rushing to get into Twitter.

I see a post on my @laMalaLuna account from last night with four of my drunk-ass mirror selfies. It's captioned, Im coming out want th wolrd to no #LGBTQtwitter. There's even an emoji of two guys holding hands and a rainbow for extra gay emphasis.

I'm dizzy. My hands have trouble holding on to the phone because I can't keep them from shaking. I have to force myself to keep breathing because my body's incapable of doing it on its own. I've never felt more overwhelmed by embarrassment and fear and frustration.

I can't bring myself to look further, letting the phone fall between my crossed legs and my face drop into my hands. Jordan's fingers lightly scratch my back, and he repeatedly presses me to answer whether I'm okay or not.

I don't know. Probably not. But I nod for his sake, unsure if even I believe that.

Chinga'o. What did I get myself into?

"Itzel mentioned a conversation y'all had in the bathroom that seemed to be leading to this. We just wanna know that you're in a stable place internally. And if you're not, it's—we'd understand, but we're here for whatever you need, all right?"

I look at Jordan, whose face is strained in that familiar *wanting to be sympathetic, how do I best help my friend* look.

"I wish I had the perfect words to say right now, Jules. But I'm at a loss, and I'm sorry. This was kind of something we were all waiting for, but I imagined it would be in a way that you had complete control over. And I don't think that was the case last night when you posted this, right? Not that you can go back on it now, but—I mean, either way, know that you're still our best friend, and you're still Xo's baby brother, and we want you to be happy. And we want to be happy with you, dude. I—I don't want you to ever question whether our friendship comes with limitations."

But I did.

"I—I know," I begin to say, hearing my voice shake. "But there was always a little voice in the back of my head that would whisper, *What if I lose them? What if they hate me because of this?*" The words become a murmur as I let this secret out into the world.

"It was easier to keep it bottled up. That, plus what everyone else at school would say or how Dad and my güelo would react." I try to keep myself from becoming too worked up picturing how this will affect the days and months to come. "And I knew I for sure wouldn't be ready for that if I didn't have y'all."

Jordan wraps both arms around me, pressing most of his weight into the side of my body. "Jules, I—I wish I could go back in time and give this big signal that everything would be okay with us. I hate knowing that you went any amount of time worried we'd bail or turn on you because of this. And I—look, I'm sorry to have to tell you this, but you're stuck with me, dude. You're my brother, and who you bang or, I guess, get banged by—depending on what you're into—isn't gonna change that."

He squeezes me tighter when he hears my short laugh at his comment. "You know that we always got each other's backs. Since day one. So if we gotta take care of someone who wants to say something stupid, then we will. Don't let whatever crap they say get to you, and we'll handle the rest. And I'm sure Xo will wanna talk to you about y'all's family when she and Roe get back."

Wait. We're alone.

"Xo and Rolie aren't here? And Itzel?"

"She's here. We thought it would be a better idea if only one of us gave you the news. We didn't wanna overwhelm you or anything. Plus, I told her I didn't want her ruining any kind of *bi-curious between bros* vibe that might happen."

I shove Jordan off me, almost making him fall off the bed. He's always been reliable at breaking whatever tension is in a room. Luckily, I can count on my best friend to be both incredibly supportive *and* the most foolish.

"I am serious, though; if I were even the tiniest bit into guys, we'd be the greatest same-gender, multiracial power couple in history."

"Pinche estúpido, Jordan. Don't get my hopes up."

"Hey, one day I could wake up and realize that girls are too much trouble."

"No, you won't."

He lets himself consider the possibility for all of three seconds. "Yeah, never mind. You're right. I won't."

We get up from the bed, and I follow him out. I tell him to go to the living room without me, needing to brush my teeth and wash some of the tired off my face first. I take deep breaths as I stand over the bathroom sink, trying not to feel crushed by the weight of knowing I outed myself last night.

I drag my feet down the hall to my friends. Itzel jumps from the couch and embraces me in the middle of the living room. My face falls between her neck and shoulder.

"You know I love you, right?" she asks.

I nod my head into her.

"And that you're still my best friend, no matter what, right?"

I nod again.

"And that we'll fuck up anyone who tries to mess with you?"

I nod a third time.

"Good. Do you want to talk right now?" She waits for me to answer her fourth question. I shake my head. It's not that I don't want to talk to her. I'm not in the right mindset.

She gently pushes me off her, holding on to my arms, and kisses my cheek.

"I know you didn't mean to post any of that, but I'm proud of you." Now that I can see her, I notice a few tears traveling down the side of her face. "I'm proud of every part of who you are and am incredibly blessed to be a part of your life, mi estúpido, estúpido Julito."

"Stop talking or else I'll start crying too," I whine as I fall into the couch.

"Ugh, you're right. You're right." She wipes her face and takes a seat beside me. "We don't need that today. No more crying."

Itzel takes immediate interest in what everyone's been saying on Twitter. We look through the replies while ignoring the direct messages after the first one was full of lewd (and not at all impressive) pictures. Although there're the occasional trolls leaving hateful comments—Itzel insists that I immediately delete and then block those—there's a lot of love and encouragement from both people I know and random strangers.

It all begins to feel not so apocalyptic.

"You're finally up, 'manito?" Xochi asks when she and Rolie come through the front door, bags of breakfast tacos in hand. "Next time take it easy on the punch, huh?" She hands me a potato-and-egg taco wrapped in foil and a couple of containers of salsa verde. As she makes her way around the couch, she stops to kiss the back of my head. "Te quiero, 'Lito. We'll talk later, yes?"

I give her a hesitant thumbs-up, mouth already full of taco.

It happened. I came out. Whether I meant to or not, would have preferred this happen any other way or not, felt ready or not. Sure, I'm scared. And even more angry with myself for being this irresponsible. But I feel undoubtedly lighter. Freer.

The heaviness from the fear that my friends or my sister would reject me is gone. I'm still worried that going back to school on Monday will be a nightmare. Disappointing Güelo and the millions of ways this will not go well with Dad. But I have right now. And when I manage to block out all the negative thoughts vying for my attention, my happiness is incalculable.

Jordan leans his head on my shoulder as we go through all the pictures Itzel took last night and the stories from everyone's Snapchat and Instagram. "I can't believe we thought these were good, Jules," Itzel says. She swipes through the photos on my phone, texting some of her favorites to herself.

"Luna," Jordan mumbles into my shoulder. "You know I love you, bro, but I have to be honest and let you know that you smell like four different types of alcohol. Speaking for everyone when I ask in the nicest possible way for you to please go shower, dude."

This earns him his second shove of the morning as I pick myself up from the couch. I grab some clothes from a dresser drawer I keep stocked in Xo's spare bedroom and return to the bathroom. Craving one of those *stand under the water for half an hour* type of showers.

I hear a ding from my phone as I'm undressing. It's a direct-message notification. From @sunnysideup213 to @laMalaLuna.

The anxiety's returning. As if someone karate chopped me in the throat. How did he find this account?

It only takes minimal diving to see that I retweeted the pictures onto my @andwhataboutittt account, adding dis me who wants to be my BF? to the post.

The desire to further beat myself up for how senseless I was is second only to wanting to open the message. Needing to know what my Twitter crush sent.

OK where have you been hiding all my life? Now I'm crossing my fingers that you end up in LA for college. And if you happen to still be looking for a BF at that point I'd like to preemptively volunteer! Congrats on coming out too. Hope it's been nothing but kindness.

My phone almost drops from my hands and into the toilet. I try to keep my breathing pattern regular. My mouth is agape, mind malfunctioning and eyes skimming the short message over and over again.

8

It's not as if I hadn't received countless similar messages throughout the past eight hours. But most of them were from sketchy guys whose attempts at compliments left me more grossed out than flattered. This, though, is different.

This is @sunnysideup213.

The guy who's been in my head for days now. Someone who's not creepy, my age, *so good-looking*. And he seems to be at least into me enough to slide into my DMs, considering what my relationship status might look like a year from now.

However, there's one crucial box that remains unticked: lives in Corpus Christi. Or even Texas. Or at the very least not two time zones away. Social media can give that immediate connection to someone while making me ask myself daily why every single one of my soul mates lives hundreds, if not thousands, of miles away.

I list all the potential next steps as I scrub off the lingering scent of beer, whiskey, and whatever was in Lou's punch. Ignoring his message is off the table. I'm not stupid. But I don't want to say something that makes me look brand-new to this in the saddest way.

I can't deal with this right now. I'll come back to him when my mind isn't on the verge of exploding. No matter how desperately I want to respond.

~

"Want coffee, 'manito?" Xo asks, pouring herself some while I sit on the counter next to her.

"No thanks," I reply, pretending like I need to throw up. "Coffee's muy asqueroso."

She gives me a confused glare, opens the fridge, and hands me a carton of cran-apple juice and a cup.

"So I'm going to be the chismosa older sister and ask. Is there a boy?"

I choke on the juice. Some comes out of my nose as I struggle to clear my throat. "No, Xo. That's not happening. No boy."

I mean, except for the boy volunteering to be my boyfriend next year. But that's not real. And not something I'm telling her.

"Huh. Smarter anyways to wait until college. Better options, bigger pool, and condoms are way more accessible—"

"Oh my God," I interrupt, hands covering my ears. "I am for sure not having this conversation with you."

"Hey, I had a lot of gay friends in college who left very little to the imagination on the specifics of what goes where. I could go on and on about how important lubrication is. Oh, and with your fingers—"

"I will give you any amount of money to please stop!"

Xochi smirks as she brings her coffee mug to her lips. "Only trying to help you out, baby brother," she says with a wink. Moving toward the coffeepot to top off her mug, she takes a long, deep sigh before the sound of my phone vibrating beside me gets both of our attention.

Dad shows up in the middle of the screen. The last person I want to talk to right now. I hit the side of my phone, letting the call go silent, and we both wait for it to go to voice mail before saying anything.

"You telling him?"

I know she chose not to start that question with *when are* on purpose.

"No sé. You know how he is." I stare at the tile floor.

Xochi places a hand on my chin and lifts my face so we're looking straight at each other.

"'Lito, that's perfectly fine. The time and place for that talk, and if it happens at all, is up to you. And if you need me there with you, I will be. And I don't care if you've already been told this by all your friends this morning and are getting tired of hearing it, but I love you, I support you, I'm proud of you, and if you *ever* need anything or want to talk through whatever is going on with your life, you can come to me."

She places her mug on the counter next to me and hugs me. There's been a lot of hugging this morning, but I'm not complaining. It reminds me that this is real. That my coming-out isn't some confusing dream. And that I'll be okay.

~

Oh my God. @sunnysideup213. I've ignored him all day.

I nearly throw my dinner onto the floor rushing to get to my phone and open his message. My thumbs quickly start typing, then deleting, then typing some more. Editing it until I have something that's close to ideal.

You know, existing in my cocoon for 17 years. Guess now I'm making my grand entrance. And if LA works out, you'll definitely be the first to know. Coming out was . . . well didn't play out exactly the way I'd ever pictured it, but good. I'm lucky to have some rly supportive people in my life.

My eyes stay glued to the screen as if I should expect to get an immediate reply when I've made him wait hours. Not happening. I put it under my leg and try not to fixate on whether I'm actually feeling my phone vibrate or if phantom vibrations are making a joke out of my life. Because, surprise, it's *always* phantom vibrations.

I've nearly fallen asleep when my phone dings. I'm cussing as I throw pillows across the room and pat around the comforter, searching for my phone in the dark as the sounds continue. And I'm glad no one is present to witness the big, elated smile on my face when I see it's another message from my Twitter crush.

I'll be keeping an eye out come August then. Not that I'm hoping for you to be single or anything. Actually . . . maybe hope is an accurate word. Just trying to shoot my shot. He follows that with a GIF of a basketball player throwing a ball and whose arms go up and wide when it lands right through the net.

And glad you finally broke outta there. The metamorphosis looks good on you, he continues, followed by a third message. Wow I'm realizing I've been using your coming out as a reason to very openly hit on you. And then a final reply: And now I'm gonna continue typing as if it'll make me seem any more normal. FUUCKSJKSJSKS k thx bye.

He's awkward. And that's such a relief and really funny and actually makes him even more attractive.

Normal's overrated. And don't worry you've been way less cringey than most of Twitter today. I press reply before continuing. And if it helps, since you posted those senior pics, I've spent way more time stalking your social media than I would ever admit.

Oh well I'm definitely interested tho in hearing how much time you've spent staring at my pics. Maybe its equal to the number of hours I've spent today going through yours, he responds within seconds.

Yeah? Anything in particular catch your attention? Not sure when I grew the balls for that one.

The pics from your friend's pool party. Never seen anyone make an avocado floaty look so good.

Nope. This can't be reality.

Your turn! he sends. Which pic is your fav?

All of them. They all tie for first.

Mm the one of you in front of the Hollywood sign. Big LA mood.

Solid choice. Glad we both have preferences for each others shirtless pics. I'm Mat btw.

PURELY FOR ARTISTIC REASONS. And I'm Julián, but everyone calls me Jules.

It's nice to know you, Jules. And for sure. Arts great.

Talking to @sunnysideup213—I mean, Mat—is like when you make a friend in kindergarten: spontaneous, unforced, naturally comfortable in an instant. Attraction aside, this is my first time having an actual conversation with another out gay person. And someone who's never known me as anything else. Which is *huge*.

But also, he's *so* attractive. And that's the best added bonus.

He tells me about his own coming-out. A pretty straightforward event, since his older brother and sister are both queer-identifying. And how amazing growing up in Los Angeles is, while not being at all subtle about dropping praise on all the city's universities—UCLA being his top choice too.

And he tells me how he goes by Mat in public, or even Matthew if he's feeling forgiving enough of people colonizing his name. But his given name is Mặt Trời. It means *sun* in Vietnamese.

So why LA for college? Not to seem against the idea bc I'm v pro Jules being in LA. Just curious.

Would you judge me if I told you I let a Buzzfeed quiz decide for me?

ABSOLUTELY. Yes.

Then forget I mentioned it. But honestly if Corpus was, say, a Charmander, then LA would be the Charizard. I'm used to living by the beach, being in the Southwest-ish part of the country, heat, but I want something bigger and better and less conservative where I can have the freedom to evolve. I considered Chicago, New York, and Boston but the idea of being somewhere with an actual winter sounds horrible. Gave some thought to Miami or Orlando too, but Florida? Hard pass.

Loving the Pokémon comparison. Now I'm wondering what a Charmander version of LA is like.

A beach. And a Selena statue. That's it.

By the time four thirty comes around, my eyes are struggling to stay open. Mat keeps apologizing when he remembers the two-hour time difference, realizing that it's not actually only two thirty everywhere.

Would you be cool texting instead of DMing over Twitter? If not, no worries. I get it. But it'd be easier, you know. And yes, this is me asking for your number.

I'm more certain than not that he isn't some sixty-year-old man pretending to be a Vietnamese American teenager, so I tell Mat it's fine and message him my phone number—not without a small internal scream, realizing this is the first time I'm giving my number to a boy who's not my straight friend, classmate, or family member—before closing out of the app and setting my phone down beside my head.

The screen brightens and displays a two-word text message. The last thing I see before falling asleep: goodnight, Jules.

9

Bojo-what?

BO-JUT-SU, Mat replies, stressing each syllable. It's a type of martial art using a really long stick. My ma and ba signed me up for it when I was little because I was hyperactive and always getting in trouble. And I do wrestling now with my school.

You as a problem child makes complete sense, I reply while my mind goes straight to him in a wrestling uniform.

Mat replies with one of those emoji faces that looks super frustrated and has air coming from its nose.

We've been texting basically since he woke up. What started out as a Morning! turned into a back-and-forth that, two hours later, still hasn't stopped.

Okay, he starts. Favorite place to eat. Go.

Mm, oh there's this frutería here called Viva Chamoy. And besides the obvious great things like aguas frescas, mangonadas, cucumber cups, and Takis and cheese, they make the BEST nachos. They even started using vegan ground "beef" and they make it spicy and load it with jalapeños. It's SO GOOD.

You had me at aguas frescas.

Your turn!

In-N-Out. Obviously.

I *wish* he could see my dramatic eye roll. Out of ALL the food in LA you pick that? As a Texan, I need you to know that even as someone who doesn't eat meat, it's a fact that "your fav" is TRASH compared to Whataburger.

Hold on, he replies. Give me one sec.

A couple of minutes later, he catches me off guard with a FaceTime request.

Did me wishing he could see my eye roll do this? Did I conjure this?

Mild freak-out. About to *talk* to him. I guess at least he didn't call when I was on the toilet?

When I answer, Mat's smiling while walking out of an In-N-Out, bag of food in hand. He's wearing glasses, and—swear—no one has ever pulled off poor vision so well. Damn, he's way too attractive.

"Listen, I get that you Texans are all obsessed with Whataburger or *what-a-ever*, but it doesn't even have *animal-style*. I mean, I find it hard to believe that it's better than this." He displays the white bag, making sure to get as much of the logo as possible. "Oh, and just putting it out there, looking real cute today, Jules."

"I—you—" Hearing my name come out of Mat's mouth for the first time has me forgetting how to exist. "I'm pretty sure you added that last part only because you knew I wouldn't continue to correct your drastically wrong opinion. And to be honest, it worked. *Mat.*"

He laughs as he sets the bag down on the roof of his car to reach for his keys, and I'm so enamored at the way his cheeks rise and make his eyes close. *I'm cute? He's cute.*

"Glad to know it worked. I'll be sure to keep that in mind if I ever piss you off. Anyways, sorry for making this quick, but gotta get back home. I'll talk to you in a bit, though. Are you gonna be busy tonight?"

"No, I don't think so. Some guys from soccer want to get a game going later, but that's it."

"Cool. Well, if you feel compelled to take any locker-room pics while you're changing and need someone to send them to, you got my phone number."

"Are you always this shameless?"

"I prefer to think of it as confident," he says. "Talk to you later, Jules."

"Bye, Mat."

I like how his name feels. How it's him who I think about when I say it. His smile and boldness.

And the little voice in the back of my head that may have still been *slightly* concerned he could be a sixty-year-old man pretending to be a Vietnamese American teenager is very relieved to know it was actually Mat on the other end. But I have to throw my head back and groan at my depressing reality.

Why do you have to live so far away?

~

"Can I get serious with you? Just for, like, a sec," Mat asks.

"Uh, yeah. Sure."

"I was remembering one of your messages from yesterday. You mentioned that your coming-out wasn't exactly how you pictured it. Wanted to make sure that you weren't implying, I guess, something disastrous or otherwise comparable."

"Oh. Well, *otherwise comparable* might be a good way to put it. I got *way* too drunk on Friday night, which led to me convincing myself that coming out would be a good idea. I can't remember posting any of it and had never told anyone before then, so the morning after wasn't great. And not only because of the hangover. Honestly, if I had been sober, I doubt I would've come out at all."

Mat stares at me. His eyes full of worry. "I—that sucks, Jules. Although, thinking about it, I should've realized something was off.

You misspelled half those words. Too focused on the pictures. My bad. And not that coming out sucks. Unless it's putting you in an unsafe situation. But it doesn't sound super ideal. Which is, well, shitty. You're fine, though?"

"I'm trying to not beat myself up over how reckless I am. But I'm fine. At least, for the time being. I'll get back to you when I finally tell my dad and abuelo."

While I will forever look back at this past Friday and beat myself up over how no one can wreck my life as well as *I* can wreck my life, I know I wouldn't change anything about how the weekend played out if the opportunity magically presented itself. I still have my friends, my sister, and I got to spend the larger part of the past forty-eight hours talking to Mat.

A week ago, I knew him only by a Twitter handle. So obvious pros and cons.

"Well, I'm here for you, in whatever you might describe this capacity as, when you finally tell your family. It can be hard telling people you're gay, as I'm sure you've realized this weekend."

"Actually, even though I'm out now, I don't think I've said the words yet. At least, not out loud."

"For real? Well, if you want to get some practice, you could say it to me."

"What? You aren't serious."

"Yeah, I am. This is as inconsequential as it gets. Trust me. You won't catch me by surprise."

I open my mouth and can feel the sentence travel down from my brain to the tip of my tongue, but I find myself having trouble letting it out. Even to this fellow gay person over the computer. I can feel my head strain and my gut clench.

"Why is saying it this hard?" This isn't new information. I've always known. I've said this sentence in my head daily for as long as I can remember.

"You have to let go of everything negative you associate with being gay. All that makes us resent this part of ourselves. And then come to terms with who you are. Reject all the hate you were raised to believe. It won't be something that happens overnight, but you'll get there. I believe in you, Jules. Take that first step."

Mat must've read my face, wondering when he switched from clown to counselor. "My brother and sister were already in their mid-twenties when I came out," he adds. "I had lots of people to lean on and be my therapists."

He's right, though. There's knowing and accepting, and there's knowing and burying. I've been doing the latter my entire life. Long enough that saying anything different seems unnatural. But it is natural. It's who I am.

"I'm—" I take a deep breath and exhale. "I am gay. I'm gay. I'm gay." Each time I repeat the words, they come out a little easier. With a little more confidence.

"Congrats!" Mat claps and gives me a high-spirited smile. "You did the damn thing! On behalf of the LGBTQ-etcetera-etcetera community, we welcome you to the coolest club on the planet. I'll make sure they send you your complimentary Pride flag, champagne, and OJ. Think you're ready for the first day of school as openly-gay-Julián?"

"I hadn't put a lot of thought into that yet. Praying it turns out no one cares."

"Maybe it'll turn out a classmate has a crush on you."

"No way," I mock. "And even if there was literally anyone else gay in the entire school, I'm not interested in any of them."

"You'd be surprised. It only takes one person to live their truth before more people start realizing they can too. And then you'll be all, *Huh, you're cute. Please date me.*"

"Did your coming-out lead to boys admitting their crushes on you?"

"Kinda. I mean, since coming out my sophomore year, I've had two boyfriends, and one did come out to me only days after I did. They were both cool. Not for me, though."

"Then I guess I'll let you know how the day goes and how many boyfriends I have by the end of school tomorrow." I lie down on my stomach, looking into Mat's eyes brightly displayed on my laptop. "It'll be fine, right? I have nothing to worry about?"

"Nothing at all. If anything seems not right, stick with your friends. And if you need to talk to someone who's been there, call me. I'll tell my teacher I have diarrhea or something, but I'll answer. Or when you get home tomorrow if you need to process everything. What you did was a huge deal but in the best way. And you deserve all the happiness in the world for it."

I may not know what to expect tomorrow or the days after, but with my friends and sister and Mat at my side, I'm more than capable of handling whatever it brings.

10

Okay, still nervous. Feeling less capable. I text Mat, asking for strong thoughts. He replies with a GIF of SpongeBob lifting a barbell with teddy bears attached to the ends. I guess that'll have to do.

Acting calm in front of Dad before he leaves for work takes some real effort. I don't even notice him until he's doing one of those *pretending to clear my throat so you'll realize I'm watching you.*

"What's wrong? You're doing that finger tap, tap, tap on the table and your breakfast is just sitting there. That yogurt's gonna turn back into milk soon."

"I'm not hungry."

Dad's head goes back, and he squints his eyes. I know exactly what he's thinking. "You're always hungry." He takes a slow sip of coffee while continuing to try to read into the situation.

"Something got you nervous?"

Of course. You. You got me nervous. Life's got me nervous.

But I can't tell him *feeling crappy today because I came out a couple of days ago and, I don't know, I might be heading into some conversion camp today, maybe?*

My phone vibrates on the table, and I swear, against the wood it's never sounded louder. My hand rushes out for it, and I quickly swipe the notification from Mat off the screen. I'll come back to it later.

"Texting someone special?"

"*What?* No. No. Definitely not."

"I don't know. You're reminding me of when I used to look all tonto y bobo when your mom gave me any amount of attention."

"That's not it. I promise."

"Whatever you say, mi'jo."

~

When I get to school, there's no mob. No **God Hates Fags** picket signs. It's, well, a usual Monday.

I get a few supportive pats on the back, high fives, and fist bumps. Some classmates even voice their acceptance, shouting, "Born this way, Jules!" or "My older brother is gay. Y'all are so much fun!" It's obvious that this isn't a big deal to most, or at least not enough to make a scene out of it.

So yes, I was overreacting. Yes, I was expecting the worst. Whatever. I had good reason to be scared. I'd rather everyone prove me wrong than validate my fears.

The one person who couldn't keep things low-key today: Lou. She dances over to our table at lunch. "I'm Coming Out" blasting from a Bluetooth speaker. Giant rainbow balloons and rainbow frosted cupcakes in hand.

I'm pretty sure I've never been more mortified in my life.

And because I couldn't go all day without *some* drama, in theology class, Sara Salinas, one of my holier-than-thou classmates, thought to put in her two cents during small-group discussion. "I don't see why some Catholics are becoming lax with people who, what's the phrase, divert from a *biologically natural lifestyle.*" She looks me up and down as she speaks.

"What the f—" I begin to respond, not concerned with filtering my reaction in front of the entire class. I'm interrupted by the third member of our group, Silás Adame. His arm presses against my chest like those commercials when a mom slams the brakes and tries to make sure her kid doesn't fly forward.

"Sara, if our eighty-year-old pope who's been a religious for half a century says who is he to judge a gay person, then you can get off your high horse for a second. Yeah?" His voice is sharp, and he's not nearly as quiet as he thinks he is.

Did not expect the head of the Martin Students for Life club to drag this girl in front of our entire class and God. And by the look of her surprised face, she didn't assume this reaction either.

"Speak on it, Si!" someone yells from across the room, breaking the tension and getting laughter from most of the class.

Silás pats my arm. A small smile forms at the corner of his mouth.

"U-um," he stutters. "So, next question?"

~

I couldn't wait to FaceTime with Mat when I got home. Let him know I survived. Assure him that I did in fact not have to swat away hordes of suitors.

See his face again.

"*Hey*, that means I still have a chance." He winks. And, God, I can't concentrate. "What'd I tell you? No reason to worry. I mean, except for that Jesus-y girl. But she seems pretty harmless? Plus, on the other side of that, *cupcakes*! I'm gonna tell my friends that they're fake for not doing that for me when I came out."

"Lou's a special kind of extra. Everyone else was pretty tame. My friend Itzel was trying to get me to list every guy I've ever had a crush on—"

"Was I on that list?" Mat interrupts, his voice full of interest.

"I'm not answering that." I mean, he is, but no one needs to know that right now. "And then there's Jordan, who's ready to sneak into a gay club and help me live my *best queer life*. And Rolie, who's kinda been quiet through it all."

"Good quiet?"

"Eh, he's the introvert of the group. I'm assuming it's nothing bad."

"You're doing all right, then?"

I am. Eight hours where I could be myself. Not having to make sure I passed as straight for the first time in my life. It was the freest and most relaxed I've ever felt. But—

"Home life is still stressful. My walls involuntarily come up when I drive into my neighborhood. I hate having to be cautious around my dad."

"Well, if you ever wanna run away to LA, I got space in my bed."

Did he really—

"I mean, speaking as a well-intentioned, purely platonic friend, of course. Or not. It's all hypothetical."

"I'll keep that in mind."

Us. In his bed. That's for sure staying in my head for a while.

Mat tells me how his day was (equally uneventful). And we talk. About nothing important: what movie we last watched, the songs we're obsessed with right now, which queen of pop we stan, and why the only right answer is Ariana Grande.

"Ariana? She's all right, I mean—"

"I will hang up on you. I swear to God, Mat."

He's so easy to talk to. Opinionated on everything, and I'm finding a lot of joy each time I can call out another one of his embarrassingly incorrect beliefs. Like how if he had to go straight for someone from *Elite*, "It'd be Carla all the way. I am very bi for Carla."

"How, when Lucrecia is *right there*? She's the only right answer."

And then watching him make this *bitch, please* face? So, so great.

"Okay," Mat says when we hit a pause. "One weird fact. Go."

"I went first last time," I reply. "You first."

"Hmm." He looks up from the screen, as if he's thinking seriously about what fact to go with. "Got one. When we were, I don't know, in elementary school, there was a show on MTV called *America's Best Dance Crew*. Maybe you remember it or saw it. My older brother got me into it. Well, my friends and I were high-key obsessed. We started our own group called Beach Boyz, which we later learned was not at all creative or original. We'd practice on Saturdays and stuck with it up to maybe when we got to seventh grade. And we were *not* good, Jules. I mean, *I* wasn't bad. But we definitely weren't making it to TV with our skills."

I've been sucking in my lips, trying not to laugh at imagining a third-grade Mat horribly break-dancing in his parents' garage. "I—uh, that's gonna be a hard fact to beat."

"I know," he says back. "Realizing that yes, I have always been this cool."

"That's a word for it, sure."

"A few of us still kinda do it. Mainly TikTok dances now, though. Have you seen mine?"

"Your TikToks? No. I didn't realize you had one."

"Yeah, I need to get better about posting them to Twitter. It's mattroi213. Prepare to be impressed. Like, you might wanna be sitting down when you start watching."

"Thanks for the warning," I tease.

"*I'm serious.* Anyways, your turn."

I mentally flip through all the random things about me. Something more than my favorite colors or what my go-to stores at the mall are. "So, fact about me. I was born in Mexico."

"No way?"

"Yeah. To two US citizens. But in Matamoros. It's a border city where my dad's dad, Abuelo Julio, lives. I wasn't supposed to be born until January; my parents thought it'd be fine to visit him and decided to go down for an early Christmas. Except I was tired of being in a uterus or I guess I *had* to be a Sagittarius. A few hours later and I'm hanging out in a Mexican hospital."

"Huh. That's a good fact. Are you named after your abuelo?"

"Both of them, technically. A mix of the beginnings of Julio and my mom's dad's name, Andrés. A surprisingly clever way of getting to a name that's actually pretty common."

"I like that." Mat takes a moment to look to the side, at whatever's next to him. "Speaking of Mexico, you wouldn't happen to be fluent in Spanish, would you? I didn't want to assume."

"It's cool. I am, why?"

"I have a Spanish test tomorrow."

"Oh, quieres que te ayude a estudiar?"

Mat stares blankly, mouth agape. It's fucking adorable, and I'm trying not to laugh at him slowly translate in his head.

"Yes! Exactly."

"Then, would you be able to help me with my physics and calculus?"

"Way to stereotype, Jules!"

"Shut up. Or else I'm *only* speaking in Spanish for the rest of the night."

"No, please don't."

Mat texts me his review sheet, and we go over everything on the page. Correcting him on a couple of conjugations, an *el* that should be a *la*, and a word here and there. But he seems pretty prepared. I assumed he was waiting until the last minute to even start studying. Because that's definitely something I've done plenty of times.

I'm not so easily taught. I'm giving him confused looks as he tries to explain science and math concepts and attempts to help me figure out my own homework. That he doesn't make up some excuse to leave a few minutes in says a lot about his resolve.

"I'm jealous that you're a STEM genius," I tell him after finishing the last of my assignments.

"Nah, that's not me. Biology and that sort of stuff, sure. Everything else takes a lot of effort, but I know I'll need to stay ahead when I get to college."

"You plan on majoring in something science-y?"

"Health related, for sure. Eventually get into STI and HIV testing and counseling. Research would be cool if I can get into graduate school, but that's thinking years down the road. Like, it's still a huge deal in the LGBTQ community, and people knock getting tested and knowing their status. I don't know. I watched *Pose* once and it got me all interested in how this is still a thing forty years later."

"I—how do you go from someone who couldn't stop cackling because you said *pussy* instead of pasé to, like, that?"

"I'm a complex man, Jules," Mat answers. "I wanna keep you on your toes, or whatever the saying is. But hey, I have to be up early tomorrow, and it's probably late for you already too, so call it a night?"

"Sure," I say, fighting to keep a yawn down. Realizing that I am actually pretty sleepy.

"Again, really happy your day went well. And lemme know how that homework turns out."

"Thanks. I will. Good luck with your test. Good night, Mat."

"Night, Jules. Dream about me."

I have no doubt that I will.

11

Talking with Mat becomes a consistent and best part of my day. He'll send me Snaps between classes. Usually of random thoughts he's having—*there's this great Honduran place I'll take you to next year; wanted to make sure everything's still low-drama at school; I was stalking your IG story and you're looking extra lindo today, FYI.*

A*nd then I'll take a picture of the Whataburger sign every time I pass by one and caption it* better than In-N-Out. Or tell him how good he looks that day. *And* in Vietnamese, because he's not the only one who can go multilingual, but it only got me a row of skull emojis and were u trying to say cute?

Never trusting Google Translate again. *Never.*

I'll send Mat a song I heard on my Discover Weekly playlist that is now on repeat. Or any that makes me think of him. Looking for any reason to interact with him.

I'm falling. Hard.

Pretty sure Dad's noticed. I'm constantly getting asked *What's her name?* whenever he sees me smiling at my phone while I'm messaging Mat. Assuming he knows exactly what's going on in my life.

Not that he's wrong. Just wrong gender.

No one, I repeat, each time hoping that he continues to leave it at that.

And school stays as normal as I could've hoped. At Wednesday's StuCo meeting, Mirella asks me if I want to start an LGBTQ student group.

"Thanks for the gesture of solidarity, Mirella," I answer. "But we'd need more than one gay student to form an organization."

"I'm cool with exploring my sexuality for the cause!" Lou yells from the back of the room.

I give her such a dirty look, whispering, "Qué pinche perra, la pendejita," under my breath. That she was elected a senior class rep really makes me question the sanity of my classmates.

~

On Friday, I hold in a scream and a string of cusses when I open my locker and find a giant dildo attached to the backside of the door. There's a note taped to it. A bunch of stupid slurs and threats and—damn it—I couldn't go five days? *Five days?*

I'm trying not to let someone who couldn't even say these words to my face scare me, but—

"What is that?" Itzel asks.

I jump and yell out a "chíngale!" not hearing her approach and already on edge.

I quickly crumple the piece of paper and toss it into my locker, slamming the door shut. "Nothing. No te preocupes."

She stares into my eyes, studying me. I know she can read right through me.

"Stop lying. What happened?"

I open the door, moving aside so she can see the silicone dick and paper lying on top of my books. "Someone put it there. Late after school or this morning. I don't know."

Itzel straightens out the note to scan it over. "Nope. No. We're not doing this today," she says while tearing it up. She throws the pieces and the sex toy into a trash can. Everyone's staring at her as she yells about *I hate everyone* and *Why aren't we allowed to have LOCKS on our LOCKERS* while she gathers up the trash bag, taking it to the dumpster outside.

For the rest of the day, Itzel, Jordan, and Roe never leave my side. Looking around, needing only the smallest reason to blow up on someone. Asking if I'm all right every time they see me looking lost in thought.

I know they're trying to help, but I wish they'd stop asking that.

After school, Lou and Piña join us at my house. We all made plans to go to tonight's football game together, and everyone wanted to hang out until then. Fine with me. Helps get this morning's prank off my mind for a while.

I stretch out on the couch, careful to not mess up the now nearly dry, giant white C with a navy border Itzel painted on me and the rainbow stripes on the front of my left shoulder. The voices of Piña and Jordan, currently getting an H and S on their own, and of Roe—who got an M—and Lou in the kitchen already blurring as the thought of a power nap sounds nicer and nicer. Until I hear Lou asking me who *Mat-yellow-heart-emoji-sun-emoji* is.

Chingada madre. I left my phone in the kitchen.

I jolt up, falling over the table as I sprint toward her.

"It—he's no one. A friend, and that's it."

Everyone stares at me as I grab my phone from Lou's hand.

"Dude, a heart emoji doesn't usually imply a friend," Piña says in the middle of chewing an avocado egg roll.

"Wait, is this Mat, Mateo Rincón from StuCo?" Lou asks.

"What? No. Of course not."

"You sure? Because I could've swore he was checking you out at this week's meeting now that he knows what team you play for."

"Lou, you're imagining things—"

"Then tell us who this heart-emoji-sun-emoji Mat is, bro," Jordan says, taking a seat on the arm of one of the couches.

"I told y'all. He's a friend. No lie. We started DMing on Twitter and then that became texting and FaceTiming. It's not serious, though. Like, it's been nice to have another gay guy to talk everything out with, you know?"

"Hold up," Jordan says. "Did you slide into his DMs that night you were drunk?"

"No. He actually DMed me first." The entire house roars in excitement. *BRO*s come from the guys, a *BITCH* from Lou, and Itzel boisterously commands me to tell them everything immediately.

I wish we could all agree to brush this off. To recognize that it's not *that* big of a deal. That there's not much to say on an almost-week-old friendship.

But as I'm forced to tell them about this Californian who initiated a conversation, I realize how much I've looked forward to talking to him every day since then. As I assure them that *it's casual; there's nothing more*, I think how all it takes is to see his face and I'm immediately happier. And as I give them the most minimal of details on our conversations, I start really missing him.

The last time we were able to FaceTime was Tuesday. Neither of us has had a lot of time between trying to get a moment when Dad's not around and Mat working a couple of evenings at his brother's food truck.

"Well, if his text message is any indication, he's wanting to make time to see that face real soon, chiquis. Unless it's not your face you've been showing him."

"That's *not* what's happening, Lou. Cochina. I'll talk to him when I get home tonight from the game."

"Oh, you're gonna put on a show for him while you wash off the body paint. Good call, Luna." Jordan extends his arm, waiting for me to give him a high five.

I'd very much like to die right now.

12

During halftime, I walk down from the bleachers with Jordan, Piña, and Roe. Jordan left his phone in his Jeep by accident before the game and was going to lose his mind if we didn't get it the moment the first half was over.

Piña and I are in front, all of us talking and joking on the walk back into the stadium. I'm not paying much attention to my surroundings, which is why I don't notice the guy walking past me until his body knocks into me and pushes me to the side. Piña catches me, and then things start happening very quickly.

"Watch where you're going, faggot," he says. He's your average small-town tractor-enthusiast white guy. I'm assuming from the other school. One of the Saint Caucasian High School white supremacists.

Rolie rushes at him, pinning him to the wire fence near the entrance gate.

"*Say that again.* I dare you." His eyes are seething with anger, and his forearm presses into the guy's neck.

"Roe, cálmate. He's not worth it," I plead, stepping away from Piña to grab Rolie's shoulders, attempting to get the larger boy to let go. My heart's trying to pound right out of my chest and my hands are shaking against his skin.

A couple of people who are making their way between the field and parking lot eye our small, suspicious crowd. And the last thing we need is for cops to see a white boy surrounded by a bunch of shirtless teens with varying degrees of melanin. "It—it's okay."

Rolie doesn't move. I can see in his eyes that he's calculating. Weighing his options. Or maybe trying to convince himself to be rational.

"Urgh. Pinche cabrón," Rolie grunts as he lets him go. The guy starts coughing and tries to move away from us, but Jordan's quick hand grabs him by the collar of his shirt before he's managed to be out of arm's reach.

"You're gonna *never* use that word again. And if you don't want your ass kicked, you'll make sure we don't ever cross paths again, all right?" Jordan throws him to the side, watching him take off into the stadium.

Jordan turns and looks at us. Walking up to me, still latched on to Rolie. They look at each other, and Jordan shakes his head and lets out a bothered breath through his nose.

"Roe and I are taking a walk," he tells Piña and me.

The anger in his voice is palpable. I wish I could tell him it's fine, but we all know it isn't. His and Roe's reactions were completely reasonable. Admirable, even.

He hands us his debit card. "Get everyone drinks and nachos. Or popcorn. Whatever. We'll meet y'all at the concession stands." He puts a hand on Rolie's shoulder and walks with him back to the parking lot.

"Don't ask me if I'm good," I tell Piña as we head the other direction. I could tell he was trying to look for the right time to do so. "Please."

I'm not. And I don't want to have to lie about it.

I thought I could stop putting up this rigid, straight facade when I'm out with my friends. I should be able to. But I'm feeling myself want to shut it all in again. I don't want to be the person who needs to be protected all the time.

I jump slightly when Piña's arm wraps around my shoulders. "Sorry. Is this okay? You looked like you were just—"

"It's fine," I tell him. Mentally, confusing and weird. But physically, this is really comforting, and I can feel myself leaning into his side subconsciously and then his head leaning on mine.

"You aren't worried about what people might think?"

"Not really. I could do a lot worse than you."

"That's not what I meant."

"I know. I was joking, Luna. And people can mind their business. If I wanna comfort my bro by rubbing my shirtless body against his, I'm gonna do it."

"Straight boys are so fucking weird," I say, just loud enough for him to hear. "But thanks, Piña."

~

After the football game, we stop for food and take it with us to Walmart, lining up our cars at the far end of the parking lot. Itzel and I sit in my truck bed while Jordan and Piña are dancing along to the music coming out of Jordan's Jeep, and Lou is sitting on the lowered gate with handfuls of dollar bills, sticking them into their waistbands. They all look so unconcerned. Unbothered. Happy.

And usually this mixture of shirtless guys and fast food would be the perfect recipe for a better mood. Not only twenty-four hours ago, I would've been right there with Lou, living my best life.

I wish I could be like them.

I wish I could push these qualms out of my head as easily as everyone else. But all that's happened today keeps replaying in my brain. Making me apprehensive about every little thing, to the point that it's making me twitchy. I guess I should at least be glad I had a good first few days.

I was convincing myself that the years of rumors and assumptions and bullying and harassing were over. That if I was out, it wouldn't be such a taboo subject that everyone felt they could hold over me. That we were past this bullshit as a society.

I look at Roe, who's quiet as usual. His back leaning against my truck as he takes a big bite of burrito. Making one- or two-word comments to Lou. He notices me and gives a tight-lipped smile. Maybe I should talk to him.

"Hey," Itzel says as she throws her arms around me and her head falls onto my shoulder.

"You're gonna mess up my C," I whine.

"The game is over. I think you're good." Her fingers scratch at my biceps, and we say nothing for a minute. Watching everyone else. "I'm sorry this is happening to you."

"I know." I take a deep breath as I look up and away from everyone, into the sky. My mind has been wanting to break, but I can't in front of everyone. Not yet.

"What's going on in your head?"

"Nothing. Sorry. Tired, I guess."

"It's been a long week."

"Understatement of the century."

"You know all those stupid asses aren't worth any amount of your time, right? I'm gonna sound like Jordan, but don't let them get under your skin, Jules."

How? How do I not let them have that power over me? I've felt vulnerable and angry all day because I couldn't go a week without people making a joke or an insult about my sexuality. Not that this was anything new, but now it seems *extra* pointed and personal.

"I'll try" is all I'm honestly able to promise.

~

I lie on my side, clutching my pillow to my chest—now washed clean of the paint. It's pitch-black in my room, except for the small amount of light coming from my phone facedown on my nightstand. It'd be silent too, if it weren't for the sound of the vibrations against the wood. I ignore it, turning my body away from it in an attempt to block it out. But only a few seconds pass before another, shorter pattern of vibrations occurs.

Curiosity gets the better of me. I turn back around to grab my phone, interested in who's seeking my attention.

It's Mat. A FaceTime request followed by a text.

Assuming you're asleep. Wanted to say I've missed your face, if that's not super creepy. Anyways, good night. Or I guess good morning if you aren't gonna read this until you wake up.

I do want to talk to Mat. And I want to see his face just as badly. He would let me vent about everything that's happened in the past fourteen hours. And then he'd distract me from those concerns and make them all seem unimportant. But what I need most Mat can't give me. Because he isn't here. I need a comfort that I imagine can only come from being embraced, kissed, and told that nothing else in this world—outside this room—matters. But that all seems so tragically unattainable.

So I don't. Not tonight, or tomorrow, or the days after.

13

It's six in the morning, and I'm wide awake. On a Sunday. Internal clocks are a bitch.

And my first thought is how it's been eight whole days now since I last had a conversation with Mat. This is what I get for dreaming about him.

I throw on some shorts and an old Martin soccer shirt and grab my keys, wallet, phone, and AirPods. My head's already going at full speed, and I'm past the point of forcing myself back to sleep. So I'd rather go for a run if the other option is lying in bed with my very awake brain.

I leave my truck at the entrance of Cole Park, along the beach. A few other people dot the waterfront walking path, but it's otherwise empty. I look out into the Gulf water and an indigo sky brushed with pinks, oranges, and yellows announcing the slow arrival of the impending sunrise. Feel the salty breeze that helps the air seem not so awfully damp.

Once the Bad Bunny album starts playing, I raise the volume high enough to where I *probably* won't damage my eardrums. I let the music and the exertion of energy take priority, instead of thinking how I'd barely given Mat the time of day since the football game last week. Instead of thinking back on all the excuses I made for why I couldn't FaceTime or why I wasn't being as consistent as usual with texting.

I hate myself for it.

Not only because of how I've been with him. I've kept Jordan, Itzel, Roe, and even Xo at a distance the past eight days. If not physically, for sure mentally and emotionally.

The day after the football game, a text from Rolie, trying to be supportive, went ignored. I got angsty with Itzel when she called later the same day wanting to check in on me. And I up and left Jordan when he asked me to hang out, repeating his same *wanting to be sympathetic* lines.

And as much as I know it bothered them, they let me exist under my gray cloud all week at school. I could see Itzel and Jordan wanting to have a come-to-Jesus moment and Roe struggling to act at least minimally normal. The cringiest eight days I've had in a while.

It's because they wanted to make sure I was fine. But what if I told them I wasn't? What if I told them that for some reason, this was triggering some lengthier-than-usual depressive mood? I don't need to put that on them.

I distract myself with anything and everything that will keep my mind from thinking. Sing along to "Caro." Complain about how muggy it is right now. Ask to pet every dog I pass. Count how many steps I take in a single minute.

An hour of nonstop running, all the way to the Selena Memorial, and then I start back. I stop at McGee Beach, taking a seat at the seawall steps. I turn off the music to listen to the waves crashing against rocks and cement. Mat returns to the front of my mind as the sun starts making its way into the sky and I get to watch his namesake welcome Corpus Christi.

I'm an idiot for distancing myself from him. For convincing myself that his value as a friend should be measured by whether or not he can sit here with me right now. And for maybe being scared of making someone so far away the person I pour my heart and soul out to.

But I have to let it out to someone. If I'm going to be anything close to functional again, I need to. And as much of a dick as I've been brushing him off, I know he'd listen.

I make sure I look halfway decent before calling. Hoping I don't look as tired as this front-facing camera is making me look. No, I probably look worse.

Ni modo.

Five rings go by before I see Mat on the screen. He's lying in bed, half his face buried in his pillow. He squints as he looks into his phone.

"Hey, it's you," Mat mumbles through a yawn. I can tell he's struggling to keep his eyes open. But then comes a smile that provides an immediate warmth and security. God, I've missed seeing that smile.

"Why're you up this early?"

"Seven thirty isn't *that* early. Well, for the weekend it is. But still. The sun was coming up, and it made me think of you."

"That's nice. But time difference, Jules. Remember? It's five thirty here."

"Then I guess you can be the first person in California to see the sunrise today," I tease. "But if you'd rather go back to sleep, that's fine too."

"No, don't hang up," he implores, sounding a little more awake now. "This is the first time I'm seeing you since last week."

"Sounds like you missed me?"

"I'm not gonna confirm or deny that. But I need to pee real quick and put on my glasses." Mat raises himself up from the bed. "Don't go anywhere," he demands.

He places his phone facedown, and I'm left looking into darkness until he arrives back. "You're sweaty," he says bluntly, looking at me.

"Oh, yeah. I woke up earlier than I wanted and decided to come to the beach for a run."

"Woke up early? I could never."

"I'm cursed with being a morning person."

It feels like hours go by with neither of us speaking. It's awkward. I've made this awkward. My pendejismo is ruining everything.

"I-I'm sorry for being such a dick to you," I start. "And avoiding you all week."

"It is what it is, Jules." There's sadness behind the words. Behind the tired. "Everything cool with you?"

If this was any other person, I'd lie. I wouldn't want Itzel to start crying, or Jordan to try his best to be comforting, or Xo to start worrying because someone messed with me. But being truthful is all I know with Mat. And I don't want to break that.

"No, it's not."

"Well, I'm here, at least half-awake, and you have an entire week of bailing on me to catch me up on. Spill."

The words and emotional baggage I've carried around since last Friday erupt out of me. The locker prank, the note, the douche at the football game, how my friends reacted, this incessant pressure to make them believe that I'm holding it all together even though I can't help but feel that literally everyone is out to get me. I can see the empathy in Mat's face behind the fatigue, and although that doesn't fix any of my problems, it's comforting to know that I'm speaking to someone who might be able to relate.

"I don't have to pretend to be straight anymore—at least, ninety percent of the time—and that's great and such a relief. But now I'm pretending to be happy because I know my friends won't understand. Pretending that this doesn't affect me, otherwise they'll want to get involved with my problems even more than they already do. It'd—life would be immeasurably easier if I had someone who had some of these same experiences here—not that you aren't great, Mat. I'm so, so lucky to have someone who I can call or text or tweet to, but—"

"I get it, Jules." He sounds frustrated. Remorseful. I already felt horrible for ghosting him all week, and now even more for bringing up the distance. "I wish you had someone there too. I don't know what it is to be without another queer person around, but I do know what it feels like to be lonely. Even when I'm surrounded by people who care for me. And I know what it is to feel that way because I'm gay. I—I know this doesn't help, but I'm sorry that I can't be there with you through this."

"You don't have to apologize for that." I attempt an encouraging smile, wanting to not make him feel bad for something he has no control over. "It's not your fault, Mat. You've been such a huge help and an amazing friend the past couple of weeks. And *especially* now, after I've been a dick to you. Way more than I'd ever expect from someone trying to hit on me over Twitter."

A short laugh escapes under Mat's breath. "I know, but—" He takes a long pause, as if trying to carefully consider his next words. "I wish I could do whatever you needed to forget about all these jerks. I wish I could grab your hand every time you get in your head and feel alone. Or, I don't know, do anything that would take your mind off it all. Dildo unicorn or something. And I wish I could've grabbed your face and started making out with you in front of that dumb homophobe because one, that would be cool and, I'm assuming, enjoyable. Personally speaking. And two, making those kinds of people as uncomfortable as possible—"

"Wait. You—you want to make out with me?"

"Jules, dammit. Is that the only thing you got out of what I'm trying to say?"

"*Of course not.* But it's a good thing you saved it for last because I would have gone blank after that."

"Dumb. I needed to let that out, though, and it's too early to process and refine what I'm trying to say before speaking. But in the future, I get it if you need to have some time to digest stuff. Or you mentally might not be in a place to talk, but you've got people who will try their best to understand. Even if it's at five thirty in the morning. You don't have to make up excuses, all right?"

"I know."

"Good. That said, I'm gonna fall back asleep now. So unless there's other serious stuff you need to get off your chest, can we continue this later?"

"Sure. That's it with the drama for today. For hopefully a while, actually. And I should get going anyways. I've still got to get to my truck. Thanks for answering. I promise I won't make a habit of avoiding you again."

"You better not."

"I won't. Pinkie promise. I'll forever assault you with Twitter mentions, IG comments, texts, and FaceTime calls."

"Good."

"I'll talk to you later, Mat. Dream about me."

"I'm hoping the one I was having before *someone* decided to wake me up will continue where it left off," he says drowsily but not without a mischievous smirk before hanging up, leaving me staring at a blank black screen, taking a moment to process his continued shamelessness.

14

My friends can be rowdy, but all our dads together for the backyard barbecues mine hosts at least once a month? It's like a frat house but made up of a bunch of forty- and fiftysomethings. They've been talking and yelling and laughing for hours now, huddled around the grill. Mine is kind of at the center of the group: he works with Lou's dad, we go to the same church as Rolie's and Itzel's families, and he met Jordan's and Piña's parents because of soccer. All the games, Confirmation meetings, carpooling, their kids becoming friends and always hanging out, them doing the same was probably always more of a when than an if.

I support it. Dad's always more relaxed and noticeably happier when he gets to be around them. And he's never got to have much of a social life. Before I started high school, we lived in Gregory with Güelo and Abuelita—this small town of maybe two thousand on the other side of the Harbor Bridge. I went to a little Catholic elementary and middle school in Ingleside. The most excitement he got was probably when Xochi went to Gregory-Portland High School, and even that's a reach.

Whether he's ever dated isn't anything we've talked about. I imagine trying to while his dead wife's parents babysat his kids was a weird line to cross. And now maybe it's easier to wait a few more months until he's got an empty house.

I mean, he's only forty-three, and he doesn't even look it. He's always been fit from constant physical work. Buzzed hair that actually gets curly like mine when it's grown out, but the only times I've seen him like that are in old pictures. Somehow he has never once had a cana, and I pray every day I got that gene. A mustache and nearly always present stubble at his jawline, chin, and neck (genes that I definitely didn't get). And even though his style preference is thrifted short-sleeve button-downs left open with a white tank, Xo makes sure that the prints aren't awful.

I look like him, which sometimes is a thing I hate. Those moments I look into a mirror and see his eyes, his facial structure. Remembering how he looked at my age and see myself: same hair, same smile, same ears, same body structure except he's a few inches taller than I am. I'm him but shorter and a little darker and less body hair. *How I'd look if I was more Indio* is how he used to describe me. *A perfect mixture of your mom and me.*

Other times I can appreciate the fact that I kind of won with genetics. I mean, if I could be five foot nine like him, that might be nice, but I've learned to live.

"¡Mi'jo! Julián, siéntate," Dad says while patting the foldout chair next to him, a veggie burger and chips on a paper plate sitting there with a Jarritos in the cupholder waiting for me.

"Have you ever eaten one of those Impossible Burgers?" he asks Rolie's dad, sitting on his other side. "Julián came home with a pack of a couple one time, and, not shitting you one bit, compa, they're pretty good. *Not beef*, pero ya sabes, if all the cows in the world disappeared one day, I'd be all right living off those."

Jordan tilts his body toward me, trying to scoot his chair a little closer. "Luna. Luna. Lemme try it."

"It's got grilled jalapeños and habaneros *and* sriracha mayo. I don't know if you're gonna like it."

"Nah, I got it. Come on."

Jordan opens his mouth, waiting for me to let him take a bite, and I give him a smirk while shaking my head. I'll be telling this pendejo *I told you so*; I just know it. I hold the burger up to him and feel him take a huge bite, waiting for a reaction.

He lets out a "hmm" as he chews, doing these small nods like he's really thinking about it.

And then I see it.

His chest puffs up in a deep breath. His eyes get large and then squint like he's holding back tears. And then he leans forward, his elbow resting on his knee and his fist covering his mouth.

"You good?" I ask through a laugh.

Jordan only raises his other hand, his pointer finger up like *give me a minute*. And then he finally picks himself back up, shaking his head and wiping his eyes. "Bro. *How do you eat that?*"

"I got into my abuelita's pico de gallo once when I was a baby, and when she realized I liked it and wasn't screaming in pain, that was pretty much my go-to meal when she took care of me. Gave me a really high tolerance."

"No kidding. Burger's good, though, I'll give it that."

"Stupid," I tell him while turning to my drink, but, at the same time, noticing Dad's daggerlike glare. It's as if time stops completely and has vacuumed out all the happiness I was feeling up to now. Left with only me and the messages he's sending.

I know I didn't just see you feed that boy.

Fucking playing esposa with him or what?

You really gotta be testing me all the damn time.

"Are there any more grapefruit Jarritos?" I hear Itzel ask.

"Yeah." I throw the word out as I come back to reality. "Yeah. Uh, I can show you where."

~

Jordan stays over for the night. A choice that Dad obviously wasn't thrilled about, but he decided against making a scene in front of

Mr. Thomas. "I work in the morning, so don't be all animales all night. And he sleeps in Xo's old room. ¿Entiendes?"

We stay outside for a while, hopping over the chain-link fence into the empty field on the side of my house, kicking a soccer ball around, practicing passes and steals until we've run off the burgers and smell like sweat and grass. And then a little longer in the backyard, catching our breaths and downing a couple cups of water. Listening to Jordan recall every detail of what we were doing, going into coach mode like usual and suggesting pointers for next time, as if he were taking this as seriously as a real game. Which he probably was.

He comes into my room from the shower, wearing a pair of my shorts to sleep in that are already made to be slim on me. With the extra inch or so of waist he's got, though, I'm glad Jordan doesn't catch the one, two, seven times my eyes involuntarily glance over while he's busy staring at a YouTube video he's trying to show me. Some soccer match or a clip from an Avengers movie. I don't know. There was no way any of my attention was ever going to be on that screen.

"Huh," Jordan chuckles, now looking at some group text. "My cousins. They keep asking when I'm visiting Spartanburg next so they can take me over to Clemson."

"Is that where you're set on?" He's mentioned Clemson before. They have one of the best soccer teams in the country, so, added to him having family there, it's an obvious choice. But, being completely selfish, if Jordan ends up in South Carolina for college and I'm in California, that's going to hurt.

"I'll go with whoever gives me the best offer. I'm not trying to have my parents pay for me to go to school when I know I've got the talent for a full ride. *But* having my cousins and my granny less than an hour and a half away would be nice. Although, being around that much soul food is for sure gonna give me a gut, no cap."

"You've managed while being surrounded by Tex-Mex and barbecue."

"Look, nothing against y'all, but Mexican food comes second *after* soul food. I'm weak for good grits, corn bread, mac and cheese—"

"I make corn bread and mac and cheese."

"You make, *yeah*, you do," Jordan responds, stumbling from trying to speak and think of the right words at the same time. "And it's good. You cook better than anyone here who's not my mom. Which is saying something because you don't even cook meat. But it's not *Southern* mac and cheese made by my granny. Just like the barbecue."

"What about the barbecue?"

"Again, your güelo is the king of Texas barbecue, but it's different in South Carolina. It's better. Not the white Carolina barbecue, though. Important distinction. And no one in the state comes close to my Uncle Cookie. Actually, no one in the country."

"I disagree. *Hard.*"

"You're a vegetarian, bro. I don't think you get much of an opinion about this anymore."

I hit his arm with my elbow while letting out a "shut up" in a whispered yell, and then he's falling on his side on top of me, his arms clamped around me, holding me down as I try to break free. Whisper yelling back, "Admit that Carolina barbecue is better." Until I almost fall off the bed and would've if it wasn't for how tightly gripped Jordan has me, and we realize we might be being too loud for how late it is.

"So, uh, seems like things have calmed down," Jordan says while we lie down, both of us on our sides, facing each other. "Right? I mean, there might be some stuff that you're seeing that we aren't, but it feels like anyone at school who cared about you being—"

"Can we not?" I interrupt. "Not while my dad's here."

"I can hear him snoring, Luna. I think you're fine."

"I just—yeah, I think most people have realized their existence isn't going to come crashing down on them because of me. But, ya, that's it. Okay? We can process another time if you want."

"All right. Only wanted to make sure, you know?"

"I know." A long yawn follows the words, making them sound only half-intelligible. "Thanks. I think I'm gonna crash now, so just go to Xo's room at some point and I'll see you in the morning."

"Yeah. Night, Luna."

~

The first few minutes of the morning happen almost too quickly and chaotically to process.

A voice calling out "Julián, Julián" wakes me up. And after those initial few seconds of figuring out my environment—my face in my pillow and arms around it, hugging it as I lie on my stomach; the feeling of someone's hand and arm on my back; the realization that that someone is Jordan and that voice is Dad seeing us half-naked and basically cuddling in my bed—I wish I could fall back asleep and never wake up.

Dad's entire face looks like he wants to explode. And his voice is hinging on it as he tells me to get Jordan out of the house. "It's time for him to go. *Now.*

"I gave you instructions," he says as soon as Jordan is out the door, standing in between there and me, at the other end of the living room. "Is something going on between you two?"

"*What?* No. Of course not."

"You sure? Porque vi dos putos."

"He just fell asleep, Dad. That's it. We didn't—"

The force of his palms slamming into my chest stop me from talking.

"¿Y tú?" he yells as, again, his hands hit me. This time right at my bottommost ribs, and I'm trying to not cry or throw up while also gasping for air. "You could've went to Xo's room instead. Let him sleep there. Instead I fucking find you—are you gay?"

"What?"

He grabs on to my left wrist, making me tilt down, feeling even smaller compared to him. "Dime, Julián. Is my son gay?"

"I—*no*."

That lie has never hurt so much. It's one thing to deny something that no one else in the world can prove. But when I've gotten a taste of what it is to be able to say yes to that question . . . I've seen a life where I can be open about it and still have my friends and my sister and Mat. I think of how I worked up the courage to tell him before I said it to anyone else in the world. And I feel like I'm betraying both of us right now by saying the opposite. I know I shouldn't feel that way. I'm doing what I have to do, but still.

"You sure?" Dad asks. "If I went into your phone right now, I wouldn't catch you lying to me?"

"No. I promise." I'm pretty sure he can hear my heartbeat. Hear me think how he can do whatever he wants *except* go take my phone. "It's just Xo and Güelo and my friends."

"Yeah, so if I go into your texts between you and Jordan, I won't find some joto shit?"

"No. He—we're not, Dad."

The way he looks down at me, it's a look I've seen a lot in seventeen years. Those eyes that see a person who falls short of everything he imagined his son would be like. That wish they could blink and I'd be different. More like Rolie or Piña.

"If I ever catch you two doing anything like that again, he's never coming back into this house. You hear me?"

"Yes."

He lets go of my arm and sighs as he shakes his head before starting for the door, not even saying goodbye before slamming it shut. Leaving me to stare at the space where his face used to be. Feeling the bruises that are going to last a few days starting to form.

I go back to my room and fall onto my bed, staring at the wall and holding a pillow in my arms. Trying to not let the thoughts of *You should have told him to go to Xo's room* and *This is all your fault for not saying anything* stick to my brain like mental bumper stickers.

And then my phone starts ringing. Mat, wanting to FaceTime. I want to hit "Reject," but I promised him. I told him I wouldn't run away. I can do this.

"I woke up early for the first time in my entire life and wanted you to be proud of me for it," he says as soon as his face is on the screen.

"Hmm. You aren't going back to sleep?"

"Thought about it but then was like, Jules is probably awake already, and I just wanted to talk to you. So I—actually, you okay? You look a little, I don't know."

"Bad morning."

"Wanna talk about it?"

"Not really."

"Do you want me to let you go? We can talk later; it's cool."

"I—" I wanted to hit "Reject" at first, but now I don't want to exist alone. I want someone who makes me feel the opposite. I want Mat. "No. Don't."

"Okay," he answers softly. "Can I help at all?"

"Tell me your favorite places in LA."

"Which ones? Restaurants, malls, beaches, parks, hangout spots?"

"All of them."

"How much time you got?"

"All day."

So he starts. Talking about the trails he likes to hike and the Vietnamese restaurant that's better than his mom's cooking (*but don't tell her I said that*). His favorite spots around UCLA. Everything.

And for a while, I can imagine a life where I'm not so scared. Where I'm happy and free and maybe get to hold Mat's hand while we walk through The Grove. A life fifteen hundred miles away from what's felt like continual gray and where I can finally be in the sun.

15

We like this one the best, right?" I tell Itzel, looking into my reflection as I model in front of the mirrors in the hallway of Express's fitting rooms. We've spent the better part of the last hour going through their selection of suits, with Itzel providing her always honest opinions, ranging from *I'm obsessed* to *Please take that off right now.*

"Yes," she affirms, scanning me up and down in the slim-fitting light-gray suit. "Oh, with what tie? Maybe the—"

"Navy tie with the floral pattern going on?" I finish.

"Yes! You're gonna look más que sexy."

I take the suit and tie, plus a new white button-up and navy socks from the store (thanks, Güelo, for the credit card), and then we go to Johnston & Murphy for cognac-brown Chelsea boots. No doubt Lou and I will be two of homecoming's best dressed.

We *have* to go to every other store after getting everything I need because Itzel and I will always convince each other that we don't have enough clothes or shoes or bags or bath bombs. And yeah, soccer is tiring, but try walking at a *normal gay pace* with arms and hands full of bags. Then, on top of that, while keeping up with Itzel in an H&M.

"I'm tired now," I whine as we leave American Eagle. "And hungry. Let's go eat."

I'm multitasking between eating my tofu poke burrito and talking to Mat on Instagram, who replied to my story posts of fitting-room selfies modeling three different suits, asking for opinions on which looks best.

TBFH you look hot in all three. But you in that navy suit with the black lapel is doing things to me.

Sorry to disappoint a fan, but I went with the gray.

Whenever someone tries to tell me that my vote matters, I'm going to show them this conversation as proof that they're wrong.

"Your *sunshine*-Mat?" Itzel la metiche asks.

"What? Yes. I mean, it's Mat. Yeah. Why you being nosy?"

I'm not sure what part of her question got me falling over my words. That she referred to him as *my* Mat, maybe. Or that I'm now thinking of how appropriate of a nickname Sunshine is for him.

"You're *into him* into him, aren't you?"

Also yes. Very much yes.

"No. I told you. He's only—"

"Don't BS me. I know that smile you had going on. The grin of someone clearly crushing hard."

The stuttering coming out of my mouth as I try to form a response does little to convince her she's in the wrong. "Itzel, that's not what this is. I—ugh, shut up and stop giving me that look. I don't know. It's way too complicated to be anything. And stop making that smirk or else I'm gonna throw soy sauce at you."

"Trust me, the unattainableness, the complexity of all the *Wait, but what ifs* are what's making him seem so attractive. We like to want what we can't have."

"I guess you'd be the one to relate," I say. "Not to be shady or anything. But—"

"I got it, Jules." The nicest way possible of saying *shut up and eat*.

"But let's say, for argument's sake, I am into him. What do I do? I don't want to let that attraction ruin our friendship. And it's only been two weeks. How do I even know that I really like him?"

"No, you do. That much is obvious. You're gonna have to, I don't know, be realistic with it. How likely is it that something between y'all would work out? You'd go months—could be up to almost a year—before you meet him in person. Not worth the drama. Stay friends. Don't put yourself through that sort of trouble."

I groan. She's right. It'd be way too much drama.

"But," she adds, "tell me what has you hot and bothered. You know, between two friends who can be empathetic in these situations."

"And because you're a pinche chismosa."

"Whatever, I'm taking an interest in your life while acknowledging how much I love that I can talk about boys with you. Dígame."

"I think it's that I allowed myself to put a lot of trust in him immediately, you know? Whether with coming out or everything that's happened. Where I am with all this—"

"You can come to us about that stuff too."

"But he gets it." I try to make the words sound not as insulting as she's probably taking them. "There's some stuff that I'm more comfortable letting out with another gay person. Nothing against y'all."

Itzel rolls her eyes. "I guess. Continue, though."

"I mean, he's hot. And funny. We seem to have that connection, you know? If he lived here, I'm certain he'd fit in perfectly with our group. Oh, and he may have mentioned that he wanted to make out with me."

"Don't be a thirsty ho. I can find someone here to kiss you if you want."

"Cállate. That's not what I want. I'm not trying to kiss some random guy. I'm just saying."

"I'm kidding, oh my God. And forget I ever admitted it, but I know how hard it is to have feelings for someone who's more or less unattainable. You gotta focus on what's priority. Don't ruin a relationship with someone who's obviously good for you as a friend—"

"You *and* Jordan are gonna die on that hill, huh?"

"You're not funny," she replies. "Where was I? Don't hold yourself back, but be optimistic. If you're single a year from now, you have someone waiting for you. But don't *stay* single because of him."

Being optimistic isn't the hard part. Being patient is.

Regardless, I know what I need to do when it comes to Mat. Nothing.

I'm not going to make this into something it's not. I'm not going to get hopelessly romantic with someone I've known for only a couple of weeks. I'm not going to fall head over heels because Mat said he wanted to hold my hand and make out with me and I really, *really* want to do the same. It means nothing when he's states away. We can't. It's not possible for either of us to act on that. It's not possible for me to act on any of the thoughts that have crossed my mind involving him. And I doubt he'd want to wait almost a year for the opportunity. I doubt I would either. I won't ruin what's become a great friendship.

Even if it already feels like I've known him my entire life. Even if I've been able to share myself with Mat without thinking what I'm going through doesn't matter or that I'm overreacting or worrying that he'd judge me. Even if he's without question the cutest boy I've ever met.

I stand *firm-ishly* resolute that I will not get into something that has no hope of being successful.

16

Doing nothing is hard.

It's been more than a month now since I came out and my friendship with Mat began, and every day of it, I fight back against how much I want to tell him how I feel. Every time we stay up later than we should, talking about our day or whatever's on our mind. Every time we send each other a selfie on Snapchat or one of us tags the other in a tweet. Every time something happens that makes me think of him, I crave more. Even if that doesn't include him being instantly teleported to me or me to him. At least I'd know he would be mine and I, his. And that's better than nothing, right?

I pose in front of my mirror, adjusting my tie and trying not to loosen it, before taking a quick picture. Not saying I was wrong or you were, IDK, whatever, but the navy suit did look better.

So what you're saying is I WAS RIGHT, Mat texts back. You look hot AF regardless. If you're free in a couple weeks, bring the suit and come with me to my HoCo.

For sure I'll see you there.

Cool. I already got a date, but I can let her down easy.

Tonto.

He sends a laughing face emoji, and then, go have fun Jules.

FaceTime when I get home?

I'll be here.

I don't know why I'm surprised that Lou is not near ready when I arrive at her house. Although I have to admit, for as long as she takes, she does good work. Lou looks gorgeous in her navy dress, hugging and accentuating her body as it comes down from her boobs to waist to hips to knees. Dark-brown extensions that look just as natural as her real hair fall all the way down her exposed back. As always, her makeup is flawless, and she's painted her nails a burgundy color with a pearl accent nail that matches a few of the flowers on my tie. Lou's never been one to let her natural curviness diminish her confidence, nor care what anyone's opinions are of her or how she presents herself. It's a quality I've admired since I've known her.

"Chiquis," Lou starts as she sorts through more cosmetics than I'm sure anyone could ever need. She pulls out a bottle of navy nail polish and shakes it in her hand. "Can I paint your nails?"

"What?"

"You don't have to si no quieres, but this color is a perfect match with my dress and your socks and tie. Plus, you'd look muy hermoso with some painted nails."

I think of every reason why I shouldn't. How my classmates will react. What everyone at the dance would say. And I realize they all center around what other people might think. But I've let those thoughts bring me too much anxiety and control my life, especially recently. And to be honest, I'm over it.

"Y-yes," I answer before I can allow myself to change my mind. "Paint my nails, Lou. Porfa."

She scoots herself to sit by me, laying a towel under my hands to catch any excess polish before it ends up on her bed or my pants. We gossip and talk colleges and boys while she paints. I've never put it together until now, but while Jordan and Itzel might be my emotional-support straights, and Rolie the boy who will throw hands and ask questions later, Lou shows she cares in her own way. She doesn't do anything because she wants to force me to embrace myself. She does it because she wants me to know it's okay to.

I stare at my nails, admiring her work. She watches me. I'm sure noticing the smile on my face.

It turns into a horrified gape, though, when I notice the time on Lou's phone.

"Why didn't you tell me we were running late?" I ask as I jump off her bed. "¡Córrele, Lou! Everyone's probably almost at the dance by now."

"¡Ya voy!" Lou yells back. "I need to check my chiches real quick." She takes one last look in her mirror before grabbing her clutch, slipping on her heels, and taking my hand as we leave her bedroom, rushing out the door.

"No one is, comó se dice, punctual about these things anyways," Lou says as she buckles herself into the passenger seat of my truck.

"Is that how you justify your life?" Trying to hide how serious the question was behind sarcasm.

"Most days, chiquis. Now, unlock your phone. We need some pregame music," she requests, holding out her hand. "Promise I won't look at any of the tasteful nudes you got on your phone."

"Lou, I'm begging you to please shut up. Here."

I pass her my phone and hear her say, "Ooh, yes, this one," before "La Carcacha" starts playing.

"I hope they don't play a bunch of country music again," she says over the music. "Remember last year? When the school brought that DJ who had a hard-on for Blake Shelton or something. We ain't putting up with that this time."

"Bangers and bops only," I reply.

"And cumbias."

"Oh, cumbias are very mandatory."

We both laugh and settle into a comfortable stillness as I turn in to the school parking lot. Lou and I haven't ever been *super close.* She's got other circles of friends to maintain. Showing up for socializing at lunch, parties, and anything where her pendejisma can thrive is about the extent to which our own friendship goes.

But Lou's been great this year. I hope she sticks around a little more than usual.

"Are you sad you aren't going to homecoming with a boy, chiquis?" Lou asks as I park.

"There's not a guy at school I'd consider going with."

"Pero in an ideal situation. Would you rather be going to the dance with a guy?"

Mat comes to mind and how his not-even-half-serious invitation to his own homecoming really, really excited me. Thinking of a reality where he'd be in this truck with me. How fulfilling it might be to show him off to the school. To slow dance with him. To see him having fun with all my friends. To not have distance invalidate these thoughts.

"Ideally, I suppose so. But in a perfect world, I'd go with whoever I wanted to go with. And no one would care who they are or what gender they are. They'd only care that we're both happy to be together."

"Bueno." She sighs. "Well, if it's any consolation, I'm sorry that you can't get your perfect date."

"I'd say it's pretty close to perfect," I tell her. "I wanted to go with you, Lou. We've gone to pretty much every high school dance together already, and it's always a disaster in the best way."

"I do what I'm good at, Julito. But escúchame." She grabs my hand in hers. "In all seriousness, you're gonna meet a guy who'll make you as happy as you deserve. I know it. Be patient. He's out there."

"Thanks, Lou. That means a lot."

"I know," she boasts. "Pero, that's enough real talk. Everyone is most likely wondering where we are by now. And they know we ain't getting frisky porque, tu sabes, no soy un hombre."

"We get it, Lou."

"I mean, who knows what conclusions they're coming to? Not that I'd say no. I enjoy a good pocket papi every once in a while."

"Lou. Ya basta, pendeja. *We get it.*"

"I'm just saying. Pero let's go. We got a dance to be the life of, HoCo Co-Ho."

17

When Lou offered to host a homecoming after-party, I made it clear that I wasn't drinking. I'm still recovering from her last party. I don't think my body could handle another. And most importantly, I don't need another opportunity to make more confessions over Twitter while trashed.

I'll be designated driver. Y'all have fun.

I sit in the corner of one of the couches, can of Red Bull in hand, listening to Roe, Jordan, Piña, and a couple of other guys from school have an intense debate about anime, video games, or some drunken mixture of the two. Only feet away, the girls are dancing, ignored by their dates. Itzel winks, grinding against Avery and motioning for me to join them, no longer trying to get their dates' attention.

This entire scene is being completely wasted on me. The guys are too busy arguing about Naruto and Deku or Daku or Dick-oo that they don't realize these two are literally dry humping a yard away. *Straight boys.*

I only stick around for a few songs. If I were drunk, I'm sure I'd be all over this. Instead, I'm unable to stop thinking about the bags of Hot Cheetos and the Crock-Pot of melted cheese in the kitchen.

All my friends are getting trashed but I have food so I guess it's cool, I text Mat, along with a selfie. Wishing he was here.

He'd be yelling with the boys, though; both his love of being right all the time and anime would compel him to need to get in his two cents. One of his hands would be resting on my leg, absentmindedly gripping and gently rubbing his thumb while I'd want to be as close to him as possible, scooching until there's no more space left and reaching an arm around his back. And when he wasn't busy making points and getting way too into the conversation, he'd kiss my cheek every few seconds and I'd kiss him back.

Then I'd pull him away from them, and we would dance some more, ignoring how tired homecoming would have made us. And once more, into some empty room where we would—

"All right, putos," I hear Lou call out. "Canceling the sausage fest for right now." When I get back to the group, I see her holding an empty bottle of Corona. "Everyone circle around the coffee table."

"Are we really gonna play spin the bottle like we're back in middle school?" Jordan asks her.

"None of us is beau'ed up yet, so I don't see a problem with getting a little frisky."

"And Luna?" I hear Freddie Hernandez ask as he walks toward us from the bathroom.

"What's that mean?" Itzel asks defensively. I squeeze her hand, trying to send telepathic signals to please stay calm. He's inconsequential. We don't even talk to him, and the only reason he's here is because he's dating one of Lou's other friends.

"Que la—house rules!" Lou interrupts. "Because I don't have a problem kissing whomever, I'm gonna say where the bottle lands is who you're kissing. We're all human, verdad? But because consent is law in this house, the person the bottle lands on may pass if they want. The bottle spinner has the same right, but if they do, they have to take a shot of my choosing and they miss out on their turn. Oh! Last rule: if any of y'all been cochinos with your mouths tonight, please do us a favor and skip. We ain't judging, but we *will* ask for details. Anyone got a problem with that?"

When no one speaks up, she sets the bottle down on the table, and the game begins.

Lou proves her point when her first spin stops, pointing to Carolina, Roe's date. They both move toward the middle of the table, locking lips to screaming, whooping, and clapping. The mood of the room about playing this game takes a quick one-eighty.

Carolina is next, landing on Rolie. Then his spin stops on Ben Martinez, the guitarrón player in mariachi. Roe opts for a shot, and I can tell from Ben's face that he's thrilled about that decision.

Nearly everyone's gone by the time the bottle lands on me, spun by Jordan's date, Avery. She reaches an arm out, wanting me to help her shift her body into a more comfortable position over the table.

"You good, Jules?" she asks me, our faces inches apart.

"I'm great. Y—"

Avery is grabbing my face and kissing me before I even finish talking. And I'm surprisingly not hating it. Her lips are soft, and she smells good. Fruity and flowery. We don't separate until we hear someone yell for us to get a room.

I pull away from her and fall back into my spot on the floor, cheeks flushed.

"Not bad," Avery says as she takes her seat back on the floor, giving me a drunk, playful wink.

"Girl, cálmate. You ain't gonna turn him," Lou tells her, garnering an eruption of laughter from the entire house.

She looks at me and then to the bottle, signaling my turn. I take a deep breath, holding on to the Corona. My hand flicks, making the bottle spin in fast circles around the table. And I realize I haven't let go of the breath yet. Holding it in and feeling the nerves build as the bottle starts to slow down.

Nothing to worry about. It'll land on some random straight boy. He can pass. No harm done. Save us both, and I can go back to texting Mat.

The room becomes quiet when the Corona almost stops at Itzel but comes to a halt on Piña.

We stare at each other.

I stay still, waiting on him. Certain he's going to refuse. Piña's eyes go from me to the bottle, and he keeps fidgeting with the class ring on his finger. But then he squares his shoulders and takes everyone by surprise when he says, "Screw it. I'm comfortable enough in my sexuality to kiss a dude."

My mind is going a million miles a minute as I hear someone let out an "oh shit" and another with an "aaall right." I watch him and Itzel switch spots so we can sit side by side. It's all giving me a headache. Yes, I just kissed Avery, but this is a guy. And it's not at all how I pictured my first kiss with a boy would be.

Not romantic in the least. Nothing distinct about it. With someone who isn't *that* special to me.

I mean, Piña's definitely good-looking. Maybe it makes this a little better that he's sort of my friend? But he's gone through a lot of beer, and I don't want us to be awkward around each other after tonight.

"Are you sure?" I whisper, loud enough to keep it between us over the music still filling the room. "You're not too drunk to be making these decisions?"

"I'm fine," he stresses. "And I'm not drunk, I promise. At least, not yet. We doing this?"

"Looks like it."

"Cool."

He tilts his head down, still somehow nearly half a foot taller than me even when sitting. One of his hands goes behind my head, taking the lead of whatever is happening right now. Really going for it when I expected him to prefer a peck and call it a night.

He's clumsy about it, but I have to give it to him. Piña is a talented kisser.

I wonder if Mat's a good kisser. Probably. And he's not a giant like Piña, so he wouldn't have needed to lean in so much to meet me. And—

Piña's tongue is fully in my mouth. I'm trying to go with it, but I can taste the Modelo he's been chugging all night. And his other large hand he's been using to stabilize himself on my leg is now traveling back toward my ass.

My eyes open, and I place a palm on his chest, pushing him away. I don't think anyone saw that progression of his hand, but still, I'm too sober for this not to be embarrassing. The entire room is staring at us. A few people let out small, drunk giggles.

"Damn, y'all," Lou says as she hands the bottle to Piña. "I have to be honest, that was hot. I'd pay you both money to do that again but with your shirts off."

"Te lo sico, Lou," I say, glaring at her as I get up, in need of a soda to wash out the beer still lingering in my mouth.

~

The drive post-after-party is calm. A welcome change from the noisy past few hours. Carolina, Itzel, and Piña are knocked out in the back seat of my truck, and Rolie snacks on limón potato chips beside me. Being sober makes me realize how tired I am.

Focus on the road and get everyone home.

"Piña really got into that kiss, huh?" Rolie asks, breaking the silence. His normal quiet demeanor replaced by a louder, tipsy persona.

"Different topic, please, Roe?"

"Yeah, man. But do you think he could be gay too?"

"I'm not going to make any assumptions. He'd been drinking. We all do stupid things after too many beers." I look at the back seat from the rearview mirror, making sure no one, especially Piña, is awake while we're talking about him.

Did that kiss give me not-hetero vibes? No doubt. But does it matter? No.

All that's been on my mind is how much I'd have preferred kissing Mat. Kissing Piña only made me realize how much I want to kiss Mat. How much I want to be in his company. How I definitely wouldn't have pushed him away if his hands started roaming my body. And that I'm a little more peeved than usual that I can't.

"Pero, if he was gay, would you go out with him?"

"No, I—" I definitely don't want to tell him how I'm strongly considering taking my chances with someone halfway across the country. "The optics of two guys on the soccer team together aren't the best. And again, until he says otherwise, I'm not gonna be all metiche about his sexuality."

"You're right," he replies, mouth full of chips.

"Are you and Carolina anything?" I ask after letting him finish chewing.

"Nah, we're nothing. I'm comfortable being single, you know? Having a girlfriend would be cool, and my family would love it, but I'mma do me for now. With mariachi, shot put, college apps, graduation, trying to protect my number three spot in the class, that's enough for now."

"That's respectable, Roe."

"But I mean, if you want a boyfriend, I hope you get one. You deserve to be happy, compa. And if that's not what you want, well, we can be single together. Bros before—what is it for gays? Before other bros? Oh, bros before boys! Like, fuckboys!"

"Roe, shut up and eat your chips."

18

I get home a little after three. Exhausted beyond belief from the dance and the party and dropping everyone off and stopping by Walmart to buy nail-polish remover. All I want is to shower and go to bed.

But I want to talk to Mat too. No, *need*. The exact words aren't yet planned out. I can try to work on some sort of outline of a conversation in the shower. Even though it's way more likely I'll end up winging it.

Once I'm cleaned up and changed into a pair of sleep shorts, I settle onto my bed and open my laptop, sending a FaceTime request to Mat. He answers within a couple of seconds.

"Hey! I was starting to think you'd fallen asleep. How'd the night go?"

"The dance was fun, but Lou could make being stranded on an island a good time. A night as DD was as enjoyable as you'd assume. And—wait, where are you right now?" It looks like Mat's outside somewhere. Streetlights lining wherever he is give enough visibility to be able to see him and not much else.

"Beach. Hanging out with some friends, so, of course, no one's sleeping tonight. They're behind me somewhere right now. But, hey! I saw the Texas coast. Now you can see the SoCal coast!"

"You realize that it's just a big black void right now."

"Huh. True. My bad for not being able to keep the daylight around for you," he jokes as he holds his phone with one hand while steadying himself onto the sand with the other. "Oh, did you realize it's a full moon tonight? And thanks to first-year Spanish, I can confidently say that I knew your last name means *moon*. So, needless to say, you've been on my mind. Not as cool as a sunrise. But still, it's pretty beautiful."

"Happy to know you were thinking about me."

Actually, *happy* is too basic a description. There isn't a word for it, though. For that tingle of electricity that rushes through my entire body.

"It's not a bad way to spend my time." He gives a flirty smirk that sends my brain into overdrive. "What else happened? Tell me more."

"Well, I kissed a guy."

"No way? At the dance?"

"After-party. He's one of my soccer teammates. And he's straight. At least, pretty sure he is. We were playing spin the bottle—"

"People still play that?"

"Drunk teenagers."

"But you were sober, so—"

"Anyways," I interject, "back to what I was trying to say. The bottle landed on him, and he kinda got real into it."

"Were you into it?"

"It wasn't terrible. Doesn't matter, though, because he's not the guy I like. He isn't who I wanted to kiss."

I stare at my laptop screen, waiting for Mat to say something. Anything. Hoping he might get the hints about where I'm going with this and validate my own feelings for him.

"Can I admit something to you?" he asks.

"Yes," I answer almost too eagerly. "Of course."

Mat takes a long pause before starting to speak. "I tried to write this all down earlier, but that didn't work out." His shoulders rise with his breath, and his mouth forms a soft smile. "I—I like you, Jules. In a way that's unfair to drop on you in the middle of the night, as much as it's probably been obvious for a while. And I thought I could hold it in, but shit, it's all kind of soul crushing, you know? That all I get is, what? Texting? To FaceTime with you a few times a week or tag you in some tweet that made me think of you, and then I can't get you out of my head for the rest of the day. When, at the same time, some guy gets to kiss you. So I'm sitting here jealous as fuck of some boy I've never met. And ugh—that sounds super selfish, I know."

I want to tell him that it's not selfish. That I have entire days when I can't get him out of my head too. That I would kiss him a million times over if it helped us get past this one time someone else got the opportunity.

He doesn't look at me as he continues. Staring down at the sand or out into the ocean. He scratches the back of his neck and slides his hand through his hair.

"If there is a god out there, I did something and pissed her off because in the short amount of time that we've known each other, we've connected in a way that normally takes months to get to. We started whatever this is without any walls, no hesitations to hide any part of ourselves. And I'm honored to have been the person you gave your trust and vulnerability. But—who gave me the evil eye to now be in this situation where here's this guy who's hot and funny and seems to be super compatible with me, and in any regular situation I would have wasted no time trying to get to be my boyfriend, but fate thought it'd be cool to put us fifteen hundred miles apart?"

"So then you don't want that?"

"I—I don't know, Jules. I've been trying to figure that out all day. A part of me is screaming to forget these feelings, or at least put them on hold. That a few weeks ago, I was cool with the prospect of seeing where you are a year from now. Until I started thinking, *What if he wants this too? Maybe we're both tired of being only friends.* And that I want to spend all my time with you, even if it's from a distance."

I listen to the sound of waves crashing into the shore and digest his words. He wants more too. We could be more.

He's been struggling with the same thoughts as I have. Considering the same options. The same potential disastrous conclusions.

But he's right. Itzel was right. I was right in thinking that being more will ruin what we have. I don't know how to be a boyfriend. Especially to someone from a distance.

And if he knew how chaotic my home life is, would he bail? Probably. I would.

"I do want that too, Mat. I want that *so badly*. But I'm gonna mess this up, and—I need you."

He sighs. "You won't mess anything up. I mean, you could. I should take that back. But I could too. I'll try my hardest not to, though, if you'd let me. You make me happy, and I can't get over how cute you are and how you've managed to have the courage to start living your life—as hard as it may be—and seeing you and talking to you has become my favorite part of my day. And looking at you. And how you can make even *necesito ir a baño* sound so hot. No one else in the world can do that. Can . . . tell me if you're certain that you want me as much as I want you."

I do, but damn it. I'm supposed to do nothing. I'm supposed to want to be friends and nothing more. I'm supposed to not let myself get romantic feelings for someone when I know how hard it's going to be to make this work for even a little bit. I'm supposed to keep myself from getting into something that has almost no chance of being successful and will most likely ruin this friendship.

Screw supposed-tos.

"I do. I want you, Mat."

He smiles but bites his bottom lip at the same time. He's trying not to seem *overly* happy about this. And then he pumps his fist, and there's no hope left of hiding how he's feeling.

Pretty sure he thought he was out of view.

"Good," he says.

We stare at each other, realizing we're doing this. No going back now. For better or for worse.

"I want you too, Jules."

19

Hi, *boyfriend.*" Saying that word is my second-favorite thing. Being able to call someone that word. And that that someone is Mat.

"Hey, boyfriend," he says back.

Hearing him call me that word is my first-favorite thing.

"What're you up to today?"

"Thinking about you," Mat answers. "Going to the beach later. Usual Saturday stuff. You?"

"Hanging out with my güelo in a little bit. And mowing in a few minutes, I think. My dad's picking up pan dulce, and that usually means he's about to persuade me to do some manual labor, so I'm getting my Selena Spotify playlist ready."

"Damn, yard work? My man's masc as fuck."

"Shut up, estúpido."

I barely got any sleep last night. After Mat and I finally forced ourselves to say bye for the hundredth time and hung up, I spent the following few hours replaying it all in my head. Mat saying, *I want you too, Jules.* How his eyes looked vulnerable but hopeful. Excited and relieved and ready.

Regretting keeping myself awake right now. Not that I would've gotten much sleep regardless. And I'm already thinking about how good it'll feel to get back later this evening and fall into my bed and sleep the rest of the weekend.

I hear the short honk of Dad's truck locking and wish that I could pause time to get sixty more seconds with Mat. But then the sounds of the front door opening and closing and Dad's voice calling my name shatter any hope of that happening.

"I gotta go," I say quickly. "I'll try to call you tonight, but if you don't hear from me, it's because I'm drooling into my pillow."

"I guess I'd forgive you," he replies with a smirk. "Talk to you later, boyfriend."

"Bye, boyfriend."

I keep my phone up at face level for a minute, staring at the black screen. At my tired reflection. One that, on this side of my bedroom door, is free and happy. Is someone who still struggles but has reason after reason to smile while having to hide this part of me the moment I open that door and leave my room. At least, until Dad leaves.

I wish that I didn't have to. That I could just go exist and be.

"One day," I say before taking a deep breath and slowly exhaling. "I'm one day closer."

~

"¿Qué estás mirando?"

"Nada, Güelo."

I need to stop looking so concerningly but blissfully checked out from the world every time Mat Snaps or texts me. But I got lost in rewatching the video he sent of him trying to look cool and show off in the ocean only to be knocked down by a wave, yelling as he falls into the water. And I'm sure Güelo was curious about what had me quietly laughing and smiling.

I stick my phone into my pocket and follow him into Casa Fe, an immigrant youth shelter I've been volunteering at with him since freshman year. Güelo helps with the paperwork and, as a retired immigration lawyer, occasionally offers pro bono services in court. I usually either get put to work organizing files and boxes or, my favorite, supervising a small group of kids, none of them older than twelve or thirteen.

I help them with their English-learning assignments or whatever other homework they have. And when they're done with that, we pull out board games and I get my ass handed to me in checkers by a ten-year-old going through Capri Sun packets and bags of Cheez-Its like nothing. Or, if the weather's right, I'll get to bring a soccer ball out and run around with them.

Sometimes they'll tell me about coming here from Mexico or Guatemala or Honduras. About riding La Bestia. Parents or older siblings being threatened or killed, and their families packing their lives up in a night, leaving home for what should be an opportunity to be safe and free and without worry. And then getting here only to be separated. Alone in a place where every day is filled with uncertainty.

Originally, I started volunteering because the hours were a graduation requirement. But it quickly became so much more. The kids, their stories, Casa Fe. I realized that I want to help in a way that's greater than being their tutor or glorified babysitter.

Because when I see them, I see Güelo. I see my dad. I see the couple of decisions that put me here instead of in their shoes. And I want all of them to be able to have the same opportunities my family was given.

I want to help them get those opportunities.

How? I don't know yet. Not looking to follow in Güelo's footsteps. Becoming a lawyer has never been in my life plan. But something immigration related. Like, as I've been narrowing down majors, my mind's been less interested in political science or philosophy and more into Chicanx studies, sociology, or Spanish.

I think with law, Güelo has to try to convince someone else that these kids are human. And that's important. They're lucky to have someone like him fighting for them.

But I'd rather do something that helps remind these kids that they are human. Because that's important too.

After a few hours, they all leave for dinner, and Güelo will come find me and help me put up chairs and tables. And he'll tell me stories he's repeated hundreds of times of coming to the United States, working in the cotton fields or digging graves while spending any spare time he had studying if he wanted to catch up to his American classmates. Of teachers whipping him for speaking Spanish in school and constantly being told he'd never measure up.

Of leaving home right after he turned eighteen to get involved in the workers' rights and immigrants' rights battles that were starting to gain momentum. The marches and late nights and brawls with business and ranch owners and police. Of feeling this need in his soul to do something. To act.

I think, even though Güelo doesn't know exactly *why* I've wanted to move to Los Angeles for college, he understands. This trait that we share, a quality that's almost genetic. A need to grow and experience. Which, I think, is why he's always supported that want.

"Los niños te gustan," he tells me as we walk back to his truck.

"I do too."

"I'm happy you've stuck with this, mi'jito. That you keep coming. They're lucky to have you and your heart."

"I just think they should be allowed to be kids. You know?"

Güelo's arm reaches around me and grabs on to my shoulder, pulling me into this sort of one-armed hug. "One day, God willing." He kisses the top of my head and squeezes me one more time before loosening his grip. "Everyone deserves happiness."

20

Jules. How are you *not* excited about going to a haunted house?"

"Because," I groan at Mat. "I don't do scary. I'm gonna be screaming and hitting things the entire time."

"Have someone record that for me. I need to see this."

"Sure. Lemme tell my friends that the boyfriend they don't know is my boyfriend wants one of them to get a video of me crying in the middle of a haunted house."

"I mean, maybe figure out how to word it a little better," he replies. "You dressing up too?"

"Jordan, Piña, and I are all wearing Real Madrid jerseys and calling it a costume."

"That's the least creative outfit idea I've ever heard of."

"What's the point if I'm not getting candy out of it?"

Mat's face looks like I've insulted his entire existence. "There are *so many* reasons. Because it's fun. It's basically *the* queer holiday. Dressing up as a demonic nun doesn't have that same fulfillment every other day of the year. You get to express yourself in the wildest way possible. Or the sluttiest. Like, either way, you're doing Halloween right."

The truth is, I did originally plan on being more creative this year. Itzel and Lou had convinced me to go as Peter Pan because they wanted to be Tinker Bell and Wendy. But a few days ago, I found out Lou's dad showed my dad a picture of me and her at homecoming. Painted nails on full display.

Didn't even have a chance to say hi before I was being slammed against a wall. Looking into eyes seething with anger. Hearing slurs and threats come out of his mouth. The large cut and bruise he left on the back of my shoulder are a reminder of how careful I'm still forced to be. Just in case I've forgotten or become too comfortable because so many parts of my life now thrive in my newfound freedom.

I haven't told Mat. And don't plan to. I do my best to not bring my dad up when we talk, and that's not something I'm trying to do only two weeks into our relationship.

I'd rather take the shade over my uncreative costume choice.

"I'm good," I tell him. "What're you supposed to be going as?"

"A vampire, obvi." Mat gets up from his computer, making the outfit more visible. It's corny as hell. Grandfather-collar white shirt, dollar-store cape, this gawdy gold statement necklace that probably came with a store-bought Marie Antoinette costume. "Thought I'd go with a classic this year. All that's left are the fangs and some fake blood."

"Where are you going dressed like that?"

"My friend Garrett's throwing a party," he taunts. As if I'm supposed to be jealous of a bunch of teenagers who raided Party City to get drunk. "I helped him turn the entire place into a haunted house. Made some kind of scary-looking punch. And I heard there's gonna be a keg, maybe? I don't know, but it'll be great. He had a Halloween party last year, and I think he's gonna try to make it an annual thing, which means when you're here a year from now, I'm bringing you with me."

"You know what? Sure. I'm in. I'll let you try to sway me to the dark side. But if you even suggest we go as Mario and Luigi, I'm breaking up with you."

"I mean, we could make them sexy—"

"Not. Happening."

~

The next morning, I'm up early for All Saints' Day Mass with Dad, Xo, and Güelo.

My patron saint is Óscar Romero, a Salvadoran bishop and human-rights activist. I picked him only weeks before Confirmation, when we had to choose a saint to forever be our spiritual role model. And I didn't want someone simple. Be one of those kids who picks Saint Francis of Assisi because they *love cats* or someone who seemed great but was actually super problematic.

San Óscar isn't perfect but definitely not the worst. The ideal amount of relatable.

I've found myself talking to him more and more since applying for colleges. Hoping he'd have an idea of what I am supposed to be doing with my life, and I want it to be clear that I'm very open to suggestions (or shoves) in a certain direction. As long as he knows that following in his vocational footsteps is a nonstarter.

After Mass, I leave with Güelo to help set up the altar for Día de los Muertos. When Abuelita was still alive, I'd help her decorate and make pan de muertos and sugar skulls intricately painted with colorful faces. This is the third year without her, and I've yet to set an altar or bake pan as well as she could, but I think she'd appreciate the effort.

I cover the small foldable table that becomes our altar with two cloths, one red and one green, laying both down before bringing the pictures of Mom, Abuelita, Abuela Marisol, and my great-grandparents. Bottles of Modelo, Budweiser, and merlot and canisters of jasmine and mint green tea—their favorite drinks—are placed near the frames, and then the rest of the table space is covered with snacks, sweets, Coca-Colas, flowers, and Luna and Vela family heirlooms.

The faces in the photographs watch me as I decorate and meticulously set everything in place. I stare back, seeing if I recognize any part of myself in them. Abuelita used to tell me that I was the spitting image of Güelo's father, except for his six-foot-four stature, but I don't really see it. I think I got way more Luna genes than Vela.

I spend the entire day making sure the table is flawless for tomorrow, when it's officially Día de los Muertos. I've been known to get overly obsessive about it and will stay right in this spot the entire night looking for any imperfection or anything that's even the slightest bit off until it's picture-perfect. Which, the first year I did this by myself, kept me up all night.

"Mi'jo," Güelo calls from his kitchen. "It's good enough where it's at. Come eat."

I want to tell him *five more minutes*. That it's not good enough *yet*. But he's gotten used to this and isn't above dragging me away from the altar.

Also, the smells of fideo, vegetarian charro beans, and tortillas have been calling me all evening.

~

I am always amazed at how many people can fit inside Güelo's home. Tíos, tías, and cousins all crowd inside the house, eating and drinking and talking so loudly, I'm sure the neighbors the next block over can hear us. We light candles and open bottles of alcohol, pouring a cup for the departed. Güelo turns up the stereo, and a chorus of gritos fills the home when the rancheras start playing. Dad tells some stories about Mom, Güelo about meeting Abuelita, and lots of other memories of great-grandparents, -aunts, -uncles, and other extended family members no longer here.

After dinner, Dad, my tíos, and most of my older male cousins head outside. At any big family event, the men migrate to the garage, drinking through cases of beer and shooting the shit. Then at some point between their twelfth bottle of Tecate and third tequila shot, they'll start hollering the lyrics to some Pedro Infante song.

The rest of us turn the house into a bingo hall, playing some high-stakes, life-and-death Lotería. I set my jar of coins on the table in front of me, ready to take all my tías' money. And they've all had plenty of rum tonight, so I'm sure I'm coming into this with the upper hand.

Once I've won an impressive pile of pennies and dimes, I slide my cards to Xo and step away from everyone. Get away from the noise. But with a promise to come back for the rest of their change.

I glance at my phone. A couple of texts from Itzel and Rolie wishing me a good Día de los Muertos (Itzel's filled with lots of added heart emojis) and some from Mat with pictures of Los Angeles's festival that looks straight out of *Coco* or *The Book of Life*.

Can we PLEASE go to that next year?

Of course! You'd love it. How's the party in Texas?

It's been a fun night. Lots of sugar and currently destroying my family at Lotería.

Damn no prisoners even on a holiday. Oh! I was wondering, do you think they extend the invite to the deceased from other cultures and races?

For sure. The more the merrier at Latinx parties. Even in the afterlife. My mom and abuelas might force them to sing Gloria Trevi songs all night tho.

I don't think they'd mind. Seems like the kind of party my grandparents would be the life of. I'll tell them to be on the lookout.

They'll be ready with open arms.

21

The beginning of our relationship hasn't really changed that much from when we were friends. But maybe it'd be different if it weren't long-distance. That transition from *talking* to walking into school one day and holding hands in the hallway. Hangouts when parents aren't home go from tiptoeing in awkwardness because no one's confessed their feelings to way less studying and way more making out.

Which would all be nice. *Really nice.* But I'm happy. Mat makes me happy.

Like a Kacey Musgraves "Happy & Sad" kind of happy, though. When Mat texts me, was thinking how good it would feel to hold your hand, or I hate that I'm at work rn. I'd rather be talking to you. Your voice is my favorite sound. Or when I try *really hard* to concentrate in physics, but then the bell rings and I realize I've spent the entire class looking up how much a flight to Los Angeles would cost at this very moment.

I'm, at the same time, better than I've ever been while being tortured by longing and the stupid Earth being stupid big and California being stupid far away from me.

"Hey, babe," Mat says as soon as his face shows up on my screen. I'm not sure when we started using pet names for each other, but how I ever existed before then, I'll never know.

"Hey, cariño," I reply with a smile. "What're you up to?"

"About to go see some friends. Which is actually why I wanted to talk to you right now. I was wondering how you'd feel if I told them about you? About *us*."

My concern about people we know knowing has never been about his friends. It's *my* friends. And it's that if his friends find out, that means I have to tell mine too. Right?

"I—I don't mind."

"You're sure?" he asks in that drawn-out way of really stressing the doubt in what I'm telling him.

"Yes. It's cool. You're good if I tell my friends?"

"Extremely. But don't think you have to go do it right now." Didn't realize Mat's a mind reader. "I know that this is big for you. Do it when it feels right."

"Okay."

"Okay. Then I'm gonna tell mine in a few minutes. I'll FaceTime you later when I'm back home."

"Yeah. See you later, cariño. Good luck."

"Bye, babe."

Right after we hang up, I get a text from Xo. Come bother me I'll buy you a sofritas bowl from Chipotle and I promise not to make fun of how you crush Takis over it.

It's not like I was planning on doing anything else today, and Chipotle sofritas bowls are one of my top three favorite foods, so I reply first with EVERYTHING TASTES BETTER WITH TAKIS and then a thumbs-up emoji, followed by Be there in fifteen. AND I'm getting chips and guacamole.

We've gotten through half an episode of *British Bake Off* when Mat calls me again. Way earlier than I expected. I hop off Xo's couch and rush to the spare bedroom, closing the door behind me.

"Hey," he says, not trying to hide the awkward nervousness on his face. "Are you busy?"

"I, uh—no. Not really. Everything all right?"

"So, random question. Would you be cool with talking to my friends?"

"Wait. Right now?"

"Yes. Don't worry. It's nothing huge. *But* they may or may not be convinced that you're some creep catfishing me. Which you're obviously not. Like, hi, I see you. Only if you don't have a problem with it, though—"

"It's fine," I answer quickly. I don't want to overthink this, and I can tell it's important to Mat. I don't want to give myself a second to think about telling him no. They're just people. And if Mat likes them, then they're probably great.

It's the weirdest thing, going down the line, friend to friend, taking turns meeting them, and they make sure I'm real and ask me a million questions while having a chance to get a whole new perspective on Mat. Hearing stories he might not have voluntarily told me. Like when he walked into a glass door a few months ago or hearing them mimic the baby voice he goes into any time he sees a dog.

"So you're *really* his boyfriend?" Mat's friend Garrett asks.

"Unless he changes his mind, yeah. I'm really his boyfriend. I—" My neck snaps around when I hear a throat clearing and see Xo standing in the doorway. Her head tilted, eyes big, and lips pursed, debating between whether she's trying to say *what am I witnessing right now* and *this was bound to happen sometime.* She smiles and shakes her head as she closes the door behind her.

Ay la motherfucking verga.

~

Xo has two fingers pressed to the inner corners of her eyebrows. A tick she's had for as long as I can remember. The thing she does when she's stressed or having a moment internally. And she's been doing this in silence for a couple of minutes now, since I've told her the whole story.

"'Manito, escúchame. I know that you probably don't want to talk about boys to your sister who's seven years older than you and has been pretty in and out of your life since before you even hit puberty, but you *can* come to me. I've got some experience with dating guys. And I don't want you to think you have to keep this hidden anymore. Not from me. You have my support. And I'm gonna always look out for you."

"I know, Xo. I—I was pretty sure you'd think I'm making a really dumb decision."

"Oh, I do. One hundred percent. I don't know why you'd choose a long-distance thing when you could get any guy you want here and do all the stupid things high schoolers in their first real relationship do. But I know that as unlikely as you are to talk to me about this, you're even less likely to listen to whatever it is I have to say about it. What I'm going to *try* to do—unless I need to get *big sister* on someone—is promise to hold my tongue." She makes an X over her heart and then pretends to lock up her mouth and throw the imaginary key over her shoulder.

"Would you believe that I think he's worth it? He's worth holding off on all those things."

Xo looks me in the eyes, giving me those same pursed lips until they form a smile. "He better be." She scoots closer to me, her smile getting more and more suspiciously big. And then she squeals as she throws herself on me. "But my baby brother has his first boyfriend! This is so exci—wait. He is your *first* boyfriend, right?"

"Yes, Xo," I groan while being crushed by her arms and body.

"Making sure. Who knows what other exciting things happening in your life you've been keeping from me. Oh! Piece of advice, especially relevant in this situation: don't send him anything you'll regret taking if you two break up. And of course, by *anything* I really mean, you know, nudes and vide—"

"OH MY GOD. XO. STOP."

22

Julián, who're you talking to?" Dad asks as he steps outside. In the middle of me FaceTiming with Mat. I thought, backyard, AirPods in, hanging out on the hammock we put up a few summers ago, I'd be good. Guess not.

I toss my phone facedown behind me. "Roe," I lie. "There's a Black Friday sale on the new PlayStation, and he and Jordan are getting it tonight. Wanted to see if I'd go with them."

He looks reluctant to believe me. *Don't question it. Don't question it.*

"Hmpff," he huffs. "Have him tell his parents happy Thanksgiving for me."

"I will." He bought it. Thank God.

"Sabes que, I haven't seen Ernesto in a while." Dad takes a seat by me on the hammock, making sure we don't fall out of it as he steadies himself. "Have Rolie tell his dad to call me sometime. We'll have a barbecue, drink a little—"

"Okay."

He continues to eye me. I'm acting way too impatient. I need to calm down.

"Güelo left you some shopping money."

"Cool. I'll text him *thank you.*"

Dad grabs on to one of my shoulders. I flinch, but I don't think he notices. He kisses the top of my head. "Just wanted to tell you today I'm proud of you, mi'jo. All right? We—well, I get that sometimes we butt heads. But I hope you know I'm trying my best. For you. For your mom. And I've always only ever wanted you to have the best life possible. I care about you and your future. I'm thankful for you, Julián. Today and every day."

"Thanks, Dad." I know he means it. And it is hard to not be minimally thankful for him too. As much as my life can suck sometimes. As much as it does because of him.

"Even though you're, you know . . . vegetarian," he teases. Not realizing how that joke and that pause gave me a two-second anxiety attack, wondering what he was about to call me. "But sabes qué, those lentil potpies and your mac and cheese? Almost as good as your güelo's fried turkey."

He pats my back. Brushes his hand through my hair. "Anyways, got called in to work. I'll be gone until the morning. Call your sister if you need anything."

"I will. See you tomorrow, Dad." I'm sure that came out more like *okay cool, please leave me alone now*.

I watch him go back inside, waiting to pick my phone up until I'm alone again.

"Sorry," I tell Mat.

"It's fine. Everything good?"

"Yeah. Yeah. My dad's going to work."

I fix myself to lie across the hammock. "I wish you were here," I say in a whine. "There's plenty of room for you on this too."

"Sounds perfect," Mat replies.

There's not much I wouldn't do for a minute with him. We've both been feeling the distance extra hard recently. Sixty seconds is all I'd need.

"Hey," he calls. "One day we won't have to wish. But don't get mad when I'm immediately the clingiest."

I laugh. "I think I'd be more offended if you ever let go."

"Never."

~

I'm running late, I send to the group. Text you when I'm on the way.

I meant to get off the phone, change, maybe have one more slice of pie, then take off for the night. But my usual timeliness went out the window when Mat blew up my texts with pictures of himself right out of the shower, with only a towel wrapped loosely around his waist.

I don't know why I was surprised about them. When he mentioned working extra hours with his brother this weekend, I told him that he'd better send me some shirtless selfies if he expected me to not be mad about it.

So here I am, with those selfies. Finding myself needing to take a few minutes. In the spirit of Thanksgiving.

When I finally get to Sand Dollar Diner, one of the few places still open on major holidays, Itzel waves me over to the booth she, Jordan, and Rolie are at, and I slide in next to her. She looks thrilled to have someone else here. I doubt the guys have been talking about anything besides their new video games.

"I need to tell y'all something," I say after ordering a milkshake and fried jalapeño bites. The words come spilling out. It was now or never.

"What's up, Luna?"

"I—uh, you know how I've been talking to Mat for a while—"

"The LA guy?"

"Yes, Rolie. The LA guy."

I'm so nervous. *Please don't bite my head off for being honest with y'all.*

"Well, I like him. A lot. And—"

"Oh, dude. That's been super obvious."

Jesus. Can they stop interrupting? Do they have that ability?

"Whatever. So we gave it some thought and—" I take a deep breath. "We decided to, um—to get together."

"Get together?" Rolie asks.

"Hold up," Itzel says. Her voice carrying a major bite to it. "Jules, you and him? Y'all are *boyfriends*?"

"Y-yeah. He's my boyfriend."

"When did this happen?"

"Same night as homecoming."

"Wait," she continues. Her hands slap the table and she pivots toward me. "That was more than a month ago. You've been hiding this from us for that long?"

"We agreed to keep it between us for a while, Itzel."

If she wants me to, then I will admit I was very much hiding it from them. I don't care if she thinks that was crappy of me, but it's my life. It was something I wanted to be sure would work out before telling the world.

"So you what? Go and latch on to the first boy who gives you attention?"

Is she really—

"Itzel," Jordan interjects. "That's a little harsh."

"No, it's not. Chinga'o, can you do *anything* low profile? Coming out. This. What happens if you get hurt? Did you think about this at all?"

"Of course I did."

"Then when did you decide it'd be nice to be this chaotic with your life?"

My hands clench onto my legs. I look up to the ceiling and take a deep breath. Sure, I didn't expect a pinche party. But I didn't think I'd be getting dragged by my best friend because she wants to talk mess over something that has nothing to do with her.

"At least I'm trying to be happy. And I'm not letting other people tell me how to live my life anymore. Maybe you should give it a try sometime."

"Luna. Bro," Jordan says. It probably took a lot out of him to say only those two words rather than whatever cuss words are hanging on his tongue.

Yeah, I shouldn't have said that.

"I mean, whatever, Jules," Itzel yells. "Continue to be a detriment to yourself."

Jordan and Rolie are both trying to get us to calm down. I'm doing my best to not start yelling back at her. Why is it so hard for her to be supportive?

But she's not. There's no use in trying to convince her to be. And I shouldn't have to.

I get up from the booth. If I stay, I know I'll say something even more regrettable. "Sorry for trying to keep you involved in my life. Expecting at least a little excitement for me."

"Jules, don't leave," Rolie implores.

"No, it's cool. I'm tired." I pull out a ten and place it on the table. I don't even look at them before turning around to head out. "I'll talk to y'all later. You can have my milkshake."

I pull out my phone. I know Mat's busy with his brother, but I don't care.

My friends suck.

23

I knew this would be hard for them. They know how complicated relationships can be. How easy it is to get hurt. And this is an entirely new level of complexity. This is uncharted territory within uncharted territory.

Itzel and I haven't said anything to each other since our fight. It's not as if we've never butted heads before. We're friends. And friends can push each other's buttons.

Sometimes we need to take a day. Or three.

Jordan's the first to try and make peace. He and I hang out on Saturday, and I find out I ruined his entire plan of telling all of us that the University of Denver came in with, basically, the best offer he could've hoped for—enough that even Clemson seems out of the picture now—and wanting us to celebrate with him. So I'm the worst.

But he promises he's brushed it off. And next time, we'll coordinate who gets to make big life announcements when, so we aren't stealing thunder. We get some one-on-one in before varsity practices start on Monday. And he tries his best to be as easygoing as possible about me being in a long-distance relationship.

Jordan's protective. And he doesn't know anything about the boy I'm dating. I'd honestly be a lot more worried about what he'd do if Mat ever fucked up than I am about Itzel.

She texts me Sunday. One condition: if he hurts you, I have every right to take Roe, Jordan, and Lou to LA and we're slashing his tires.

If saying yes to that helps her come to terms with Mat and me, then fine. Okay. Hypothetically slash away.

Rolie texts me a few hours later. Mind if I come over?

I'd been trying to finish reading *Brave New World* since hanging up with Mat earlier. *Trying* being the key word.

No, ven pa'ca!

Thank God. A distraction. And when Rolie gets here, he hands me a bag of empanadas as he enters. No one gets me like he does.

I set the bag down on the kitchen counter and take out a couple along with some Dr Peppers from the fridge before returning to the living room and falling onto the couch.

"So what's up, Roe?"

"I—I thought we should talk, Jules."

"Is this about Mat?" Rolie isn't the person I'd expect to want to have a heart-to-heart about my boyfriend. I thought he'd be more like *cool? cool.* And we'd be good.

"No. Well, not exactly. More about this entire thing. I want to be honest with you, compa. Because you gotta know that I support you—"

"Roe, I've always known you do. You almost punched a guy for me at the football game, remember?"

"But the thing is, Jules—" He takes a deep sigh and pops his knuckles. "I, ugh. I did feel uncomfortable in the beginning. Those first few days, I don't know. It's not that I wasn't cool with it, but—actually, that's a lie. There's no great way to explain where my mind was. The morning after you tweeted what you did, I wouldn't have known how to talk to you or what to say in the same way that Itzel or Jordan could. And then this revamped version of you came out when you, well, came out, and I wasn't seeing where I fit into it or even that I wanted to. I was sort of glad that we didn't have to have a *moment* or something. I thought, maybe this was the point where we slowly and eventually drifted apart, you know."

My heart cracks hearing him say that. Finding out that I was so close to losing one of my best friends. My arms involuntarily cross over my torso and my eyes strain to fight the reaction they want to release.

The thought went through Rolie's mind. That maybe he didn't want to be a part of this. Maybe we'd reached the end.

He's looking at his Dr Pepper can, trying his best to avoid eye contact.

"Do you still feel uncomfortable, Roe?"

"No, dude. Estoy contigo para siempre. The night that guy tried to mess with you, I realized I was either with you all the way or not at all. And that was the easiest decision I've ever made. I know me sticking up for you doesn't make the fact that I had that mindset in the first place go away." He pauses and lightly knocks into my arm with his elbow. "I'm sorry, compa. For that and for knowing I should have told you something that night. Made it known that you're supported, even if that meant admitting the shitty part. I'd already felt bad because maybe if I'd stopped you from getting drunk at Lou's party, you wouldn't have come out the way you did—"

"I don't blame you for me getting drunk or coming out. I'm over being stressed out about it. Also, you've been one of my best friends for three and a half years. You can tell me anything. Good or bad." I lean into his side and throw my arms around him. "Thank you for being real with me. And I don't care if this seems gay. I'm not moving."

"Cállate, Jules." Rolie tilts his head so it's resting on mine. "We're okay?"

"Are we?" I ask him back.

"Claro. Compas por vida."

I stay hugging him, enjoying how comfortable he is. I'm not moving until he makes me.

"Oh, question," he starts. "Out of the three of us, Itzel is obviously kill. But then who's bang and who's marry between Jordan and me?"

"You're doing this *right now*?" I ask into his arm.

"Hey, I'm trying to make an effort. I want to have a moment with you, güey."

I groan. "What makes you think Itzel is kill?"

"Are you saying I'm wrong?"

"Ugh, I hate you. And . . . marry you. I'm forcing you to sing to me every morning, though."

"You cook. I sing. That's a marriage I can get behind." He chuckles. "Pun intended."

"Cochino, don't be gross!" I yell, throwing myself back to lie across the sofa. "Get me another empanada, porfa. Camote."

"Anything for you, mi esposito."

We let the past stay there. However Rolie felt months ago is behind us. I have him here now, grown and a better friend than I could've ever hoped for.

He and I lose track of time talking about the universities we're applying to and his upcoming trip to College Station. "My amá's been doing nonstop novenas so I'll get early acceptance to A&M."

"You'll get in. And bring me back a hoodie so I can see Itzel and Lou make faces whenever they see me in it."

We even talk about Mat for a little bit, and I show him a few pictures. I try not to get overly emotional when he mentions how we're going to look really good together.

"He's taller than you, right?" Roe asks. "Tu sabes, eres chaparro, so most people are, so—"

"Te lo sico. He's not a mountain like you or Piña. Five-eight, maybe another extra inch with his hair up."

"Short kings," he jokes while laughing. That gets him a slap to the chest.

Rolie leaves around ten, when we both realize how late it's getting.

"Thanks for coming over, Roe. Don't keep secrets next time!"

"I could say the same to you, Señor Let Me Get Drunk And Tell Everyone I'm Gay."

"Whatever. That's different." I give him one more embrace before letting him leave. "I'm lucky to have you around."

"I am pretty great, huh?" he asks.

I roll my eyes at him as I close the front door in his face.

24

Good morning, cariño soccer season starts today. Wish me luck.

It'll be fine babe. But if I need to kick anyone's ass, lemme know. Oh and see if Itzel can get some pics of you in your uniform. Preferably from the back. For . . . reasons.

Reasons that, if they weren't obvious before, are made very clear when he follows with a line of peach emojis.

I'll consider asking her if I get some of you in your wrestling uniform. Text me after you get out of practice.

I will.

"Isn't the first day only for Coach Rodriguez to go over y'all's game schedule, hand out uniforms, and then let you go home?" Itzel asks as we walk to English class. She's spent the entire morning trying to get me to tell her why I'd been acting all spaced-out.

Just counting how many ways today could end horribly.

"Still. What if he brings up me being gay?"

"I don't think that's something he's allowed to do, Jules. Breathe and focus on class."

I make it through my last two periods without a mental breakdown. I'm able to get all the books and binders and spirals I'll need tonight out of my locker and into my backpack without a mental breakdown.

Head to the school's gym, feel the cool wind on my face, no mental breakdown.

But when I walk into the athletics meeting room and feel the abrupt tension when my teammates see me, I almost turn around and run.

Piña calls me over, waving a hand and pointing to an empty seat. I rush to the chair between him and Jordan at the front. Falling into it and slouching, as if that might make my presence a little less noticeable.

"You all right?" he asks.

I nod, staring straight ahead at the blank chalkboard. "I'm fine."

Coach Rodriguez walks in not too long after and begins exactly as Itzel had predicted. Housekeeping stuff. Our schedule, uniforms, papers that need a parent's signature. But after, he leaves it to Jordan, our team captain, to decide if we should let out early.

Not one to ever waste any time, he chooses to have us stay and make the most out of our first day back.

Jordan and Piña talk between each other while we change into our practice gear, joking and laughing. Acting way gayer with each other than I ever have in this locker room. Oblivious to the stares and whispers and hushed laughs of my teammates.

I can feel everyone keeping me in their peripheral. Waiting to catch me doing something *homosexual.* Preparing to defend themselves from the lust I must assuredly have for them.

I try to keep my head down as we run through warm-ups and conditioning exercises. Even when we break in half for a scrimmage, I keep my focus straight ahead. It's fine. It'll all be fine.

And it is. Nothing more than the usual passive-aggressiveness that I've gotten used to the last three years. They can think what they want about me. Out here, on this field, I'm as good, if not better, than them, regardless of who I'm dating.

"Hey, Luna," I hear Adán Solís call from behind me as we're walking back to the locker rooms from the practice field, and I know that whatever peace I've gotten used to today is about to crash into a wall. "I hear you been busy getting Eiffel Towered by Piña and Thomas. Which one you sucking off and which one you riding?"

"Shut the fuck up, Adán," I tell him, not bothering to look back.

"Just trying to find out when I get a turn with the team joto."

Nope.

I turn around. A heat starts building up from my gut to my chest. My fists tighten. My breathing comes harder. I want to punch him in the face, tackle him onto the ground, something.

But then an arm wraps around me and pulls me back.

"C'mon, Luna," Piña says, picking me up and carrying me with him. "Don't waste your energy on him."

He ignores my yells to let me go until we make it to the locker room and I promise not to get all lucha libre with anyone today. I try to get back to something close to levelheadedness. Regulate my breathing. Stay facing straight into my locker and change as quickly as possible.

Don't think about how, in those times I get angry and immediately want to punch someone, I'm just like my dad. Regardless of whether Adán deserves it. Which he does. He fully deserves and needs to get the shit beat out of him.

I don't, though. And that's what makes it different. I'm not him. I'm not him and Adán is inarguably the worst and—

I slam my locker door and leave without waiting for Jordan.

He yells for me as I'm walking to my truck. I toss my backpack onto the back seat and lean against the side of the bed, waiting for him to catch up.

"Why'd you rush out?" he asks, leaning beside me.

"I—it was too much, Jordan. I'll never be normal to them. I stepped into *their* space, and the moment I did, they became worried they'd catch the gay or I was going to jump them or something. And then Adán—"

"They're all idiots, Luna," Jordan says, interrupting me. "Don't let them get you pressed. And they can either start acting right or leave. Especially Solís."

"Jordan, I can't tune it out." I rub my temple, feeling my frustration becoming less controllable. "You keep telling me to brush it off. For years, telling me don't worry about it. But now, now that it's out there, now that I'm not pretending and they all *know* I'm gay—it's easy for you to preach this *Screw what they say and do* mentality when you're not in my shoes."

"I know. I'm sorry, Jules. But—tell me what to do. Tell me what you need from me, all right? Whatever I can do to make you know you belong anywhere, I'll do. I'm not letting them ruin my last high school season by chasing away my best bro."

"I—I don't know what to do."

Jordan sighs. "We'll figure it out. I'll make sure they know that's not gonna fly with me. Deadass. But I can't have you quitting on me. You're better than all them. As a player. As a person. In every capacity. Here, I—"

Jordan moves to stand in front of me. He grabs my shoulders and begins to shake me around. It's a strange ritual Jordan does whenever I fall into a soccer funk. He calls it his method of doing a sana sana on me. I've told him that this isn't in any way similar—he doesn't have eggs or Vicks VapoRub—but for a strange substitute, it's usually pretty effective.

"I won't quit," I moan to get the shaking to stop.

"Promise me."

"I promise I won't quit."

"You better not." He hugs me, patting my back and messing up my hair while he has me in a hold. "And don't worry. I told you I'd have your back and that I'd take care of anyone who wants to talk mess, and I will."

"Promise *me* you aren't gonna do something stupid?"

"Sorry, Luna," Jordan says, taking out his phone. "I'm getting a phone call."

No one is calling him. He's just being puro pendejo. Trying to get out of answering me.

He holds his finger up to me when I attempt to continue, pretending to talk to someone, and mouths that he has to go and starts jogging to his Jeep.

"¡Prométeme, tonto!" I yell as he takes off. He only waves back. Still ignoring me and still pretending to be on his phone.

25

I need to get my mind off my teammates.

I don't have a lot of homework tonight. I could waste an hour at By the Bay Books before going home.

The large, two-story store is one of my favorite places, if only to spend way too much time looking at every single book with a pretty cover. I go up the escalator to the second floor and look over the table of new releases, touching one or two of the covers before getting lost in the aisles. My eyes are scanning through titles when I feel myself bump into another body and hear a few books drop.

"I'm so sorry!" I say, spinning around and reaching down to help pick up the books.

"No worries. It happens," replies the guy who fell victim to my mindlessness. I get a good look at him after he grabs the rest of the books. He's cute. Could be a senior at another school or even a college freshman. The facial hair and A&M Corpus shirt indicating the latter. He's a couple of inches taller than me. Fair-skinned. Big fan of the gray cardigan he's wearing.

His eyes scanning me don't go unnoticed, but I ignore it for now.

"I'm Carlos, by the way."

"Julián." My hand reaches out to shake his.

"Were you looking for anything in particular?"

"Nope. Why, do you work here?"

"Oh, no." He lets out a nervous laugh. "Sorry. That's really how it sounded, huh? Lame attempt at making conversation."

I smile and give a snorted laugh back. "It's cool. I'm not any better at small talk with strangers. But I was just killing some time."

"Me too. Though that turned into finding a few books on my TBR list. I came with some friends but left them at the Old Navy and Ulta next door. I was more interested in finding something to read when studying for finals gets too hectic."

"Same, but it usually involves bingeing something on Netflix."

"Whatever works, Julián," Carlos says. He has a charming smile, mixed with a little awkwardness of not knowing whether he should stand or lean against the bookshelf and where to put his free hand.

"Anyways, assuming you're here because you don't spend all your time glued to a television screen rewatching *Black Mirror*, have you read anything good lately? Always here for recommendations."

"Mm, well, it's sort of difficult to give you a really exact suggestion without knowing you. I wouldn't want to give you a crappy rec." I scan one of the shelves next to us, seeing if any names pop out to me. "Oh, here. I'd say anything by Adam Silvera. But only if you're in the mood to have all your emotions knocked out of you like a piñata."

"Love the imagery. I'll be sure to look for his name as I'm walking around, then. Thanks."

And then we get to that point where neither of us knows whether to keep talking, stand there awkwardly until we drop more books, or leave. I'm going with option three.

I begin to move away from him and toward the other end of the aisle when I hear Carlos call my name.

"Sorry, but—I'm gonna throw it out there. If you're free sometime, or right now, even, would you want to get some coffee? My friends are still gonna be a while. We could talk books and get to know each other. I can return the favor and rec some books for you."

"Oh, I—" I'm frozen, figuring out how to respond. "Carlos, I don't think—"

"Wait, please don't tell me you're fifteen or something, because that's gonna be awkward, and—"

"No! No, it's not that." Do I really look fifteen? "It's—I have a boyfriend."

"Oh. W-well, this is only slightly less awkward, then." His blushing is super obvious as he stammers over his words. Looking at the books lined up on the shelves rather than my face. "Thanks for being honest. I guess. Um, so . . . Adam Silvera. Better go find the S section." He walks away with a little less grace in his demeanor, forcing a smile and a wave as he turns the corner.

I rush to the exit. I don't want to look back and see Carlos and make things any weirder. Today has been too much for too many reasons.

When I finally make it to my truck, I lean my head into the steering wheel, with just enough effort to not sound the horn. I need to mellow out before driving.

Someone hit on me. Real-life hit on me. I hope I didn't come off as rude? What if he was only looking for a friend who's into reading?

No, he definitely had those eyes of interest.

And it was . . . nice? Not that it makes a difference. But—ugh, chinga la madre. If I had been watching where I was going, this wouldn't have happened and—whatever. I can't think about this right now.

I buckle up and begin to drive home as fast as legally possible.

~

"Do you ever get hit on?"

"Are you asking that seriously?" Mat has an inquisitive face. One that's asking if I really want to know the answer to my question.

"I mean, I'm pretty sure I know the answer already. But, I don't know. Being with me—does this seem less real when someone is standing right in front of you, giving you a sign that they're into you?"

"What? No, never. First, that's assuming I've had any interest in a guy who might have hit on me. At least since you've been my boyfriend. And I haven't. That's the truth. Second, if I felt that this wasn't what I want, then I'd end it. To be blunt. I'd want you to do the same too if it was the other way around. We both knew this would be something that takes patience and trust and want. I still want you, Jules. Even more than I did a month and a half ago. And over anyone else in Los Angeles or even in California. I want you."

"I want you too. But I don't want to hold you back. I didn't want you to think you had to stick with this because you don't want to be the heartbreaker in my first relationship."

"That's dumb, Jules. If anything, you're gonna have to be the heartbreaker here. Are you feeling as if this is too much for you? Because it's cool if you are." He keeps fidgeting. Crossing his arms and then uncrossing. Giving me that uneasy half smile. "I wouldn't hate you for needing something easier. And I'm sure you have guys in Texas waiting for their chance."

"That's not it, Mat."

I watch him as he sighs, looking at something off-screen, probably needing to take a break from being present. His hand is up to his forehead like he's got a migraine. Mat seems so certain of our relationship. Why can't I be the same? Can he send some of that my way? "I—I worry that one day you'll realize I'm not worth your time. That there isn't a lot to like about me. Some days, being optimistic is hard."

"Jules." Mat's voice breaks, and my soul may have cracked. "I know. There are times when it feels like you're planets away from me. When I start thinking, *What if I never get the chance to actually be with you?* When I feel all gray and cloudy. And it's the worst feeling in the world."

"Really? You get those thoughts?"

"Why wouldn't I? I'm human."

"Yeah, but you're always so bright and positive."

"I—I don't know. I don't like making it obvious, I guess. Plus, it usually goes away when I get to see your face, and I remember that you aren't an uncountable number of miles away from me. And you're worth it: you're smart, you're ambitious, you obviously have good taste in favorite cities that's only surpassed by your taste in guys. You're hot. And I like your strength. As much as I wish you didn't have to be so strong, and even though there are days where I know it takes a lot out of you to be so resilient. Our lives are different, and seeing how much you've overcome, how much you're still fighting because being who you are is important to you. It's bold and gutsy, and it's attractive. Your strength is goddamn sexy."

I want to reach into my computer screen and touch Mat. Feel his face and hair against my fingers. Do whatever it takes to make sure he doesn't have those cloudy days. He doesn't deserve those. He's supposed to be my *sunshine Mat*.

"I spend a lot of time thinking about something as simple as how much I want to hold your hand," he continues. "How much I want to hold on to as much of you as possible. I *crave* that opportunity. And you know what? Every time, I've come to the same conclusion: the wait is worth it. Because I know I'm going to get that chance. Some day. And I want to be clear that when the occasion presents itself, I'm going to hold on to your hand and I'm not letting go. I'm going to hold on to as much of you as possible and I'm not letting go. And I'm gonna keep holding on to your heart as long as you'll let me. I'm not letting go."

I fall down into my bed. Exhausted physically. Even more exhausted emotionally.

But I know everything's going to work out. It has to. As we look into one another's eyes so deeply and intimately through our screen, Mat erases all doubt from my mind. Like he always does. And for a moment, it's as if he's actually present with me.

"I'm honestly not strong," I say.

"No, you're just humble. The one thing you are definitely not is weak."

"I guess."

I close my eyes. The fatigue and anxiety keep fighting for my attention.

"Someone hit on me today. Don't worry, I turned him down. Politely. But—it was after I'd already had a sort of crappy day and wasn't in the best headspace. I think that's why it all turned into . . . this."

"Are you okay?"

"Mostly."

"I don't need to go over there and fight someone?"

"No. I mean, come over here, yes. That'd be great. But no, you don't need to fight anybody."

"And *we're* okay?"

I nod. My yawn keeping me from answering in words.

We are. You're the one thing in my life I'm most certain of. I'm sorry if it doesn't look that way. That the distance makes me doubt. That I'm scared. And that sometimes I feel as if I'm going to mess everything up. That I'll lose you.

I told you I'd be bad at this.

But it's because I love you. Even if I'm not ready to tell you yet. Even if I'm not sure you'd be ready to tell me you love me back yet.

26

My first day of Christmas break (and last day as a seventeen-year-old) is spent nonstop talking with Mat while scrolling through university websites, looking at classes. Both make it easy to obsess over how different my life will be eight months from now. Something comparable to *Pitch Perfect* but with less singing and no horrible sequels. It's easy to be excited with him about some of the names of these sociology and Chicanx-studies courses at UCLA while he talks about the science classes that he somehow finds appealing.

At least, it is until we're interrupted by Itzel calling.

She's either using a voice-changing toy speaker or trying to muffle her own voice with her hands. "Jules Luna," she says. I recognize Jordan's laughter in the background. "I am giving you orders. Obey! Prepare to be picked up and hauled away at eight sharp for the most fabulous of prebirthday celebrations! Until then, we sashay away!"

She hangs up without giving me any time to respond.

"What was that?"

"I'm getting kidnapped tonight," I answer, shaking my head at my phone. "Smart kids always end up being freaks."

Eight sharp for Latinx teenagers and our honorary Latino friend ends up being closer to nine thirty. I'm lying across the recliner. My eyes are beginning to close when I'm jolted up by hands banging on the front door and Itzel, Jordan, Lou, and Roe all screaming "Las Mañanitas" and pulling me out of the house.

It's nonstop talking and shouting once we're all crammed into Jordan's Jeep. As if the whole day since the fall semester ended has actually been an eternity.

"Guys!" Jordan shouts, interrupting further discussion. "What if this is our last Christmas break we get to spend together? You know? What if I have to stay in Denver for soccer, or Luna's too busy living it up in LA to spend his birthday with us?"

"Jordan, I'll be here for my birthday," I assure him.

"I mean, we're gonna be starting our last semester of high school soon. And then we're all going off to college. I don't want to lose touch with y'all. Itzel will be busy at Harvard—"

"Not true. But thanks for the confidence boost."

"Whatever. And Roe'll be inventing Westworld at MIT."

"College Station, dude. But—also—thanks."

"And then Lou's gonna, I don't know, accidentally set fire to UT because she didn't know Everclear was flammable."

"That one's accurate," she admits.

"We still have eight months left together, Jordan," I say to calm him. "So we'll keep spending as much time together as possible until August. Or until we get tired of each other."

"You don't get tired of me!" Jordan exclaims confidently.

"Yeah, sure. Of course," we all tell him.

The route he's taking is extremely familiar. Going up Airline and then turning onto Alameda. I know this drive.

"We're going to my sister's house?"

"Well, your abuelo offered, but he parties too hard for us to keep up with," Roe answers.

It's dark when we enter Xo's home, except for some faint light coming from her dining room. There, she's waiting for us with a pile of conchas in every color and candles stuck into the topmost bread. To the side is a bottle of Don Julio.

"This"—Xochi waves over the table—"is all your güelo's doing. We'll open the bottle at midnight but make a wish and blow out the candles now. I want pan."

What do I want to wish for? Too many things. We should get a wish for each year. Although I don't know if even eighteen would be enough.

Happiness. That should cover it. That's all I really want for the next year of my life.

Xo runs to the kitchen after I blow out the candles and grabs a pink concha. I hear the clinking of glass and see her pulling out more liquor from her freezer.

"I know this is what y'all would be doing anyways. At least I can provide an adult, supervisory presence for whatever bad decisions come out of this."

"You and supervisory presence are not two things that go together."

"Shut up and come take a shot with me, almost birthday boy."

We don't get wild, but when Jordan brings out *Mario Kart*, things do start getting loud. Mainly among him, Rolie, and Xo (who's surprisingly good with Toad on a motorcycle). I'm over it after a few races, having been placing in a consistent fourth all night.

"You wanna go outside?" I ask Itzel.

"God, yes," she replies.

We refill our drinks, put on our jackets, and head to the backyard.

"You're not wasted yet, right?" Itzel mocks. "Don't need you posting any more serious confessions on Twitter."

"Shut up, pendeja," I yell at her. "That was a onetime disaster." We walk toward the wooden railing of the deck, and I hop onto the planks, letting my feet hang by her side. "You didn't invite Piña?"

"No. Gabi's y'all's teammate. I assumed Jordan would've invited him if he wanted."

I look at her suspiciously. "Are we not going to acknowledge the fact that you two haven't been talking since y'all went to homecoming together?"

She looks away from me and takes a large gulp of her drink. "There wasn't anything mutual happening between us."

"That's vague."

"Ugh. *I* didn't like him the way he liked me. But we aren't talking about him tonight. All right?"

"Sure. He's off-limits."

She gives a big sigh. "How're things with the novio?"

"As good as they can be, I guess." Itzel and I have been struggling to figure out how to best bring Mat up in conversation. She wants to be metiche but, at the same time, not have to hear his name. And I'd love to talk to her. Especially as a friend who's dated. But I know how she feels.

"You realize how bad of an idea it all is, yes?"

Still being very much an ass. Okay.

"I've always realized that it's a bad idea. But it's the best bad idea I've ever had."

"And you're still convinced there's no one here worth your time?"

I glare down at her. "Itzel, what's your problem with him?"

"I—" She exhales. "It's not him. It's that this whole thing is kinda problematic, no?"

"That's it? You *care so much* and that's why you're staying this defensive?"

"It's the truth." She turns around, giving me the back of her head instead of her face. She sets an elbow on my leg. "Maybe I'm jealous too. Not in that weird straight-girl *Why'd you have to be gay, you're my backup plan* sort of way. But because there's a new person in your life. Someone I don't know now expects me to share you. And then, if you go to college in LA, he'll become your priority. He's going to get to experience the next four years with you."

I lean toward her and wrap my arms around her neck. Rest my head on hers. Take in the silence.

Yes, it's pretty self-centered. But the last thing I want is for her to think I'm kicking her out of my life. I can't imagine existing without her. Hell, I'll probably need her *more* next year.

"Itzel, no one will ever take your place. There will always be room for you in my life. I promise."

"You better," Itzel says. She pushes me off her and brings her cup to her mouth.

"Pinkie promise."

We stop talking when we hear everyone stampeding to the back. The screen door slides open and Xo, Lou, Jordan, and Rolie step outside, all carrying shot glasses.

"It's officially December twelfth, baby brother," Xo says as she hands me a shot. "Be a consistent voter, try your best to make good decisions, and use protection."

"Cheers to that," Jordan adds. I shoot back my tequila in one swig before grabbing a lime wedge from my sister.

Rolie yells, "COMPA!" and holds out his arms—definitely far too many shots in—walking toward me. And in one of the few times I'm taller than him, my mouth ends up in his hair as I tell him to be careful. I'm locked into one of his strong, drunken hugs and carried to the middle of the patio.

"Rolie, I—my phone," I try to say while wriggling myself loose.

"¡Qué precioso, Julito!" he yells when he sees Mat's name and picture displayed, feeling it necessary for some reason to announce this to the world. "His guy is calling him right at midnight!"

Everyone lets out a loud "aww" as I escape into the house. Los odio. I rush to Xo's room, closing the door behind me.

"I was going to play you 'Happy Birthday' on my guitar while completely naked, but I can't find my guitar, so I guess I'll have to try again next year."

"Baboso," I reply to Mat. I plop down onto my sister's bed, trying to make myself comfortable. Hoping it's not obvious that the thought of him naked while currently actually shirtless and wearing athletic shorts that give me plenty of thigh visual has me *very* turned on.

But that's not something I'm going to acknowledge while my friends and Xo are only feet away.

"*Your* baboso." He winks. "Anyways, how's eighteen treating you?"

"No complaints yet."

"Good. Lemme know if I need to beat anyone up for ruining your day. Oh—I almost forgot—expect a box with two smaller boxes inside it tomorrow. Or, I guess, later today in Texas time. You can open one for your birthday but leave the other for Christmas."

"What if I open both today?"

"Then I'll open the package I got from you a couple days ago."

"Touché, cariño."

I was worried the plush dog I ordered him, complete with a Texas T-shirt, would end up at the wrong house or something. I can relax about that now.

"You better not be doing anything nasty on my bed!" Xochi shouts as she opens the door, a hand covering her eyes.

"Xo, stop being a pinche cochina."

She uncovers her face and lies beside me. "Sorry to ruin your fun. Stealing your boyfriend back for the night," she tells Mat.

He knows better than to argue with an older sister. But I can see the small bit of reluctance in his face while telling me happy birthday again and good night.

"It's weirdly adorable seeing someone call you *babe* all romantic-like," she says as we leave the room. "I swear, if you get married before me, I'm going to scream."

We walk into the living room, where Xo's TV is turned all the way up, "La Chona" playing, Rolie and Lou singing along, and Itzel and Jordan doing some weird Chicken Dance–looking moves to the music. I have exactly zero normal friends.

And I can't think of a better way to start my eighteenth birthday.

27

"What the—*aah!*" I'd forgotten about the gifts from Mat, wondering what the large box at my front door was for longer than I should have. I almost trip over the curb rushing toward it. "Come on, come on, come on!" I snap at the front door, taking what feels like actual minutes to open it. Finally, I hear it unlock and shove it open, grabbing the box and running into the house.

I rush to my bedroom, unsure if I've even closed or locked the door behind me but too preoccupied to check. After I rip off the tape across the top of the large box, I see the two smaller ones Mat mentioned inside with a note on top.

> *One is for your birthday and one is for Christmas. Thinking back on it, I should have designated a box for one day or the other, but now I don't even know what's in which. They're both great presents, though, not to kiss my own ass or anything. Anyways, happy birthday, babe.*

I shake each box, seeing if the weight of one over the other could help me choose, but both seem to weigh the same. One box, though, sounds like it has at least a couple of items inside, which I use as the determining factor, placing the other inside my closet. I pull some more tape off the cardboard and finally get to my birthday present.

On top is a photo envelope and another note, with a heather-gray hoodie folded underneath.

Okay, first, the hoodie. I thought, since it might be a while until we're finally physically together, I'd give you something to make my presence a little more . . . almost real? In the envelope are a lot of my favorite places around LA that I can't wait to show you and take you to. Hope you like the gifts, babe. Let me know when you get this!

I was definitely going to text Mat to let him know I opened a box. But the moment I hold the hoodie, read Los Angeles High School Wrestling on the front and his last name, Pham, on the back, feel its comfort, and smell my boyfriend on the fabric—like flowers and the ocean or any of those blue bottle colognes I've never been a fan of until right now—I'm closer to him than I'd ever experienced before. There's no way I could do *anything* after this.

I'm completely enamored.

I fall asleep with my face buried in his hoodie.

~

The faint sounds of someone knocking on my bedroom door barely register. At first, I'm unable to distinguish whether the blunt tapping is actually happening or something I'm dreaming. But a hand tugging on my arm and hearing my name lets me know it's reality. I only make small noises into the hoodie still firmly in my grasp, trying to dissuade any more attempts to wake me.

That seems to work, but I can still feel someone sitting on my bed. I juggle between pretending to be asleep a little longer and seeing who's here. Curiosity wins, and I turn my head to my sister next to me.

"Mind if I look through these?" Xochi asks, holding the envelope of photos Mat sent me.

"It's fine," I say through a yawn and watch as she looks through each of the pictures. She turns them around to read the notes he left on the backside of the photographs. I watch her take in each image. She smiles as she reads his words about kissing me on the Ferris wheel at Santa Monica Pier and watching the sunset from Griffith Observatory.

"He's a charmer, for sure," she remarks as she pats my cheek. I nod, eyes closed, hoping she'll let me rest for a little while longer. It doesn't work. "'Manito. Time to wake up. It's almost five o'clock."

Five o'clock? How did I sleep *all day*? I pick up my phone, seeing a screen full of messages from Mat. Asking if I got the gift, if I fell asleep, if I died, if I'm actually spending my entire birthday sleeping, and requesting a birthday-suit photo.

Yes I got the gift, I reply. I opened the box with the hoodie and photos. It wins the award for best present ever. And yes I did fall asleep, but I blame your hoodie. No I did not die. And you are not getting that picture, baboso.

I was hoping you'd open that one first. And you can't blame a boyfriend for trying. Oh, happy medium: picture with only the hoodie? Nothing else. Wow, the image is already in my head and I can tell you with all confidence that you've never looked better.

I'm not talking to you for the rest of the night.

YOU DON'T HAVE TO TALK TO SEND ME A PHOTO.

I set my phone down. I need to look like I haven't been sleeping the entire day at dinner with my friends and family.

"You have half an hour," Xo tells me as she walks out of my room.

I hastily hop out of bed. Step over to my closet, picking out a black shirt with Como La Flor and a rose on it and a red windbreaker to match. A pair of ripped jeans from my dresser and I'm set.

But as I'm about to open my bedroom door, I decide that Mat might have earned a couple of pictures of me modeling the hoodie. I mean, he deserves to see how good it looks on me.

28

Can y'all not?" I whine at everyone as we exit the restaurant. Everyone's laughing nonstop at a video Jordan got of me getting on a saddle as the entire waitstaff hollered about my birthday to anyone who would listen.

The first thing he, Itzel, and Lou did when we got there was make sure our waiter knew *exactly why* we were here tonight and ask to make this dinner as rowdy and embarrassing for me as possible. I gave a considerable amount of thought to hiding under the table.

"Xo, *really*?" I groan when I see her watching another video of me. This one when the waiters dragged me up—against my will—for a line dance to "Copperhead Road."

Even my dad was giving the least amount of effort to hiding how amused he was by it all. And maybe it was just him getting to live his best gluttonous life eating bread rolls and cinnamon butter, but this is the most laid-back and happy I've seen him in a while. Who knows, maybe today will mark the start of a new relationship with Dad. Maybe God heard my birthday wish and decided to give me this one.

I say goodbye to Roe, Lou, and Güelo before following Xochi back to her car. Jordan and Itzel don't want to stop celebrating, so they follow us and our dad back to my house. On the drive home, I respond to Mat's reply to my Instagram story of me dancing. He sent this cheesy pickup line involving a cowboy and lassoing and two-stepping that I try my best not to smile and let out a laugh at, but, true to who he is, it was so brilliantly idiotic.

I hear Xo mumble something about Dad and his car and look up from my phone. Being the speediest driver in Corpus Christi, he's beaten all of us home and is now standing in our empty driveway, staring at the cement. His truck's parked in a way that blocks anyone from using the space.

He hasn't looked up at us. His eyes are locked onto the ground at something neither of us can see, and his hands are gripped behind his head.

"What do you think that's about?"

"I don't know," Xo answers, turning off her car and opening her door.

I get out with her and hear Jordan's Jeep idling behind us. I can see him mouth *What's going on?* and I shrug and hold a palm out, telling him to wait there. We start walking, approaching the driveway.

Then I realize what's going on, and I feel Xo's hand rush to forcefully grab my own.

I want to throw up when I see what has Dad's attention. My legs almost give out. And my gut feels like the wind has been physically knocked out of me.

Happy Birthday, Maricón is spray-painted on the concrete. Dad's eyes are still glued to the words. My own flick between him and the cement.

I don't know what to do. I feel compelled to both walk toward him and sprint in the other direction until the entire world is behind me. I want to be anywhere but here right now.

Xo's hand relaxes and lets go of mine. I hear her footsteps fading. She must be on her way to let Jordan and Itzel know about the graffiti.

"This meant for you?" Dad doesn't even bother to look in my direction as the question leaves his mouth. The words cut into my lungs as I try my best to keep control of my breathing.

How am I supposed to answer that? *Of course not, Dad. I have no idea what this is.* Or a more forward *it sure is, Dad. I'm a maricón. Happy birthday to me.* But neither comes out.

Nothing does.

"Julián, answer me. ¿Sabes quién hizo esto?"

I shake my head. Bullying might be nothing new to me, but I have no clue who would care this personally to vandalize private property.

"Well, tell me why this is here." His voice is sharp. He's trying to not let his anger get to him, but I'm painfully aware of how limited his ability to contain himself can be.

I know what the most efficient answer would be. To say those three words I've grown accustomed to saying to almost anyone else. Anyone but the man in front of me.

And I hate myself for it. For being scared. For letting one word and one person have this tight, invisible grip on my throat. For feeling so small.

The wall that's always existed between us, the one that keeps me from opening up to him about who I am, is still there. It's still too hard to get over. But it's quickly crumbling. Forcing me to face this truth with him.

"I—people are dicks, Dad," is all I'm able to mutter. When I look at him, his face is too emotional to pinpoint one specific reaction.

"We should go inside," I tell him before turning around and walking to the front door. I try to piece together some sort of mental conversation, knowing how ill-prepared I am for what comes next.

My phone vibrates in my hand, and I see a message from Xochi, still with Jordan and Itzel at the curb. Do you need us?

I'll be okay. I think. Give us a few minutes.

We'll be around the corner getting some coffee. Let one of us know if you need us and we'll rush back, k? I love you, baby brother.

I place my phone in my pocket as I go into the kitchen. I need a glass of water. I bring an extra glass for Dad, placing both on the coffee table, and take a seat. He stares at me from the other end of the couch while my thumbs twiddle in my lap.

"You got something on your mind, Julián?" His voice is stoic. An eerie contrast to the stern glower of his face.

I place my hands under my thighs when they begin to tremble. I wish I could say this without crying. That I wasn't telling him because someone deprived me of a conscious, planned, and ready coming-out plan.

Stolen by some douchebag with a can of spray paint. I wish I could say these words with confidence, knowing that he won't care. That he might tolerate or, better, embrace me.

"I—" Fuck. I can say it. I can tell him. "I'm gay, Dad."

I've never seen a more disturbing look of frustration and anger. Knowing I've destroyed us. "Yo—no, I don't accept that." He stands and takes a step toward me, making his presence tower over me. "I didn't raise you to want to be this way."

"Dad, I didn't *want* this. I didn't ask for it." I can hear my voice crack and feel one tear already escaping my eye. "All I wanted was to not hate myself anymore. I spent too much time thinking I was broken. Unnatural. Unlovable. Tiring myself out from trying so hard to force myself to be anything else."

"So you'd rather spend your time under some boy, then? Julián, you have to see how disgusting, how fucking—who is it? Jordan? Rolando? Who's screwing you into thinking you'd prefer that life instead of being with a girl?"

I stand up at that. Still scared but able to bring my head up to look him in the eyes. "Don't bring them into this, Dad. It's me. Only me."

"Julián, I'm not going to pretend I've never seen the way you look at that negrito—"

"Dad, *shut up*—"

"No, *you* shut up." Dad paces back and forth in front of me. His hands put pressure at the top of his head, and his fingers tap on his buzzed scalp. "I don't want to hear another word about your joto-ass bullshit, all right? I don't accept this. Not for a son of mine."

"Would you rather I continued burying this part of me? That I keep lying awake at night, in so much pain? Thinking of how easy it could be to stop it forever? That I let you keep slowly chipping away at my desire to be alive every time you insult and damn us and—"

"That is not a life I will allow my son to have!" Dad screams. He rushes at me, hands clenched. I know he's holding himself back. I know if even a little more of him believed he could beat the gay out of me right now, he'd do it. "Yes. I would have rather you never acknowledged it. That you tried harder. Julián, what Heaven can you ever hope to reach?"

"If that's what I'd have to do, I don't need Heaven, Dad. It's not worth this. I wouldn't survive the life you want for me."

He grips my upper arms, squeezing them tightly. Bringing my face even closer to his. I can feel the anger in his eyes. The fragile fury barely holding it together. He's terrifying. So much more imposing this way. When he's angry and in my face, it's like confronting a bull. One that, at any second, won't hesitate to use its horns on me.

And then he lets me go. His chest rises and falls with a heavy sigh. "Escúchame. I did not raise a maricón. And I won't have one staying in this house."

"Dad, you—"

"Get some shit together and *go*, Julián," he says in a quiet and calm tone that scares me more than the yelling. He's not saying this out of unfiltered, quick anger anymore. He fully means those words.

"Dad," I say again. For the sake of my own dignity, I'm trying as hard as I can to keep from crying. To not seem like some little chillón. "Why? Is it so hard to accept me?"

"I will accept every good part of you," he says, still softly, mixed with intense rage. "Pero if you want to be a faggot, go be a faggot. But you aren't doing it in this house. Make that choice yourself."

I tried. And I couldn't stop it: I'm crying, and I feel so pathetic. "So, what? You're gonna kick me out?"

"I'm not kicking you out. I want you to be here, Julián. I do." His hands brush over his buzzed head before clasping together at the back of his skull again. The emotion in his eyes hasn't subsided. "*Those people*, the people you want to go fuck around with, they end up dead on the streets—not because their families didn't want them. We do. I do."

"No, you don't. *You're* abandoning *me*." I wipe at my eyes to see Dad's more clearly. And in them, it's clear that those three words won't ever register. "You really don't see that, do you?"

"If you're going to choose this life over a home, that's on you. I don't want that for you. I tried. I did. But if you're deciding to go against all I've taught you, I won't have you here as a constant reminder of my failure to shape you into a real man. Vas. Leave. Die trying to find belonging and love, knowing full well you rejected it yourself." We knock shoulders as he walks past me. "So if that's what you want, you have five minutes to get some clothes together before I throw you out the door myself."

I wait until he's in his room before willing whatever strength remains to not break down, and I rush to my room. I close the door behind me and try not to collapse on the floor. After dragging myself over to the dresser and closet, I grab whatever clothes I can fit into a backpack. The photographs I got from Mat go on top before I zip it up and toss it over my shoulder. His hoodie stays under my arm.

My entire body is shaking. As if it's all about to fall apart at any minute. Even more so when I stand outside and the cold bites at every bit of exposed skin. Trying to unlock my phone and get to my texts.

I can't be here.

I don't know how much time passes. Sitting outside, I put on Mat's sweatshirt, draping the hood over my head to mute myself from the world and bring my knees to my chest and face-plant down into them. I consider calling him, but I know that hearing his voice won't be enough right now. Anything he might try to say to make it all seem all right won't be enough right now.

I hear a vehicle pull up, then a door opening and slamming shut. A body runs into me. I hear my sister crying. I feel her hand rubbing my back. And I become a whole wreck. I'm crying with her. Screaming.

"I've got you, 'manito. Take as long as you need," she says. "We'll leave when you're ready."

29

Xochi enters her guest room—now my bedroom—to set a suitcase full of what was left of my clothes beside some trash bags full of possessions. Not saying anything. Only setting the luggage down and looking at what's become of my life.

She turns to me. Still silent, arms crossed, fingers tapping against her skin, staring. Her eyes are bloodshot. A mixture of not sleeping last night, spending all that time she should've been asleep crying, and probably a morning of yelling.

"Can we talk?" she asks.

I nod and sit up on the bed. Xo pulls at the comforter and slips under with me.

"I—" She takes a long, heavy sigh. "I know I haven't been around a lot before August. I missed the better part of a decade of your life. But don't think I was ignorant to the things Papi told you and called you. I had plenty to say to him."

"I know, Xo. It's—"

"No, 'manito. Let me finish. There were things he kept me from seeing. But there was also what I chose not to see. And what I'm trying to say is, I'm sorry there were times when you needed someone, and I looked away. That you had to go through this alone for your entire life. I know you can take the words. Even from him. I know you're strong.

But did—" She grabs my hand in both of hers. They're soft. Warm. Safe. "Did Papi ever hurt you? Did he—"

"Hit me?"

"Yeah."

My heart is beating so fast. I feel the room is closing in on us. I'm having trouble breathing. Speaking.

I'm scared of saying yes. I'm scared of what that says about me. That I let him. That I didn't tell anyone. That every time I thought I could try to accept myself, the fear of what he'd do to me kept me closeted and afraid.

That it takes so much out of me to be happy with who I am. To not let it all defeat me. To tell myself that it's okay to be me.

That even after all those times, hearing all those things that made me believe otherwise, I still love Dad.

I try to say yes, but all that comes out are more tears and sobs. I nod and fall onto her shoulder. Holding on to her. She's crying again too. For me. Because she couldn't or didn't protect me. Because she doesn't want me carrying all this on my shoulders any more than I already am.

"You're safe now, 'manito." Her hand brushes through my hair. "I'm so, so sorry."

I cling to her. And as destroyed as I am, I try to let myself feel safe for what might be the first time in my life.

~

"What do you need from me?" Mat asks when he calls later that afternoon.

"Stop asking that question."

Instead of hearing how much fun eighteen has been so far, he got most of the details of how my night actually went. And a slightly deeper understanding of who my dad is.

I tried to hide it. I tried to act as if nothing was wrong. I didn't want to tell him then.

But I did tell him. Because it took no time at all for Mat to tell that something was very much off. I really wish I wasn't this bad at hiding what I'm feeling.

I recall every word. All the fear and pain. Only about last night, though. I'm still not ready for him to know the entire story of who my dad is to me.

To see him so angry, sad, and powerless really cements how shitty this is. Because I don't need Xo, or Itzel, or Jordan, Roe, or Lou right now. I need my boyfriend.

And dammit. I can't stop crying.

"I need you here with me," I say. It comes out almost like a whisper but loud enough to know he heard me. "But you aren't. You can't be. And even then, you can't understand what I'm going through."

"I know, but—"

"You can't fix everything, Mat!" I shake my head. My arms cross at my stomach. My entire body hurts. "You're always trying to put on this front of being strong and smart and always knowing the right words to say. And you put this belief in my head that everything will be fine because you say so. You said you'd be here for me when I came out to my family. But where are you? In fucking California.

"I need you to stop making these optimistic promises that you can't keep," I continue. "I need you to stop playing into my stupid emotional vulnerability. Stop trying to be my goddamn superhero. You can't fix this. I need you to realize that. That's what I need." The words come out harsher, struggling to escape through my throat. "I'm not some pet project for you. Something to pat yourself on the back for because you helped some baby gay with his daddy issues and taking his first steps after coming out."

"For real?" He turns away from his screen, lips pursing, almost completely sucked in. He tilts his head back and starts mumbling. I can tell I've stepped over a line. I wish I could go back in time fifteen seconds and never have said that. "Jules, you know that's not what this is. I know you know. I—"

"Stop," I demand. I have to turn away from my own laptop and wipe the tears and mocos off my face. "Can you just give me some space right now?"

"Fifteen hundred miles isn't *enough* space for you?"

I think this is the first time I'm seeing him angry. Hearing it in his voice. Being the cause of the pain in his eyes.

I can't take this.

"F—bye. I'm leaving." I slam my laptop shut. Hang up on him while I'm able to get the last word in.

I hate that this is all having such a vicious effect on me. That the actions of one person are causing me to be so violent toward people who care for me. People I love.

Like father, like son. Fuck, I'm starting to hate myself.

I don't call him later that day. Or the next day.

I distance myself from him. Again. After I promised I wouldn't.

30

Jordan throws a towel over the shower curtain when I turn off the water. I let out a startled gasp and then groan when it lands on top of my head. He practically threw me into the bathtub after finding out I hadn't gotten out of bed once in the few days since my birthday.

Thanks for being a snitch, Xo.

"I'll be with everyone in your room," he tells me. I listen for the door opening and closing before stepping out.

I'd rather eternally exist in this tub. Lock myself away from the world. Burn my skin with hot water until I forget Dad. Until I forget how I treated Mat.

Putting on clothes seems like a monumental thing right now. Brushing my teeth. Anything.

Everyone already thinks I'm helpless. And they're right. I don't need to keep reminding them, though.

Itzel and Lou have changed the sheets and pillowcases and replaced the comforter on my bed in the time it took to shower. The room smells like lavender and cedarwood. Some Bath & Body Works candle one of them brought in. Roe offers a bowl of tortilla soup.

"I'm not hungry," I mutter.

"Jules," Jordan responds. Little patience left in him. Only twenty minutes ago, he undressed me and forced me to stand under a stream of hot water. He's not above strong-arming me into eating.

"I got it," Itzel tells him, taking the bowl from Rolie. He and Lou follow Jordan out, closing the door behind them. We stay looking at each other for who knows how long. I want to go back to sleep. That's it.

"Can I lie down with you?" she asks.

"Whatever," I say, walking past her. The new bedding feels amazing. There's a good chance I'll never take my head off this pillow. "You're not gonna tell on me for refusing to eat?"

"No," Itzel says as she settles in next to me.

Kind of wish I said I'd rather be alone, but at least she isn't making me eat right now.

"I'm gonna ask you something," she starts. Itzel turns to face me, but I stay looking up at the ceiling. "And if you don't wanna answer, then don't. But—why? Why does someone who has spent years hurting you get this reaction out of you? You're free, Jules."

"You wouldn't understand."

"I can try."

I cover my face with my hands. Maybe if I create this pseudo darkness, everything else will go away. I won't have to explain myself to her.

I won't have to explain this all to myself. I won't have to confront the truth. I won't have to relive every day that's brought me to where I am now.

"He was the one parent I had. The only parent I've ever known. And I've only ever wanted to make my dad proud of me. Whenever I could tell that he was or that he loved me, it felt *so good*, Itzel. And . . . yeah, he's a trash person. I had to make up stories, covering up too many bruises he caused. But when I imagine his face after a soccer game where I really kicked everyone's ass, or when we'd watch movies together or drive to Port A or South Padre and sing badly along to 'Fotos y Recuerdos' and 'Dulce Niña,' I thought, *I can keep this up. I can at least pretend to be the son he wants. I can try my best to hide who I am for a few more months.* Because I thought the good times were worth it. And who knows, that could make me a trash person too. But at least I had a dad around. And one who provided for me. Who gave me everything I could need . . ."

When the tears started coming out, I don't know. I quickly go from minimally coherent to unable to talk anymore, though. I can't go into any further detail about how fucking weak I am.

Itzel scoots closer to me, her hand gently rubbing my chest. Her chin rests on my shoulder. "You don't have to say anything else," she whispers. "Close your eyes."

~

I have no idea what time it is when I wake up. It's dark. But it's winter: it could be six in the evening or four in the morning. Itzel is still on my left, cuddling with Lou. Jordan is on my other side, an arm thrown over my stomach. Rolie looks uncomfortable but managed to fall asleep at the foot of the bed, using Jordan's feet and ankles as his pillow.

It takes some Navy Seal–level maneuvering, but I manage to squeeze and hop out of bed while only minimally disturbing everyone. My stomach clenches and growls with hunger. There's only so long my body will let me cope with depression by not eating.

In the kitchen, I find some flour tortillas that Itzel's mom probably made. A couple of bags of shredded cheese, jalapeños, some butter. That's all I need.

I turn one of the nozzles on Xo's oven counterclockwise and cut the peppers into slices while the stovetop warms up. Soon, tortillas are warming up, cheese and chiles in between them, and I have a couple quesadillas.

The final thing I need, the jar of salsa verde. Abuelita's recipe. She used to say that there was no sadness a good salsa verde couldn't cure.

That if you want to stop crying over unhappy things, cry over the sting of blended peppers kicking your throat's ass instead.

A true Mexicana.

I take the jar and plate of quesadillas with me back to the room, carefully sitting myself on the floor while balancing it all. They're set beside me, and I pull one of the bags Xo brought over. Grabbing a fistful of black plastic, thinking about how all it took was my being open about one aspect of who I am for me to be in this position right now.

I take a deep breath and exhale before tearing through it. There's a bunch of random stuff inside. The soccer ball Jordan and I always used when he'd come over. Permanently stained brown and green from years of practice. A Chicharito jersey Dad got me last Christmas. Framed pictures of Mom. One with a young her and Selena from one of her final concerts that used to sit on my desk. And the other of her and baby me that once hung on the wall at home.

Digging further, I find the plush bull Abuelo Julio gave me when I was born. I wonder what he'd think of Dad right now. If he'd be just as tied to stupid ideas of masculinity and gender norms or if maybe he wouldn't see who I am as a reason to hate me.

Then more pictures. Itzel, Roe, Jordan, and me looking almost four years younger, dressed in matching royal blue for Itzel's quinceañera. And a box with MILLENNIAL LOTERÍA printed on top. A game Lou left with me months ago. At the very bottom, the *Spider-Verse* Blu-ray. Dad must not have been watching very carefully, because there's no way he'd have let Xo take this.

"Hey," my sister's voice whispers from the door. Her eyes are half-open, arms crossed, looking confused at why I'm up right now. "What're you doing?"

"Looking through some stuff. Wanna sit?"

"Mm," she says, nodding and quietly dropping next to me. I offer her my other quesadilla, but she holds up a hand. "I'm good, 'manito. I know how you fill those with every pepper you can find. I'm not trying to have fiery caca later."

I finish my food while she looks through the stuff. "I'm getting y'all a new one. This one's gross," she says as she pushes the soccer ball away. And: "All of you were babies in this picture," while staring at the quince photos. "I mean, still are. But—y'all have really grown up. Become this cute little familia. You did good in the friends department."

"Yeah," I answer. "I lucked out."

I look up and see them all, still passed out on the bed together. And I think about how Dad gave me everything I could need. Except for the one thing that shouldn't have terms or conditions. That should be a given. That should be *so easy*.

Acceptance.

At least I have a few people in my life who are happy to give me theirs.

31

On Christmas Eve, when I would usually be with family at my house—no, Dad's house—I stay in bed. I'm not strong enough to face him. It's not like he'd even let me through the front door anyway.

Xochi doesn't say anything about it. She only lets me know she won't be gone long and that she'll bring whatever's left of my things back with her. I'm in and out of sleep for most of the day, rooting myself into the mattress.

I wake up to the smell of pozole warming up in the kitchen. There's a box at the foot of my bed. My Christmas gift from Mat.

Since our last conversation almost two weeks ago, I haven't talked to him. I didn't know what to say after blowing up at him. He sent a text that night, letting me know that whenever I'm ready to talk, he's only a phone call away, and he messages me good morning and good night every day.

I don't respond. Again, maybe it's because I'm a trash person. Or maybe it's because I'm scared that one day he'll find out how broken I actually am and realize this isn't for him.

But I've spent hours staring at the messages he sent. I replay in my head how his voice would sound saying those words. How his laugh sounds and how his cheeks rise and his eyes close.

I sit up and reach for the box to open it. A sea of packaging peanuts buries whatever's inside. But another note is lying on top.

I hope you know how much of an inspiration you've been to me, Jules. In the three months (give or take a week or so depending on when you open this) we've known each other, I couldn't have asked for a better friend and boyfriend. Although your location could be better TBH. Hope this helps inspire you through our last semester of high school, reminds you that good things are coming, and potentially helps you make an important decision in the next few months. Not that I am in any way partial to this choice.

I dig through the box and pull out a large bear wearing a blue UCLA shirt.

I squeeze the bear tightly against my chest and fall back onto my pillow. Tears gather in my eyes. I try to focus on my own slow breathing and find a calm after days of feeling like crap.

Good things are coming. Good things are coming.

A quiet knock on the door interrupts the little peace I'm able to create.

"Coming in," Güelo's voice announces as he opens the door. He places a bowl of pozole on the desk beside my bed and brings a chair around. One of his hands reaches out and pets the bear's head.

"Me gusta el osito."

"Me too."

Güelo brushes my hair with his hand. "Recuerdo cuando naciste. Your abuelita and mom could have hoped for ten more girls. But I was so excited to have a grandson, as great as your sister is. All the women, gets loud sometimes." He lets out a small laugh. One of those *if you know, you know* laughs. "Desde el momento en que te vi, eras mío. You were our baby. And Abuelita and I were unconditionally in love with you. In the eighteen years you've existed, that hasn't changed. *Nothing* will ever change that, mi'jito."

"¿Usted sabe?"

"Well, you weren't at your dad's. Makes an old man curious. Tu abuela connected the dots a long time ago, though, Julián. We told each other that, whenever you were ready, we'd let you know that it didn't matter to us. Your dad might have his way of dealing with things, and I have my opinions on that. Pero, your abuelita would haunt my dreams if I didn't tell you and keep reminding you how much we love you. And that all we want is for you to know love in this life. The gravest sin of all would be to keep you from experiencing the fullness of this life. As long as whoever you give your heart to is good to you and for you and doesn't put ketchup on his tamales, then bueno."

He gets up from the chair and kisses my forehead. "Now, eat some pozole, get some rest, and if you're feeling up to it, I'll see you and your sister at Mass tonight. Te quiero mucho, mi'jito."

~

"Hi, M-Mom," I stutter. "It's me."

My teeth chatter as I take a seat on the dry grass in front of my mom's grave and the cold wind hits my face. Dim lamps on posts around the cemetery give off enough light to see, making being here after dark a little less creepy. I pull my knees up to my chest, trying to keep myself warm.

"It's been a while," I start. "And sorry I'm not at Mass tonight. I'll say a couple Hail Marys."

This never gets any easier. I forever have a hard time figuring out what I want to say. I've never known how to have a conversation with a woman who missed hearing my first words. Whose voice I can't recall the sound of.

"So, uh, not to put any stress on you or anything, but, one, I'm gay. And I hope that's okay with you. I like to believe that it's okay with you. That you—that you'd still love me." I pause, letting myself take a couple of breaths before continuing. "And two, I—I could really use you right now, Mom." I sniffle and let a tear travel freely down my face. "I could—I wish you were still here. I—I really just want my mom right now.

"But, uh, don't worry. I have Xo, and she's been great. Better than great. I'm sure you'd be really proud of her. Güelo's awesome too. Like always. But—I wish this wasn't such a big deal, Mom. It's not supposed to be a big deal anymore. I see all these TV shows and movies and they get hugged by their parents. They get told it doesn't matter. I want that."

I slowly trace her name—Adelia Flor V. Luna—with a finger. Picturing her image from the old photographs. Wishing I could tilt my head and feel my cheek against her shoulder.

"Why don't I get to have that? Why do I have to get hurt? I spent eighteen years being someone else because I thought—I thought maybe Dad would come around. Maybe he'd figure out how to love me unconditionally. He'd realize that we're all we have. He's all *I* had. And now I don't have either of you. I have to go the rest of my life without a mom or dad."

I let out a cough, feeling a little bit of congestion in my throat. Xo's going to be pissed if I get sick because I had to come to a cemetery in the middle of the night.

"I try to list out the good things in my life when I start getting in my head. Xo says it helps her, so I thought I'd see how it works. Better than nothing. I've got her. Soccer's going surprisingly well. I have all my friends. Mat—*oh*, I haven't told you about him yet. Um, I mean, you probably know already. None of this is new to you, since you're up there and all, but I met a guy. And it's complicated. *Really* complicated. But I like him. I like him so much. His name is Mat, and he's helped me find courage and pride and happiness in who I am. I don't think I would've gotten through coming out if he hadn't reached out. It was all overwhelming and suffocating, even with Xo and my friends there. But we started talking, and then when I saw his smile and heard him say my name, and when he told me that everything would be okay, I knew I'd get through it."

I wipe my face, getting the few tears that have started making their way down. Thinking about the boy I haven't spoken to in so long.

"I mean, at one point I knew I'd get through it. And then everything with Dad happened and it didn't seem so certain again. It all made me sad and angry and we—I tried talking to Mat about it but ended up being kinda an asshole to him. I'm still being an asshole to him. I don't know if you can send any cosmic energy to him, let him know that your son is sorry he's such a pinche pendejo and that—that your son loves him. That he hopes he didn't ruin everything.

"He's such a good guy, Mom. In my mind, you would've loved him and wouldn't have been able to hide how thrilled you are to see me happy. I hope you're not mad if I keep living in that assumption. Who knows, maybe you sent him to me. Maybe you knew he was exactly who I'd need right now. I—I need to think my mom would be okay with this."

I fix the poinsettias that have started sagging and rotate the pots so the prettier ones are facing forward. And then I look at my phone, checking the time: 12:56 a.m. Xo and Güelo will be out of church soon, and I don't need them realizing I'm not home.

"Anyways, thanks for listening, Mom. I hope you're proud of me. I hope I'll continue making you proud of me. And I promise I'll come see you before August. Tell the Big Guy if he could get me into UCLA, I'd be really appreciative. I think y'all both know how much I need to get out of here for a while."

I kiss my fingers and place them on the top of her headstone. Hoping to feel something. Any sort of vibe that might tell me she's here with me. Listening to me. Embracing me.

"Te quiero, Mami."

32

Merry Christmas to me.

When I wake up, there's a large envelope lying on the pillow next to me. From one of the Los Angeles colleges I applied to: Loyola Marymount University.

"No mames," I gasp, throwing myself up and sitting in a kneel. I open the packet as quickly but with as much caution as possible, emptying the contents onto the bed. A letter addressed to me lies on top of the pile.

> Dear Julián,
>
> Congratulations! You have been accepted for admission to Loyola Marymount University. The undergraduate faculty are looking forward to your arrival—

"OH MY GOD!" I fall off my bed in my excitement, thudding onto the wood floor with an *oomph*. My frantic screams continue as I pull on a pair of Adidas pants and run into the kitchen, where Xo is pouring a cup of coffee.

"Congrats, baby brother," she says as she kisses my cheek and hands me another envelope. Inside is the printed itinerary for two flights to Los Angeles in March. "Time to start planning your campus visits."

"You knew already?"

"I know what a big letter from a university means. And I bought the tickets months ago. Was waiting for your first acceptance to arrive before getting you all excited."

I cling to my sister. I'm one step closer to college. To being in Los Angeles. To existing in a place that won't ever have known me as I once was—closeted and worried about every choice I made being scrutinized. Where I can be me and feel the freedom of it all in the warmth of the California sun.

"How long did you plan for? I'll need a few days to see Loyola plus UCLA *and* USC."

"Oh, not so you can spend more time with your boyfriend?"

My boyfriend. I need to tell Mat. He's the one person I want to share this with most. Hopefully he'll want to talk to me after how distant I've been.

Ignoring her question, I grab a few leftover tamales and an entire jar of jalapeños and run back to bed.

I open my laptop and whisper a Glory Be as I call Mat, praying that he'll answer. That he hasn't realized I'm the worst person in the world.

When he answers, a "what the fu—" comes out of my mouth as I see a plush dog wearing a shirt designed as the Texas flag waving into the screen. Forgetting about the Christmas gift I sent him. And then there's Mat, center screen.

"Howdy, stranger," he says in a fake Southern accent that's bordering on obscene.

I'm already on the verge of crying. Just hearing his voice again—especially when he's being stupid—is making me lose it.

"This is an excessive level of Texan, Jules," he says as he holds on to the dog. "But I'm obsessed. Although a little disappointed he didn't come with a cowboy hat. I need to buy him one."

"Glad you like him," I say. My voice only manages to barely crack.

"*And* you named him Yeehaw? I can't." He laughs. And hearing his laugh makes me both happier and sadder than I've been in a while. "That's basically Texas's *aloha*, right?"

I smile. "No, that's not in any way right."

"I've been pressing its paw all morning, since you've deprived me of your voice," he says as he presses the paw. My voice comes out of the animal, saying, "Hey there, Sunshine."

Ugh. I was so rude to him. I was ready to admit I couldn't do this. "I'm sorry I've been shitty."

"I'm sorry you've had to go through such a shitty situation. And that I can't be there for you more—"

"You've been as present as possible since day one, Mat. I—" What else do I say? Sorry for making you a part of all this. Toda la mierda that is my life. "I said a lot of terrible things that I didn't mean, but I still need you. Even during the times where you can't guide me through whatever crap is going on. I promise not to be a douche to you anymore, but you have to know that sometimes it's all right when you can't be there for me."

"But it's not, Jules. As cool as it is that you have your sister and your friends, I want to be there for you too. I need to be there for you."

"You were, though." I think about all the time I spent the past couple of weeks staring at his good morning and good night texts. And how much I relied on them. How much I relied on him. "You remind me every day that this life and being gay isn't all that terrible."

"I—" He bites his bottom lip. "Tell me that you're safe. And that mentally you're—you won't do anything harmful."

"I'm not going to hurt myself. I promise." I wipe my eye and swear that I will break a window if this chillonismo doesn't stop immediately. But, chíngale, I hate that I worried him so much. "And I'm safe. I've got Xo and my abuelo. I've got my friends. I've got you."

"And don't you ever forget it." He looks straight into my eyes. "You know that I don't hang around because I'm trying to fix you, right? That I do actually like you? More than I've ever liked anyone."

"I know. Again, that was super out of line for me to say."

"You were hurting."

"That doesn't make it all right." I grab my UCLA bear, sitting it in my lap. "I—I shouldn't have taken it out on you."

"Not hearing from you for two weeks was worse, to be honest. At least the read receipts were on. So I wasn't worrying *as much*. But you're doing better, right?"

"Yeah. I am. It's not perfect, but I'm feeling happier. Or at least not as depressed. The bear helps. Good things are coming, right?"

"The best things." He smiles, but it's a tired smile. A sad smile. "But I need you too—can you promise me you won't shut me out again?"

"I won't. Never again. Mat, I—"

"Mean it, though. Take it out on me, whatever. But don't do this ghosting lite with me anymore."

I'm gonna mess this up, and—I need you. I almost did. And so whatever I have to do to convince both of us that I'm capable of not screwing this up, I'll do.

"I promise."

"Okay. Good." He resituates himself in his chair. "Now, talk to me. Did you get anything good for Christmas?"

Wait—the letter. "Oh! *Yes!* I did. And I need to tell you."

"Then tell me!" he says, getting himself into a good sitting-up-straight, paying-attention position.

I hold up the acceptance letter, putting it in view of the screen. "I got into Loyola Marymount!"

"What? Jules, congrats! That's great! Are you going with LMU, then?"

"I mean, UCLA has always been the goal—"

"Of course."

"Still is my first choice—"

"As it should be."

"But the thought of going to a smaller school is pretty cool. It's what I'm used to. I guess next, I need to find out how much financial aid I qualify for. That'll determine whether it's a realistic option. My counselor who recommended Loyola Marymount helped me out with applying for scholarships. Fingers crossed they'll be throwing cash my way. But even more exciting, I have a set date for campus visits now."

"Oh, cool. LMU's really pretty."

I'm staring at him, concerned. I thought I'd get a larger reaction. He looks at me, knowing he's missing something. Trying to read my face.

"Wait—" I can see him actually putting all the context together in his mind. "You're gonna visit LMU. That means—YOU'RE COMING TO LA!"

I laugh and almost fall back onto my pillows at how long it took Mat to process it all. His brain is a little slow before nine a.m. But the hysteria that follows is infectious. He wants all the details: dates, flight times, as much as I can provide.

He's so focused on the excitement for my upcoming trip that he doesn't register a voice calling for him, requesting his presence, gradually becoming a yell.

"Oh, sorry, parents. I have to go, babe. But call me later."

"I will," I reply. "I promise. I'll talk to you soon. I love you—"

We both freeze when the words leave my mouth. I would doubt I said them at all if it weren't for Mat's eyes, locked on my own. His mouth goes from agape and surprised into a wide smile.

"I love you too, Jules."

The response brings me back to reality. Although, my ability to react is still impeded by how entirely unreal this situation seems.

"Agh, got to go now. I'm really happy you're doing better. Talk to you later. Bye. I love you. Again."

I told him I loved him. And he told me he loved me back. Twice.

I had always envisioned planning the first time I said those words. But this, it was word vomit. Coming out of me without even thinking before speaking. Okay, not word vomit. Spilled word glitter.

I do love him. He's been my biggest support. The person who invested himself from the beginning in wanting to know every detail that makes up who I am. Who's made me feel safe and accepted in a way that no one else could. I do love him. It didn't have to be this big event. I meant it. And Mat meant it back. And it was perfect in a way that's uniquely us.

I love you, Mặt Trời Phạm.

33

Fireworks explode over the Gulf of Mexico waters as I sit on the beach with my friends, celebrating the arrival of a new year. I've never understood the significance people put on one day to make dramatic differences in their lives. Why wait? What makes January first anything more than some arbitrary moment in our lives?

That is, until now. The next twelve months are going to bring a lot of good things: seeing Mat in a couple of months, graduation, college, moving to Los Angeles.

Not on that list: knowing that I'm nowhere near ready to say goodbye to everyone yet.

To Rolie, on my left, mesmerized by each explosion, and Lou sitting next to him, recording it all for Instagram. And then on my right, Itzel making herself comfortable, leaning on Jordan, and his arm around her, both whispering to each other. Those two have been all *canoodle-y* since my birthday, but neither of them has told me anything about where they are yet. Like, *what are you waiting for? Y'all are so obvious.*

They're really making me feel some type of jealous. I'm happy for them. *So*, so happy for them. Even if I'd push them both into the water if it would bring Mat here right now.

After the show, Itzel, Lou, Jordan, Rolie, and I hang out at Xo's house. We gorge on tamales, nachos, buñuelos, and Abuelita's hot chocolate and talk about New Year's resolutions—Lou promises to try to not fall asleep in calculus anymore, and Itzel is going to attempt to cut the number of selfies she takes in a day.

"Have you told your novio happy new year yet?" Rolie asks.

"No, I'll tell him around two, when it's midnight in California."

"You're not gonna take some ass pics in the bathroom for him, Julito?" Lou asks.

I choke on the Coca-Cola I'm drinking, coughing as the carbonation scratches my throat.

"Oh my God, Lou, no," I tell her while still trying to clear my esophagus. "That's not something that's happening."

"Chiquis, Steve Jobs invented the camera phone because he *wants* you to sext with your boyfriend."

Everyone glares at her, trying to understand where these thoughts come from. Lou holds her hands out like *what part of this am I not making clear* before throwing them up in defeat. "Pues, fuck me, then," she says, getting up from the couch and heading to the kitchen.

"Can we talk?" I whisper to Itzel.

"Claro." She follows me to my room, and I close the door behind us.

"So can I ask what's going on between you and Jordan right now?"

"Since when have you been a chismoso?" Itzel asks back defensively.

I glare at her. Ain't no way she's pulling that card on me.

She groans. "*Fine.* It's nothing official. We don't know what we're going to want in half a year. I—pretending I wasn't attracted to him was getting tiring. I'd had enough of trying to make something work with someone else because I needed to get my mind off him."

"And you were, what, never going to tell me?"

"You weren't going to say anything about Mat! So don't come for me. We were going to tell you. But it's a little weird when we aren't calling each other boyfriend and girlfriend."

"I'm guessing it wouldn't be any less odd than a guy from California and me calling each other *boyfriend*."

"You're right. Love is a complicated romance journey for us."

"I hate that we're so alike sometimes."

"Well, stop trying this hard to be me," Itzel teases, bumping our shoulders together. She grabs my hand, inserting her fingers in between mine.

"Do you want to be his girlfriend?"

She sighs and stares at the wall covered in the pictures Mat sent me. "I want it to not be difficult to see him leave this summer. And maybe using or not using a specific title will make things less hard. But that's all I got right now."

"Okay," I tell her. Not that I have any say in this—because I, unlike her, recognize where that line is—but that's fine with me. I want them to be content. In whatever way that plays out.

I hug her. "I love you both. No matter what."

It's almost two a.m. by the time we start making ourselves comfortable, sleepiness finally catching up to us. I give the bedroom to Itzel and Jordan, Rolie takes a couch, and Lou and I share an air mattress in the middle of the living room. Roe's snores fill the room almost as soon as the lights go out, and Lou's follow soon after. I hold on to my phone, ready to text Mat right as midnight hits California.

Happy New Year, cariño. I hope you know I'm adding the kiss I missed out on at midnight to the ones you'll be making up for in a few months. Hope you have a fun night! Be safe. I love you.

Ten weeks. Ten weeks and I'll be where you are. This is going to be our year, Mặt Trời Pham.

~

I dream of my dad. Of his yells. His eyes. How he starts tapping his hip in a quick rhythm that gets faster and faster as his anger rises until—

I dream of purple and burgundy bruises on my body. The memories of each one replaying in my head.

You don't fucking walk like that, with your arms like a maricón. He told me that almost thirteen years ago. The first time I remember him hurting me. In his old truck, outside of my day care. Grabbing my wrists and not letting go as he yelled. His grip getting tighter and tighter. Even as I started crying. Yanking my arms, trying to get him to let go.

A loud gasp escapes me when my back hits the wooden floor of Xochi's living room, startling me awake. My heartbeat races with my breath. I touch my wrists, my biceps, ribs, shoulders, and jaw with trembling hands. Feeling sweat all over my body. But no pain.

"I'm fine. It was only a dream," I say aloud. Putting it out into the universe so I know *this* is reality.

I grab my Martin Soccer jacket, throwing it on and opening the front door. When my feet touch the cold concrete, I immediately regret not putting on shoes too. Too late now, though. I don't want to make any more noise.

I walk to my truck and around it, up to the gate of the bed, opening it slowly and quietly. A small *hmmp* comes out as I hop on, my legs dangling off the ledge.

I think about calling Mat. Starting off the year with an *I should fill you in on why I'm a complete mess.* He's probably drunk. It's about to be four here, two in Los Angeles. So actually, he's probably still partying.

The sound of the front door opening and closing comes from behind me. And footsteps getting louder as they get closer.

"'Manito, why—no, *why are you barefoot*?"

"One of my many late-night-slash-early-morning poor choices."

Xo takes a seat next to me, looking comfortable in an old sorority sweater, sweatpants, and a colcha wrapped around her.

"You aren't cold?" she asks.

"I'll survive."

She eyes me with disbelief and then scoots closer. Her arm nearest me reaches around my shoulders to share the quilt.

"How many pairs of those Adidas joggers do you own?"

I chuckle and shrug. "A lot."

We look at all the neighbors' homes, their Christmas lights and decorations still up, and soak in the silence.

"You gonna tell me why you're out here?"

"I, uh—I had a nightmare about Dad. All of it stays on repeat in my brain. I want to not think about those times anymore, Xo. I wish I could forget them."

She rubs circles on my back and takes a long, drawn-out sigh. "I know, 'Lito."

I fall onto her, wrapping my arms around my sister.

"You're warm."

"Because I'm not an estúpido como tú."

I close my eyes for a minute. Concentrate on her breathing. Try to match it.

"I think I want to go to counseling."

"Good," she replies. As if she's been waiting for me to say those words for a while now. "I'll look into it. We'll make it happen."

"Thanks, Xo." I try counting the number of icicle strands lining the roof of the house across from hers until my eyes start to feel strained. Anything to get my mind off why I'm awake and outside shivering. "Are you okay?"

She scoffs as she sniffs and wipes her nose. "*You* shouldn't be asking *me* that question. I'm the big sister. And you're the one going through it right now."

My big sister. My guardian angel. The person who is here for me when I need her most and has probably stood up for me more times than I'll ever know.

As much as Xo hates it, she deserves someone making sure she's all right. Someone to protect her when she needs it. Even if it's only once every eighteen years.

"I know, Xo. Thank you—for everything. I love you."

"I love you too, 'manito." She pats my back and then grabs my hands to loosen herself from me. "Let's go inside now. Güelo will kill us both if I let you spend the rest of your Christmas break in bed with the flu."

34

After living with Xochi for a few weeks, life starts becoming something close to normal. Though having to sit with her while she explained to my principal and our school counselor why she needed to replace Dad as my guardian on their records was agonizing. And Father David feeling the need to reiterate *how Catholics should support LGBT people* was a little over-the-top.

I wasn't the person who needed to have that talk.

Also, trying to get me on her insurance so I can start counseling has been the worst. Not that I couldn't go now, but using Dad's insurance to go talk about him and why I'm not living with him anymore to a therapist seemed odd. And the least amount of connections I can have to him, the better.

Xo's become a regular in the stands at my soccer games, which is interesting. The last time she saw me play, I was still in the YMCA kids' league. But she gets into it. You'd think my sister was watching the World Cup or something.

Having her around at normal times of the day is really different compared to Dad's all-over-the-place work schedule. Pro: hanging out with her after we're both home from school. Con: every time she gives me that *get your ass to bed right now* look whenever she catches me FaceTiming with Mat past midnight.

I miss the kitchen, though. Xo's is so modern, which is cool, but something about a gas stove is so much better than using a flattop. And it doesn't feel the same using her equipment rather than all the utensils and holders and bowls Abuelita left me that are still at Dad's.

Then finding out that Xo actually has a social life? Don't know why I was so surprised to learn she has friends. But seeing her walk out of her room in a dress that showed Jordan, Piña, Rolie, and me nearly all her chiches *and* her nalgas was never anything I asked for.

"Going on a date. Don't break anything while I'm gone."

"Who are you going on a date with?"

"Don't worry about it. Just a guy."

And Piña was all, "I'm just gonna say it, Luna: your sister could get it," the second she was out the door, with those bobos Jordan and Roe nodding in agreement. "Like, I know we hate your dad, but, no cap, your parents made some pretty kids."

Spent a solid five minutes screaming into my pillow after that.

~

"'Manito," Xo shouts as she approaches her dining table. "You have letters from Southern California and Loyola Marymount."

I shove away the Tupperware container full of fruit I'd been working my way through and grab the envelopes. In between Christmas, when I got my first letter, to now at the beginning of March, they and UCLA have been silent. Every day started as *this is when I'll get more acceptance* letters, only to end with wondering whether they forgot I even applied. UT's showed up a few weeks ago, but the only ones excited about that were Itzel and Lou.

The size of the letter from USC is an automatic discouragement. Plain, regular white envelope. Not the huge, colorful packet LMU sent.

I take a deep breath. A finger slowly tears into the top, and I remove the paper and scan the words.

> Dear Julián Luna,
>
> Thank you for your interest in attending the University of Southern California. After a review of your application, the Admissions Committee has decided to place you on the wait list.

"What did they say, 'Lito?"

"It—I've been wait-listed," I answer, pushing the letter aside. I know this doesn't *technically* equal rejection, but it feels the same. Like a defeat. Officially one and one.

I try to remember every detail of my application. Where did I go wrong? What about me wasn't enough for them?

"Hey. Hey. 'Manito." I glance over to my sister, who's trying for my attention. Snapping near my face. "Stop getting in your head. You still have one more school. Keep putting all the positive vibes toward that and you liking LMU, yes? ¿Qué dicen ellos?"

I open the second letter, seeing a long list of numbers printed onto the paper under the LMU logo. "It's my financial aid awards."

"A ver." Xo holds out a hand and I give her the paper. She scans the list and starts writing down numbers on one of the envelopes. Head down, lost in calculations.

"This . . . hmm," she says, tapping the end of the pen against the table.

"That doesn't sound like a good *hmm*."

"It—schools can be pricey. Especially when it's a private college in a city with a much higher cost of living than Corpus. But we still have your FAFSA, the private scholarships you applied for, and everything else that could come up between now and August. So say lots of prayers, put what you want out in the universe. When the actual number becomes clearer, hopefully it'll be more manageable, and Güelo and I can take care of it."

"Xo, you don't have—"

"I'm not asking your permission, 'Lito."

Putting Xochi in this position isn't something I wanted. I'm already living under her roof, eating her food. I don't want her to have to pay for me to go to school.

And—as much as I hate to think about it—going to UT, staying in state, would be a lot cheaper. I might even be able to go without paying anything. I could, I don't know—

"'Manito." Her hand rests on top of mine. "Don't worry about it. You hear me? Focusing on that isn't going to do you any good. Send all the positive energy to UCLA and to, cómo se dice, the Hispanic Scholarship Fund and everyone else we'll be waiting on. Focus on what you need to do to get where you want to be."

On going to Santa Monica with Mat. Sitting in huge classrooms, learning about social movements like the Chicano Blowouts. Decorating my dorm room.

Don't think about options C or D. Austin or staying here isn't on the table. It can't be.

There's only UCLA or, if I have to, LMU. There's only Los Angeles. I can see the sun, and I'm almost close enough to feel its warmth. I'm not taking any more steps back.

~

"Aren't you supposed to be working? Or did you almost burn down your brother's food truck again?"

"That was only twice!" Mat yells back. "It slowed down, so Khan's giving me a break." He swallows a bite of spring roll before continuing. "Do we need to drag a college for a minute? Because I can tell you every reason why not going to USC is the best thing that could've happened."

"No, I'm fine. Only positive thoughts. Like getting a million-dollar scholarship. I'm actually looking at LMU's website right now. Do you think double majoring would be too hectic?"

"I'm sure you'll kick ass at whatever you do. We're gonna be that educated brown gay couple Boomers have nightmares about."

"Big power-couple mood," I reply. "Anyways, waiting on UCLA now. Your letter come in yet?"

"We've still got at least a week before they start sending the emails. Sorry if you were expecting another piece of paper. But they've got, like, four times as many students to admit compared to Loyola Marymount. We got this, though. Don't get all fidgety waiting for them."

"I'm not—ugh. I'm more anxious waiting for my trip to get here. My patience is basically nonexistent at this point."

"Same. I hope your sister didn't buy you a round-trip ticket. You won't be needing it. After you're done seeing all the cool places around the city, you're never gonna want to leave."

I'm for sure not above skipping my return flight. Xo will have to pry me off my boyfriend if she thinks I'll be going home willingly.

"Holding you to that. I'm expecting to be completely awestruck the entire time."

"Well, you'll already be seeing me, so that won't be too hard."

"Shut up, necio."

"Oh, have you talked to your sister about staying with my brother and sister? Tien's got a sofa with a bed in it she can use, and Khan and Ruben already said it's cool if you stay with them."

"I'll bring it up. She mentioned wanting to go to West Hollywood, though. Is that something they're into?"

"My lesbian older sister, bi older brother, and gay brother-in-law taking a straight girl to WeHo for the first time? Yeah. They'd be *very* into that."

"Cool." *And* if they're all out partying, that means Mat and I get more alone time. Not that pushing my sister on his siblings is in any way a method of making sure I have as much privacy with my boyfriend as possible. "I can't wait."

"Me neither. Thirteen days to go."

"Thirteen days."

35

I'm surprised Jordan and I have never gotten kicked out of an H-E-B. Every time we go shopping together, the first thing he does is hop into one of the carts like he's four. Asking for me to throw him fruits and vegetables so he can try to juggle them. Then give it half an hour max, and he'll get bored of sitting in there, stand up, and try to hop out. Which almost always brings both him *and* the cart crashing to the floor.

And it's not like I wasn't pushing him as fast as I could before hopping on the edge and riding with him down the parking lot. Or that I can say I wasn't recording him almost busting his head in the middle of the store instead of helping him out of the cart.

But he's the one who asked me to get a Boomerang video for Instagram.

Jordan is splitting housesitting duties with Güelo while we'll be in Los Angeles, and Xo promised to stock up the fridge for him.

"No parties," she told him with a serious face, knowing it'd be the first thing that'd happen in an empty house. "And I'm going to assume you'll be staying there by yourself. I'm going to make myself believe this. Do not make me regret that."

"Do you cook?" I ask him, pushing the cart through the meat section of the store, pointing at the animal parts. "Like, you know what to do with these?"

"I made spaghetti once."

"How did that turn out?"

"It was . . . edible."

"We should probably stick with frozen chicken strips, then?"

"I'll go home for dinner. Let's get eggs, some cereal, sandwich stuff, snacks, and we'll call it a day. I know you haven't finished packing yet, so—"

"You don't know that."

"Tell me I'm wrong, Luna."

I turn away from Jordan and face straight ahead, ignoring him trying to drag me. Flipping him off as I take a right into the cereal aisle.

We get him a box of Honey Nut Cheerios. The twenty-grain bread he *has* to have. Sliced turkey, cheese, pickles, and a bottle of mustard. Chips and fruit snacks. Everything he'll need to survive for eight days.

"You excited to be finally getting dicked down?"

"*Jordan.* I'm not talking about that."

"What? It's a natural thing, bro. Oh, and I heard that there's a gay version of those exercises people with vaginas do. The, uh, Kegels but with your—"

"I get it," I snap, throwing a bath sponge at him for emphasis. "But I'm not having this conversation in a grocery store. At least wait until we're back in my truck for—"

I'm going to throw up, faint, and choke to death all at the same time. In the instant that my mind registers what I'm seeing, I let go of the cart, fling myself against the nearest giant shelf—knocking down whatever my back runs into—and squat on the ground. My elbows are resting on my legs, hands clenching my hair, and my eyes are looking straight down at the tile floor.

Breathe. Breathe. Breathe.

"Luna." I can hear Jordan's voice, sense him kneeling down next to me, feel his hand on my back, but I can't respond. "Jules, talk to me."

My mind is telling my head to shake from side to side. *No.* But I'm having a hard enough time trying to remember to get air into my body.

"What is it?"

"M—Dad."

His hand leaves, and I want to scream for him to put it back. I want to be able to move. To sprint out of here and to, I don't know, Xo's, the beach, Los Angeles. Keep going until my legs give out. Until I know that if I look back, I won't see my dad a few feet away from me.

But I can't. I'm stuck. Heavy with panic and fear.

I can hear Jordan moving in front of me. It has to be an eternity that he's standing there before he's back down to my level.

"He's leaving through the other side. Won't see us," Jordan whispers. "What do you need?"

"Stay here for a minute. Please."

"Yeah. Of course, Jules."

~

"Are you sure you're okay?"

"*Yes*, Xo. I'm fine."

My eyes are red. I barely got myself to stop shaking. There are parts of the last forty-five minutes that are completely black.

But I'm fine. I have to be.

"We can figure something out if you don't feel up to getting on a plane right now or traveling—"

"Xo. We're going," I say definitively. It took long enough to get Jordan to go back home, and now I have my sister thinking we should cancel the entire week. I want to pretend this never happened. "I need to eat something, pack, and go to bed, and I'll feel better."

She lets out a long, bothered exhale. "No me mientas, 'manito. I'll check on you later."

Xo shuts the door to my room, and I lie down on my bed, the lower half of my legs hanging off the side.

This isn't how I wanted to start my spring break. It's supposed to be nonstop fun and excitement. Filled only with people who matter.

I don't want to go to Los Angeles with Dad at the front of my mind.

My phone starts vibrating in my pocket. I pull it out and, for the first time in my life, am wishing that I wasn't seeing my boyfriend's name with a sun and a yellow heart emoji on my screen. That he could've waited five minutes for me to get in the right mental headspace. I wipe my face with the bottom of my shirt and press "Answer."

"Hey! You finished packing?"

"Of course I have."

"Why don't I believe you? And—are you good?"

"What? Yes."

"You sure? You look—not trying to be insulting, but a little off."

"Long week." I know I need to tell Mat. I need to figure out a way to get this all out with him. But not right now. "As long as I get some sleep, I'll be set for tomorrow."

"Then I don't want to take up too much time, but . . . I got into UCLA!"

"Mat, I—oh my God. That's amazing!"

I know how much it means to him to be going to the same school his brother and sister went to. How he tries not to talk about the expectations that his family has for him. That he has for himself.

"I'm so proud of you, cariño. There was no way they *weren't* letting you in. You found out today?"

"I got the email this morning. Khan, Ruben, and Tien are taking me out to dinner to celebrate. But this means you should be hearing from them soon too, and we can both go visit campus sometime during the week."

"Sure. Sounds great."

I'm mentally saying every prayer I know so I get my acceptance email soon. And that stepping foot onto the university I've dreamed forever of attending will be everything I've ever hoped for. Even more, because now it includes being there with my boyfriend.

"Maybe we can *get lost* and see if there's an empty dorm room we can test the beds out in."

"Don't push your luck," I say in the sternest voice I can give.

Stupid ass. I can't wait to see him. Not because of the implied *getting lost* stuff. At least, not *only* because of that.

Everything will be better when I see him. I know it will.

He laughs. "I'm kidding. But not really. Anyways, I'm hyper because of how happy I am. This, and you'll be here tomorrow. For an entire week. *Ahh,* I'm gonna want to keep on talking when I should let you go. You have to be up in, what, seven hours?"

"Yep, and already hating it. You remember our arrival time, right?"

"I think so. Text it to me just in case."

"Don't you dare leave me stranded at an airport."

"If you think I'm going to waste even one second of you in the same city as me, you don't know me at all, babe."

"Whatever. I'll see you in a few hours. I love you."

"See you tomorrow. I love you too. Dream about me."

36

I hear my alarm go off. See 4:30 on my phone.

"Fuuu—" I groan into my hands, covering my face. It feels as if I only blinked rather than actually slept. Too busy obsessing over how excited and nervous and anxious I am for this trip.

"Get dressed!" I hear Xochi yell from the other side of the door as I force myself out of bed.

My yawning makes my reply of "shut up, I'm going" incomprehensible. I trudge over to the dresser, staring at my choices, knowing this'll be what I'm wearing when I first see Mat.

Screw it. It's too early to think about impressing anyone. I grab a T-shirt and running shorts. I bet he'll be showing up in a tank and joggers anyway. This is fine.

The smell of coffee is overwhelming when I open the bedroom door. Did a Starbucks move in overnight? Güelo must already be here.

"Buenos días, mi'jito," he says between sips of his gross unsweetened bean water. "Listo para tu viaje?"

"Sí, Güelo," I answer. The words mix with another long yawn.

The three of us grab bags and suitcases, hauling the luggage out the door. Xo Tetrises it all into the trunk of her car.

"You have everything?" my sister yells as she shoves a bag between two suitcases.

"Yes, I have everything."

"Your charger, earbuds, laptop?" Güelo lists off.

"Sí, todo."

"Tienes sus boletos, Xochi?" he asks.

"On my phone, Güelo."

We get to the departure gate as the line is forming to enter the plane. The lady at the entryway looks way too smiley for six thirty in the morning. She scans each of our tickets and motions for us to keep moving forward.

"Take the window seat," Xo orders, following me into a row. I set my backpack at my feet and take my phone out of my pocket. "And wait until we take off to put your earbuds in."

I give her a tired glare before sticking my AirPods in. Sticking my tongue out at her and then turning to my phone, going to Spotify and picking an album at random. I just need some noise.

On the plane. I'll let y'all know when I'm in LA, I text to the group chat formerly known as "Itzel y Los Dinos" and now labeled "Casa de las *Whore*-es" (Lou's creativity really shone with that one). They won't be seeing it for hours still, but I know how insulted they'd be if I don't give them a play-by-play of this entire trip.

I open my email app and do a quick scroll through the H&M, ASOS, and Fastweb mail that's come through since yesterday afternoon.

"Oh my God," I whisper when my finger abruptly stops. Hovering over an email from UCLA.

Subject: Decision Letter.

My heart beats like a bass drum in the marching band as I tap on the email.

Finally. I can't wait to tell Mat, and see the school, and figure out which dorm we like best, and—

Dear Mr. Luna,

After careful review of your application for admission, we regret to inform you that we are unable to offer you admission for the upcoming Fall quarter.

What? Wait—what? No, I had to have read that wrong.

"¿Qué pasó?" Xo asks, concerned. I didn't realize my hand had started shaking.

"I—" The disappointment mixed with how sleepy I still am makes me sound like I'm choking up. I am, but . . . "It's UCLA. I didn't get in."

Xo wraps her arms around me, her head leaning against mine. "'Lito, I'm sorry," she says. "That school is so, so hard to get into. Literally everyone applies there. But you've still got Loyola Marymount, and we'll get to see it in a couple days."

"But—I thought if I had at least two LA schools to pick from, I wouldn't have to worry about one not working out. I could go to the other. What if LMU ends up being too expensive? We still don't know how I'm going to pay for it." My ability to handle my anxiety is about to clock out for the morning. Something as simple as breathing is becoming difficult to do without putting all my concentration into it. "Or what if I don't even like LMU? What if I don't even want to be in Los Angeles? What am I supposed to do, Xo? I can't stay in Corpus. And this is what I've wanted for forever. I thought I had everything figured out and now I don't know."

I can't handle this. Something's going to go wrong. I know it is.

"It's—and then what if I get there and Mat realizes he doesn't like me and I've wasted the past five months of his life? Or if he realizes he does love me, and I have to tell him, *Hey, this isn't gonna work out. I'm actually staying in Texas. Bye.* There's so much pressure right now for this to work out and—"

"'Manito, breathe," Xochi interrupts. She hands me her venti Starbucks cup of ice water. "You're having a slight freak-out. Take deep breaths. You need to not overwhelm yourself."

"How? It *is* overwhelming."

"It's growing up, 'Lito." She lets out an exhausted, sympathetic chuckle. "It's complicated. You want to have your entire life planned out, but life isn't something that will take orders or that we can construct in a way we'll always be comfortable with."

"But, Xo. I—"

"No, escúchame, 'manito. Do this for me: go into this week excited to see a brand-new place for the first time. Be excited for all the experiences that are waiting for you and everyone who's been waiting to meet you. But be open to reality. Don't force something. Because—and this is very important—you're eighteen. Right now, focus on yourself before anyone else."

"What if this is a reality where I don't go to Loyola Marymount?"

"Then don't. Don't think that only being a few hours from home or sticking with a couple of old friends makes you any less capable of breaking out of your shell. Don't forget, you got accepted to UT. You can always go to Austin. Or if we have to consider community college for a year and transferring to UCLA or USC, that can be on the table too. I get what you want and why you want it and, yes, anything else is scary. And I'm fully supportive. But I'm equally supportive of every option that could be out there.

"What we're not gonna do is spend the next nine days worrying about money, because you're way too young for that, or what if you hate this school, what if you don't end up in a certain city, what if you have to stay in Texas, what if you break a boy's heart or if he breaks yours. You've been waiting for this for years. Have the time of your life. Can you do that for me, 'manito?"

I nod and take one more sip of water. I hand Xo the cup and lean back into the seat. "When did you get smart?"

"Cállate, tonto. Take a nap. I'll wake you when we get to Houston."

37

We haven't had a five thirty a.m. conversation in a while," Mat says when he answers my FaceTime call. We got to Houston with three hours to kill before leaving for Los Angeles. And I knew if I didn't break the news to him, I'd be thinking about it all morning.

"You're not as moody when I've let you sleep. So I try not to make it a habit."

"I don't get moody."

"Okay," I reply, emphasizing the sarcasm in my voice. "But I need to tell you something real quick."

"What's up, babe?"

"I—I didn't get into UCLA. Found out this morning."

"What?" If he wasn't awake before, he sure is now. His screen gets shaky while he sits up and situates his glasses. "Are you serious? That—that . . . I'm sorry, Jules."

"It's—whatever. I'm not gonna let it ruin this trip. Just wanted to tell you in case you scheduled a tour with them or something. I don't mind going with you, but—"

"No, it's cool. I'll go some other time. Don't worry. I've already seen it plenty. Get some breakfast and then get your cute ass to LA. I've got plenty planned to take your mind off this."

I laugh. "Shut up. We'll be there in a few hours. Want me to bring you some Whataburger?"

"I'm good, thanks," Mat says with the mild distaste of someone who's never known good fast food written on his face. "See you soon, Jules. Love you."

"Love you too, cariño."

I find the closest Starbucks and buy a bagel and a passion-fruit lemonade. Browse through the small bookstores and gift shops, finding a Texas key chain for Mat. But after that, the limited number of distractions aren't enough to keep my attention.

"I will force you to take some Benadryl or NyQuil if you can't calm down," Xo tells me, bothered by my constant leg bouncing.

"I'm sorry. Impatient."

It feels as if I've been waiting an eternity by the time we're on the next plane. I send a short text to Mat so he knows we're on our way. The next time I'm on the ground, I'll be in California. The expectations and excitement running through my head are making me nauseous. Or it could be the sudden change in oxygen levels as we take off.

~

I'm not sure when I fall asleep again, but I wake up to endless city. Palm trees. Hills. California. I can't take my eyes off this sight.

I'm here. This is actually happening.

When the plane lands, I'm shaking as I stand waiting to get out. I've done enough waiting.

"Cálmate, 'manito," Xo says when she feels me try to shove her into the aisle. "We have an entire week. A couple more minutes isn't going to kill you."

"You don't know that."

After entering the terminal lobby, we follow signs leading to baggage claim. We wait an ungodly amount of time watching luggage make their orbit around as slowly as possible. Xo's come first, and I'm about to start screaming when my own finally come around.

We're here! I text Mat.

He quickly follows with a line of heart eye emojis. Driving back around rn. Hang outside the arrival doors.

I look at every car driving by, as if I have any clue what vehicle I should be looking for. I get antsy standing and waiting and checking my phone every two seconds. The voice of their mayor greeting us over the intercom system on repeat is going to be stuck in my head for the rest of my life.

Every part of me is nervous and excited, and I'm sure I look like I have to pee. But I can't stop moving. And I can't stop smiling.

Then I hear a honk. A car stops at the curb in front of us. And I see him.

I'm lost for breath. But in a good way. I don't *want* to breathe until he's in front of me. Until we're sharing the air. Knowing that the same oxygen sustaining him is keeping me alive too.

Mat steps out from the passenger side of his brother's car. Smiling that smile I've seen from miles away. The one that makes my heart and soul go wild without even trying.

He's barely got a foot on the sidewalk when I drop my luggage and run to my boyfriend. I didn't even have time to think this over. Consider how I wanted it to play out. Another *I love you* moment. But it would've been pointless to think I'd have any control over my reaction.

I jump onto him. His hands grip under my thighs and my arms wrap around his neck to support me. And we kiss. A kiss that's been put on hold for almost half a year but was so worth the wait.

The same beach-scented cologne from his hoodie fills my nose and, *damn*, that mixed with whatever his body chemistry is doing, plus his hands on me and mine on him and fully making out in front of everyone arriving to Los Angeles has my mind already craving things that would require a lot more privacy.

"Sure, 'Lito, let me get your bags for you," I hear Xochi say from behind me as she makes her way to the open trunk of Khan's car. Mat starts laughing against my mouth, but I'm not letting him end this yet.

"Hi," Mat says. Finally taking his lips away from mine.

"Hey."

"Should I put you down?"

"Are you giving me a choice?"

"*I'm* content with this for the rest of the week, but I don't think your sister or my brother is loving my hands on your ass right now."

I see them in my peripheral. Definitely not huge fans of the PDA. "Yeah. I think you're right."

I land back on my feet and pivot to my sister and Khan, both looking thrilled that their younger brothers have finally managed to tone down the hormones. I've only ever seen the few pictures of Khan that are on Mat's Instagram. It's easy to tell they're brothers. Not in a *this is what my boyfriend is going to look like ten years from now* way, but how they carry themselves. Confident. As if they could take on the world.

Mat gives Xo the passenger seat, so he can sit with me in the back. I brush my hand through his hair, fuzzy and soft without any pomade in it. I bet he just woke up and walked out like this. It's cute this way. I look at him, loving how his eyes squint when he really, *really* smiles. Loving that I get to see this while sitting next to him.

And I play with Mat's hand. Tough from years of wrestling and that stick fighting he does. I slide my fingers in and out between his. Playing with each, comparing the differences of our palms and fingers.

He leans to my side, his mouth on my shoulder. His eyes watching me study his features. Saying very little. Just . . . looking.

Khan's voice sounds almost distant as he points out which way the museums and beaches are, where their favorite Korean restaurant is, and the Filipino restaurant that Mat's brother-in-law swears is as good as anything his family back home cooks. Like listening to morning school announcements coming through the intercom, I hear him, but it's all going in one ear and out the other. I have plenty of time to familiarize myself with the city. Right now, nothing is tearing my concentration away from my boyfriend.

I knew all I needed was to be here and I'd be good. Dad doesn't matter. All those times my brain tried to bring me down don't matter. The worries don't matter.

This is where I'm supposed to be. There was nothing but certainty about it when I saw Mat's eyes inches from mine. Touched him.

At least, enough certainty to not let anything bother me right now.

I already never want this to end.

38

I'm trying not to think about how any of this is too good to be real life.

Standing in the middle of Khan and Ruben's spare bedroom. My bags thrown to the side as soon as we ran in and closed the door behind us. Our arms wrapped around one another. Going right back to making out.

"Em!" Tien's voice from the living room interrupts the mood. When Mat pulls away, I can see his eyes roll as he lets out a bothered huff. "Let go of your boyfriend so we can say hi properly!"

He sighs as his hands slip from my back, into my hands. "I wonder how long I could ignore her before she kicks the door down."

"If she's anything like my sister, it's a miracle she hasn't already."

Mat looks at me and then to the door, repeating this a couple of times. Thinking about whether or not he's planning on listening to his sister. I'm rooting for us to ignore them. Sixty more seconds. That's all I want, and then we can go back to them.

"All right," he says with a lot of reluctance in his voice. "Let's go say hi."

I get a very Lou-esque confidence from Tien. Except with a much more casual, *baseball cap and flannel over a band tee* demeanor.

"This is the Texas boy our brother's been obsessing and thirsting over for months."

"Chị," Mat snaps. His eyes telling her to *quit your shit.*

"Don't pretend it's not true, ading," Ruben says while coming in for a hug. "*Ob-sessed.* Very 'a gay kid discovering Britney Spears for the first time.'"

"Oh, trust me, 'Lito was the same way." My head twists to glare at Xo as she adds to the conversation. Mat getting called out doesn't mean I have to be. "He didn't need too much of a push. His friends were telling me it was only, what, two weeks in before he was crushing *so hard.*"

I need Itzel to stop talking to my sister.

~

The bright, cool Los Angeles weather is addicting. It's on the ocean, yet, unlike in Corpus Christi, a damp cloud of humidity isn't trying to suffocate me. I honestly wouldn't say no to spending the whole week outdoors.

And hanging out with Mat's family is great. Ruben is the wittiest person I've ever met in my entire life. I can tell that my boyfriend's been on the other end of his shade for years now. Tien is equal parts laid-back and serious. An *almost* PhD who is the first one to get tipsy at lunch. And Khan gives off that big-brother vibe that makes me feel immediately comfortable around him.

Ruben and Khan bring us to one of their favorite spots in West Hollywood—kitchen something. I wasn't paying attention to the name. More into the pink-and-pecan-brown aesthetic and all the pride flags that remind everyone—if we'd forgotten—that we're in the gayborhood.

"So I'm thinking Griffith Park and the Observatory tomorrow, and then you have LMU on Monday. But after that, we can do whatever you're in the mood for," Mat says, pulling up his Notes app that has a list of all the potential things we can do and places we can see. Hollywood

Boulevard, LACMA, the Broad, the Getty, Venice and Santa Monica, Olvera Street, an LAFC or Galaxy game, downtown, and about fifteen other ideas.

"You'll love it, Jules," Ruben says, sitting across from us, taking a quick moment from talking with my sister about growing up in San Antonio. "I think the city is going to treat you well. And you've got an *all right* tour guide."

"Hey, I'm a damn good tour guide!"

"Reads one Thrillist article and becomes real cocky," Ruben retorts.

Mat and I share a Nutella waffle with strawberries and bananas. Nothing huge, since we'll be having dinner with his parents tonight and apparently his mom is making *enough food to feed all of Koreatown*.

"What're we doing after this?" I ask Mat, separating from whatever it is our siblings are talking about. I cut off a square of waffle and stab it and a banana slice with my fork.

"I didn't put a lot of thought into today. Wasn't sure how exhausted you'd be from your flight. We could be lazy and hide in your room. Or drive around, show you a few spots nearby."

"I'm a little tired, but I like option two. Show me around."

"Cool. Then when we get back to Khan and Ruben's, I'll grab my keys and we'll take off."

~

So much for that plan.

Mat had all the energy while we walked back to his siblings' cars, Tien and Xo splitting up with us to head to his sister's apartment until dinner. But on the drive back to Khan and Ruben's home, he falls asleep in the car. His face drops onto my shoulder, and I try to regulate my breathing, not wanting to wake him. My hand rubs his leg mindlessly, that area between his knee and where his shorts start. And every once in a while, I'll turn so I can kiss his head.

"He was excited about you coming," Khan says, looking at us from the rearview mirror. "I'm not sure if he was ever able to fall asleep last night."

I shake my boyfriend awake when we're back at his brothers' home. Reach for his hand when he slides out of the car after me and lead him back to my room.

"Sorry I took a power nap," Mat mumbles. "We can still go if you want."

"It's fine. We've got the rest of the week. And I heard you might need some sleep right now."

"Probably. Kiss me some more first, though."

"As much as you want."

Mat's so good at it. It's not fast or aggressive. He's slow, methodical, intimate. His lips are soft. Thank God my boyfriend believes in Burt's Bees. My fingers glide up and down his wrestler arms as he holds on to the sides of my midriff. His tongue moves slowly against mine, the remnants of chocolate, hazelnut, and fruit lingering and, *Wait, how do I breathe again?* He holds mine between his lips, briefly, before going back at it.

And then he gently bites and pulls at my lower lip.

Oh. My. God.

I let out an involuntary moan. I couldn't help it. He lets go, looking at me with that *oh yeah, I did that* smile.

"Stop being proud of yourself," I say.

Mat drops onto the bed, and I fall with him. He looks into my eyes, and I stare into his.

I could do this for-*fucking*-ever.

"I love you," I tell Mat. The first time I've said those words in his presence. While being able to entangle my legs with his. Feel his hand on my hip.

I've never meant those words more.

"I love you too." He sounds half-asleep saying it. And his eyes are struggling to stay open. Using all the strength he has left to stay awake.

"Take a nap, cariño." I lightly hold a finger over each of his eyelids, trying to force him asleep. "I'll be right here when you wake up."

He lets out this part groan, part laugh while moving his face away from my hand. "Don't jinx it. I'm still not entirely convinced this isn't all a dream, and I'm gonna wake up and you'll still be in Texas."

"Shut up. It's not. I promise."

A minute later, he's given up on his battle against fatigue. His mouth stays open a little bit, and quiet snores create this oddly comforting rhythm. I make small, minimal movements to get comfortable, feeling his hand still on my side holding itself in place subconsciously when I do anything too drastic.

Any idea I might have had, any imagining of what something as simple as lying down with him might feel like pales in comparison to reality. I try my best to stay awake. To commit as much of this to memory as possible.

But I've become too comfortable. *He's* too comfortable.

I'm unable to fight my own exhaustion.

39

I wake up to Mat's hand on my head. His fingers twirling my curls. With his other hand, he scrolls through his Twitter. Absentmindedly taking in whatever chisme people are posting.

"Anything interesting?" I ask.

"Not really."

While I was asleep, Mat rolled onto his back and I clung to his side. My head at the top of his chest where his arm meets his shoulder. And my hand up under Mat's shirt. I wasn't even aware of it until now, but I keep it there, letting my fingers wander aimlessly along my boyfriend's stomach.

"What time are we going to your parents' house?"

"Um, maybe half an hour? Khan mentioned a specific time this morning, but obviously, I wasn't listening."

"Should I change? This is huge. I don't want to screw up."

"Don't go for formal. And don't worry. It's only dinner and hanging out with my family. Nothing big. Anyways, wear what you want to wear. I have to pee."

"Can't you hold it?" I whine, throwing a leg onto his waist and wrapping my arm around him.

"You can go with me," he replies.

"Ew, no. I'm good."

I roll off Mat, allowing him to leave for the bathroom while I squat next to my suitcases, unzipping one open and then digging through my clothes for something to wear.

Wear what you want to wear. Cabrón. I'm not falling for that. I have parents to impress.

I pick out a pair of jeans and a navy-and-gray gingham shirt. Casual, while making some sort of effort.

"Cute," Mat remarks. He comes back to the room as I'm putting on my shirt. His fingers hook in between buttons. "One more kiss before we're surrounded by my family?"

"One more. *That's it.*"

The most obvious lie I've ever told.

Ruben is waiting for all of us when we get to the living room. He complains about his husband always being the last one to be ready for anything and telling me the story of how Khan was half an hour late for their first date (*a date* he *asked* me *on*). True to form, Khan joins us twenty minutes later. Ignoring Ruben mouthing, *Told you.*

I squeeze Mat's hand as we pull up to his parents' house.

"They're gonna love you," he whispers and follows me out of the car.

"Má! Ba! We're here," Khan exclaims as we enter. Their home has a welcoming air to it. As if all the family gatherings that have taken place left a permanent inviting and comforting aura.

"Oh, shoes off, babe," Mat tells me. "Or else Má will flip her shit."

I hear who I'm pretty sure is their dad yelling, "I'm coming, I'm coming." And yep, that's definitely Mr. Pham. With a smile identical to Mat's but features closer to Khan's and Tien's. He's speaking in Vietnamese while he hugs Khan and Ruben before turning to Mat and me.

"You must be Julian! It's good to meet you." Mat's father shakes my hand and hugs me, patting my back.

"It's *Julián*, Ba," Mat corrects his father politely.

"Oh, sorry, sorry. We know what it's like, people not getting our names right. Annoying." His dad is rolling his eyes while speaking, as if he's imagining everyone who's ever butchered his name.

"It's fine," I reassure. "Most people call me Jules."

"Perfect. Make yourself at home. Mặt Trời, I know I don't have to tell you to keep your bedroom door open, but—"

"Ba. *Really?*"

I laugh as my boyfriend grimaces at his dad.

He pulls me with him to the kitchen, where it smells like his mom is already hard at work. We pass Ruben leaving with a glass of wine and a couple of bottles of beer, heading to his husband and father-in-law. I see him mouth *Good luck* to me as he walks in the other direction.

Mat clears his throat, getting the attention of his mother. Her back is to us as she says something in Vietnamese. Maintaining her deep focus on cutting vegetables.

"Hi, Má." Mat hugs his mom from behind and kisses her on the cheek. "And it's Khan's fault we just got here. But this is Jules." He moves out of the way for me to introduce myself.

Mat's mom looks exactly like him. Or I guess it's the other way around. Would it be weird to thank her for the good genes?

"Chào em, Jules. Welcome to LA," she says, setting down her knife and stepping toward me for a hug.

"Hi, Mrs. Pham," I reply. "It's great to meet you."

"We're happy to have you here. Mặt Trời's never brought a boyfriend home before. So when he finally decides to and says you're coming all the way from Texas, well, we have to roll out the red carpet. Hollywood-style."

Learning I'm the first boyfriend Mat's parents have met is a little nerve-racking. But I'm going to proudly flaunt that title.

"What're you making?" I ask, eyeing the huge variety of vegetables, meats, sauces, noodles, and rice paper on the counters.

"A little bit of everything. Let me show you." She grabs my hand, showing me the mint, Thai basil, and cilantro she grows herself. "Do you cook?"

"I do. Not a lot of practice with Asian food, but I love it."

I look around at the different pots, pans, and woks, and the rice cooker hard at work. The herbs, the tofu and jackfruit. Mat must've told her I don't eat meat.

"If you want to stay, I can teach you how to make some of this," she offers.

"No, I don't want to get in the way." As much as I honestly do want to learn, I don't want to leave Mat.

Even though declining a mom asking if I want to help in the kitchen feels horrible. Itzel's mom would think I was sick if I said no to her.

"It's no trouble. I haven't had a sidekick since Khan was still living at home. Mặt Trời, on the other hand, you'd think no one would be able to mess up tearing lettuce leaves. We don't even let him make rice by himself."

I love how everyone in his family teases him. This boy who seemingly had no faults. Still doesn't in my eyes.

"Don't feel obligated to stay," Mat tells me. I can tell what he means is *I completely support your decision to say no to my mom.*

"I—" I pull Mat aside. "Would you be okay if I stay with your mom?"

"I mean, if you want to." He's trying to hide his reluctance. I'm sure I'll be making it up to him later. He kisses me. "You sure?"

"Yes."

He looks at me and tilts his head a little. Waiting for me to change my mind.

"Then . . . I guess I'll leave you two here?" Mat asks neither of us in particular.

"Yes, I'm stealing him away from you for a while. Go talk to your ba." She shoos him out of the kitchen before giving me directions on cutting vegetables. "Cut these thin for me first, and then we'll see how well you do with the gỏi cuốn."

"The what?"

"Gỏi cuốn. Unfried spring rolls."

"Oh! I love spring rolls."

It's basically the same as making egg rolls, but I know enough to not say that out loud. It'd be like saying that all of Latin America's tamales and empanadas are the same. And they actually look nothing like any egg rolls or spring rolls I've ever seen. But they're really pretty. I add a few more to the mountain she's already created, while she makes some slightly different ones and dips those down into a pot of oil.

Mrs. Pham shows me the Ziploc bag of tofu and lists everything in the marinade, telling me exactly which type and brand to get, how she does it, and how long to leave it for. Then she guides me through cooking jackfruit for bánh bao, going heavy on the peppers and chili oil after she finds out I'm a fan of spice, and how to form the steamed bun.

"This one gets hard—watch first," she says, expertly frying onions, shallots, garlic, and tofu in her wok for a minute and then ladling some batter-looking liquid, quickly picking up the wok and spreading everything around. She adds mung beans, bean sprouts, and a couple of other things, and soon it becomes this giant clam-looking crepe thing.

"Bánh xèo. The vegetarian version," she says to me, tearing off a piece, wrapping it in lettuce, and dipping it in what she tells me is a homemade vegan fish sauce. "Found the recipe online."

It's incredible. The crepe part is crispy, and there're all these flavors from the turmeric in the batter, the tofu, garlic and onions, the mint and cilantro she wrapped with the lettuce, and the salty umami of the sauce.

"Wait, so there's bánh xèo, which is this, and then bánh bao, which are the bun things?"

"Bánh is very common. The other word describes the bánh. Bao? That's bun."

"And xèo?"

"Like the *shh* of the wok. It means, uh, sizzle."

Mat checks in a couple of times, making sure I'm still alive and stealing a fried spring roll, but other than that, we're left to ourselves. While we share the bánh xèo and cook, his mom tells me stories of her youngest son as a child—their surprise baby ten years after Tien was born. She washes her hands before going to grab a few pictures of him in his single-digit years. I hear him tell her something on her way back, and even though I don't understand the words, I can tell by his voice that it's something close to *you're embarrassing me, Mom.*

And when she finally has enough confidence in me, she lets me at the wok by myself—with her standing inches away, observing in case she needs to jump in.

"Turn, turn, turn," she says quietly when I pour the batter, mimicking her flick of the wrist.

I put in all the filling, flip one half over the other, and get it onto a plate. The sizzling still audible as it rests. And a promising crisp sound comes when Mrs. Pham breaks into it with her chopsticks.

She puts together her bite, dips it into the fish sauce, and goes for it. I hold my breath, waiting to see if it meets her standards or if I've poisoned my boyfriend's mom. Those are really the only two options here.

More Vietnamese words come out of her mouth, but by her smile, I think they're good words.

"This stays between me and you, but"—she leans in closer, as if someone might overhear—"it's better than Khan's."

40

Mat's head lies on my shoulder on the drive back to Khan and Ruben's. His hand is on my leg, fingers tapping to the beat of the radio.

"Your parents are okay with you staying the night with me?"

"They were pretty confident it was going to happen regardless. So they'd rather this than me sneak out in the middle of the night."

When we reach his brothers' house, they park only to drop us off, already prepared to go to Tien's and pregame for WeHo with our sisters. The two turn around to face Mat and me. Everyone in the car is certain what conversation is about to take place. They aren't oblivious to the fact that they're leaving two gay teenage boys alone in their home for at least a good six hours.

"Let's get this out of the way now," Khan says. "We all know what's about to happen in our guest bedroom tonight. Both of us were eighteen before. We know we can't change your minds, and we're not gonna try to."

"But remember the four Cs for good gay sex," Ruben adds. "Consent, cleanliness, communication, and condoms."

"Did you come up with that on the spot?" his husband asks.

"Yeah, it just came to me."

"That's brilliant. Write it down somewhere. But work in lube somehow. Because that's important too. Obviously. Maybe *condomsandlube*. Say it real quick together."

"Or how about you *lubriCANT* have good gay sex without the four Cs."

"*Yes.* That's so good, I think—"

"CAN WE LEAVE?" Mat screams at the two, who are now completely ignoring us.

"Yes, you may go," Khan replies.

"And don't forget the bag, Mat!" Ruben calls before my boyfriend slams the door. He grabs my hand, and we rush inside the house. Neither of us looks back until we've locked the front door, made it to the bedroom, and the two of us are out of sight from the world.

"What is *the bag*?"

"It's—ugh, so when I told Khan that you were coming, he and Ruben put together an *everything we'd need for sex* bag. Which is fine in that I didn't have to spend money on it. But having my brothers do it all for me was, well—"

As he describes it, he grabs an unassuming canvas bag from the closet floor and hands it to me. I immediately freeze up when I look into it.

SO MANY CONDOMS. And oh my God, that is a lot of lube. Did they rob a CVS? And what is thi—never mind. They really thought this all the way through.

It's not like this wasn't exactly what we were going to be doing. But having an entire Planned Parenthood inventory sitting in my lap is slightly more than completely overwhelming.

Mat takes a seat next to me on the bed, hand back on my leg, rubbing gently.

"Hey, we don't have to do anything you don't want to do. Yeah, we talked about tonight, but if you're realizing right now you aren't actually ready, I get it. Like Ruben's stupid ass said, the first C is consent."

"No, I do. Honestly, I *really* do. But, I don't know, I'm nervous now."

"I am too. We can take it a step at a time. And if you need to stop, tell me."

"Okay."

His hand moves from my leg to my cheek. "Can I kiss you?"

"Y-yeah. Yes. Of course."

And then from my cheek to the back of my neck, pulling me to him. The kisses are soft at first but quickly progress into hungrily making out. He pushes me down onto the bed and situates himself over me. My hands go under his T-shirt, exposing most of his upper body.

His hands travel down to my legs, encouraging me to lift and bend them up to the sides of his torso. I wrap them around his midriff, pulling him in as close as possible, feeling him rub against me.

Mat breaks our kiss. He sits up and silently stares at me.

"What?" I ask.

"Nothing," he answers before coming back and pecking at my lips. "It's just that this is a million times better than all the scenes that've played out in my head."

"Me too. But—don't stop, though."

That's all he needs to hear. Mat begins to unfasten each button on my shirt, spreading it out to get as much access to me as possible. His hands are on my skin, and then his lips and tongue travel down from my throat to my belly button.

"Fuck." It comes out just louder than a whisper. I'm not going to make it. My boyfriend is going to kill me, and he'll have to tell the police it was because of foreplay.

He starts fiddling with the button on my jeans and I grab him. "Maybe I should go to the bathroom first." Trying to think with a clear mind is difficult when there's not a lot of blood left up there. "Right? I need to, you know—"

"Oh, uh—yeah. You're cool with that?"

"Yes. Very. *Completely.* I—it'd be kind of awkward to get further and then—anyways, I'm—I'll be right back." I grab the bag from the floor and rush out of the bedroom.

I slam the bathroom door, locking it behind me, and take long, deep breaths. I stare at myself in the mirror, mentally pepping myself up. I take a small box out from the bag, open it, and remove the bottle with the long nozzle and a note from Khan and Ruben on how to use it.

I hate them.

This isn't embarrassing. This is totally natural. I repeat the words to myself. Second C is cleanliness. This isn't weird.

But, oh my God, THIS FEELS SO WEIRD.

It'd make no sense to put my jeans back on, so I walk back to the bedroom in my briefs and unbuttoned shirt, pants flung around my arm and bag in hand.

Mat stumbles through his words when he sees me come in.

"Are you good?" I ask with a smirk. Satisfied that I've managed to leave my usually bigheaded, overconfident, *always knows exactly what to say* boyfriend lost for words for once.

"I'm—I am so good. So. So—the most good," he stumbles out.

I toss my jeans aside and straddle Mat's lap, wrap my arms around his neck, and we start making out again. My breathing is becoming heavier, almost erratic, when his hands grab and begin rubbing my thighs. Then venturing up and down my chest and back. I'm hoping he doesn't feel the—completely unintentional—slight trembling happening as he travels lower, at a slow pace that's borderline torturous. When he reaches the waistband, Mat pulls down the back of my underwear, taking handfuls of newly exposed skin.

Parts of me that no one else in the world has ever known. *Only you, cariño.*

Mat pulls away, smiling as he gets some air back in his body and using the break as an opportunity to pull his own shirt up while I let mine fall behind me. He grabs me and turns us over. I tug him to me, wanting to feel his skin against mine. The beating of his heart and the rise and fall of every breath he takes.

"Fucking fuck, fuck," he mumbles in annoyance as he tries to pull off his pants. He tosses them to the floor before returning his focus to me.

He pulls my legs back up. Perfect for grinding himself onto me. The layer of fabric we each have remaining doing little to hide our excited anticipation.

"Anh yêu em," he whispers in between gentle bites on my shoulder and neck.

"También te amo," I manage to reply through moans.

He comes back up to my mouth. Kissing me like his life depends on it. Like he's making up for every kiss we missed out on the past five months.

I force myself to pull away from him, placing my hands on his chest as I catch my breath. Feeling the rapid thump of his heart.

"We're gonna start slow, right?"

"I had to wait half a year for this—we have the house to ourselves. I'm going to take my time. I won't rush even one minute of tonight. Talk to me, all right? If you want to go slower, *faster*. If I need to be gentler. *Or go harder.*"

"Shut up." I look at those light-brown eyes of his I've spent months staring at over Twitter and Instagram and FaceTime. Eyes I've been in love with since I first saw them. I graze a thumb across his lips.

I'm really here right now. With him. I'm about to do this.

"You good?" I ask.

"The most good. You?"

"Perfect."

"Yeah, you are," Mat says as he lowers his head. I can barely concentrate as his mouth goes back to the dip between my collarbones.

My hands roam his body. From his face, down to his shoulders and arms, every part of his torso, into the front of his boxer briefs. Every part of him I've patiently waited months to touch.

41

I carefully reach over Mat to grab my phone, mumbling, "Dios te salve, María, llena eres de gracia," hoping I don't wake him. How did my phone even end up on the opposite side of the bed?

My thumb taps on the lock screen to display the time. Five in the morning. It's only been two hours since I fell asleep.

Even in California. Even after a night like the one I just had, I'm still up early. I dig through my luggage for a pair of shorts, putting them on and taking quiet steps out of the room.

As I leave the bathroom, I have to hold in a scream when I see a shadowy figure that turns out to only be Ruben stumbling down the dark hallway. I almost forgot that I was in his house.

"Well, look at this fully bloomed child of God," he says with a noticeable slur to his words. "Your hair is telling some explicit stories. Didn't think you'd be awake already, ading. You walking okay?"

It's too early to acknowledge him bringing up my sexual awakening.

"Technically it's seven in Texas."

"Doesn't change what I said. Are you hungry? Do you need coffee or something?"

"No, it's fine. I'm gonna try to get a few more hours of sleep. What time did y'all get back?"

"An hour ago. *Ish.* I won't lie to you, I'm still *very* tipsy. Your sister knows how to club. Anyways, there's cereal, eggs, Pop-Tarts, whatever you want in the fridge and—what're they called? Pantries!" He chuckles to himself as he maneuvers past me into the bathroom (not without a few more stumbles).

I get back into bed and wrap an arm around Mat. My face falls into the back of his neck. When his left hand moves to cover my own, I still myself, waiting to see if I've awakened him. I'm nearly convinced that it was subconscious when I hear Mat mumble, "You're already awake?"

"I'm going back to sleep," I whisper as I leave a trail of kisses along his shoulder.

"Mm-kay." His breathing pattern calms almost immediately. He murmurs a string of words I can't understand, and I try not to laugh.

Pretty sure he's sleep talking.

I wake up again around nine. My stomach is begging for food and I'm trying my hardest to ignore it. I don't want to get out of bed and I *definitely* don't want to do anything that would require me to let go of my still-sleeping boyfriend or put clothes on.

Always being hungry is annoying.

I groan quietly as I pick myself up. Ruben mentioned cereal. That sounds good.

I take a quick trip to their kitchen, search for a bowl, milk, and Frosted Flakes, and bring it all back to bed with me. My concentration splits among the cereal, my phone, and watching Mat, who's now completely turned onto his stomach, face planted in his pillow, unbothered by my movement.

I go into my text messages. There are notifications from the group, starting with one from Lou. SO YOU GOT THE D OR WHAT CHIQUIS? And then a couple of GIFs from Jordan and Roe.

WHY ARE Y'ALL LIKE THIS?

I close out of my texts, ignoring the dings and notifications of everyone wanting to know how my first day was. Switching between

Instagram and Twitter, I look through the pictures Mat and I posted yesterday. Us leaving the airport, a video Mat took while I was still asleep before dinner, cooking with his mom, everyone at the table, me looking around his bedroom after dinner (where his dad definitely didn't almost catch us making out).

Being here, able to touch him, meet his family, actually be present in Mat's life—it all cements how real this is.

I have a boyfriend. And he's literally right next to me.

My phone starts ringing. Itzel is trying to FaceTime me. She must've gotten annoyed by my ignoring all their stupid texts. And la pendeja will keep calling if I don't answer.

I don't want to wake up Mat, so I hurry out of the bedroom, making myself comfortable on a recliner before answering.

"Are you naked?" are the first words to come out of Itzel's mouth.

"What? Estúpida, no. I'm wearing shorts. What're you doing?"

"Jordan and I are with Roe and his family in Port Aransas today. We're on the way right now." She turns the phone, giving me a view of Jordan driving and Rolie in the back seat. "Say hi, boys."

"Sounds fun."

"We figured we should try to go on with life without you."

"I'm sure it's been a difficult twenty-four hours."

"You wouldn't believe," she mocks. "Oh, we've been stalking both of y'all's socials, because you can't be bothered to keep us updated. But anyways, OMFG you two are the actual cutest."

"Luna!" I hear Jordan call from outside the screen. Itzel turns her phone again to face him. "Bro, we're all waiting to hear if your dude was all about your churro y pan dulce yet."

"You're disgusting. And you've obviously been hanging around Mexicans way too long. And, most important, we are not getting into this conversation."

"Aw, c'mon, Luna. Our baby's growing up, and we're all excited for your first time."

"First time *and* second time!" Mat shouts as he walks into the bathroom. I jump, alarmed by my now-awake boyfriend.

"What was that?" Itzel asks nosily.

"Nothing. A burglar, I think. I should go check on that. Y'all have fun in Port A. Send me Snaps!" I hang up before they see my flushed face and realize Mat's awake and he gets a chance to brag even more.

He takes my empty bowl when he enters the living room on his way to the kitchen. He comes back with a reheated bánh bao and sits on the floor, back against the recliner. I scratch his head as he bites into the roll.

"You wake up early."

"You've known this for half a year already."

"Still weird. How're you feeling?"

Like I got *just enough* sleep to be functional. Like I put my body through the world's strangest and most intimate workout. And I'm experiencing this attachment to Mat that came with everything that happened last night. It's a little frightening and incomparable to anything I've felt before.

"I'm perfect."

"Yeah, you are," he replies. "Anyways, up for Griffith Park today? Hang out around the Observatory and then hike for a while. If you aren't sore or anything from last night."

"Bet you'd be real full of yourself if that were the case."

"I mean, if I remember correctly, it was actually *you* who was full of—"

My hand swipes at the top of his head. "Stop talking." Should've seen that response coming. "It's fine; I'll survive. Whatever you want. Following your lead."

"In that case, round three first?" Mat asks as he tilts his head back as far as he can, looking at me wantonly, waiting for a reaction.

I stare back. Give him only silence. I want him to think that I'm actually having this debate with myself.

But those eyes. That bedhead. I'm weak.

I jump off the chair and run to the bedroom, Mat right behind me.

~

I'm such a tourist, taking videos and pictures as Mat drives up toward the park.

"These aren't even the cool parts of LA," he says, taking a quick glance at me when we get to a red light.

"Let me live. Every part is a cool part."

"Whatever. Hold my hand."

I let my left hand fall and feel his fingers lace between mine. My right hand keeps the phone stable, continuing to capture anything even remotely picture-worthy.

Mat parks at the Greek Theatre. From there, we take a bus up the rest of the hill, dropping us off at the Griffith Observatory. It's gorgeous. This templelike building existing in the middle of wilderness. Overlooking a city that seems to go on forever.

He takes me around to the back of the Observatory, and I know he's watching me look so awestruck as I take in Los Angeles. We continue on to the roof deck, the terraces, the promenade. It's as if every new angle is like I'm seeing the same view for the first time.

"I'm sorry for being repetitively impressed by this," I tell Mat while taking pictures of the Observatory.

He laughs, never taking his eyes off me. "It's cool. I like seeing you into this. I was kind of worried I'd end up boring you. But inside is a lot of science-y stuff, so we can skip it if you want."

"Definitely skipping. I'm not spending my spring break learning. Where to next?"

"To the trail," he declares, pointing to the hills.

My hand flinches when I feel him trying to hold it. Because even though I might not have been actively thinking about it, I'm aware that this is the first time we've done this in public without our siblings around. This is *my* first time *ever* existing hand in hand with a boyfriend, just the two of us. And I'm not so blissfully ignorant to think that Los Angeles has zero homophobes.

But I don't have the same worry that I would have in Texas. I know I'm safe with Mat and vice versa. Anywhere together, we'd be looking out for one another. And I *want* to hold his hand. To show us off.

So I do. "Come on," I tell Mat, pulling him toward one of the dirt paths.

We have lunch—and a photo shoot—at a rest stop with a view of the Hollywood sign. Some cute ones of us kissing with the sign behind us and then a few of Mat caught totally off guard. One of him holding his chicken wrap, midbite, and another of his excessively judgmental face after I joke about the Spurs being better than the Lakers.

When we reach the Mount Hollywood summit, I take a seat on one of the picnic tables at the top of the trail. Mat sits next to me. I can feel him again watching me stare at this amazing view of buildings and homes and mountains.

"I can see the ocean from here," I yell, looking toward the Pacific.

"It's one of my favorite views," Mat says. "But it's never looked better than it does today."

I turn my head to kiss him, and I entertain, very briefly, the idea that no one else is up here right now and that this picnic table seems pretty sturdy.

"Thank you for bringing me here."

"Thank you for letting me."

42

What happens if Loyola Marymount doesn't work out?"

I'd been able to get through almost an entire day and a half without thinking about it. Out of sight and out of mind. Entirely happy.

But now, here I am, interrupted from enjoying the best burrito I've ever had in my life, thanks to Danny Trejo (who knew the same person in *Machete* could also do some surprisingly great vegetarian Mexican food?). Forced to consider, *What if everything I've hoped for comes crashing down tomorrow?*

"Do we have to do this right now?"

"Look, I get that this isn't something either of us wants to get into, but I—" Mat holds my hand. He's biting his lip, looking down at our table. "This has all been so perfect. Yesterday, last night, today. But tomorrow—be honest with me, all right. If you come back tomorrow realizing LMU isn't gonna happen, what then?"

I shake my head and push back the sadness I'm feeling as much as I can. It only takes *thinking* about the what-ifs to make this entire day start spiraling downward.

"Being realistic, I go to UT."

"And then?"

"What do you mean, *and then*? I stay in Texas. Let Austin be my consolation prize, I guess. I've thought it over, and the idea of going to a community college for a year and trying again isn't something I could do. I don't want to be continually rejected. I can't—"

He's understanding. I know he was waiting for me to say it. Letting me be the one who puts this ultimatum into the universe. Tell him what *and then* is.

And then that's it. We admit that fate had other plans for us. We figure out how to go on. I stay mad at God for a long while.

"I wouldn't want you to," Mat says. "I wouldn't want you to put yourself through that. Especially if UT's where you're supposed to be. If you're meant to stay in Texas. I don't want to be a reason you hold yourself back from happiness."

I hate this entire conversation. That we're putting these *what-ifs* out into the universe. Giving actual thought into breaking up.

And that Mat sounds ready to do so. As if he's already given up.

"I—I can't do this right now."

I stand up and walk off, toward the gate at the patio and then the sidewalk. I need air. Okay, not really. I mean, we were already outside. I need to not be surrounded by people.

Which is a little hard in the second-largest city in the country.

I hear Mat's voice, calling out "babe." But I keep walking. Not because I need to get away from him. But if I stop walking, I'm going to start thinking.

"Jules," he yells as he grabs my arm. "Where are you going?"

"I don't know. But—I don't want to talk about tomorrow." Whatever eye muscles keep me from crying are quickly giving up. Cool. In the middle of Los Angeles. Super normal.

"Maybe if this trip had never happened. If all I ever knew of us was existing between screens, then it wouldn't be as bad. But here we are. More than anything I was ever prepared for, and—I can't have this on my mind. Now that I have you right in front of me. After kissing you for the first time. After last night. I—"

He grabs me tightly, and I hold him too. Remembering how he told me he was never letting me go. And I want so badly for that to be true.

"I'm sorry," he says. Mat's eyes are red. He's a lot better at keeping the tears locked up than I am. "I'm scared. Really scared. And feeling a little selfish. Trying to fight my want for you to stay with me, even though I know you have to do what's best for you. But—whatever happens, we'll get through it. Together."

I look at him and wipe a tear falling down his cheek. Maybe he's not as good at holding it in as I thought.

We really got ourselves into the best worst idea in the history of the world.

"I wish today could pause. Just for us."

Mat kisses me. And it almost does feel like time stops as we stand here, kissing on some Los Angeles sidewalk.

Until a car driving by us honks and some girl hanging out the back window yells, "Yas, gay rights!"

Way to ruin the moment.

We laugh, our lips still touching, not ready to let go yet. But when we do, and I look up into the evening sky, I see the moon and the sun. Together. Sharing the same sky.

And I know that, no matter what, we'll be all right.

I hope.

"I have an idea," Mat says. "Now that you got us out here." He grabs my hand and leads us up La Brea Avenue. A few blocks north and then we turn onto Wilshire Boulevard.

He's looking for something specific. His head goes back and forth at the different signs and businesses. And then he points to a place a couple of buildings down.

"Here it is," Mat announces. **BOBASAUR KARAOKE**.

"Wait, we—"

"C'mon," he says as he pulls me in. "It's the only under twenty-one karaoke bar in the city."

"Why are we here?"

"Why not?" he replies. He ignores my hesitant, reluctant looks and turns to the cashier to get us a room. Mat hands her his debit card; we're given a room number and then told to walk down the hall.

It's a small room. A green sectional, glass table in the middle, and large flat-screen TV on the wall. The lights flash and flicker to the beat of the techno music playing.

The cashier comes in with two bubble teas. Almost too peppy as she goes over how to pick a song and how to call for someone. "No questions? Love it! You two are adorable. Have fun!"

Mat scoots as close to me as possible, grabbing my hand again. "I realize that I forced us to consider some crappy things, and maybe we weren't ready for it yet. I'm sorry. Let's—I'm fine with ignoring this for the rest of today and tonight. No more mentioning tomorrow. Only you and me and right now."

"You think *karaoke* is the best way to do that?"

"Yeah." He smiles, grabbing the remote. "It's silly, right? And kinda intimate. And good for getting our minds off *things*. I don't know."

I smile back. And it turns into a laugh.

"Sure. I've only ever done this on video games, though. So you pick a song first."

"How about," he starts as he types, "we do one together first? Get any nerves outta the way."

He clicks on "Dance to This." Great choice.

"I call Troye's part," I yell as I grab a microphone.

"Would've thought you'd go straight for your girl Ariana's verses."

"Shh," I tell him just in time for the vocals to start.

I stand up. Because how do you sing this song while sitting? And I start dancing in front of him while singing. Ignoring all the fears that were stampeding through my mind until they're forgotten. Doing my best Troye Sivan impersonation.

He comes in at the refrain and then goes into Ariana's verse. We dance together and sing. And laugh. And kiss.

And it's perfect.

Mat picks "I Wanna Dance with Somebody" as the next song. I guess we're going with a theme tonight. He's way too cute, getting real into it. Doing these stupid little shoulder moves to the beat of the beginning.

It'll be hard to pick a better song.

"Don't pay attention to the lyrics," I tell him as I type. "It's an anthem, and we're gonna go with it."

"Whatever you say."

I pick Robyn's "Dancing on My Own." Again, the words aren't important. She's a gay icon who can do whatever she wants.

Plus, I've sung this song hundreds of times while washing dishes. I got this.

And I might have ended the song on my boyfriend's lap. Because, damn it, *I'm* gonna be the guy he's taking home. I know the same thought went through both our minds. Wondering how far we could get before someone sees us.

We sing through "Baila Esta Cumbia," "Dance, Dance," and "Lose Yourself to Dance" before tiring ourselves out. Share a cup of matcha green tea ice cream. And for the last ten minutes we have the booth, I rest my head on Mat's leg while we let random instrumentals play in the background.

I don't say it. We said we wouldn't talk about it anymore, so I keep it to myself.

But if this is the last time I'll look at Los Angeles fondly, as a place where I could be and not as a place that might turn me away and break my heart, then fine. If these are the last few hours I can hold on to my dreams and my boyfriend and the memories we've made with any kind of happiness, I can make peace with that. Because this is as good as I could've hoped for.

And this is exactly how I'd want it to end.

43

I don't want this to end.

As I get dressed, I can't stop thinking how this is my one shot at being in Los Angeles next year. My one shot at leaving Texas behind and all the struggles and triggers there.

I said I was cool with yesterday being where it all ends for me, but I need to redact that. I was kidding. I didn't mean any of it.

I take one final sixty seconds to lie next to Mat, scratching the back of his head and trailing my hand down his back. Glad he's not awake. I wouldn't know what to say to him.

The drive to Loyola Marymount is pretty much the same route Khan took from the airport, only the other direction. My mind drifts for most of the car ride as Tien and Xo relive the past couple of nights and start planning where they want to go today.

I wrap my hand around my San Óscar pendant. *Call in whatever saintly favors you have. I need this to work out.*

Tien turns onto the main road into the university. The large Loyola Marymount sign and fountain on either side of the street greet us. *I'm excited. I'm excited. I won't hate this.*

We find a nearby parking space and walk the rest of the way, following directions given to me by the admissions counselor I'd been emailing. It's a small, homey campus, half the size of the university in Corpus and a few thousand less students.

At least I wouldn't get lost here.

We arrive at a small lobby, where a receptionist offers a seat on the couch while she finds our guide. I'm texting Itzel when I hear footsteps approaching and a guy's voice saying, "Good morning! You must be Julián."

I stand up and shake the outstretched hand of my tour guide.

"I'm Tristan." He has a strong grip. "Welcome to LMU, and—I guess—welcome to California too, right?"

"Yeah." I'm sure I sound nervous, as hard as I'm trying to seem chill.

"I'll be showing you around. Hopefully convince you that this is the *best school ever*, and don't think I'm above treating you to Jamba Juice as persuasion. Then we'll come back if you need to talk to someone in financial aid or whoever, and we can get you a meeting. You ready?"

"Sure." As ready as I'll ever be. "Let's get started."

Xo and Tien let me go by myself, waving bye as Tristan leads me outside and goes right into it. He mixes rehearsed lines with personal stories on different buildings and areas around the university. I get introduced to a few of his friends we cross paths with during the tour. Most of them fraternity brothers. At least, that's what I assume from their shirts with embroidered letters that remind me of Xo's.

"Are there any LGBT groups here?"

"The Gender-Sexuality Alliance is the main one. And there are a couple of social justice clubs that get involved in gay and trans issues. LMU tries to be pretty inclusive with identities. They have Instagrams, I think, if you want to look them up. And we actually have a Student Services office solely for LGBT students. Which is pretty cool, in my opinion. We can swing by there while we're out."

I spend the whole morning following Tristan around campus. He takes me to the LGBT Student Services Center so I can meet the director, we run into a sociology professor and end up getting to talk with her for nearly twenty minutes about classes and "oh yeah, double majoring with Chicanx studies would be great for you" and where my head's at about my future career ("truthfully, not really sure yet"), and then we go to the edge of the school, on a walking path with views of Los Angeles and the mountains, and even though I just got the best views of the city I could've asked for yesterday, I'm still floored.

Maybe it's a different school than I've always imagined, but standing on this bluff, sunshine and the soft breeze against my skin, the only thought that comes to mind is that I'm here. I've arrived. I've made it.

And there can't be any going back.

~

"Your name is Ram? Like the goat?" I ask the financial aid counselor after he introduces himself. He turns around and glances at me with a confused look.

"A ram is actually a male sheep. But sure." He offers me a chair and falls into his own, spinning to his computer. "So how'd you enjoy the tour?"

"It was . . . everything I could have hoped for. I got a lot of information from Tristan and felt really at home walking around."

"Love that." He's still staring at his monitor, clicking and typing. He must have an unbelievable WPM rate. "Tristan enjoys being thorough," he says with a hint of annoyance. "He could go on and on about this school for days. It can be a hit or miss with you guys. And it's your first time in Los Angeles?"

"Yes. First time on a plane too."

"Exciting," he says, almost in a songlike way. "Liking the city?"

"So much. It's only been a couple of days, but yeah. I love it."

He toggles among the countless windows covering his computer screen. "Sorry, I'm listening. Getting your information here. Excellent student. Ranked ninth in your class. No wonder we want you. Where else did you apply?"

"UCLA and USC and the University of Texas, Saint Edwards in Austin and Texas A&M back home."

"What kind of money are the other area schools giving you?"

"I actually wasn't accepted into either of the other LA colleges." My voice drops in volume. The remorse over getting rejected is not going to stop stinging for a while.

"That's confusing." Ram looks back at the screen. "Either they're seeing something we're missing completely or, I don't know. Admittance rates can be a bitch, I suppose. Sorry—pretend I didn't say that." He turns back around to face me, pages that he's printed in front of him on his desk.

"You realize we accepted you into our honors program, yes?"

"Do—wait, what now?"

"It's part of one of your scholarships. If you didn't know, you do now, but—all I'm saying is, if you've pulled a fast one on us, good job. Anyways, thoughts on your award package?"

"I'm still waiting on private scholarships," I reply. "Even with what y'all've given me, it still leaves a lot. But my sister and abuelo think it should be doable."

"And your father? He's the one we have listed with your records and your FAFSA."

"He's out of the picture now. Or, I guess, he forced me out of his picture."

"So your living situation is—"

"With my sister."

He's silent. Reading me. Trying to process the situation.

I hadn't noticed until now, but his bag behind him has a small Pride flag pin attached to it. Hopefully he gets what I'm saying without needing to actually spell it out for him.

"I'm trying not to be an asshole," he starts. "But at least right now, with your father tied to how much aid you qualify for, you may be better off at an in-state school for a year. Until we can help you apply for financial assistance yourself. And a school like UT, of course, comes with name recognition that we don't have. Unless you're *really into Catholicism*. It's something to consider."

"I get that. But—this has been the dream. Not necessarily LMU, but now it's the one option I have of going somewhere. Doing something new."

"And that's important to you?"

"It's all I want. It's been my obsession for years. And since I came out in September, and with the drama between my dad and me—" I stumble over the last part, not wanting to get emotional in front of someone I've only known for not even fifteen minutes. "Some kids grow up wanting to be in New York or, I don't know, Paris or Washington, DC. This has always been where I've wanted to be. I can't imagine myself anywhere else."

Ram's been nodding and taking in my words with silent intensity. He turns back to his monitor, again clicking through windows. I watch him making notes and calculations before he spins back around to face me.

"Hold on for me, all right?" he says as he gets out of his chair, not waiting for me to answer before he's power walking out the door. A couple of minutes later, Xo's following him in and taking the seat next to me.

Ram taps on his keyboard a few more times, and after a couple more mouse clicks, his head is pointed up at us. "One option I have right now is what we call an early deposit scholarship. If you can manage to make a deposit to the school *this week*—and I'll take your word for it right now—we can provide an extra four thousand annually, contingent on continued academic achievement."

Xo and I look at each other, thinking the same thing. *Is that possible for us?*

"We can do that," she tells him. "Just let me know how much is needed, and we'll have it in by the end of the week."

"Perfect." Ram goes back to typing. "We'll hope for those nonuniversity scholarships to come in as well, and worst-case scenario, because the deposit is coming in before the decision deadline, if you end up having to go somewhere else, we can work out getting it refunded. I'll take care of it. I only say that because I don't think I'd be doing my job of adequately preparing you for the horror that can be paying for college—*any college*—if I didn't tell you that you might want to have a backup plan. A public, *in-state* backup plan."

"No." The word comes out quicker than my ability to think about what I'm saying.

"'Lito," Xo snaps, her eyes daggering into me.

My left foot starts tapping, making my whole leg shake. My arms cross, and I try to look anywhere besides Ram or my sister. "I wish just one person with some authority over my life could tell me, *Yes, you're good; you win; welcome to your best life, Julián Luna.* Can everyone take a break from being realists and ruining any good coming into my life? Just for a day. *Please.*"

"I have a lot of kids come by with similar situations. Lives that have been tough but they're somehow so capable of achieving greatness. So many of us wouldn't survive a day in your shoes. And I say that as someone who wants to give you and everyone like you the world but knows I can't. That I'm going to let some of you down and be added to the long list of people in your lives who've already done so. But I'm going to try my best, and I hope you'll walk out of here knowing at least that.

"I'd like to talk to your sister privately, if that's okay with you," Ram continues, bringing my head up from staring at the floor. "There's some information I can give her to help plan for what your out-of-pocket cost might accurately look like, and I want to make sure that she leaves with my number. I'm not giving up, all right? So you don't either. I am *not* going to be the one blamed for a potential honors student having to decline an offer because of finances. If you decide on UT even after we've done all we can, then I wish you the best, and if you get something from, say, Harvard or Stanford, then by all means go. No hard feelings. But you've put in the effort, come from a diverse background, seem pretty resilient, and if this is where you want to be, then I want to see you succeed here."

"This is," I reply. "This is where I want to be."

44

Well?" Mat asks excitedly while hugging me as soon as we get to Khan's truck, BANH | BUN | BOY, to have lunch with him and Ruben. "You're gonna be an Angeleno?"

I turn to Xo, waiting for her to hint at whether Ram gave her any better news than he gave me.

"It's looking promising," she tells him. "So I need you to make sure this one stays optimistic. Good thoughts only."

"Got it." He doesn't let go of me until we get to one of the picnic tables near the truck, and even after that, he tries his best to eat a bánh mì with one hand while his other stays around my waist. It's not successful. At all.

My eyes widen when I take my first bite of the sandwich.

The tofu is marinated in some kind of sauce that's honestly better than their mom's. If Khan invented it, this proves he's a genius. The pickled vegetables, cilantro, jalapeños. The bread. I'd never heard of bánh mìs before meeting Mat and never had one until today. Now I'm mad at myself for taking eighteen years to discover them.

"Khan, this is amazing!" I shout.

"Thanks, Jules," he replies. "I can teach you how to make them before you leave. Super easy."

"It's no torta, but he does all right," Ruben remarks. Khan kicks his leg, telling him that he's not above divorcing his husband over irreconcilable differences.

Leave. I don't know how to feel about that word. What should I be feeling?

It's something that I'd like to believe holds only temporary meaning. I have to go back to Texas, but once I graduate and get through those few months of summer, I'll be back. Right?

I have to focus on a future where I'm living here. Where I get to come back to LMU, bánh mì, and Mat. Where I never have to be anyone else other than me. Where the culmination of my dreams, ambitions, wants, and strides forward don't all trip over themselves because I've hit a dead end.

I'll be back.

I hope.

~

"Hey, sleepyhead," Mat says when I wake up on the couch. He's sitting on the floor, playing some Link game on his Switch, but takes a brief pause, long enough to turn his head and whine, "Lemme kiss," until I lean forward to meet his lips.

"You got a few texts and missed calls." He hands me my phone and I scroll through messages of TELL ME HOW YOUR VISIT WENT and so is LMU official now? from my friends. A missed call and voice mail from Güelo. Lots of likes and comments on my IG post of pictures Xo took of me at Loyola Marymount.

This time yesterday, I expected to have a clear yes or no answer for them. I could say *yep, I'll be in California for college!* and start preparing myself to leave my friends and family and figuring out how to say goodbye. Or I could say *no, my entire life plan came crashing down today* and spend the rest of the week on the phone with Itzel processing the grief and end up okay with knowing that at least I'd be going to school with her and Lou.

I can't say either. I can tell them that it's not no *yet*. That visiting campus was amazing and if I don't get to go, getting that glimpse of what my life could've been is going to make this hurt a thousand times more. Turns out this is going to be a lot more complicated and far less black-and-white than I'd like it to be.

All I know is I'm not ready to leave Los Angeles yet. I'm not ready to leave Mat. To go home and have to wait and figure this out without being able to grab his hand and feel all the fears disappear when I touch his skin.

"How long was I asleep for?"

"A couple hours, maybe. But you were up early this morning, so I let you rest."

"And you keep me up late," I tell him accusingly.

"Oh yeah. It was definitely *only* me who had us up until three. You didn't seem super concerned with your *time differences* when I was—"

He yells when I hit him with a pillow. "Te lo sico, smart-ass."

Ruben comes out of his bedroom with a bag of clothes and a bottle of vodka, whistling something that resembles "Toxic."

"All right, adings. Khan and I will be having dinner with your sisters and returning to WeHo. I'm sure you're both *incredibly disappointed* that we'll be leaving you alone for the night again." Both of us attempt to agree but convince no one. "Pray for our livers, Jules. Mat, be good. And boys," he says teasingly as he exits the house, "try to take some time to wash the sheets."

We look at each other, trying not to laugh.

Doesn't work.

"We can do that later. Right now, what do you want for dinner?" Mat asks as he takes a seat on the couch. I rest my feet and calves on his legs. "We could go somewhere or make something here."

"Let's cook something. I'll raid their kitchen and see what we're working with."

I'm able to come up with a few ideas. We go to Ralphs to buy some pita bread and the remaining ingredients needed for falafel, tzatziki, and a feta salad. Setting everything on his brothers' kitchen counter, ready to get all domestic.

When Mat's mom said he wasn't the greatest kitchen helper, she was a hundred percent accurate. But we manage. He's at least able to roll the chickpea mixture into mostly similar-size balls.

And I don't know if it's because I'm with him or it's the bottle of whiskey we found in his brothers' freezer (and are hoping they won't notice is now missing), but I'm sure I've never made anything this good before.

45

The rest of the week flies by.

On Tuesday, I meet Mat's friends at an LAFC soccer game. Afterward, we walk around the Arts District (and my Instagram aesthetic has never looked better). Then to Boyle Heights for the biggest bean-and-cheese burrito I've ever seen in my life.

Coming into their circle feels natural. Even though I'd technically already met them before, I still felt like the new one going into it. They're all pretty foolish, and there's more joking and shade throwing than anyone could keep up with. Not that I don't love my group, but spending a day with pretty much all queer teenagers is a little bit revolutionary.

"You excited to finally be leaving Texas?" Garrett asks. I catch Mat glaring at him, like this was on their list of *things not to bring up in front of everyone because reasons.*

I put a hand on my boyfriend's leg and give him a small smirk. "I—um, I will be."

We watch the sunset at Dockweiler Beach, huddled around a firepit. I lean back on Mat, sitting on the sand between his legs. A serape drapes around him and onto me, keeping us warm in the cold West Coast evening.

We toast marshmallows and make s'mores. Talk and laugh even more with his friends. Sing along and dance to the music blaring in the background from all the other groups using pits.

This will need to be a regular thing in the fall.

Wednesday, Mat takes me to LACMA. We have an impromptu photo shoot with the streetlamps in front of the museum before walking through what must be hundreds of exhibits. Then he takes me around Hollywood, where I start fangirling *hard* when we find Selena's star on the boulevard and make him take tons of photos of me with it.

On Thursday we start at Mat's favorite museum, the Broad. Works by Jeff Koons and Andy Warhol are on display, plus the coolest part, infinity-mirror rooms. Walls and a small path that goes to the middle of the room are mirrored, the rest of the floor covered with water, and a countless number of lights hang from the ceiling, everything reflecting off each other.

We stay downtown for the day, going to Mat's favorite ramen shop, then Olvera Street, the city's cathedral, and a bookstore that doubles as an art installation. He watches as I walk around in awe of a tunnel made entirely of carefully placed books.

On Friday, I wake up to Mat on top of me, shaking my shoulders.

"Why are you up already?" I ask, still half-asleep.

"It's Venice and Santa Monica day! And it's sunny! Hurry and get ready so we can go."

By the time I make myself look presentable, slip on a pair of swim shorts, and put on a short-sleeve button-up, he's waiting in the living room with a backpack full of snacks and a few towels in his arms. He rushes me out the door, in a hurry to get the day started. As if the knowledge that our time together is approaching its end is compelling us to get as much in as we can.

The Venice Beach Boardwalk is full of life and energy and little bits of everything and everyone imaginable. Like he's been doing all week, Mat watches me take it all in. Sometimes he mentions something about the different street vendors and performers but otherwise lets me observe and lightly swings our hands.

We stop by a table where a woman inscribes each of our names onto a grain of rice. She drops the grain and a miniature flower into a vial filled with oil, then knots it onto a necklace. Mat gives me the necklace with his name, and I give him the one with mine.

It's super cheesy. But I'm never taking this necklace off.

I pull him toward the sand after I've seen enough of the boardwalk. I'm ecstatic for this. The water looks so pretty. And even though we'd spent time at a different beach earlier in the week, I've yet to actually go into the ocean.

So I rush forward, excited that I finally get to dive into the Pacific—

Only to immediately recoil back onto the sand as soon as my foot touches the water. Yelling a bunch of *chinga'o*s and *pinche*s. It's *freezing.* How do people get in there?

Mat jogs over, laughing, wrapping his arms around me. "Too cold for you?" he teases.

"Why is it like that?" I reply. "How do you people just jump in? It's not normal."

"Mm, you get used to it." His eyes squint like he's thinking. "I know a good method."

I knew I should have been suspicious of his hug. But I catch on too late. I'm trapped in his grip as he carries me back to the water—ignoring my yells—and falls into the ocean with me. Submerging both of us in intensely cold water.

"You're really asking to be single again, Mat Pham," I say as I take his hand and shake the excess water from my hair. He can't stop laughing, even as he tugs me in and pecks at my salty cheek.

"Give it a minute and you'll be good."

"I don't think so. It's not—" A wave knocks us both back into the water before I can finish my sentence.

And the water might not seem *that cold* anymore. It might have worked, *maybe.*

But I'm not giving Mat that victory.

After getting our asses kicked by a few more waves, I take my boyfriend's hand and lead him back to the sand. The sun against my skin is healing, already warming me up. Mat passes me a Topo Chico and a bag of Takis, hogging the dried mango slices for himself.

We spend the next hour lazing on the beach. Mat rests his head on my thigh, his fingers lightly tracing secret messages onto a palm he's pulled to his chest until he falls asleep. Should've known him waking up early would mean he'd eventually need a nap.

I watch the waves come in and people walking around. And my boyfriend, looking like an entire meal in his seafoam-green swim shorts. My hand stays resting on his chest, subconsciously counting the beats of his heart, while his hand keeps ahold of mine.

"Agh," Mat groans groggily when he wakes up, rubbing his eyes. "Didn't mean to do that. You ready to move on?"

"Sure. Where to next?"

He sits up and points to a Ferris wheel in the distance. "There. Santa Monica."

He jogs over to the electric scooters lined along the bike path. "I'll race you."

"Okay," I reply, grabbing one of the scooters. "But don't get mad when I beat you."

The beach, the cool SoCal air, the sun providing a perfect amount of heat, Mat's smile, and then his *pretending to be bothered* face when I beat him to the pier. I've had a million *I don't want this to end* moments all week, but all this might be near the top of that list.

Mat grabs my hand when we reach the amusement park, making sure we don't lose each other in the crowd of people moving in every direction as we enter. It's like a rodeo carnival jutting into the Pacific Ocean.

The roller coaster is the first thing to catch my attention, and I immediately drag him to the entrance. Then the bumper cars and a dragon swing. And finally, this ride where you sit inside a spinning shark head that's like those teacups at Disneyland.

After going through all the rides, we share cotton candy, walking in view of the carnival games. I catch Mat staring at a few.

"I bet I can win more of these games than you," I taunt.

He's immediately intrigued. "Someone's feeling confident. You're gonna lose so bad, babe."

Our competitive sides come out immediately. I win the water-gun race and the penalty-kick game. Mat beats me at the Wiffle ball and basketball tosses.

"Whac-A-Mole as a tiebreaker?" he suggests, leading us over to the foam mallets.

It's an intense game. I take an early lead, not letting any of the moles escape. But then they start getting faster, and I notice Mat getting ahead.

Too ahead.

I push him right as his hammer is coming down on a mole and he almost trips.

Worth it.

"Cheater," he yells, trying his best to get back into his groove.

"Street rules," I tell him, now regaining my advantage.

I'm too busy dominating this game to see his outstretched arm. All of a sudden, his hand is covering my eyes. "Street rules," Mat says back to me, not letting his hand down for the rest of the game. Even when my mallet swings at his stomach.

Didn't help, though. In the end, the score wasn't even close. And I make sure to boast about it every chance I get as we continue walking around the park.

The sun is beginning to set along the ocean's horizon when we make it to the Ferris wheel. The view is unbeatable. Especially of Mat, who's nothing short of beautiful in the golden hour. I lay my head on his shoulder, and he places his own on top of mine. When our pod pauses at the very top of the wheel, I get lost in the unmatched view of the ocean that goes on forever. The sun submerging itself into the water.

And when our cart starts moving again, I hold Mat's face as I kiss him. And we keep kissing all the way down.

This is it. This, right here, tops my *I don't want this to end* list.

And hopefully it won't have to.

~

Mat and I lie side by side, looking straight up at the night sky. Santa Monica Beach is nearly empty. The only other people remaining are a good distance away from us. Neither of us has said anything for a while, preferring to listen to the sound of the waves.

"Thank you," he finally says.

"For what?" I turn my head to face Mat, who is still staring at the sky.

"For everything. For taking what had to be one of the most terrifying experiences of your life and rising above it. For embracing yourself. For trusting me to be your friend. For making what has to be the stupidest decision you've ever made letting some kid you've never met, who lives fifteen hundred miles away, call himself your boyfriend."

"You made that same decision," I tell him.

"Yeah, but if I were in your shoes, I don't know if I could have been as brave or as strong as you were. As you are."

"You sure do enjoy pretending that you are."

"Don't ruin my speech. You know I'm not, though. Virgo tendencies. But I had my doubts. I mean, we've both felt that way. We've talked about it before. There were days where it took real effort to convince myself that we were, I guess, valid. But when I saw you outside the airport, and I got to kiss you, touch you, hold you, look into your eyes, tell you I love you, fall asleep and wake up next to you, I—I'd never felt more certain of anything in my life."

"You know you can talk to me about the shitty stuff more often, cariño. Don't think you have to seem indomitable all the time."

"You've had a lot on your plate," he responds. "I didn't want to pile on more."

I'll give him that. But from now on, I'm going to make sure he knows I'm here for him. Next time, he can be the one with the chaotic life.

"What—when you had those doubts, how'd you get past them?"

"Talking to you helped. Hearing your voice was—is—therapeutic. Oh. I—this is gonna sound really weird—but I'd look at the moon."

"Like, the actual moon?"

"Yes, Jules, the *actual* moon. *Ass*," Mat replies. "It makes me think of you. When it was really bright, it was almost as if those were the nights you knew I was struggling, regardless of whether I'd mentioned it or not. And you were sending me a signal, screaming, *I'm right here, stupid!*"

I sit up, remaining quiet. Digesting his explanation. "You're right. That was weird."

"Shut up, dick," Mat replies. He turns onto his side, pulling me back down. Throwing an arm and leg over me. "I don't know if you remember, but there was a full moon the night we got together. I had been grappling with whether I should come clean. And I almost decided on keeping how I felt to myself. But when I saw it staring at me, I knew I had to. Plus, I didn't want you kissing any more boys unless they were me."

"Kinda possessive, no?"

"More determined." He turns my head with his hands and kisses me. "You're my moonlight, Julián Luna. A brightness in the dark. I knew if I kept trying, one day I'd reach out and you'd be there. You'd be here."

I look up at my boyfriend, thinking of when I first liked his senior pictures six and a half months ago. That were taken only a couple of miles from where we're at right now. Half a country away from where I was.

And how every choice I've made since then has led me here. With him. With @sunnysideup213.

"Then you're my sunshine, Mặt Trời Pham. Since the day I met you, when I would wake up feeling scared, anxious, or alone, you've been my warmth and clarity. I'm lucky you found me."

"I'm lucky you finally allowed yourself to be seen."

46

I need—I want to tell you something."

"Okay," Mat answers. "What's up?"

His fingers trail lazily up and down my spine. After a Saturday filled with walking around the neighborhood, Mat showing me some bōjutsu, a final dinner with his family and friends, and then coming back to Ruben and Khan's for my last night with my boyfriend, I'm feeling great. Loved. Never better.

A lot of me would rather I just forget about saying anything.

Too late. We're already here. Mat's waiting for me to start speaking. For the words to unclog themselves from my stomach and throat.

The mattress makes quiet squeaks as he scoots himself closer to me, and one of his arms falls over my body. Properly situating himself as a big spoon.

"I, um. I don't know how to start."

I'm glad I'm not facing Mat. It'd make getting this all out even more difficult. I grab ahold of his hand and grip it tightly as my eyes already start reacting.

"There are some parts of myself that I kept from you. That I didn't want you knowing about because—because it felt like a lot to put on you. Even though I've known for a long time that I needed to let you in on it eventually. On what my life has been. Not because I expect you to fix it or *put me back together*. But . . . you deserve to know the crappy parts of me. And I want you to know those parts. I trust you."

I start from the beginning. From the first moments I felt scared for being someone and something my dad hated. The first time I ever worried that who I might be was wrong.

I tell Mat about moments that no one else in the world knows about. And whenever I have to take a minute, he doesn't push me to keep going. He squeezes me. Reassures me. Cries with me.

I go through all the times I wished for a different future. Thought that there was no way I'd ever be where I am now. Prayed for something in me to change. And all the times I contemplated doing something myself. Making a choice that would allow me to never have to confront who I am.

I recall all the recent memories and talk about how there are many more that are blacked out. The details my mind has managed to erase from existence but the pain that I can still place. Those are the scariest.

The time he found Jordan and me lying on my bed together. When he found out I wore nail polish at homecoming and why I didn't dress up for Halloween. All of it.

When I'm done, I turn around. Look into Mat's sad, reddened eyes.

"I love you," he says. "And thank you for telling me."

I nod and sniffle. I think I may be out of words to say.

"I—I'm glad you're here right now. That you're safe. And alive. And I know that you have all the willpower and determination to get through anything in life, Jules. But I hope you know now that you can tell me anything. Always. Everyone needs somebody, and I want to be your somebody. I want to be your person. And I want you to be mine."

I nod again. "I want that too."

He kisses me and then moves down to my neck. The front and back of my shoulders. My arms. Wrists. All the places that have known pain and bruising and hurt.

I know that Mat can't heal me. That he can't erase it all with his lips. But he can make me feel not alone in this world. He can replace those memories with moments like these.

He can be my person, and I can be his.

I want to always remember this. I *need* to remember this.

I need to remember what it is to look into his eyes and feel his presence. How his body feels against mine. What he tastes like. I need to remember how soft his lips are. I need to remember how his tongue feels against my own, how I lose my mind when it explores my skin. I need to remember how he feels inside me, how his hands feel enveloping me.

And the way he says "anh yêu em" between exhausted breaths afterward.

I need to remember how he makes me feel alive.

~

Mat takes a seat next to me on the curb outside of California Donuts, holding out an open, clear plastic container. I grab my horchata-glazed doughnut before he takes out a Fruity Pebbles one. And *oh my God*, when he said this is where to get the best doughnuts in Los Angeles, I thought he was exaggerating, but no. That might actually be underselling these.

"Why did you wait until my last night here to take me? These are *so good*."

"We'll have plenty of doughnut date nights in the fall. Don't worry."

The lights from the shop. Sitting on a sidewalk at two a.m. Hearing some drunk girl tell her *definitely not entirely but for sure more sober* friends which doughnuts she wants before adding that she needs to find a corner to pee and sprinting away and then watching one of them chase after her while the other looks completely done with existence all feels very aesthetically Los Angeles. This—after the week of landmarks and museums and touristy things—is the real pinnacle of life in LA.

"I don't want to go home."

"I'm cool with keeping you here forever." Mat scoots closer to me, getting rid of any space that existed between our bodies. "Look, I know that everything's gonna work out and you'll be at LMU in August and we'll be the cutest couple in all of Los Angeles and every week will be as great as this one was."

"But?"

"But . . . if that doesn't happen, I don't want this to end. When I said I wanted you, Jules, I meant it, knowing that distance would be a part of the deal. And it hasn't always been easy, but easy would be boring. Not having you in my life would be boring. I'm not ready to let you go."

"I'm not ready to let you go either."

"But," he repeats, "everything's gonna work out."

"I know. I believe you."

Mat's eyes focus on me. Much like both of us have been doing all week. Moments where the act of being able to look at my boyfriend next to me have been a thing I have thanked God for.

Taking another bite of doughnut, I think about a question in my head before asking it out loud. Unsure of what my own answer would be.

"Do you think the distance will be easier or harder now?"

"Easier," Mat answers. "The morning is gonna suck. I've honestly never been happier than I have been the past seven days, and I'm not thrilled it's ending. But until you're back—which you will be—I can always text, or FaceTime you, or replay the memories from this week in my head. That'll happen a lot. And in my dreams too."

"Continue existing as a come-to-life version of Selena's 'Dreaming of You' for a little while longer?"

"Exactly."

I hear him mumble something after, but he's too quiet for me to get the words clearly.

"What'd you say?"

"I'm thinking of that Frida Kahlo poem." He takes my hand and kisses my palm. "The one that's like, you should have someone who doesn't mind if you're messy, and who will make you feel safe against all the things that keep you awake. Who will take on the world with you, hand in hand. And who, every time we hug, will remind you that this—*us*—was meant to be."

"You know that poem?" I ask. I think I might be more in love with and turned on by my boyfriend than I've ever been up to now.

"Don't get too hyped. If I really concentrated, I could probably say how it actually goes, but only that part. And only in English."

"I'll teach you the whole thing in Spanish when I get back if you teach me Vietnamese."

"It's a date."

47

Lito," Xochi calls. My name soaked with sympathy.

I haven't let go of Mat for what has to be at least five minutes. "Sixty more seconds," I whine. Too quietly for her to hear me.

I want to tell her to go on without me. Mail me my diploma. *I'll see you in December.*

"I'm still not against never going back," I tell Mat.

"Say the word and we'll start running."

I groan into his shoulder and squeeze him one more time. "I'll be back in five months."

He tilts my chin up to kiss me. "You will. And I'll be right here waiting for you. Let me know when you get back to Texas. Anh yêu em, Moonlight."

"También te amo, Sunshine."

I say goodbye to Khan and Ruben. Grab on to Mat a little longer. Hoping that I can blink and it'll magically be August and this is actually me returning to Los Angeles and everything in my life has worked itself out for the first time in eighteen years.

Don't get too emotional, I repeat to myself while walking into the airport. *Don't look back,* I repeat in my head even louder. *You're going to be a big gay mess if you look back.*

I do, though. I look back. And I see Mat looking back too.

And—shit. I'm a big fucking gay mess.

~

Güelo is waiting outside the airport when we arrive back in Corpus Christi. He hugs us and begins asking for every detail of the trip as he helps with our luggage. He wants to know every sight I saw, place visited, and (especially) how the novio is. Xo drives so I can show him photos of downtown, museums, beaches, and park trails. He takes it all in with unbroken concentration.

"¿Qué es esto?" Güelo asks me, looking at trays of Vietnamese food.

"They're called bánh bao, Güelo. They're these amazing buns that're filled with carne or jackfruit or whatever you want. I learned how to make them."

"You'll have to make some for me, then," he says. "And next time, when tu novio comes here, he can try some Tex-Mex and *real* barbecue."

I love how Güelo casually mentions how eager he is to welcome Mat. How only a few months ago, I pondered whether that could actually be a reality. I don't think my heart has ever felt this full. Or that my life has felt so together.

Turning onto our block, I see Jordan's Jeep and Rolie's truck parked on the curb of Xo's house.

"They *had* to see you the second we got back," Xo says as she parks.

Bodies rush at me as soon as I walk inside. "How could you leave me with them for an entire week?" Itzel groans as she holds on to me. "At least you're only selectively messy. These two plus Gabi and Lou? I think there were entire days I spent disassociating."

"Don't listen to her, Luna," Jordan responds. "You know how she exaggerates."

They lead me to the dining table, where trays of Itzel's mom's vegetarian mole cheese enchiladas wait for us. These rank near the top of my favorite foods ever. Maybe even the very top. I think I'll miss them more than her daughter if I leave in the fall. Something I'm *never* saying out loud if I value my life.

"What'd you bring back for us from LA, compa?" Rolie asks before bringing a spoonful of rice to his mouth.

"Oh." I let the backpack I haven't had the chance to take off yet slide from my shoulders, and I bring it to my lap. After getting it unzipped, I take out a large plush dolphin I won in Santa Monica and hand it to Itzel; then an LA Galaxy shirt for Jordan, who immediately changes into it, draping his old shirt behind him; and finally a mariachi calaverito I found at Olvera Street for Rolie, who's instantly enamored by it.

"So," Itzel starts as she pushes her plate aside, "when were you planning on filling us in on LA?"

"I Snapped y'all every day. You were *constantly* filled in."

"But that's surface-level filled in, Jules," she says. "We're here for some chisme. You know we need every detail. His family. Oh, how were his friends? Not as great as us, I'm sure. And is LMU actually as pretty as your pictures made it seem? What else—"

"Did you try any of their weed, Luna?" Jordan asks. "It's legal there. Colorado too, bro!"

"Jordan, my güelo's literally right there," I snap, looking toward him and Xo, busy in conversation, sitting on the couches only a couple yards away from us.

"Twenty bucks says marijuana's nothing new to him, compa," Rolie adds. "I can see him out there en el campo, puro Pancho Villa after a long day of messing with Americans."

"That is incredibly detailed."

"Really, though," Itzel interjects while petting her dolphin. "How was meeting your boyfriend for the first time after doing this long-distance thing for almost half a year?"

"It was—there was this huge rush of emotion when I saw him, right in front of me. And it seemed . . . natural. I already knew so much about him, but finding out how it felt to have him *right there*. Once it all happened, every day of the past six months seemed worthwhile."

"And by *it all*, you mean—" Jordan makes a circle with his left thumb and pointer finger, repeatedly inserting a couple of his right fingers in and out.

"Can you stop being gross for one day?" I ask.

"Don't listen to him. Y'all are way too cute together," she says. "And I know I wasn't into the idea at first—something I will not apologize for, because there were legitimate concerns, and I will not be sorry for being who I am. But I can't deny that he's been good for you, Jules."

"Yeah, Luna," Jordan adds. "We get that he was able to help you sort through coming out in a way that we couldn't. And we're happy that it turned into something great for you. Also, Itzel is sorry that she was mean."

"You weren't thrilled either, fool," she yells. "Don't try to play all *Bro, I love you; bro, I'd do anything for you, bro*."

"Hey, I didn't like that I couldn't size him up, you know. Give my approval of this guy."

"And? You approve now?" I ask.

"I mean, if it can't be Piña or Rolie or me, then I guess this guy's fine."

"Y'all's loss."

~

After everyone leaves around three, I go to my room and fall on my bed. All the enchiladas I ate are about to put me into a food coma. Oh well, I'll run it all off during soccer practice tomorrow.

Lying down and going to sleep is an entirely different experience now without someone next to me. I'd quickly grown accustomed to it throughout the past week. It's not even about the more *intimate* moments that happened. Although I do miss those a lot too. *A lot*, a lot.

What I crave most is being next to someone. *My* someone. It's an addiction now. The cuddling that always came before naps and waking up still holding on to each other. The body warmth, the soft pattern of Mat's snores, trying to stay awake as long as possible because as tired as I was, I would not allow myself to stop looking at him.

My phone starts vibrating, and—as if he felt me thinking about him—Mat's name comes up.

I miss you already. Well, I've missed you since this morning. And I made one more TikTok, for whenever you wanna remember this week.

He sends me a link that takes me to his profile, and there—before all the dances we did and those videos for couples that're like *who's louder? who's the night owl?* and the other random stuff we did in between everything else the past week—is a new video. The cover is Mat pointing up to a text box that says my boyfriend lives in Texas and I live in California, but after almost half a year we finally got to spend an entire week together. That's how it starts, with Kid Franescoli's "Moon" playing in the background, and right after the *and it went like*—it goes into pictures of the two of us and some few-second clips. Us holding hands in his car, lying in bed together, me singing karaoke, us cooking, and all our adventures around Los Angeles. I watch it over and over again until my phone starts complaining about "20% battery remaining." And even then, I watch one more time before being forced to get out of bed and dig through my backpack for my charger.

I miss you already too, I text. A week wasn't enough.

We'll have a lot more weeks soon.

You promise?

I promise.

48

I think you should leave."

"Hmm," I moan as my eyes open and I take a deep breath into the pillow my arms are wrapped around. I thought I was dreaming, but now that I see light coming through the bottom of the door and my mind starts waking up, I realize there's a conversation happening.

"He doesn't want to talk to you."

"Xochi. Mi'jita. I just want to give him another choice."

"That's not what he needs, Papi."

Dad?

I try to fight my body going into helpless mode again, as much as hearing his voice makes me want to curl up under my blanket and let the mattress swallow me whole. My eyes close, and I slowly inhale and then exhale. And again and then again.

I push myself up and off the bed, grab a pair of shorts, and rest my head against the door for a moment, letting my hand hover just above the knob. Xo's and Dad's voices keep filling the house.

"You don't know him, Xochi."

"Says the one who would rather kick him out than let him be himself!"

"I can do this. I can do this."

The silence that follows the sound of my door cracking open is like a thick gust of wind pushing at my chest. And then I see both of them standing in the middle of the living room, already waiting for me.

"'Lito, go back to—"

"What're you doing here?" I interrupt, glaring at Dad.

"I got an email from the University of Texas about your financial aid, and I wanted you to know. I want to talk about it. Talk about your options."

"Why do you care?"

"I told you, Julián. I want you under my roof. I try to be a good dad. To care about all the good that you are, and there is a lot of it. And this"—he holds up a handful of papers, motioning them at me—"this is me trying to show that I care."

He takes a seat on the couch, eyeing the one next to him. "Will you at least hear me out?"

"You didn't for me."

"This is something you'll want to know."

"Fuck you," I mutter. "I don't want you here."

I turn around to start going back to my room, mid–first step, when Dad says, "You know that you have a full ride to UT?" and it freezes me. "It's all covered, Julián. You could go to one of the best schools in the country and not pay a dime."

I wish I didn't know this. I should've stayed in bed. Because now I have to compare the school I want to be at, and is going to cost more money than we have right now, with this. And I hate that my mind is debating it. I'm supposed to focus on Los Angeles and LMU and all that I want my life to be in just a few months from now.

"I know about that LA college," Dad continues. "I know you went and visited."

"Okay." My voice sounds nervous saying the word. Scared that he knows anything about my life now. That he does so without my wanting him to.

"And I know about that boy over there."

"*What?* No you don't. How?"

"You think I don't know what my own kids are doing? Nah. I'm fully aware. So I'll say it again: sit down and let's talk about Austin."

"I'm fine right here."

"All right. Está bien. Pero—look, mi'jo. You can't see this chance and think going to some small school no one's heard of is better. You worked hard, stayed in the top ten, and earned your spot. Take it and I will make sure that you're able to be comfortable. You want an apartment instead of having to stay in the dorms? I'll pay for it. Don't you want to take your truck? You can't go to LA with it. You'll have extra money for food and clothes and whatever that you won't have at that other school."

"Why are you trying so hard? Throwing all these things at me?"

"I can keep an eye on you if you're in Austin. And if you're living under a roof I'm paying for, I'm gonna want you to abide by some rules. Like you get rid of that boy. A-S-A-P. And there won't be any of that while you're at UT. You study, hang out with Itzel and Lou—I don't give a fuck—but there won't be any jotería. Those are my demands."

I take slow steps forward, stopping only feet from Dad.

"That morning you found Jordan in bed with me, the one thing that plays over and over in my head is when you asked me if I was gay. When I looked you right in the eyes and I told you no. And how much it hurt to say that word, *no*. Because everyone else knew already. My friends, Xochi, *that boy* you seem to hate so much. So you know what? I'm never going to put myself in a situation where I have to hide who I am because of you. We're way past that, Dad. So you can take your apartment and this idea that you actually want what's best for me and go fuck yourself."

I rush to my room, my heart beating erratically, half from fear and half from pride. I slam the door behind me and stand there, catching my breath, allowing myself to calm down. Their voices exist, but I can't make out any words. Everything is hazy. But I can hear the front door closing and then, moments after, Xo's footsteps coming toward my room and her asking if she can come in.

We stare at each other quietly for a moment when I open the door, waiting for one of us to react. Until I see the little smirk forming at the side of her mouth, and then we're both trying badly to suppress our laughs.

"I'm really proud of you, 'manito," she says. "But you're okay?"

"Yeah. I am."

She pats my cheek, holding her hand there after the fourth one. "Manifest, all right? You planted this seed a long time ago, and it's ready to bloom. So keep at it."

"I will, Xo. I will."

49

We are definitely losing this game," Piña says, running past me back to our goal.

It's not something I'm ashamed of. We made it to the TAPPS state semifinals. And if we weren't up against this team from Houston that plays like they were trained by Megan Rapinoe, we might've had a shot at the finals. But it was an uphill battle from the beginning, and at the start of the second half, we're down four to zero.

I get the ball and start running to the other end of the field. Feeling the wind against me. Dodging players from the other team as best I can.

Someone comes from out of my peripheral. He zooms in front of me, stealing the ball as if it was the easiest thing he's ever done.

"Chinga'o," I say under my breath, trying to keep myself from tripping.

"You've been off your game ever since you started riding dick, Luna," one of my teammates says as we sprint in the other direction. "Too much strain on the legs or what, joto?"

Whatever Jordan did at the start of our season managed to tone down most of their stupidity, but one or two still can't go without saying something once in a while. At least after today I'll share one less connection with these pinche dumbasses.

I ignore him and rush ahead. I catch up to the Houston player who stole the ball from me, slide into a tackle, and tap the ball away from him. Jordan is ready to retrieve it and dashes back toward our goal.

"Luna," he yells, passing the ball back to me when I get ahead. I run a few more steps, kicking the ball to get some momentum before striking it as hard as I can toward the net. The Houston goalie jumps for it. Jordan and I watch the ball graze his fingertips on its way past him, shooting straight into the netting.

"YES! LUNA!" Jordan gives me a high five as he runs past me. "*Finally!* Los MVPs!"

"Hey," I call out to my jeering teammate, approaching him as the game continues. "Not bad for a joto, huh? Maybe if you'd shut up for once, I wouldn't have had to spend four years showing you up." My glare stays fixed on him, as I take as much of his personal space as possible. Bumping into his chest for added emphasis.

"Do something for once, yeah?" I tell him while running back into the madness. Flicking him off and letting that be the last interaction I ever have with him.

To none of our surprise, we end up losing the game, having scored only two points. Way behind the seven the other team made. Jordan, the sorest of losers, mutters angrily as he leads us to our friends and families.

"Don't let the other team get to you," I tell him. More sarcastic than serious. "You gotta shake it off, *bro*. Los MVPs, right?"

I see a small smile begin to form. "Whoever gave you that advice was probably a really smart person."

"The smartest."

I hold on to Jordan's shoulders and hop onto his back. He carries me off the field piggyback-style until we get to the parking lot, where our cheer squad is waiting for us.

Mr. and Mrs. Thomas congratulate Jordan and me on our goals and gush about how well we played this season. And while they're busy talking to me about how surprised they are I won't be continuing soccer in college, I catch their son kissing Itzel behind them. *Glad I could be a distraction so y'all can make out.*

After the game, we, plus Rolie, Piña, and Lou, head to a Chinese buffet not far from the stadium. The guys and I waste no time rushing to the lines, coming back with piles of food. Itzel stares as we empty plate after plate, looking both astonished and repulsed.

"Those boys better be thanking God for that metabolism," I hear Mrs. Thomas tell her when we all stampede off to the ice-cream cabinet.

~

"I'm bored," Mat complains, chin propped on his hand. "And I miss you. What're you doing?"

Missing each other has had new meaning ever since I was forced to let go of Mat and fly home. Before Los Angeles, missing him was realizing it'd been a couple of days since we last FaceTimed. Now it's more . . . feeling incomplete. A part of me is missing. And it's all intensified by the uncertainty of ever getting to go back and knowing that there's an affordable plan B a few hours away and, even though she's told me over and over again that she hasn't, being worried that Xo's going to come home one day and say that she's given up hope and I need to prepare myself to stay in-state for college.

It all makes me want to get in my truck right now and start driving to California.

I adjust my iPad, propping it up on the kitchen counter. "I'm cooking. Rolie's family is having a barbecue later because he went Hulk mode at the district meet today. We're pretty sure he set a few new records in shot put. But since his family practically worships brisket, I'm bringing some vegetarian options."

Mat asks a million questions about what I'm making. *Do all Texans use that much butter* and *Why are you putting peppers in macaroni and cheese* and *Why didn't you make me brownies when you were here?*

"We should start a YouTube cooking channel!" Mat proclaims. "Like the Tasty or Bon Appétit videos. But less racist. Or a TikTok for cooking. Those are really popular right now. I can be your assistant and taster."

"You're just trying to find more ways to get me to cook for you."

"*What?* Okay, that's exactly what's happening. You can't tell me it wouldn't be fun, though."

"Whatever you say, cariño," I reply, giving him an unconvinced look. "Get your mom or Khan to teach you how to slice a tomato and I'll consider it."

We're still talking when Jordan texts me, and I hear the honk of his Jeep in the driveway. How mad would he be if I pretend I got sick in the three hours since we left Roe and Lou's track meet? I'd rather eat an entire pan of macaroni and cheese and talk to my boyfriend, whom I haven't hugged or kissed or held hands or had sex with for six entire days.

The *only* reason I force myself out the door is because Mat promises we can talk later, as soon as I'm back home. Jordan and Itzel don't seem to have noticed how long they were waiting on me. Whatever they're in the middle of must be more important than getting to Rolie's on time.

I'm really happy for them, now that their feelings are out in the open. Envious too, because they get to sit there and talk and be cute. But I'll keep that to myself.

Spanish music blasts from the speakers Rolie and his brothers installed on the pillars of their backyard patio, where his family's all hanging out. Roe and his dad are busy grilling, the smell of burning mesquite and cow covering the yard.

I follow Rolie's eldest brother, Tony, inside to put my dinner contribution with the rest of the food. He offers me a beer. I decline, grabbing a can of AriZona tea instead.

"So I hear you're a gay or whatever," he says as he starts opening drawers, looking for a bottle opener.

"Yeah, I'm *a gay*," I respond.

"That's cool, bro. Live and let live, right?"

I smile, contemplating a way out of the conversation.

"We were actually worried Roe was gonna end up that way too. Since he's never brought home a girl or mentioned dating anyone, you know. Even thought y'all might be a thing when we heard you were a mariposita."

"No, he's definitely straight," I say, brushing off his word choice. Again. "He has different priorities. I mean, he literally crushed it at his meet today, and he's one of the smartest in our class. Rolie being content single in high school doesn't make him any less or more something. He knows who he is and what's important to him. Better than any of us could say about ourselves."

I'm getting heated. Men are the worst. *Why am I attracted to them?*

I head back to everyone, but something inside me tells me to turn around. I'm not done ranting.

"Also, *worried*? Whether someone is gay or not isn't something to worry about. That's actually pretty fucking stupid. You know? Maybe as his brother, worry if he feels loved. Regardless of who he brings home or dates."

"Whatever, cabrón." Tony takes a swig of his beer. It's obvious he's not listening to anything I'm saying.

"*And*, for the record, Rolie and I would make a cute-ass *thing*."

I huff as I open the door leading to the backyard, taking a seat by Jordan. I understand a little more why Rolie might have been uncomfortable with me when I first came out. His family seems to be stuck in a very familiar, rigid expectation of how men should be—no, not even. How teenage boys should be.

Thankfully, he's turned out all right. Better than all right.

50

"I need to talk to you," Xo says, leaning into the doorway, looking at me on my bed surrounded by books, spirals, and my laptop. What my life has become the past few days as I prepare for the last final exams I will ever have to take. At least, until college. "You got a minute?"

"Yeah. Sure." I hop onto the floor and follow my sister to the dining table cluttered with her own computer, lots of folders and papers, and a plastic bag probably with some of her trash.

Xo takes a deep breath as she stares again. I can't tell what she's thinking. Her eyes are both happy and sad. Excited and nervous.

"What's going on?"

"I—'manito, I know this year has been difficult for you. A lot has changed. Well, not changed. I mean, yes, changed—"

"Is there a point to this?"

"I want you to know that you deserve the entire world. And that, as your older sister and basically your guardian, I would do everything I possibly could to give that to you. Seeing you become someone you are proud of has made me incredibly happy. You've gone through a lot to get where you are. Coming out, Dad, Mat. And now having to sit on not knowing where you'll end up next year when all your friends decided months ago. I know all of those are drastically different, but still. It's been a journey, huh?"

"Uh, yeah."

Shit. This is it. This is when she lets me know that California isn't going to work out. That, at best, she has a plan to trick Dad into giving me money for an apartment in Austin as a consolation prize. Because after all the dreaming and effort and pinche manifesting, this is the hand I'm given. How am I supposed to tell Mat? We talked about it, but—long-distance for years? Sounds easier said than done.

"I just wanted to tell you that, 'Lito. And how, when I look at you and see the man you've become, well, I'll miss seeing your face." I can tell she's trying not to cry. It's hurting her to hold in the disappointment. The knowledge that she has to be the one to break it to me.

"Tomorrow is Decision Day," she continues. "May's finally here, and, uh—I think we've got a really promising option here. I know it's not where you thought you'd end up, and I'm sorry I can't make this perfectly match what you envisioned this day being. But—"

Xo grabs the plastic bag from the table and takes out a carefully folded white shirt. She holds it toward me, waiting for me to take it. I start unfolding it, slowly at first, until I see the beginnings of red-and-blue lettering.

"Oh my God. This—" I rush to open it completely and see Loyola Marymount written on the front. Their lion logo in the middle, separating the two words. "Xo, you—am I . . . ?" I can't get the rest of the question out. Too surprised and maybe a little worried that if I do, I could jinx it.

"You tell me. It's been figured out, so if LMU is really where you want to be, then—"

"Yes. Yes, yes, so much yes! This is for sure? It's happening?"

"It's happening."

"Wait. Tell me you're not paying thousands of dollars for me to go to school. Because I told you—"

"I'm not," she responds. "The financial aid counselor we talked to has been helping me, and we were able to figure it out. Full disclosure, I am putting in a little, but it's nothing more than I can handle."

"You better not be lying."

"*I'm not.* Trust me. But with that being said, I'm going to expect you to keep your grades up, all right? Show up to class and do the work. And just as importantly, be happy."

I jump at Xo, squeezing her and crying, but only a little bit, as "thank you, thank you, thank you" repeatedly comes out of my mouth.

"I seriously thought you were about to crush my entire soul."

"Good. I was going for keeping you on the edge of your seat."

"You're the worst."

"Yo sé. Have to get as much of it in as I can before you leave me."

~

I have a surprise for you! Can you FaceTime?

Is it a sexy surprise?

NO don't be nasty.

Mat sends a crying face and a pouty-face emoji. *Baboso.*

Fine. I guess. I'm free. Call me!

I quickly change into my new LMU shirt and fix my hair. And then I stack a box and some books on my bed, high enough so that I can stand my phone on it when it's time for the reveal, making sure the letters aren't on-screen just yet. Okay, everything's good. Time to tell him.

"Hey there, boyfriend."

"Hi, boyfriend," I say back. "So I've got something really important to show you."

"*Okay.* What is it?"

"Hold on. Close your eyes until I tell you to open them."

"Got it." I wait for Mat's eyes to shut before getting my phone set up on my bed, making sure it won't fall. "This sounds like it's gonna be a sexy surprise."

"I told you it's not." Although—no. Never mind.

I take a couple of steps back so everything waist-up is visible. "Okay. Open your eyes."

He looks right at me, and the way his face goes from normal happy to thinking about what he's supposed to be seeing and finally to the most excited I've ever seen him in only a second is going to be something I remember for a long time.

"You—yeah? Yes?"

"Yeah. I'm going to LMU."

"OH MY—FUCK YES." Mat's phone goes blurry as he stands up and, I'm guessing, starts running around his house. "YOU'RE GONNA BE AN ANGELENO! We're gonna be in the same city! You did it!"

The sounds of someone loudly knocking from his end and the familiar voice of his mom yelling something get him to stop, and he talks to her only slightly less enthusiastically while he catches his breath.

"My mom says congrats."

"What were you doing?"

"Jumping on my bed, of course." He carefully sits down and brushes his hand through his hair. "I wish I could celebrate with you."

"I know," I say while grabbing my phone. "I really want to be with you right now."

"Soon." Just that one word, when it comes from him, reassures my whole spirit. "Soon we'll have all the time in the world. So don't let me hog you from your friends and family, yeah? If you need to go yell about this with people, I can call you back later."

"Sixty more seconds." I take my phone and sit down on the floor, bringing my face nearer to the screen. The closest I'm going to get to him actually being here. "Sixty seconds and I'll start letting everyone know."

"Sixty seconds."

"Hey," I start. "Can we get bánh mìs as soon as I arrive?"

"Sure, babe. Khan is gonna have such a big head knowing that's the first thing you want to do when you get back."

"Actually, let me correct that. It's second. There's definitely someone I want to do first."

"You mean something."

"No."

"Wai—OH! I'm stupid." He laughs at himself before giving me that smirk that, without fail, causes all my blood to rush to a very specific part of my body. "I can arrange that."

51

Does this even look good? Be honest," I say into my laptop. I use my iPad as a mirror to straighten my bow tie.

"Babe, you look fine AF," Mat encourages. "Best dressed at prom for sure."

"But—I don't know. Now that I'm looking at it, this maroon jacket and pants look a little . . ."

"Gay?"

"I wasn't going to say that."

"You're rocking the look, Jules. Honestly. I mean, you're giving me that *twink Olympic ice-skater going to the Met Gala but brown and better*."

I roll my eyes at him and look at myself one last time, making sure my black button-up shirt is completely free of wrinkles. I agreed with Jordan, Itzel, and Roe to all go together as a group. Rolie got to pick the color after beating us at rock paper scissors, and of course he went with Aggie maroon.

Itzel wasn't too happy about the decision.

"If I get bored, I'm gonna call you."

"You won't be. You're gonna have a lot of fun with your best friends and dance until your feet hurt, and you can catch me up tomorrow."

"I know. I wish you were going with me. It—" I say, but then I get a text from Jordan. "Crap, I got to go. Love you."

"Love you too. Have fun!"

I rush out the door and see my friends waiting for me in the driveway. I sit in the back with Itzel, who gave up the passenger seat for the sake of Roe's longer legs.

"You look beautiful!" I tell Itzel. I touch her dress so I don't give it ojo, staring at the long, flowy maroon silk from the waist down and cream bodice decorated with pearls and beads on top.

"Me? You, Jules! ¡Qué flaco! And the black nails? Fierce."

Our prom's at a large dance hall off Shoreline Boulevard. There's an esplanade on the side leading to the beach. Inside, lights cascade down from the ceiling. Navy-and-black fabric drapes across the hall. Keeping with the theme of "The Starry Night," the backdrop for the pictures is a giant canvas of Van Gogh's painting. The four of us take a picture, and then Itzel kicks Roe and me out for one of just her and Jordan.

Piña waves us over to the table he, Lou, and their dates are holding for all of us. Everyone's laughing and yelling over the music. Having a great time. Which they should be. It's not their fault I'm here feeling mentally not present.

I'm giving them five minutes before I spend the rest of the night on the phone with my boyfriend.

And luckily for them, it takes only three minutes and thirty-seven seconds for "Bidi Bidi Bom Bom" to start playing.

Lou and Itzel grab my hands, pulling me onto the dance floor. God must be wanting me to leave Mat alone tonight. "High Horse" comes on right after, and I can't leave while the low-key only country singer I like is playing.

When a slow song finally comes on, I start walking back to our table. I can get some punch and pretend I'm not petty everyone's slow dancing with their boyfriends or girlfriends. But then I hear Lou calling out for me.

"C'mon, chiquis," she says when she gets to me, holding on to my shoulder. "Dance with me. I'll lead."

I know there's no way out of this, so I grab on to her waist. Her hands fall on my biceps.

"I'm going to miss you next year, Julito," she admits as we sway to the music.

"I'll miss you too, Lou. But we still have almost four months left. That's a lot of time for you to be the worst influence in my life before we're off to college."

"You know I take a lot of pride in that title."

"Yo sé."

As we continue dancing, I begin to laugh.

"Damn, I wanna laugh with you, Julito. What's funny?"

"Remember the Monday after the whole coming-out debacle, when you brought the balloons and cupcakes?"

"And Diana Ross. Don't forget Diana."

Yes, and Diana. I can't listen to "I'm Coming Out" anymore without thinking I'm being gay-ambushed.

"Well, I was way too embarrassed to say it at the time, but thank you for that. Not that I ever thought you'd stop being my friend, but being *that* extra with your acceptance really meant a lot to me."

"Chiquis, when have you ever known me to be anything less than one hundred percent extra? I'd been waiting for you to come out for years. Your gayness was pretty easy to recognize."

"How was it easy to recognize?"

She spins me when we get to the bridge of "Fallingforyou." I listened to this song a lot when I first met Mat. When I was pretending he hadn't instantly claimed my whole heart the moment he DMed me.

"Chiquis, if I had a dollar every time I saw you *discreetly* checking out some boy, I'd be swimming in Gucci purses. And if I had another dollar every time you were completely oblivious to a girl crushing on you, I could buy the whole damn brand."

"Who had a crush on me?"

"Don't be nosy. You got a man." I'm spun one more time as the song ends and goes into a corrido that gets all the puro Tejanos hollering gritos. Turning prom into a quince real quick.

Lou pulls me off the floor, toward an uncrowded wall. "I want to tell you something."

"Uh, okay," I tell her, watching our friends dance. "What's up?"

"First, I haven't told anyone yet, so keep this between us for tonight. But I've been doing some researching and thinking. All that mess. And I—I think I'm pansexual, chiquis."

I turn my head to her and see that she's looking right at me. I wouldn't say I'm *surprised.* She's always said stuff that might imply her being bisexual or something, but I guess I assumed she was joking.

I'm, well, okay, I'm surprised.

"That—good for you, Lou," I say. "Honestly. I'm happy for you. Did you realize this recently?"

"I mean, for a while it's been all, *Oh, he's cute.* And then I turn my head and I'm like, *Wow, she's cute too, and so are they.* I don't know, my attraction filter doesn't seem to care about gender. It's—actually, I don't know how it's filtered. I'm still figuring it out."

"Has there been a *not-man* person?"

"There've been girls."

"What? You've had girlfriends?"

"Julito, you know I prefer to play the field right now. I'm not looking to get tied to anyone. I'll leave that to you and Itzel and Jordan."

"Fair," I reply.

I'm at a loss for what else to say. I can't give her the big celebratory moment that she gave me. But I don't think she's expecting or wanting that. If Lou wanted a big coming-out thing, she would've made it known. So I squeeze her hand and hope she knows that I'm here for whatever she needs.

52

Itzel and I walk barefoot in the beach sand. The wind blowing her gown makes her look like she's ready for a magazine cover shoot. She stole me away from a selfie with Lou and Roe, holding on to my hand while we rushed out from the hall. Needing to talk.

"Mind if we sit?" she asks.

"Only if you promise not to let me walk back in with sand on my butt."

I help her down while she keeps her dress as decent as possible. She stares into the dark ocean water, and I can hear her let out a heavy sigh.

"Jordan wants to be official. And I have no idea what to do. I kind of walked out on him."

"What in your mind says this is a bad idea?"

Itzel lets out a loud, annoyed sigh. "We're basically done with high school. He leaves in less than two months. And then what? We don't see each other until when? Mid-December? I don't know why he thought tonight would be an ideal time to tell me—as if an ideal time actually exists. But I don't know what to do, Jules."

"Because you're scared."

"Duh, I'm scared. I don't want him to feel chained to me. Regretting this decision when some hot Colorado girl with UGGs, a military jacket, and a nice scarf walks past him. Or what if I do something really stupid when I get to Austin?"

"Itzel, you're the smartest person I know—"

"Intelligent people can still get into some stupid-ass foolery," she interrupts. Her eyebrows rise. She knows she doesn't have to say any more.

Valid. I can't argue against that one.

I look up at the moon, this crescent hanging out in the sky, and wonder if it's as visible in Los Angeles. If Mat's looking up at it too right now.

"You owe it to yourself to try. I don't think you'd bring me out here if you didn't already know what you wanted. Looking for someone who's been in sort-of-similar shoes to tell you that it'll work out."

"Are you going to tell me this is all going to work out?"

"No, of course not."

I push my fingers into the sand. Focus on the salty smell of the air. It's humid and uncomfortable in a suit.

How do I explain how hard it's going to be? The days where her confidence level will be at zero. And feeling like every hour away from him is an eternity.

I think about the words I was preparing to tell myself if I landed in this same situation. The thoughts I'm glad I didn't have to say aloud. The process that was getting into a mindset that long-term distance isn't the end of the world.

"I'll tell you that I *want* it to. That y'all are my OTP. But none of it will matter if you don't give him a chance." I reach around and pull her close to me. She smells really good. I think it's the Gaga perfume. "You have to want this, though. Take advantage of the time you have to create as much good as possible before he's in Colorado. Don't waste any of it. Oh, and if you want, I'll give Jordan the condoms that ended up coming back with me from California."

Itzel shoves me, screaming at the suggestion. "Jules, cochino. Shut up. As if he should be so lucky." She grabs her heels and readies herself to walk back. "But also, yes, please give those to him. Whenever. Actually, if you want to go to Xo's house right now and pick them up, I have his keys in my purse."

"Don't you have a prom queen crown to win?"

She gasps and starts smacking my arm with her hand. "Oh, crap, you're right! Let's go. And make sure to brush the sand off your culito."

~

"Where've y'all been?" Roe asks when Itzel and I make it back into the hall. "They're announcing prom king and queen right now."

He leads Itzel to the stage, where the rest of the prom court is being lined up. I sneak through the crowd to get by him and Lou.

Mrs. Bell, the prom committee sponsor, stands center stage in front of the mic. Going through all the usual *thank you*s and terrible jokes and *how about that DJ?*

She announces the king nominees first, having them take a step forward as each name is called. We scream extra loud when Jordan steps up. Rolie nervously clutches one of my shoulders, his fingers digging into me.

Lou lets out a string of swears when Alfie Vasquez, our high school's most prized football player, wins prom king. Roe and I both glare at her, telling her to calm down. Everyone else's clapping and cheering drown out most of the words, but if anyone heard her, she doesn't seem to regret it.

The other boys move back in line with the girls, and Mrs. Bell continues on with the queen candidates. The room roars when Itzel steps up, and now Roe's burrowing into both my shoulders, shaking my entire body impatiently. Lou moves close to me, holding on to my arm. Our teacher pauses before letting the name of this year's prom queen leave her lips, and I'm actually going to break from my friends' grips.

When we hear the words *Itzel Santos*, there is a collective release of tension on my body as my friends start jumping and cheering for her. Lou screams, "YAS, QUEEN!" loud enough for Itzel to hear, and she breaks from her composed demeanor, laughing as Mrs. Bell tries to attach the crown to her head.

"Jules! Picture!" Itzel yells when she and Jordan arrive back to the group, handing her phone to Lou.

Lou moves around, trying to find the best angles. "Think *GQ*, mi'jas. Think 'break the internet.' Think 'Beyoncé's Instagram.'"

I'm posting my favorite photos, captioning it dos reinas when I see Itzel heading back outside, this time hand in hand with Jordan. She winks at me and smiles, tapping her fingers lightly on my shoulder as they pass.

I TOLD YOU YOU'D HAVE FUN TONIGHT! Mat messages. And give my best to our queen.

Always being right isn't a cute look for you.

He sends me a row of yellow hearts in response. Cabrón.

~

Jordan's parents offered to throw us a prom after-party. Which is cool, except they insisted on being there too, so no cases of beer or handles of liquor are present tonight. But that's fine. I'll drink water all night, as long as I can change out of this suit and into one of the tanks I stole from Mat and shorts. And I'm not saying no to frozen virgin margaritas in May.

I take a bag of tortilla chips and the bowl of guacamole outside. I need to get away from everything happening in the house. The loud music. Every song that comes on reminding me of Mat. Jordan and Itzel being all cute. Piña and his date being all cute. Everyone being too damn cute.

I hear the back door open and close behind me. Jordan takes a seat next to me, handing me a margarita.

"Mind if I interrupt whatever it is that's happening here?"

"Go for it." I pass him the chips and guacamole.

"Bummed your guy's not here?"

"For most of the past eight months."

"But I mean, since spring break, I'm sure it's been harder. And on prom night."

"Yeah," I acknowledge, sighing. "It's been rough."

I've been trying not to think about how much I miss Mat. Focus on my friends instead, since I have a very limited amount of time left with them. But it just happens. And of course, today is a huge reminder inflating all those feelings.

"No cap, I'm gonna be jealous as fuck if you don't miss me this much come July," he teases.

"I'm sure it'll be comparable," I tell him. "But he does do a few things that you won't, so—"

"True. I'll respectfully take the L, then. Although I'm gonna stay a little salty, since he's got you for this four-year adventure you have coming your way. But I'm happy for you, bro. You're gonna go get that new, bigger, better life you've dreamed of since I've known you. I can't think of anyone more courageous and ambitious or more deserving."

"I—" How is everyone seeing these qualities in me? "I'm not courageous. Mat said the same thing. That I'm brave. But I'm not. I'm scared. My entire life I've been nothing but scared."

"Hasn't every president and famous writer and MLK or Gandhi said that courage isn't the absence of fear but doing what you gotta do anyways?"

"Not as eloquently as you did."

"But really, it's true. I know you think that it's because you've had us to rely on, and not to knock that, but you're stronger and more resilient than anyone I know. Except for Xo, you don't actually *need* any of us. You're the hero. Itzel, Mat, Roe, and I are all just phenomenal-ass sidekicks who're happy to be here."

"What about Lou?"

"Lou's the villain. And Piña can be the Alfred."

I laugh and lean back into the chair, throwing a leg over one of the arms. "Y'all are putting in a lot of overtime for sidekicks."

"I'm sure Robin's had to rescue Batman from the Joker once or twice."

"Well, thanks for having my back, Robin."

"Always, Batman. Remember, you're stuck with me. No matter where we all end up."

"I don't know if I'm ready to leave y'all yet." The words sound strange coming out of my mouth when I can barely think of anything else that isn't about being back in Los Angeles.

"Me neither. But I'm sure Lou and Itzel will survive, and Roe's capable. And I'll plan a trip from Denver to LA to visit you. That's not a long ride. They're right next to each other."

"Jordan, that's not true. At all." I'm really concerned with how he learned nothing in geography class. "There's definitely at least two states you'd have to go through between Colorado and California."

His face is deep in thought as he pulls up Google Maps, trying to locate the two points. "Oh, you're right, Luna. My bad."

"How are you ranked number seven in our class?"

"I ask the same thing about you whenever I see that stupid blank look you get all the time in physics. We can't all be like Itzel and be great at everything."

We don't stay outside too much longer. Or maybe we do. I'm not sure. Neither of us is checking the time. Someone will come get us if we're needed.

Until then, I'll be right here. With my best friend.

53

I'm having, um—the pest-control guys spray the house later," Xo mentions before I leave for morning graduation prep. "Mind seeing if you can hang out with Jordan or someone for the day?"

"Sure, I can do that," I answer. "So I should—"

"Take the clothes you're wearing tonight, cap, gown, y todo," she finishes for me. "Yes."

Jordan was definitely planning on being alone with Itzel all day, but he lets me be third wheel. I make sure I have my earbuds on me in case they both feel the need to recall what the inside of his bedroom looks like. When I get to his house (with a dozen doughnuts and a gallon of orange juice as a *sorry y'all aren't banging right now* gift), Itzel is hunched over, writing in a spiral, deep in thought.

"What is a valediction even supposed to be about?" Itzel yells as she crumples a piece of paper. "This is stupid. No one listens to these."

"We will," Jordan replies with a mouthful of doughnut.

"And why do they make the highest-ranked student in the class do this? I didn't ask for that to be part of the deal. Who started this tradition? Because I have some words for *them*."

"Why'd you wait until today to write it?" I ask.

"Julián Luna, I swear to God, do not come for me this morning," she replies. "Because I do what I want. That's why."

Jordan and I give her some space to write. Letting her be alone with her thoughts is probably going to be more productive. He turns on his PlayStation and grabs one of his many FIFA games.

"What would you say, Luna?" Jordan asks as he hands me a controller. "If you had to write a valedictorian speech."

"I don't know. I'd probably play the *Golden Girls* theme song over the loudspeakers or something."

Jordan cracks up. "That's pretty gay, bro."

"You asked. I don't do speeches. I'd be struggling as much as Itzel."

We play best two out of three. Usually we don't make it to a third game, so when I win game two, Jordan scoots himself to the edge of his seat on the couch. Intent on not letting me have this one.

"What would *you* say?" I ask.

"Don't try to distract me, Luna."

"I'm not. I wanna know."

I glance over at him. Jordan's concentrating on the game, tongue out and everything. He jumps up when he makes his first goal.

"You're gonna laugh," he says.

"No, I won't. I promise. No judgment."

"I—so I'd mention how I'm moving soon. And that the next four years have some big shoes to fill, because the past four have been the best of my life. Which is scary. Not having my parents around, I can get used to. No more Whataburger or a solid breakfast taco place, I'll adjust, I guess. But to not have Itzel and you, Piña, Roe, Lou. Everyone who made these years great, that's terrifying."

"Yeah, it is." Relatable. We're the ones leaving, yet I don't think Jordan's ever talked to me about where his mind's at with moving for college. I know he'll fit in anywhere, but that doesn't mean he can't be afraid.

"You know, though, y'all have made me into the person I am today. So even if I don't have any of you in Denver with me, I got y'all in here."

He pats his chest with his hand. "I know I'll be all right. And you will too, Luna."

We hear Itzel sniffling behind us and turn around. She wipes a couple of tears from her face and walks over to sit between us on the couch.

"I'm not crying because you're both leaving me," she starts. "That'll come in a couple months. I'm crying because that was meaningful. And unexpected. And now look what you've done to me."

"I'm sorry," Jordan says. "It's what I felt. Not that huge of a deal."

"No, it was great," I say. "It only took three and a half years for you to let yourself be a softy around us. Oh, now that you've brought it up, I'll need someone to mail me a bottle of Whataburger spicy ketchup, like, weekly. And jalapeño ranch."

"We'll be sure to send both of you Texas-themed care packages on the regular."

Itzel kisses me on the cheek and Jordan on the lips before returning to her speech. She seems more focused. Probably doesn't want to be one-upped by her boyfriend. She brings her notebook over to recite lines, ask opinions, and edit, finishing her first and only draft with barely enough time to get home and dressed for graduation.

I take my time getting ready. It's all feeling surreal. Changing into a shirt and chinos, checking my tie for any sign of wrinkles, putting on the dress socks, making sure I don't scuff my shoes.

Hey, Xo, I'm leaving to the event center now. Graduation starts at 5:30! BE ON TIME.

She responds with only a thumbs-up emoji. She's going to be late. No doubt about it.

I lay my forest-green gown across my back seat and my cap and National Honor Society and top-ten cords on top of it. Jordan backs out of his driveway, and I follow behind him.

Here we go.

~

We're all in disarray, crammed into one of the diocese center's conference rooms. A couple of teachers are trying to get us lined up in alphabetical order in the limited space. Everyone's antsy, wanting to get this started already.

I stand right behind Lou, Luna falling immediately after Longoria in the class roll. Rolie's up near the front, and Itzel and Jordan are farther in the back.

"You ready, chiquis?" Lou asks, grabbing my hand.

"I think so. Only took eighteen years to get here."

The room goes quiet, and the line starts to make its way out of the room. I can already hear the sounds of "Pomp and Circumstance" ringing through the auditorium as I approach the doors. We walk single file down the middle aisle, cutting left up the ramp onto the stage. I follow Lou into our row, staying standing until the entire class has made its way up. While we're waiting, I try to find Xo and Güelo, but the bright lights pointed directly at my face make it impossible to see past the stage.

I tune out most of the beginning. Father David welcoming everyone, congratulating us, leading everyone in prayer, introducing some teachers. Mirella making her salutatory address. Some school awards are given out; everyone applauds because of the huge number of service hours we completed, that our entire class is going to college, and something about someone going into the seminary, maybe. Then this poet who was invited to give a commencement speech talks about beauty or life or rose quartz. I don't know.

But then the front row stands up, and I realize people's names are being called out. And now the nerves hit. Why am I nervous? This is easy. This is what everything up to now has led to.

I made it.

An eternity's passed by the time my row is standing and each of us is waiting for our turn to move to the front of the stage.

"Julián José Roberto Luna," I hear Mrs. Bell announce. She's got the pronunciation down perfectly. Teach at Martin long enough and Spanish probably becomes second nature.

I walk toward the center of the stage where Father David waits for me. I stretch my right hand out to meet his while my left hand reaches for the diploma. I turn to face the audience, the dimmer lights up front making it easier to spot my family. Güelo is only feet from the stage, taking pictures. And not too far back is Xochi and—

I have to be imagining this.

Nope. It's real.

I'm barely sure that the words *what the actual fuck* didn't come out of my mouth while standing next to a priest.

There's Mat and Ruben sitting next to my sister, smiling and clapping. I could easily jump off the stage and run over to my boyfriend, who is, right now, in the same time zone, same state, same city as me. Only yards away.

But then I feel Father David's hand pushing against my back, and I realize I'm holding up the line.

"Why'd you freeze up there, chiquis?" Lou asks when I catch up to her.

"Mat is here."

"No mames. The same Mat who is your boyfriend and lives in LA?"

"Yes, Lou. That one."

"He surprised you?"

"Obviously!"

The classmate on my other side clears her throat. Chiding us with her eyes. Lou places a hand on my leg, shaking it as she squeals.

"¡Ya! Calm down," I tell her when Itzel steps up to the podium to deliver the valediction.

Her speech is amazing. She talks about being rule breakers. Being unafraid of change if it cultivates our growth. Being confident as we enter adulthood. And being supportive of the friends we'll leave behind but who will be forever weaved into our heart and soul.

Lou and I don't even wait for her to finish saying the last word before we're up and applauding. Roe and Piña and Jordan do the same. The entire class follows, and soon the whole auditorium is standing for Itzel.

She turns to face me, beaming at the podium.

Te quiero, I mouth to her.

54

WHERE ARE Y'ALL? I text my sister, adding a couple red-faced, super-bothered emojis for emphasis.

We're outside.

That doesn't help at all, Xo. OMFG.

I walk what has to be the entire perimeter of the auditorium, staring at a blinking ellipsis as Xochi types. She sends a picture of a large angel statue, and I run back, cussing because I *just* passed it.

A bunch of other families crowd around the area. I tiptoe and see Ruben talking to my sister and abuelo.

Where is my boyfriend?

I find him standing close by. Talking to Itzel and Lou.

The girls notice me and point in my direction. Mat turns around and jogs over, almost running into me. I would've still thought I was imagining this if it weren't for his embrace. The smell of the cologne that works only for him. The words "hey, babe" leaving his mouth. Feeling him kiss my cheek.

"I'm assuming it'd be a bad idea to kiss you on the lips right now in front of this angel hanging out here and in the middle of a Catholic school graduation at the—what is this—the pope's Texas summerhouse?"

"Not what this is," I say, still holding on to him. "But that's a pretty good guess. And yeah, let's wait until we're somewhere we won't burst into flames."

I let go of him only to quickly make my way around to family, friends' parents, teachers, and some classmates. While, at the same time, keeping a careful eye on Mat and everyone crowding him. I'm sure my friends are all eager to tell him every embarrassing story they've got on me, so the sooner I get back to my boyfriend and pull him away from Itzel, Lou, and Jordan, the better.

I can sense the stares of more than a few people looking at Mat and me holding hands when we leave. But in that same moment, I feel Güelo's hand on my shoulder and notice his other hand on Mat's. And when I turn my head, I see Xo and Ruben glaring right back at those people, both ready to take off their earrings if needed.

"Deep breaths," I whisper to Ruben when I overhear him mumbling thoughts I'm sure he'd rather be screaming right now. "We don't want to have to call Khan because you got arrested getting into a fight with someone."

"I'd win too," he says. "Trust."

"So this was your pest control?" I ask Xochi when we get to my truck.

"You told him we were what now?" Ruben interjects, staring at my sister.

"I had to get him out of the house," she replies. "And it worked. But blame your boyfriend, 'manito. He was the mastermind of all this. All I had to do was make sure they got picked up from the airport, and we surprised you."

I have to give it to him. This was not how I was expecting tonight to go.

"You're such a Texan," he tells me as he hops into my truck, abandoning Ruben and Xo for our trip to my graduation dinner.

"It was either this or a John Deere tractor."

I lean in and kiss him, not caring who walks by and sees. It's been two entire months. They should be glad kissing is all we're doing.

"I guess God isn't gonna strike us dead for now," he says. "We could see how far we get before the lightning starts."

I *almost* say yes. Lay the passenger seat back myself and jump on him. But I decide to listen to my better judgment.

"Let's wait to get somewhere more comfortable." I turn on my truck and set it to "Reverse."

~

After dinner, I take Mat to the beach. We walk along the seawall and step down to the bottommost row. The waves come within inches of our feet.

When we sit, I lean on him. I kiss his cheek. He turns, giving me access to his lips. Again, and again, as much as I want. Because he's here.

His fingers scratch up and down my back. I feel safe and comfortable and a happiness that comes with being next to him. How have I survived two entire months away from this?

"It's not Venice," Mat comments. "But it's all right."

"But Selena didn't dance at a SoCal beach."

"I guess," he says. "Oh, by the way, your, uh, abuelo makes the best barbecue I've ever had. He brought so much meat over, and honestly, I can't go back to California knowing he exists. Even though he did give me the entire story of how the sausage he made went from live deer, to shot, to—anyways. I'm sneaking him back with me to LA, because obviously his talent isn't getting the recognition it deserves here."

"You're gonna take Güelo with you but not me?"

"You already have a plane ticket," he yells jokingly before kissing the side of my face. "Take one for the team, babe."

While Mat and I head back to the truck, his hand that's been holding my waist gradually starts traveling lower, stopping at my butt. When he's made his way into my back pocket, I glance at him. He doesn't look back at me, but I can see that proud smile.

"That I've been here since noon and have only grabbed your ass once says *a lot* about my restraint."

Xo and Ruben are waiting up for us when we get home. They're drinking coffee and sharing pan dulce, and Ruben is whining over how no one makes a concha as good as a Texas abuela. Neither of us wants to stay and talk with my sister and Mat's brother-in-law—there are much bigger priorities tonight—but the looks they both give say there isn't much of a choice.

Ten minutes. That's all they get before I pull him into my bedroom.

"I'm not going to make any assumptions about what's happening in your room tonight," Xochi says while yawning, finally getting up to go to bed. "But if any noises come out of there that will scar your older sister for the rest of her life, I'm getting the most horribly produced VHS tape on abstinence I can find and forcing you both to watch it. It will be very heterosexual and very Christian."

"I made sure your boyfriend came prepared," Ruben whispers to me when my sister is out of sight. "The four Cs, boys."

"The four what?" Xochi asks, jumping back into the living room, looking suspiciously at all three of us.

"CHER, CELINE, CHRISSY, AND CHRIST," Ruben hollers, more in genuine frightened surprise than actually answering her question. But I give him major kudos for the response.

Xo's eyes go from him to Mat to me. Not convinced at all. But she doesn't press any further and turns back to her room. Probably realizes she's better off not knowing.

Mat and I tell Ruben good night while running to my bedroom. I'm glad he has his headphones in, glued to some video on his phone, when I rush into the bathroom. Even more glad when I walk back out in only a towel.

Time to let out eight weeks of repressed hormones.

55

You and Mat are having lunch with us, Itzel texts. 1pm. We're going to Whataburger. The one on Shoreline.

Y'all better show up! Jordan adds. You cockblocked me yesterday, so don't think I won't spam your texts if you try to ignore us.

STFU. We'll be there, I reply. Buuuut we may be late.

LUNA. YES. GET IT IN.

It's still early, not yet nine in the morning. I toss my phone on the floor with enough care to not wake up the heavy sleeper sharing my bed. Mat's arms are tightly locked around me, his torso pressed fully against my back and his legs tangled between mine. I'm doubtful that our bodies have spent any time apart at all since last night. Mat's face is buried in the back of my neck, and his breath is warm against my skin. I want to stay up and savor this.

But I'm still tired. And more importantly, more comfortable than I've been in weeks. There're parts of me and Mat that are definitely already awake, but we can get to that later.

What's one more hour of sleep?

~

"Missed you at Graduation Lock-In last night," Itzel says as she hugs Mat and me outside the Whataburger. Rolie, Jordan, Piña, and Lou are a few steps behind her.

"I was kind of preoccupied."

"I'm sure y'all were *very preoccupied.*"

I glare at Mat, who's proudly and very happily nodding in agreement and getting a high five from Jordan.

Why are babosos my type?

"Anyways, it was pretty much a carnival," Lou continues, describing the lock-in in full detail to Mat and me while we wait in line.

"Highlight of the night was Lou getting hypnotized," Roe adds. "They got her to spray herself with Silly String!"

I'm slightly disappointed to have missed that.

When the cashier hands Mat his thirty-two-ounce medium-size cup, he stares at us. Mouth agape. Looking very concerned.

"This is what a medium is in Texas?"

"Everything's bigger here, Matito," Lou jokes.

"Mm, I don't know. Drinks, sure. But things come pretty big in California too," he says back with a wink.

It's way too early for this mixture of his shamelessness, Lou's impressed face (whether it's because of his quick comeback or what it implied, I don't know—both, probably), and Jordan and Piña behind them with more thumbs-ups and mouthing, *Get it, Luna!*

The seven of us pack into two tables pushed together at the side of the restaurant. We go over all the last-minute reminders for our graduation party while we wait for our food. Anything we're scared someone might forget, like song requests for Lou to pass along to her cousin who's DJing and what time she and Itzel are getting their hair done.

The table goes silent when our food arrives. All eyes are on Mat, waiting for him to take a first bite of his double-meat burger with bacon.

I don't think any of us are breathing while we watch him. Itzel's even got her phone out, making sure to get this all for Instagram. And when his eyes go from thinking to that *oh, OH* look, and a smile starts forming while he chews, I know I've won.

"You better not tell any of my friends I said this, but it's better than In-N-Out. And I'm gonna need to come back before I leave tomorrow."

"We'll come after the party," Itzel tells him. "You *have* to try the barbecue chicken strip sandwich."

"Here," Jordan says, handing a paper Whataburger hat to Mat. "I told the guy at the counter that we popped your cherry—"

"You told him what?" I interrupt.

"You know what I mean, Luna. Stop being dirty minded. Keep it in your pants till you get home. Anyways, they gave us this so you can take it back with you. Wear it everywhere."

"That's not happening," Mat replies. "But I'll take it. Thanks." He puts it on, looking like a 1950s diner waiter. "If I get my Californian card revoked for this, you think I still have time to apply to UT and start saying *y'all* unironically?"

"We'll work something out, cariño."

~

Mat put on a playlist I made him a couple of weeks ago, and we've been listening to it since we got home from lunch. Lying in my bed, his head on a pillow and mine resting on his thigh as I quietly sing along to the Burns Twins and Bedows and KAINA's "Honey." There are a lot of songs that make me think of him. The nearly forty that're on the playlist prove that. But this one—there's no way they weren't thinking about us when they wrote it.

I can see Mat's hand reaching toward me. His fingers grabbing air until they're locked with mine.

"Can I tell you something?" he asks.

"Anything."

I hear him swallow loudly and take a deep breath in and out. "I—I met your dad yesterday."

I pick myself up, looking at my boyfriend. "How? When? Was he here?"

"No, he showed up to your graduation." Mat sits up too, scooting close to me. "I overheard your abuelo tell Xo he saw him standing in the back. So I tried to covertly turn around and found the guy who looked close enough to you and your sister to be able to safely assume. Keep the curly look, by the way. But I noticed him leaving right after you got your diploma, so I pretended that I had to go to the bathroom and followed him."

I'm confused? Aggravated? I don't know what I'm feeling. Tense? Uneasy?

"Why did you do that?"

"I thought—I felt it was something I had to do. I needed to introduce myself to my boyfriend's dad. Even if he's trying his best to not acknowledge you. And I had to get some shit off my chest that he should hear. He should never stop hearing about how much he hurt you. How much it hurt me to see you in that situation. And—fact—I told you I'd beat up anyone who ruined your birthday, so be glad I didn't follow through with that."

I want to know what Dad told him. I really want to know. There's no doubt in my mind that Mat can take care of himself, but if anyone—especially my family—insulted or threatened him, I—

"I'm sorry if I crossed a line."

"No, it's—what if something had happened to you?"

"Nothing did, though." Mat pulls at my leg until I turn and we're face-to-face. I settle my legs over his. "He didn't touch me. And he didn't say anything I haven't heard before or that's worth repeating."

"That doesn't calm me down."

"Hey, breathe and look at me. I'm here." His hands slowly run up my legs and then down my arms, landing on top of my own. "We're here. And we don't have to ever bring him up again if you don't want to. I—I didn't want to keep that from you. Don't think about it, all right? We're gonna have a lot of fun tonight with your family and your friends. But until then, forget everyone, okay? If I can't fix it, lemme take your mind off it. Pause today for a little while. You and me."

56

Here, let me help," Mat says. He straightens my tie and fastens the topmost button of my sports coat.

I almost forgot about my graduation party completely, but Xochi and Ruben coming back home reminded me that I had to get out of bed. I leave Mat with my sister and his brother-in-law, running out the door for Lou's. My friends and I agreed that the only way all six of us were showing up on time would be if we went together.

More accountability, I guess.

Itzel and Lou are still doing their makeup, sorting through their accessories, and triple-checking their hair when I arrive. Jordan, Piña, and Rolie are sitting in the living room, at varying levels of patience.

"Line up some shots," Lou yells from the restroom. "We're almost finished!"

"You said y'all were almost finished half an hour ago," Jordan yells back.

"Don't sass me!"

Everyone looks better than ever in our Martin Catholic navy and green, crowded in Lou's kitchen. But this might be the last time that I ever choose to pair these colors together again after having them forced on me every school day the past four years.

"Escúchenme, perras, putos, y cochin'is. Get a shot!" Lou exclaims, lifting one of the small glasses. "Someone make a toast so we can go."

"C'mon, valedictorian," Piña shouts, getting a quick glare from Itzel.

"Nope. I am done with public speaking for the rest of my life. Someone else do it."

Jordan nudges my arm. "Go for it, Batman."

"What? No. I'm not good at this."

"You don't gotta be. Just give us more than the *Golden Girls* theme song."

The room's quieted, and everyone's looking at me. *Perfect.* I've been volunteered.

"Okay. Fine. I'll do it. Be nice, though, because I'm not good at this. But I—lemme just say, if I haven't thanked everyone in this room yet since September, thank you. Life's been rough and great and scary and confusing all at the same time, and I'm really happy—and lucky—that I had y'all with me. So to Jordan and Itzel, for finally getting together. I think that's the one thing our group has been waiting on longer than for me to come out. *And* for being the best support system ever. Pero, more importantly, getting together. Oh, and also, to Itzel for single-handedly making sure I never failed a science or math class. Rolie for being consistently awesome and almost beating up someone for me. Lou for helping me live my life loudly and colorfully. And Piña for being a solid kisser—don't tell my boyfriend I said that—and for making sure I didn't beat any of our teammates up. Thanks, everyone, for looking out for me."

"Baby boy, that was beautiful," Lou says, fanning her eyes with her hands. "Oh, but we need one for you too!"

"To Jules, our superhero," Jordan adds, raising his shot glass.

"To all of us," she finishes. "Mis perras favoritas. Now let's party like it's the last day of our lives. Porque tomorrow is the first day of lots of new beginnings."

We tap the glasses on the counter and raise them back up to our mouths, swallowing the gold liquid in unison, hands grabbing for lime wedges on the counter.

"¡Listos!" Roe yells when we hear Lou's brother honking from the driveway. We quickly pack in, and the excited hysteria starts the second we begin driving off.

~

The six of us stand in line outside the hall, waiting for the DJ to call our names so we can enter. They've all got one or both parents standing with them, and I'm in the middle, with Xo next to me, our arms hooked together. I tap my head on her shoulder, and she gently hits my side with her elbow.

I hope she knows there's no one I'd rather walk into this with than her.

The DJ announces "Rolando Amos de Leon," and our entrance begins. Rolie throws his head back, clearly bothered that his mom and dad got the DJ to use his given name.

I hear my name, and we begin our march forward. Xo kisses me when we reach Roe and Lou, then leaves while we wait for everyone else. I'm glad I wasn't first. Standing up here is awkward.

But once the food's brought out, we're done being the center of attention. While our families are distracted getting their dinner, a photographer tries to instruct us for pictures. Ill-prepared for how stupid we could all be in front of a camera and how much Jordan enjoys some floor-work poses.

I get maybe half an hour to sit and eat with Mat, Ruben, Xo, and Güelo before "Boom Boom" starts blaring from the DJ's sound system. My friends run from different corners of the room to the middle of the dance floor. Because fact: when Kumbia Kings come on, the party has officially begun.

"You got the steps?" I ask Mat as I get up, reaching for his hand.

"I think so. Once we start, I'll get the hang of it. Remember, I'm a former *America's Best Dance Crew* hopeful."

"That is sadly something I will never be able to forget."

We hop in line, joining Jordan, Lou, and Piña, following the herd of people dancing around the floor. Mat's naturally a good dancer, and I knew he'd have no problem if I showed him a few of the basic moves. Though we're all shown up by Roe and Itzel, who since freshman year have perfected their complex routine of turns and spins that puts everyone to shame.

"Okay, I want cake now," I tell Mat after the song ends, walking him back to our table.

"Hey," Jordan calls from behind us. He places a hand on Mat's shoulder, whispering to him. I watch my best friend and boyfriend interact, Jordan doing a hand gesture and Mat nodding but silent.

"I'm borrowing your dude for a sec, Luna," Jordan says.

"I'll be right back," Mat reassures me, letting go of my hand.

They walk over to the hall entrance, where Roe and Lou are waiting. I eye the entire thing distrustfully but let it happen and walk to my seat. Itzel comes over and joins me, taking Mat's chair.

"What're they doing?" I ask her.

"You know how those tont'is can be," she answers. A small eye roll doesn't go unnoticed by me. "They want to make sure you're gonna be taken care of."

"Y'all worry too much."

"Don't act like you haven't gotten yourself into some dramatic-ass situations this year, Jules. For someone who doesn't enjoy being the center of attention, you really don't do anything low profile."

"I'm not dignifying that with a response."

"That's what I thought." She grabs an unused fork and takes the remaining bite of cake for herself. "Let them do what they need to do. It's more out of sadness at seeing you go than anything else."

"No, because they're protective."

"Yes. That too."

I look at her curiously. "You didn't feel the need to be a part of whatever harassment is happening right now?"

"We had a thorough conversation when you were trying to find us after graduation. I said what I needed to say, and I'm as much at peace as I can be."

"Which was?"

"Don't be a chismoso. That's private."

When they get back, Mat pulls me up, tugging me back to the dance floor. I'm feeling apprehensive and more than a little uncomfortable. Yes, we've danced together, but it was in a small room at a karaoke bar.

I'm gonna be dancing with my boyfriend in front of what has to be hundreds of people, many of whom have probably never seen two boys holding hands, much less dancing together. I get that it shouldn't matter. But it does. And it's affecting my ability to have fun with him.

A hand grabs my arm. "Bro, stop thinking," Jordan says into my ear. "Have fun with your guy or else *I'm* gonna start grinding on him. If anyone has a problem, they can leave."

He pushes me to Mat. I grab his arms to keep from falling onto him.

"You okay?" he asks.

"Yeah, sorry. Just—you know."

He kisses me, and I let him pivot me, wrapping his arms around my stomach and resting his chin on my shoulder. We start moving along with the beat of the music. Jordan and Itzel are dancing next to us, and Lou with Piña and a couple of her cousins, and Roe and one of Itzel's cousins close by. It's dark, except for the strobe lights and lasers coming from the DJ booth.

And for one of only a few times in my life thus far, I stop letting everyone else get in my head. I brush off whatever opinion anyone might have of me. Of my boyfriend. Of us together.

I'm too busy making up for every dance I went to with Itzel or Lou or nobody instead of a boy.

I'm living my life. And I'm happy.

"Hang on. Be right back," Mat tells me after a few songs have passed.

He leaves the group and heads to the DJ booth. We all watch him, unsure of what he's up to. But when he starts walking back, I hear the familiar sounds of the beginning to Ariana Grande's "Moonlight."

Mat places both his hands at the small of my back, and I bring mine around the back of his neck.

"You're *the* sappiest person in the entire world. You know that?"

"Don't tell me you aren't enjoying this."

"I am, but . . . everyone's watching."

"Let them. I'm not going back to LA until they know that you're mine and I'm yours."

Mat presses his head to mine and encourages me to keep dancing. He's quietly singing along to the song, and no offense to Ariana, but she has nothing on my boyfriend.

"You're my Moonlight, Jules Luna. Always."

57

It's only three months. Not that long at all, right?" I ask Mat. This feeling is depressingly familiar. Locked in a hug. Mentally pleading for God to cancel all flights between now and August.

I'm not ready to let him go again.

"Watch. You're gonna blink and realize you're in LA already."

"And I shouldn't expect some surprise visit for Fourth of July or something?"

"No, babe. Sorry. This is the last trip to Texas for the foreseeable future."

"Fine. Text me when you get home."

"I will."

"And tell everyone hi for me."

"I will."

"Now tell me you love me."

"You tell me first."

It's a long pause. We both know those words will be the last we say in each other's presence until August.

"Te amo, Sunshine."

"Anh yêu em, Moonlight."

58

Itzel and I are on our way to Jordan's house, neither of us ready to tell him bye. To acknowledge that we have only about two hours left with him. Hanging on to whatever resolve we have left to put on smiling faces at this breakfast before his parents take him to the airport.

Lou, Piña, and Rolie beat us to the Thomases'. Everyone's wearing Denver Soccer shirts, talking nonchalantly. As if a piece of all our souls isn't about to break away.

Jordan's mom greets us, handing us matching shirts. "Something to keep Jordan close by."

We both change after saying hello to everyone and try to fill the growing sadness with waffles. Itzel is talking less than she ever has in her life. Even Lou is trying harder than usual to be her typical way-too-much self.

I try my best not to start crying when I hug Jordan in the driveway. I know he'd prefer it that way. But then I hear him sniffle, and emotions start surging.

"Don't you dare start crying, Luna," he says. "You're gonna get my allergies all out of control."

"Stop being such a guy," I complain. Today is not the day to let him repress his feelings.

"Love you, Jules. You'll always be my brother. No matter what. And FaceTime me at least weekly. More than that, preferably, but you know, college. We'll be in the same time zone, though, so it'll be cool."

"No we won't, Jordan."

"What? Aren't we in—hold up." He looks up into the sky, a finger pointing into the air at, I'm assuming, an imaginary US map. "Never mind. Either way, call, FaceTime, Snapchat, all that. Maybe you can come to a game if it's not too far."

"All that. Yes. For sure. Got it."

"Good. Now, time to let go; otherwise Itzel will get jealous."

He turns around to face his girlfriend, and neither is bothering to hold in tears. They whisper to each other as they hug, with some nodding and headshaking and small laughs. Keeping each other as close as possible for as long as possible.

Jordan's dad calls for him, and they gradually separate until only their pinkies stay intertwined for a second.

"Watch out for my girlfriend, Lou," Jordan says before getting into the car.

The four of us stand in their front yard, waving at the car as it becomes less and less noticeable, until taking a turn and *poof*. We're one less.

"Whenever you're ready," I tell Itzel. She gives the smallest of nods in response. Still staring at the road. Maybe hoping they'll turn back. Hoping that she'll get just a little more time.

59

It's three in the morning. Seven hours before I'm on a plane to Los Angeles. And I can't sleep.

My concentration keeps going to one thing. To the one person I won't be saying goodbye to. Though I feel like I need to. If I don't close that chapter myself, if I let him dictate the terms and conditions of our relationship, then I won't leave satisfied.

I grab a pen and paper and begin to write out whatever comes.

> *Dad,*
>
> *I'm leaving for Los Angeles today and thought I should say goodbye. Not that you deserve it by any means. You lost any right to that when you threw me out of your life.*
>
> *I know you were at my graduation in May. I want it to be clear that that will be the last time you'll ever be a part of anything I accomplish in life. And trust me, you're going to miss out on a lot.*
>
> *I also know you met my boyfriend, Mat. He wouldn't give me the specifics of what happened, and that's fine. Any amount of words he shared with you are, again, more than you deserve. But I want you to know that he's kind and supportive and loves me. And I love him back. And*

the love I have for him is valid and real and no less valuable because of who we are.

I want to tell you I hate you. I wish I could tell you I hate you. For beating into me such stupid and dated ideas of gender and what it is to be a man. Sometimes literally. For thinking any part of me needed to be corrected because it made you uncomfortable. For instilling such a resentment toward who I am. For every night that I wished I would die in my sleep because at least I wouldn't have to wake up still gay. Still a disappointment to you.

But I can't. To say it would be a lie. Because I still love you. And I forgive you. So it hurts knowing you won't get to know who I will become. To see all that I'll do. To meet the people who have shown me love and acceptance when you refused to.

Being gay isn't something I was able to choose. To be happy, to get out of bed every morning, to be strong and brave and proud of who I am, sure. Those were choices.

Just like being an intolerant asshole is a choice. And that's on you, Dad.

Goodbye.

I park a block away from his house. The house that I called home for eighteen years and a few hours. I walk the rest of the way, not wanting the sound of my truck or its headlights to wake him.

I carefully step up to the front door and tape the envelope carrying my letter. My hand stays pressed against the door. Remembering the good times the two of us had, the days when I could tell without any doubt that my dad loved me.

And I have to admit, I'm going to miss him. I have missed him. Not a day has gone by when, even considering every resentment I have toward him, I haven't missed him.

I hope he misses me too.

More out of pettiness. But still, hopeful.

60

This mixture of excitement and reluctance to be leaving somewhere is new to me. Roe, Lou, and Itzel come by to see me off before Xo and Güelo take me to the airport. Roe, the appointed *strong one* today, hugs me tightly, picking me up off the ground, while the girls tear up.

As usual, he doesn't have a lot of words today, but we promise to keep in touch. Lou is a mess, knocking me into Xo's car with her forceful hug.

"You take care of yourself, chiquis. And we're planning for a spring break trip to LA, all right?"

"For sure. You better come through, though. Keep me in the loop about all the shit I know you're gonna get into at UT. And if you ever need to talk, call me. Mat's much better at that stuff than I am, so I might just pass the phone to him, but we're here for you."

She kisses me on the cheek before passing me over to Itzel. We stare at each other before rushing into an embrace.

"Are you sure you have to go?"

"Are you sure you don't want to come with me?"

"Got any extra room in your suitcase?"

"For you, all the room in the world."

I hear her start to cry, right as I've barely composed myself.

"Itzel, no llores, porfa," I moan. "Or else I'm gonna start crying, and I don't want to look ugly on the plane."

She lets out a half cry, half laugh and sniffles. "You'll call me when you get to LA?"

"As soon as I hit the ground."

"I'm going to tell Mat right now that I'm expecting a phone call and that he better not hog you the minute you get there."

"I wouldn't expect anything less."

"I'll see you for your birthday?"

"It'll be the week after, but yeah. Mat and I will be here for all of Christmas break. So you and Lou start planning now. I'm expecting something big for nineteen."

She hugs me one more time, not done saying goodbye yet. "Te quiero, Jules."

"Y yo también. Te quiero mucho, mucho, mucho, Itzel."

~

Xo and Güelo are all that stand between the airport entrance and me. I'm not ready to say goodbye to them. I don't know how to say goodbye to them.

Thankfully, my güelo can read the cues. He steps up and hugs me, a hand on my back and another on the back of my head. It takes only a few sentences for him to have me crying.

"You go and learn everything you can, mi'jito, okay?"

"Si, Güelo. Yo aprenderé."

"Bueno. You're going to change the world, Julián. Güelita y tu mamá are always looking out for you. And we're a phone call away. Te quiero mucho."

Then he lets go, and all I have is Xo in front of me. My heart is beating so fast, and there's some imaginary lump in my throat. And my vision is all fucked because of the tears.

I've only just gotten used to having her around again after seven years, and now it'll be another four. Probably more.

I don't know what I'm going to do without her constant presence. Without her protecting me.

"You did it, 'manito," she says, holding on to my shoulders. "Go have the time of your life and forget anything and everything that's held you back here. Be you. That's all you've ever needed to be great."

I can only nod, unable to form words. I want to thank her, over and over again until she's tired of hearing it, and even after. For loving me. For giving me a place to stay. For keeping me alive.

I take one last look at both of them before turning back into the airport.

I'm grateful to have enough time to go to the bathroom and wash my face before making my way through security. A brown kid having a mental breakdown in the middle of an airport would be a little concerning. If I can at least wait until I'm on the plane, my instability might hopefully mean no one will want to sit by me.

When I find my gate, I stand near the windows looking out at the planes arriving and departing. Wondering if there are any other eighteen-year-olds inside those planes, on their way to start their own journeys.

I think about mine. The twelve months that led up to this. All the ones that are yet to come.

I don't know what my life will look like four years from now or even four hours from now. I don't know if I'll have the same best friends. Or the same boyfriend. I don't know the people I'll meet and lose touch with, the memories I'll make, the regrets I'll look back on.

But I do know every day is getting better. I'm happier with who I am. I can love, in spite of the hate that has defined my past. I can be strong, in spite of the struggles, pain, and tears.

I know that I am worthy. That I am enough.

And that's enough for right now.

Because I'm just getting started.

ACKNOWLEDGMENTS

An enormous, Texas-size amount of gratitude to my agent, Claire Draper. From the very beginning, you've embraced this story in a way I could have only hoped for. You've championed this story better than anyone I could've dreamed of. You've worked so hard and with so much care and with the velocity of a literary cheetah even as the world went through the entire experience that was the year 2020. I am so honored to share this moment with you.

Thank you to my editor, Carmen Johnson, and everyone at Skyscape, for taking a chance on this book about brown boys falling in love and a story that often doesn't get told through the eyes of QTPOC characters by QTPOC writers. For your dedication and support and all the time, work, and effort put into making this story as wonderful as it could be.

Thank you to my developmental editor, Paul Zablocki, for your time and heart and incredible knowledge in the few weeks we worked together. And my copyeditor, Stacy, and proofreader, Liz, for your detailed eyes and ensuring this book was ready to be seen by the world.

To my cover artist, my agent sibling, and the incredibly talented Jay Bendt, for taking my breath away with that your art, and cover designer Anna Laytham. Thank y'all for creating something better than I could have ever envisioned.

To my friends, all of whom have been such an inspiration and light and indescribable bother in my life. Reader, if Jules's friends were at all your favorite part of this book, you have this group of people to thank. And if you hated them, you have this group of people to blame. Leo*na*, my sister and someone who can be described only as my platonic soul mate, hopefully you'll finally get around to reading this book; Duchess, who has become my designated first set of eyes on any writing; gay Alex and girl Alex, who volunteered to read this book and share in my obsession with these characters; my niecey and daughter in drag, Jarred; Andy; nephew Alex and Monse; Merissa (the Snooki to my JWoww) and Amador; Jesus V. and April; DJ and Vanessa. The Jean-Ralphio Saperstein to my Mona-Lisa (or vice versa, depending on the day), Lindsay Medina-Silvas, and Joseph. To my little, Mark, the original chaotic pocket papi in my life. Consider the drunkest parts of this book an ode to us.

To those I've met over Twitter who have so lovingly helped me shape this book into what it is now, who have supported me since the very beginning, and who have become some of my closest friends. MJ, my first writer friend from NaNoWriMo 2018 during this book's initial draft; Skye Kilaen, my very first beta reader and she who taught me the difference between *me* and *I* and *lay* and *lie* and who fed me with validations; Torie Jean, for your critical eyes and wonderful friendship and inspiration for that karaoke scene; Louangie Bou-Montes, te quiero, amiga, and I cannot wait for the day I get to hold your book in my hands; Madi Leigh, for your graciousness and so, so appreciated support; Sonora, my Wonder Twin, thank you for your guidance and friendship. Let's create some of the queerest Mexican American books this world has ever seen, primx.

To everyone else I've gotten to know in the Twitter writing community, especially within LGBTQ+ and QTBIPOC spaces. I wish I could spend an endless amount of pages for you all, but know that I carry all your love and encouragement in my heart, and whether you've been with me since NaNoWriMo 2018 or DVpit or PitMad or when I got to announce this was all a very real thing that was happening, your support has been noticed, appreciated, and embraced.

To my family. Mom, Grandma, and Grandpa, for your love and energy through this entire process and in my life; Joe Michael, Britt, Uncle David and Aunt Carmen, and Aunt Sheila; Uncle Rick, for your savvy, care, intelligence, and guidance. Jennifer, Aunt Lia, and Grandmo. To dad. If you've read this book, I hope you'll leave at least with a deeper understanding of the ways you've left an impression on my life, especially those you probably prefer not to think about.

To Granddad. You were the brightest of souls in this world, and I hope however you imagined heaven, you reside there peacefully. Any success and good I bring to this world, I do in your honor. And I hope I've made you proud.

And to all QTBIPOC youth, especially my Mexican American, Chicanx, and Tejanx sobrines. Always know of your beauty and power and strength and that you are plenty enough for this world exactly as you are. This book is for you.

ABOUT THE AUTHOR

Jonny Garza Villa is a product of the great state of Texas, born and raised along the Gulf Coast, and a decade-long resident of San Antonio. Jonny is an author of contemporary young adult fiction that maintains a brand of being proudly Latinx, and the most queer, and embracing the power and beauty of the chaotic gay. *Fifteen Hundred Miles from the Sun* is their debut novel. For more information, visit www.jonnygarzavilla.com.